Advance Praise foı

MW00775077

All of us whose families came from Eastern Europe and the old Russian Empire have grown up listening to ancestral stories of mystery and intrigue, and wondering what is truth and what is lore. David Abromowitz brings such stories into perspective, tracing the lincs and breathing new life into the old legacies. In *The Foxtail Legacy*, Abromowitz has gone above and beyond to show us where we came from, and how. With clear vision and an eye for story, he re-introduces us to the wonder of a family's history, showing us where we came from, and why we arrived at "here." Every family with immigrant ancestors can see itself in the tale he tells.

— Susan Katz Keating, award-winning investigative journalist, editor and publisher of *Soldier of Fortune*

"It's an origin story familiar to many American families — a young man, armed with big dreams and few prospects, sets out from the Old World to the New — but in his debut novel, *The Foxtail Legacy*, David Abromowitz molds it into a richly detailed and deeply moving saga. Following the tumultuous fortunes of the Itzkowitz family as they migrate from one continent to another, Abromowitz simultaneously paints a portrait of life in burgeoning twentieth-century America — a portrait spanning several generations, and touching on everything from the Depression to the rise of the Ku Klux Klan — that is as illuminating as it is unforgettable."

— Robert Masello, bestselling author of *The Einstein Prophecy*

David Abromowitz has written a fascinating historical novel about the Jewish immigrant experience. It has something for everyone: love stories, lies, secrets, deception, criminals, discrimination, global and local historical context, time traveling, and many twists and turns. I'm a terribly slow reader, but it was easy to read this book in very short order. Anyone who's interested in writing their own family history should seriously take a look at this as a possible role model.

— Ron Arons, author of *The Jews of Sing Sing*

THE FOXTAIL LEGACY

To Rhoda —
Enjoy!
David Abr...

THE FOXTAIL LEGACY

by David Abromowitz

Waterside Productions

Printed in the United States of America

First Printing, 2022

ISBN-13: 978-1-958848-48-7 print edition
ISBN-13: 978-1-958848-49-4 e-book edition

Waterside Productions
2055 Oxford Ave
Cardiff, CA 92007
www.waterside.com

For Roz and Joe,
and the ones who came before them.

Point Pleasant
1966

On that mid-August Friday afternoon, Point Pleasant was swelling up with wave after wave of "bennies." For a few more weeks, throngs of weekend partiers and day-tripping families would continue to surge into town like a solar high tide. Beach badge sellers and boardwalk kiddie-ride operators worked long shifts to handle the summer inflow. Only after Labor Day weekend would the flood dwindle to a trickle and allow the town to drift gently back into its usual seaside torpor. Today was still high season. With a forecast in the mid-90s, there was more money waiting to be separated from tourists.

Route 35 was bumper to bumper with tricked-out Chevy Impalas crawling in the wake of wood-paneled station wagons and sporty Mustangs. The occasional Cadillac or Lincoln bobbed in the river of vehicles flowing non-stop all the way from Exit 98 to the far end of the Manasquan River bridge. Some cars peeled off at the Broadway exit,

heading for the phalanx of clean and tidy motels catering to family groups. Beaters packed with friends from
Patterson drove the few blocks further to Arnold Avenue,
then fanned out through side streets like mice in a maze,
searching for guest houses with vacancies. They parked on
the front lawns of stately Victorians converted into summer lodging with names like Kelsey's Kottage and Bosun's
Quarters, where young workers from Jersey City, away
for a drunken weekend, plunked down $7 a head for a
spare room and shared bath. More upscale autos drove
east nearly to the Atlantic, turning right on Ocean Avenue
before depositing well-heeled visitors at the few elegant
hotels occupying valuable beachfront turf, like the Oasis-
by-the-Sea.

The locals couldn't agree on why they all called tourists
"bennies." Old timers claimed the beachgoers used to arrive by train waving a ticket stamped from one of five main
departure points, **B**ayonne, **E**lizabeth, **N**ewark or **N**ew
York. Others asserted that it mocked Italians proclaiming
the Shore's healing ocean breezes "bene" compared to the
miasma up North. Most bet on the money theory: that the
townies' derisive term sprang from show-offs ostentatious-
ly passing $100 bills bearing Benjamin Franklin's portrait
for every little purchase. Whatever the origin, if you lived
in Point Pleasant you made your livelihood off bennies all
summer, then spent the off-season scorning them.

Especially profitable were impulse travelers who
hopped on the last train south. On arrival they'd desperately dash to the ticket counter in the ancient railroad
station, imploring the kindly gray-haired cashier to reveal
where they could buy a bathing suit. "You have a couple
of choices," she would invariably advise, "but I'd say try
Itzkowitz's first. They have the biggest selection. Just a few
blocks west on Arnold." As grateful tourists hurried away,

the cashier would silently thank old man Itzkowitz. Back in the '40s the savvy merchant had started the tradition of slipping her a generous Christmas gift for having a ready answer to such questions, a tradition his son Lewis still carried on.

In front of the white stuccoed Itzkowitz Department Store that Friday, a dapper looking man in his sixties was hand-cranking down a row of green and white striped awnings. Lewis Itzkowitz had been performing this ritual, protecting the merchandise, every sunny summer afternoon for nearly four decades. Although Lewis was President of Itzkowitz Company, Inc., he personally handled the chore, emerging through the men's store door just in time to block the intense light from saturating the lower half of the two-story building.

A few blocks away, ten-year-old Jake pedaled frantically, straining to return to the store before his father finished with the awnings. Atop his fire engine red Schwinn Stingray with its V-shaped handlebars and banana seat, he imagined himself part of a pack of leather-jacketed bikers, like the riders in the Wild Angels poster outside the Globe Cinema, as he shifted into high gear and sped past kids on clunky one-speeds. He pumped his legs extra-fast, making up for having lost track of time playing outfield at the Little League field. Zooming over the railroad tracks, he spotted his father silhouetted against the descending sun. Jake calculated that he could reach the back entrance of the store and slip in just before five, when Pop had said they'd talk about something important. He didn't want to be late, especially if it was about the Big Sea Day parade.

Next Saturday was Big Sea Day, the pinnacle of each summer. Jake's father told him once that the tradition started a century earlier when farmers and townspeople from all over the area would come together for a festival of ocean bathing, fishing and clam digging. Local lore claimed the gathering originated even earlier among the Algonquin and Leni Lenape tribes, who allowed white colonial settlers to join in their August rituals. For Jake, Big Sea Day was the special Saturday in mid-August when tens of thousands lined the streets for the mile-long stream of string bands, drum and bugle corps, politicians in sports cars, beauty queens on floats, and reenactors costumed like 19th century settlers snaking through town. Last year he'd finally achieved his dream of riding in the parade. He felt a knot in his stomach, wondering if Pop would let him do so again.

Skidding to a stop just short of the heavy windowless rear door, Jake dismounted, hastily set the bike on its kick-stand, and hustled into the back area that served as the store's office. He glanced around, exhaling with relief. He had two minutes to spare. Scrambling to his favorite perch, the seamstress' four-legged stool, Jake reached under her workbench and pulled out the large black and red volume of Sherlock Holmes he'd stashed there. The Baker Street savant was his idol. Holmes' eccentric scientific methods and exacting observations enthralled Jake and taught him to pay attention to every detail.

Precisely on the hour, Pop emerged from the Men's Store and stepped into the office. Jake waited for his father to hang the awning crank on its peg before blurting out the tidbit of department store intelligence he'd gleaned on his ride.

"Gottfried has dress racks out on the sidewalk, Pop!" he declared in full voice. His father turned, a half-smile on his face. "Good spotting, Jake."

Pop had taught Jake why he personally handled what others might consider a menial task. Standing outside on the main thoroughfare of town provided an opportunity to observe subtle signals a businessman needed to assess if their seven-decades-old enterprise was to last a few more.

"Gottfried knows full well the Merchants Association decided sidewalk sales can't begin until the weekend *after* Big Sea Day. He's desperate. I'll bet Bradlees and the other big shops popping up in Bricktown are cutting into his sales. Damn chain stores."

"Have the chains hurt us too, Pop?" Jake probed, only vaguely aware of profit and loss, but determined to show interest anyway.

"Always a good question," his father answered. "I don't think so, but I'll have to double-check the figures myself. You know we can't rely on Norman to pay attention to such details. Speaking of your cousin, have you seen him?"

He paused a moment, weighing his words. "Ages ago, Pop. When Mom was back in the bookkeeper's office. She was yelling, I couldn't hear what. He got all red in the face and took off. I think he went for one of his big walks, like when he's gone for two hours."

"I thought so," Pop mumbled, rubbing his hand several times over his thinning scalp.

Jake held his breath, sensing something alarming in the way his father fell back into his chair behind the oak pedestal desk that filled up the center of the cramped room. "Jake," Pop began, haltingly. "I told you we needed to discuss something. You'll be disappointed. I know. But with what's going on with your cousin, we just won't be able to enter Grandpop's wagon in the Big Sea Day parade this year."

A sharp "No!" burst from Jake's lips, a stricken look on his face. He had been counting the days until he would ride again alongside Norman on the wagon bench, perhaps even getting to steer the horse. It was only last year that he'd finally worn down his parents, extracting permission to join his cousin on the brightly painted buggy. Riding in Grandpop's peddling emporium on Big Sea Day was more a symbol of growing up than the bar mitzvah a few years off. Pride swelled in him when they clip-clopped along in the replica emblazoned in red, black and gold with the "J. Itzkowitz 1897" logo and signs boasting a rolling store laden with shoes, clothing, dry goods and notions. He'd felt like a celebrity last year as masses of tourists and townies waved and cheered when he and Norman rode by dressed up in vintage clothing. His cousin made a great fuss over dressing exactly like their grandfather.

Jake clenched his hands tightly, gaze snapping up-wards to the familiar photograph hanging high up on the back wall: a balding man, neat mustache, round horn-rimmed glasses, wearing an ill-fitting suit, stand-ing beside a horse and wagon. For as long as he could remember, Grandpop Jacob had loomed above shelves laden with ledgers, postal supplies and an array of busi-ness odds and ends. Jake knew he was named after the patriarch, his father's father, who'd died a few years be-fore he was born. His mother always called her father-in-law a "lousy peddler", but he figured his ancestor must have done something right to end up owning this store.

"I'm sorry." Pop said gently. "It's just, well, there's a lot of tumult with Norman. Your mother and I don't want him out in front of the crowds like he's the face of the store. You'll understand someday."

"Let me do it!" Jake exclaimed. "I can dress up like Grandpop, just the way Norman does. I know how to handle the reins and steer the wagon. Please, Pop!"

Pop chuckled. "Someday. Someday you'll not only handle the reins of the wagon, you'll run the store. But right now, you're too young. Imagine if the horse got spooked!"

Cheeks burning, Jake fled the office, not wanting to burst into tears in front of his father. He bolted to one of his many hiding places in the old building, the basement storage area where he sometimes helped the store's handyman repair mannequins. In a dank room with an odor of ink, he stopped running. Catching his breath, Jake leaned against the hand-set printing press they used to create signs enticing customers with messages like "Special Today" and "20% Off All Items on Rack".

A beat-up steamer trunk he'd passed dozens of times caught his eye. Jake remembered it was filled with antique clothes that the window trimmer turned to when evoking an historic feel in the display windows. Intent on his plan despite his father's rejection, he popped open the rusty latch and flipped back the lid. One by one he plucked out stale-smelling garments of a bygone era. A stiff-collared shirt looked too big, so he tossed it aside. He grabbed a pair of spats, putting those in a pile of items to try on. Then his hand brushed something stiff and woolen down near the bottom.

Grasping the fabric, Jake dug out a moth-eaten vest and held it up. Its tweed pattern brought a smile. He'd seen it on Grandpop in the family photo album. Unfastening three buttons, he slipped it on over his shirt. Breathing deeply, Jake noticed that underneath the staleness the waistcoat gave off a hint of cologne. It smelled to him like something fancy, a life well-lived. To his chagrin, the waistcoat hung down halfway to his knees. It was clearly too large for Big Sea Day, but maybe he could sweet-talk the seamstress into shortening it. Picturing himself decked out with the vest and bowler hat, he absentmindedly thrust his hand into the lower welt pocket and struck something.

He gingerly withdrew a metallic token about the size of a Kennedy half-dollar and held it open-faced in the palm of his hand. The detail was worn smooth, but he could still make out the profile of a bearded man. Running his thumb across the gold surface gave him an unexpected sense of peacefulness. The coin felt warm and solid. This must have been Grandpop Jacob's, he speculated. A lot of relatives talked about Grandpop as wise and generous, some sort of King Solomon businessman, but he couldn't remember Pop saying much about his own father. He decided to keep the coin his secret. It felt a lot more valuable than a Kennedy half-dollar, something to hold on to. Turning it over, running a fingertip over faded letters spelling ZUID-AFRIKAANSCHE, he felt a tug of mystery about a man he never knew.

The Mission
Ferreirastown 1894

The stocky teenager stroked the horse's neck. Daily routine finished, horse fed and groomed, he was getting ready to leave the stable. He'd been lucky, he thought, to find work driving horses here in the Rand. Back in Shavlan, he'd grown up around horses. He had an affinity for them, a sense of what would calm them and what would spur them on. His father had traded horses, and had taught Jacob what to look for when assessing a purchase. Now, a world away from Shavlan, that skill was proving valuable. It was a blessing that Aunt Sora and Uncle Helman had room for him as a boarder. Tending to Uncle Helman's horses any evening when he wasn't tending bar was something he could do in return.

Exiting the stable, Jacob paused to survey his surroundings in the twilight. The stench of dung was even stronger in the muddy street, until recently something Jacob barely noticed. Daily he trudged indifferently past the ragged jumble of tents, wagons and make-shift structures that formed the burgeoning mining town. Now it nagged at him that in barely a year he'd become inured to the squalor of the frontier outpost. Cousin Moishe's latest letter portraying the wealth and wonders of London had heightened his senses, so sharp was the contrast with the muck and mayhem of Ferreirastown.

He dearly missed Moishe. They'd grown up together, with Moishe becoming closer than Jacob's own brothers. Now Moishe was far off in the capital of the Empire seeking a better future along a different path. It had wounded Jacob when Moishe turned down his proposal that they get rich together in the gold fields, but he'd come to realize Moishe had made the right decision for himself. The mining camp life was barely tolerable for Jacob. His more bookish cousin would have been ground down by the ceaseless travails of the Transvaal. Jacob's initial feelings of betrayal yielded to a hope that Moishe's quest was leading him closer to success. Maybe, Jacob considered as he spotted another drunk lying face-down in slop, it's me who should join Moishe.

He'd barely taken two steps when a rough looking Boer loomed before him, blocking his path. Jacob tensed, unsure what to make of the stranger. The man had a military air, a serious weathered face, but did not evoke a sense of menace. Had he served the stranger in the tavern? He couldn't be sure. The man looked like many in the mining town who passed through saloon doors eager for strong drink.

"Are you the barkeep who knows how to drive a team?" the man asked without ceremony, speaking English in a heavy Afrikaans accent. "The tavern owner said I'd find you here."

He hesitated. "It depends who's asking, and why." Jacob was guarded around all Boer. Most got along well with the Jews who daily were swelling the ranks of the mining camps, but you never knew when that might suddenly change. Back in Russia, fellow Jews in *shtetls* like his largely steered clear of the *goyim*, never sure when some interaction would bring trouble. Here the Boer and the English weren't prone to treat Jews badly, at least no differently than they treated other *uitlanders*. Perhaps it's because we are useful to them, he thought, at least for now.

"Kruger is asking," the man said in a low voice. "I'm here on an errand for Oom Paul."

Oom Paul? Was this some sort of trap, or espionage, he wondered? What could the leader of the Republic want with him?

"President Kruger? He sent you to find a Jewish bartender? Is this a joke?" Jacob inched closer to the nail on which hung his bullwhip. He never used it on animals, but it came in very handy from time to time on a belligerent drunk.

"Oom Paul has some important cargo he needs delivered. He asked the tavern owner who's the best with horses, and was sent to you. Are you – good with horses? Can you drive a wagon under unusual circumstances?" the man said, eyeing Jacob carefully.

He swallowed. This could be real, he contemplated. I can handle any horses, and Mr. Momberg would vouch as much to anyone asking around. Kruger could pay well, and I could use the extra money, he calculated. Passage back home someday to get a bride wasn't cheap.

"My boss was right, I am the best around. But this sounds dangerous. I need to know more. What's the cargo, and what it pays," Jacob answered, looking the stranger directly in the eyes. He willed himself to remain calm despite the churning in his gut. Instinct told him this wasn't a trap. Or at least the risk was worth it for a chance to meet Kruger.

"Come with me."

Hesitating just a heartbeat, Jacob fell in alongside the messenger. A few blocks north they reached Commissioner Street, passing Stoffel's blacksmith shop and Goldberg's produce. Abruptly, the rugged Boer turned into a ramshackle wooden building that proclaimed itself a hotel but to all appearances was primarily another of the many shebeens in the camp. At the very back of a smoky room, in a dark corner, sat two men. Even in the dim light, Jacob recognized the bearded "Uncle Paul", President of the South African Republic. The most powerful man in the Transvaal. What could be his secret cargo needing an expert wagoner?

"Sit down, young man." Kruger gestured to a third chair. "Your proprietor speaks highly of you. He tells me that you enforce order at the bar with a whip and a pistol. I like that, a man who knows how to maintain order."

Jacob said nothing, but the comment pleased him, set him a bit at ease.

"You're probably wondering why I asked for you," Kruger continued with a slight smile. "I will get to that in a second. First you must answer a few questions."

"Ask what you want," he said flatly.

"Are you good with a map?"

"I can read and tell directions. Back home I delivered horses for my father, all over the countryside. And I traveled here from Cape Town on my own."

"Good, good. You have a gun. Do you know how to use it?" Kruger leaned closer.

"I've never had to kill anyone, if that's what you're asking," He felt nervous, but kept his voice calm. "I'm not afraid to shoot a man, if it comes to my life or his."

"Well, it won't come to that on this errand. But I need a man who is thinking about being prepared."

"You haven't told me what this is about, Mr. Kruger. I know you're an important man, so I assume this is something important," he said, placing his hands solidly on the table.

"You're young but you carry yourself with confidence. Reminds me of myself, at that age," said Kruger. "Well, Mr. Itzkowitz – that is your name, isn't it? I have a very precious delivery for you to make soon. What I am about to tell you is extremely secret. Can I count on you to keep it that way?"

Jacob nodded.

"There is trouble coming in the next few days. I can't go into detail. I will be preoccupied dealing with the English. My darling wife Gezina is at our house on Church Street in the capital. You will fetch Gezina and her belongings and take her to Boekenhoutfontein. You'll be given a map, but no notes about this mission. You must keep the details in your head in case you're stopped," Kruger sat back, waiting.

"Trouble," he said, half as a question, half repeating.

"All I can say is that Rhodes hopes to stir the pot. You know of Rhodes? He's got some fool named Jameson planning to give us a Christmas surprise. They think we are blind. We will handle them, but I can't sleep well if my dear Gezina is nearby, in case anything goes wrong. That's all you need to know."

"And if I do this…" Jacob began slowly.

"Ah yes, what's your reward. A fair question, young man," Kruger smiled broadly. "Isn't it enough that you would have the President of the ZAR in your debt?"

"That's worth a great deal, sir," he said, nervous he might offend yet determined to press further. "I have plans, for a wife back home. For that I need more than gratitude."

"That you do, young man," said Kruger, reaching into his pocket. Three gold Afrikaner *ponds* emerged when he held out his open hand. Each bore the President's ubiquitous likeness on the front. "Will this do?"

Jacob's eyes widened a bit. He swallowed, calculated, then looked Kruger directly in the eyes. "Three are good, but five are better."

Kruger momentarily scowled, then quickly broke into a broad grin and chuckled. "Ah, you Jews, you're all *smouses* deep down. At least you're better than the Kaffir. So be it – you deliver my Gezina safely, and you shall have five of these, plus my goodwill to go with it. I'll leave it to Botha here to arrange for the horse and wagon, and provide you all the details. Now I'm off."

Kruger stood, said something softly in Afrikaans to the younger man at the table, and strode away.

Botha, the one who had fetched Jacob from the stable, remained standing. He maintained the same serious mien as when he first approached Jacob, but something had shifted in his manner.

"Oom Paul seems to like you. Lucky for you, because I think you're arrogant – bargaining like a horse trader with the President! But if he sees something in you, that's fine with me. Meet me here tomorrow morning at ten and

we'll go over details. Remember, say nothing to anyone."
With that, Botha and the wordless man left the tavern.

Walking back through Ferreirastown towards his lodgings, his mind raced. Should he do this? Was it too dangerous? What if he stumbled into an armed band? This
Jameson fellow, clearly he worried Kruger. Why else spirit
away his wife to his country estate?

Quickly he dismissed any concerns. After all, he was
good with horses, smarter than most of these Boers, and
the money was a fortune. If trouble came, he would handle it. He always had.

Inside what was more shack than house he found Aunt
Sora finishing dinner preparations. Uncle Helman sat by
the fire reading a Yiddish newspaper. They'd been wonderful to him. Helman had come to the Rand early on, in the
first wave of Litvaks scurrying to find riches after the gold
strike. Helman established himself by trading horses for the
continually arriving miners. This earned him enough of a
stake to lease some land and build the small stable Jacob was
now tending. The horse trade was hardly his uncle's only
line of business. It had been costly for Helman to return to
Shavlan, marry Sora, and bring her back here. To accomplish this, his enterprising relative indulged in certain side
dealings in the liquor trade. Like many of the "Peruvians",
as the Boer queerly called immigrant Jews, Helman filled
gaps in the economy of the frontier town.

"Just like with the *goyim* back in Russia," Helman explained when Jacob first arrived. "Whatever they look down
on, but need, we Jews do it. They need it, they buy it from
us. Then they spit on us for doing it."

Helman deftly straddled both worlds, the respectable
and the under. Among miners he was known for offering

quality horses at fair prices. His liquor sideline was kept out of sight by dealing through several Malay who secretly distilled it. Helman acted as distributor to a few select brothels and other establishments requiring a constant supply to quench the insatiable thirst of miners. That is how he'd gotten to know Moberg, which in turn resulted in a barkeep opportunity for Jacob when he turned up nearly penniless the year before last.

It disturbed Jacob to witness the tide shifting against Uncle Helman and others like him. Initially mine owners were happy to have Jews supplying endless quantities of alcohol to bars frequented by black mine workers: Mine owners appreciated a cheap and easy means of fostering dependence and docility. Lately the pendulum had swung, with public pressure leading to a ban on liquor sales to blacks. The craving among brutalized miners for alcohol didn't go away because of a law. Purveyors of drink now came for their supply surreptitiously to middlemen like his uncle, making his trade increasingly risky. Many a respectable Boer and Anglo, and even some wealthier German Jews, were writing letters to the editor condemning Russian Jews as the "Peruvian Pest" – portraying arrivals from the Pale of Settlement as thieves and *boerverneukers*. The powerful Chamber of Mines denounced Jews as the chief cause of liquor abuse, source of all the crimes pervading mining encampments. Jacob worried daily for Helman, for no matter how expert his uncle was at keeping his side business invisible, how much longer this could he get away unscathed?

All this swirled in Jacob's mind as he debated what to tell Sora and Helman about his upcoming mission. He couldn't just disappear for days without explanation. They were *mishpocha*. If anything were to happen to him, they would need to know who to go to for answers. But Kruger and his adjutant had warned him to say nothing about the journey. The debate was short-lived: he trusted his family more than he did the Boer.

"Good evening, *Tante* and *Feter*," he said lightly.

"Good evening, Jacob," they replied almost in unison.

"I have some good news," he announced with a smile as they assembled around the dinner table.

"We could use some good news," Helman said attentively.

"I have a special assignment for a very powerful person. It is only for a few days, but will result in an important friend," he said, waiting for the obvious question.

His words hung in the air as Sora and Helman exchanged a quick look. He knew they thought him headstrong, with a high opinion of his own abilities. Isn't my self-confidence justified, he thought awaiting their reactions. I've seized every opportunity to get ahead. I came from Russia on my own, then talked my way into a caravan heading north to Johannesburg. Not bad for a 17 year old who'd never been more than ten miles from Shavlan before, he congratulated himself while girding for objections.

"An important friend?" said Helman quizzically. "Important friends sometimes cost dearly."

"This one pays dearly, *Feter*," he answered. "There is no one more important."

"You're doing something for the Queen?" Sora liked to tease, perhaps to bring him down a notch when she thought him arrogant. He merely smiled.

"Almost, *Tante*. The President."

"The President? Kruger? What are you mixed up in?" Helman was agitated.

17

"I'm not 'mixed up' in anything, *Feter*," he said a touch defiantly. "He needs someone good with a horse and wagon. I was recommended to him."

Helman sat back, gaping at his nephew.

"Jacob, be very careful. The Boer are friendlier than the *goyim* back home, that's true. No matter. Things can change in an instant."

"I know, *Feter*, my eyes are open. I'm careful around them." Jacob said soothingly.

"That's not always enough, Jacob. *Goyim* are *goyim*, there and here. Did you never hear how they almost murdered us in Dirvianishuk, the village west of Shavlan?"

"No, what happened?"

"It was before you were born. I was just a boy myself," Helman said, closing his eyes. "For some reason, a Jewish boy wanted revenge on his father. What did the fool do? He puts a bottle of wine inside the synagogue's Holy Ark, then ran to the local Count. The idiot claimed his father murdered a Christian boy to make Pesach wine out of the child's blood. Imagine, a Jew repeating the blood libel! The stupid Polish Count believed him and arrests the father. Our parents feared the peasants would hear about it and start a pogrom. Luckily the local Rebbe knew the great Rabbi Yankel Kovner. Kovner knew Governor General Nazimov, and got Nazimov to launch an investigation. Under questioning the boy broke down and admitted the lie. The father was released, but the peasants didn't care, they still believed it. A big lie never goes away. For years we steered clear of every drunk Russian for fear he'd beat us up for killing Christian children. Like what happened with the Cossacks in Kiev not even a decade ago."

"Kruger is like Nazimov, he's not a dumb peasant," Jacob said a bit defensively.

"Maybe not," said Helman. "The average Boer, though, he's not so different. Look at how they treat blacks here, like dogs. Will they turn on the Jews next? Even if they don't, someday the blacks will get back at the Boer, and the Boer will toss aside the Jews to save themselves."

"Someday will be someday, *Feter*," he said. " Today I have a job to do for Kruger, and it pays well."

Wagon Trek
1894

Botha strode into the dingy room, precisely at 10 am. His right hand dangled at his side clenching and unclenching, occasionally touching the pistol on his hip holster. Jacob, sitting alone in the rear where he had met with Kruger, glanced up as Botha approached but didn't stand.

"Are you ready?" Botha asked, stepping close and looming over him.

He nodded. "Where do I find my special passenger?"

A scowl crossed Botha's otherwise blank face as he eased into a chair and took out a map from a leather pouch. "I hope your memory is good. Take a good look at this, study it carefully while we sit here. You cannot take this map or any documents with you. If you are captured, you'll have nothing to give away the plan. We will go over the story after you've mastered the route and these details."

"My memory is perfect," he said audaciously, looking Botha in the eye.

"Good, it has to be. Your life means nothing to me, but her life may depend on it."

Botha proceeded to outline the essentials. At 7 the next morning, Jacob was to meet two men at the stable on Fox street at the end of the camp. He would recognize one as the wordless third man from the meeting with the President. The pair would provide a covered wagon with a fresh horse and supplies for three days. He was immediately to set out alone for Pretoria. The route marked on the map was designed to avoid detection in case Jameson's men had advanced. He should arrive at a plain, elongated house on Church Street by mid-morning. It would be easy to recognize the house – a train car would be sitting behind it.

"Go to the front door, a Kaffir man will greet you. Tell him you are looking for *Mevrou* Kruger, she is expecting you. The servant knows only that his mistress is going on a short trip for supplies," Botha paused.

"And her? Does she know the plan?" he asked.

"She knows that a man matching your description will fetch her in a wagon, and that her husband wants her to go with you. Mevrou Kruger is an obedient wife and will not ask questions. It is better she knows as little as possible," Botha replied. "The wagon, as you will see, looks like a supply wagon from the outside. Inside it will have a decent seat for her. She's a sturdy woman – after giving birth to sixteen *babas* she's strong, not afraid of a rough ride."

Botha traced his finger over another route on the map, this time from Pretoria to the Kruger farm. The roughly 60-mile journey was anything but direct. The path Botha sketched out required a crossing of the Magaliesberg range to the north and then a meandering passage west. Botha warned that if there were to be any trouble, it would be in this stretch. As best they knew from Boer scouts, the rabble with the Englishman would advance well to the south of this route. Of course, scouts could be fooled. Could Jacob use a rifle if need be, Botha asked? He had his hand gun, but if it came to it he could aim a rifle quite well, he said. Botha assured him there would be a Spanish Mauser with ammunition under the wagon driver's seat, within easy reach.

"We can't make it all in a day," he observed after studying the map. "Where is there a safe place to rest?"

"Ah, we've planned for that. There's a farm of a friend along the route. Just a few miles past Silkaatsnek. The farmer is a good Boer named Schoeman, a friend of the President. He will put up Mrs. Kruger in the house, and there will be a place for you to sleep as well."

"That's all I need," he said.

"Good," said Botha. "Anything else?"

"And after?"

"After what?"

"After she is safe at their farm – when do I get paid?"

"Always the money with you people. Come back here, tell Moberg you delivered your cargo safely. We will find you. You do your job and you'll get your reward."

By the time he reached Church Street the next morning, the sun was midway to noon. The house was easy to spot, a long low milky white structure with large triangular turrets at either end connected by a shallow covered veranda. Behind it was not only the train car Botha mentioned, but several head of cattle roaming idly around a pasture. The Krugers are prosperous with someone's money, he thought while dropping a weight in the road to which he hitched up the horse. A well-dressed servant emerged from the ornate front door. "You are the man here for Mevrou Kruger?" he asked stiffly.

"Yes. Is she here?"

"Wait by your wagon," replied the servant, disappearing back into the house. After a few minutes, the servant re-emerged followed by two pairs of sturdy men. Following directions in a language he did not comprehend, each pair loaded a large steamer trunk into the back of his wagon. She must plan to be gone a while, he thought. Maybe Kruger expects a long battle?

The baggage handlers retreated, leaving him standing alone wondering what would happen next. He had only a moment to consider this when a short, rotund woman dressed entirely in shades of black and wrapped in a Victorian shawl shuffled out onto the front walk. In one hand she held an unopened parasol, in the other a thick book. With purpose, she walked directly to him, halted, and looked him over appraisingly.

"You're young," she said in heavily accented English.

"I am experienced," he replied, pleasantly. "May I help you into the wagon?"

Ignoring his offer, the matron placed her parasol carefully on the wagon seat, grabbed on to its back, and gingerly hauled herself up and into the covered cargo area. He was taken aback by how remarkably agile she seemed. "There's a comfortable chair for you back there," he called after her. In one motion she retrieved the parasol and settled into the seat, immediately opening her book. She looks as much at home as if she were in her drawing room for an afternoon of solitary reading, he thought bemusedly.

Realizing nothing more would be said, he climbed into the driver's seat, flicked the reins, and set off on the memorized route. As the horse slowly hauled its load down the wide hard-packed dirt streets, he observed the mix of shanty tents adjacent to magnificent stone buildings. He chuckled as they reached the intersection of Church Street circle and a thoroughfare named Paul Kruger Street. How strange, he thought, that fate has entrusted me with the most precious cargo of a man so powerful he has streets named after him during his lifetime. How was it possible that I, a fellow thousands of miles away from home desperate to eke out a stake in the gold rush frontier, have been chosen for this mission? I pray and observe most commandments, but never until this moment would I believe the Holy One, *baruch hashem*, might have some plan in mind for me, he thought with a sense of awe. The very idea was far-fetched — it wasn't like he was a figure in the Torah. Yet as they traveled along he dwelled on the idea that maybe he was meant for greater things than tending horses and selling drinks to miners.

Lost in this reverie, he gave his horse free rein to make steady progress westward at a slow trot. After a little over an hour, he noticed a pasture with a small roadside stream nearby. Steering the wagon off to the right, he pulled to a halt to allow the horse to drink.

"Why did we stop?" Her words from behind broke the long silence.

"The horse needs to rest and drink. I need food. This would be a good time for you to eat as well," he replied, not looking back.

"I'll eat when we stop for the night. No need to waste time." Her tone betrayed a slight pique.

"Suit yourself," he said, jumping down from the wagon to unhitch the horse and let it graze on the tall grass. While the animal fed, he retrieved a basket of food that Botha's men had stashed for him under the seat and began his own simple meal.

"What's your name? No one told me your name." The voice of the President's wife emerged disembodied from the shadows, sounding more like a command to a servant than a question.

Peering up into the canvas covered area where she sat with a stiff back, he wondered why she cared. In the dim light inside the wagon he could discern deep wrinkles on her weathered face. She's much more a farmer's wife than a royal on a throne, he concluded.

"Itzkowitz. Jacob Itzkowitz."

"Itzkowitz. No one said a Peruvian would be driving me," she said.

"I'm a Jew, if that's what you mean," he responded.

"You Jews, you used to be the Chosen People. Then you turned your backs on the Lord and killed our Savior Jesus. We Boer are now God's chosen," Mrs. Kruger said stated this as if she were instructing a schoolboy in basic facts of history.

"Are you? How do you know that?" He could not restrain rising disdain seeping into his tone of voice.

"It is well known since the Great Trek. We were liberated by God from the English like the Hebrews from Pharaoh. He guided us through our wandering Exodus. We conquered the Bantu just like the Israelites conquered the tribes of Canaan, with the might of the Lord. We came north and found the Nylstroom and the ancient ruins in the Israelitishe kloof. Those were signs that this is our Promised Land. It is all foretold in the Gospels," she said, holding up the thick volume in her hand.

He was dumbfounded. He had observed that many of the Boer in the Transvaal were devout Christians, filling up their numerous churches on Sundays. This nonsense about them being the new Chosen People, that was something altogether different. The Tsar was a religious fanatic, but even he hadn't claimed that Russians were the Chosen of Heaven. In his view being Chosen wasn't even much of a blessing for the Jews, rather more a burden. It fostered resentment among gentiles back in Russia, who spat "chosen" out like an epithet. These Boer, he grasped listening to their leader's wife, proclaimed themselves endowed with special status, a light unto the world. What the Boer are really doing, he told himself, is concocting a story to give themselves a license to rule. Uncle Helman was right. They justified treating blacks like dogs by preaching that God had singled out the Boer above all others. Soon enough they would find some need to put themselves above Jews, and their doctrine would entirely justify that too. After all, he thought, you can only have one Chosen People at a time.

He crafted his words carefully.

"You Boer built up this land. It is flourishing. Now we must be on our way, to get you where I was hired to take you," he said evenly, walking off to fetch the grazing horse without waiting for a reply.

They resumed their slow trek across the barren plain once again in silence, climbing towards the notch in the

Magaliesberg range that would let them pass through towards the Kruger farm. Mrs. Kruger offered no more opinions on religion, seemingly content to read her bible and doze on and off, judging by the soft snoring he heard from time to time. A little before nightfall they arrived at the estate of the friendly farmer with a welcome bed. Mevrou Kruger was greeted like royalty by a sturdy short man and his plump wife. The trio chatted loudly in Afrikaans as they whisked her inside the solid stone farmhouse with a stuccoed upper story and a red metal roof. He contented himself assessing the farm, impressed by its tidiness and good repair. Finally a worker, possibly a son of farmer Schoeman from his looks, took charge of the horse and wagon. The taciturn youth grunted in Afrikaans while leading the animal off to a stable, presumably to be fed and watered. The words "slaap" and "eet" and a few others he had garnered tending bar indicated he would spend the night in the barn and find what he needed there.

He was up just after sunrise, eager to get underway for the final leg of their journey through an even more desolate stretch of terrain. To his mild surprise, when he emerged from the barn heading to the main house to rouse his passenger, Jacob found her sitting fully dressed and waiting for him in a rocker on the farmer's front porch. She must wake the roosters, he quipped silently.

"I was getting ready to send Schoeman's boy to wake you. We should go," she said as if chiding a schoolboy for being late to class.

"We will be ready in ten minutes, after I tend to the horse," he replied, trying not to sound chastised.

The morning journey passed much like the afternoon before, with a few brief stops for water and to graze the horse, the barest minimum of words passing between driver and passenger. At midday he steered them into a grove of trees near the road, seeking a cool shaded location in which to eat. Again the old woman tersely informed him she had no need of food until their destination. Undeterred, he opened the re-provisioned basket for his own meal.

"When did you come to our country?"

He was startled by her question, not expecting any further dialogue. How much should I tell her? I have no secrets, but then again who knows why she's asking.

"I've been in the Rand for about a year and a half," he answered carefully.

"And before that?" she pressed on.

"About four months earlier I arrived in Cape Town," he said. "But it wasn't for me."

"No? Why not?"

What was she looking for, he wondered? He decided a simple explanation and a little flattery was best.

"My older brothers were there, so I went. Cape Town was too built up for my taste. I wanted frontier. Your gold mines offer more opportunity. People said the Boer welcome anyone willing to work hard."

"My husband is a kind man, so he welcomes anyone. That means we get too many Peruvians. That kind want to make money off the hard work of others."

"If I didn't want to work hard, would I be out here alone driving you all day?" he said, unable to hold back a flash of anger.

"Sitting on a wagon letting the horse pull us is hard work? You've never been a farmer." She broke away from his gaze, opened her book and pointedly set about ignoring him.

Flustered, annoyed with himself for letting her words get to him, he snapped the reins. Hours more silence descended on their passage, freeing his thoughts to churn. Speaking of his brothers brought pangs of guilt. Natural traders, they quickly earned enough surplus from peddling to seize opportunities to import and export goods. The rising tide of wealth from diamonds and gold created surging demand for luxuries procured from Europe. Their plan was to capitalize on the flow of goods into the local market to build their fortunes. Their younger brother fit into the plan, but their plan didn't fit into his. He had told the President's wife the truth: He wanted to be his own man. Why that was, that was not her business. The wide open Transvaal sounded like mecca for achieving independence to his young ears, at least it had a few years ago. Since arriving in the teeming camps of Ferreirastown he had come to believe he may have turned up a little too late.

Engrossed in these thoughts, Jacob almost missed the far off wisp of dust wafting above a ribbon of scrub trees. He could not see through the thicket that wound along a riverbank, but he was certain what the dust cloud signaled. Riders were at a gallop along a path that would intercept their wagon just after it crossed a short rickety bridge lying a few hundred yards ahead. Instinct told him the crossing would offer men on horseback a perfect spot for an ambush, if that was their intent. Slowing the horse just a tad with a light tug on the reins, he anxiously surveyed the terrain, searching for better options. He saw none. There was no alternate path for a wagon along the near bank, no boulders behind which to attempt to hide, and no possibility of outrunning riders.

"Mrs. Kruger, there may be some trouble ahead, stay quiet," he instructed calmly over his shoulder.

"What sort of trouble?" came the unruffled reply from the shadows.

"Men on horses. I'll handle it."

Another wisp curled up above the low trees, now just a hundred yards from where they were soon to cross a small stream that cut a sharp V into the flat terrain. Jacob eased back on the reins, further slowing the horse. In one smooth motion, he secured the reins under one leg and leaned far back, snatching his bull whip in his left hand and the Mauser under the seat in his right. Now armed, he took the reins back with his whip hand and brought the wagon to a standstill just shy of the narrow wooden crossing. As he did so, two riders with faces obscured by bandannas broke past the last of the trees. They turned into the lane directly opposite him, revolvers drawn.

On either side of the bridge, armed men stared each other down in silence. He held the rifle steady, calculating his best move. Guessing the older of the two was more likely to be in command, he took aim for that one's chest. The riders in turn seemed to be sizing up the situation, perhaps unsure why a lone man with a small covered wagon would be trekking along a fairly desolate route. He decided to make the first move.

"I have no gold or diamonds. Nothing of value," he shouted in as steady a voice as he could muster.

"Then what are ye doing out here?" replied the one he believed the elder. It sounded to his ear more an Irish brogue than a Boer or English accent.

"Just delivering cargo to a farmer up ahead in Rustenberg," he called back, remembering the name of the town near his destination.

"Cargo? What kind of cargo?" the man asked, his revolver leveled at Jacob. He had a nasty scar on one cheek, a slash that peaked out above his mask and nearly touched his right eye.

"I'm the cargo." Her voice rang out clearly from the rear. Suddenly her bonneted head stuck out from between the flaps in the canvas covering the rear frame of the wagon.

Jacob was startled by her outburst, but managed to hold his bead on the bandits. Her magical emergence had more of an effect on the pair on horseback. They exchanged confused glances, momentarily looking away from him. For a second he considered squeezing off two quick rounds, letting the thought linger a moment too long to act on it.

"Who are you?" the younger one called out, as both outlaws regained their wits enough to resume the stand-off posture.

"Just a farmer's wife" she said. Simultaneously he blurted out "She's my aunt."

The older one laughed. "Which is it?"

"It's both," she answered brusquely before he could speak. "He's taking me back home. We've got nothing you want. Just some clothes and things I had with me for a visit with my sister in Pretoria."

The scar-faced rider spoke up. "I don't believe you. You're a Boer, and this one, he sounds like the Jews we run into around here."

"I don't care what you believe," Jacob called out, leaning slightly forward as if to get better aim. "Like she said, we've got nothing you want. What I do have are five rounds in this rifle, more than enough to get you both. Is it worth your lives to find out?"

The younger one's eyes darted sideways, looking for a cue. The older one stared hard at Jacob's rifle and the head peeping out from the flaps, as if weighing odds of a bluff in a poker game.

"Alright," he said, relaxing his shoulders and his grip on his revolver. "We'll take your word for it. But be warned that our men patrol this area. If you're ever back here with valuables we'll have our share or we'll have your life. Now lower your gun."

"I'll lower this rifle when you're gone. I don't shoot men in the back, so just turn around and go back the way you came."

Hesitating a moment, the older one gave a flick of the hand holding the reins. With that the two highwaymen wheeled their horses around and trotted back along the riverbank path, soon disappearing behind the thicket.

Jacob exhaled. He dropped the rifle into his lap, slumped forward, and closed his eyes. The effort to blot out the images racing through his mind of what almost happened failed, and a hollow shiver of fear ran through him. Then he caught the sound of breathing behind him.

"Why in hell did you do that?" he growled, not turning around to face her. "I was handling it. I didn't need you interfering!"

"You have a good head, that was smart to stop the wagon. You took charge with the gun," she said nonchalantly, as if assessing his performance on nothing more serious than a training exercise.

"You should have kept quiet, like I told you!" he interrupted, agitated.

"I have eyes. From back here I could see two hardened outlaws with guns. They saw a man all alone, no one for miles, with a wagon full of who knows what. What man risks his life to cart worthless junk to Rustenberg? They weren't going to believe you."

"You don't know that."

"Them? Those fellas were part of the Irish Brigade. Couldn't you hear the accent? The Irish Brigade are a dangerous bunch of bandits, like that killer named McKeone. The one who got hung for attempting to kill two of our policemen. That caused my husband a lot of trouble, people didn't like the judge hanging a white man."

"Doesn't matter. I would have scared them off," he replied, still taking offense.

"More likely they would start shooting, figuring they could get you faster than you could get them. Killing one Jew out on his own would mean nothing to those two."

"I had the older one in my sights, I would have gotten him and then the other one if I had to," he replied, feeling less assured than his words.

"Maybe. Don't forget, I'm sitting behind you. If they are shooting at you, they are shooting at me. What if they killed you and then found me? They'd have no choice, they couldn't leave a witness. But seeing I'm your passenger, they're not likely to start off murdering a farmer's wife. They'd know my family and the Boer sheriffs would come after them."

Unwilling to concede to her logic, he simply muttered "We've got to make up some time." Their journey resumed, a bearable silence enveloping most of the remaining passage. Am I crazy, risking my life for some gold coins, he questioned himself. And if I don't take risks? Will I end up just toiling away for someone else? The choices were equally bleak, driving his mood fouler as they plodded along.

The sun was edging close to the horizon when the silhouette of the hill resembling a pyramid topped by farmhouse buildings fitting Boekenhoutfontein's description came into view. "Is that your farm?" he barked over his shoulder, the first words spoken between them in a dozen miles.

Seconds ticked by before he heard her rustling, so he suspected she might have been dozing. Once again her head poked out from between the loose flaps. "We're here."

He maneuvered up the winding drive to the main building, a house typical of Transvaal farmhouses, with a pitched corrugated roof and plain stuccoed walls. The structure reminded Jacob more of the style he had seen further south in the Cape Colony than those typical of the Boer in this area. Out its front door tumbled a husband and wife, the man resembling the President, followed by scurrying servants. No one seemed surprised to see a strange man driving a covered wagon, even though he had been assured this mission was a secret. Perhaps Kruger dispatched a messenger to precede him? He had no time to ponder this, as one of the servants took charge bringing his horse to a halt while the couple hurried to the rear and threw back the flaps.

"Mama!" bellowed the husband in a deep bass, dropping the back board and opening his arms to embrace his mother. Amidst this tumult of welcome, he waited, wondering where they would lodge him. Immediately a second servant beckoned at him to follow. Jumping down from the seat, he dusted himself off and prepared to accompany his guide, expecting to be consigned to another array of hay bales. Before they could set off, Mrs. Kruger's voice rang out. "Itzkowitz, come here."

What does she want to bother me with now, he wondered. Was she going to complain to the son how he almost got them killed? Jaw clenched, he changed direction and marched stiffly to where the Kruger woman was stationed behind the wagon, surrounded by a gaggle of children. Reaching this cluster, he planted hands on hips and waited.

"Itzkowitz, this is my son Pieter and daughter-in-law Cecilia. They were just asking about the man who drove the cart here. What should I tell them?" she said.

"I am Itzkowitz, Jacob Itzkowitz. For the time being I work in the mining camp for my Uncle, a horse merchant. Someday I will own land and a farm, maybe as grand as this," he replied confidently.

Pieter laughed. "Good to meet you, Mr. Farmer-to-be. Mother tells me you are level-headed."

"Itzkowitz," the President's wife spoke up before he could respond. "You're a Jew, but you're not like the other Peruvians. You're brave. You could have turned me over to the bandits, maybe gotten a reward. You lived up to the bargain and protected me."

"A deal's a deal," he said simply.

"Everyone says that, but not everyone acts that way. My husband will be pleased, he will reward you with gold. I want to give you something myself." She held out a coin in her palm, roughly the size of an English crown, bearing the profile of Kruger rather than Victoria. "This is a special piece. It's not a Kruger *pond*, but rather a medal of friendship. The President mints a small number of these to give to persons who perform special service for the

ZAR. Whoever possesses one is blessed by good fortune. If you ever need a favor from an official, show him this."

Jacob stared dumbly at her open hand. Looking up, he saw her smiling at him for the first time in their trek. A sense of excitement welled up in him, an energy he had not felt since arriving in Africa. Maybe he really was destined for greater things.

Overboard
Crossing the Atlantic 1897

As Jacob approached the dock, he noticed a familiar looking man deep in conversation with two others. Fashionably dressed, with pince-nez and a fastidiously trimmed mustache, the man radiated authority. Hard to place him, thought Jacob, but I've seen that face before.

Jacob scanned the grand Union Steamship waiting room. Hundreds were milling, some with just a small tattered satchel in hand, others attended by black servants wrestling a herd of steamer trunks. The vast gaps in status and wealth of the passengers were familiar to him from having made this voyage in reverse just a few years before. This time he would embark in third class, a cut above steerage, an accomplishment that gave him inordinate satisfaction. A few years of hard work compounded by his luck in crossing paths with Kruger and he was rising. On my next passage, he thought, I will dine with the captain.

That's when it struck him. Barnato. The familiar face belonged to Barney Barnato, the Jewish diamond magnate. Barnato was lauded in Uncle Helman's Yiddish newspapers as emblematic of what was possible for Jews to achieve in southern Africa. Articles always noted he'd been born Barnett Isaacs in London's slums. For a time Isaacs/Barnato tried his hand as a performer, while never shying away from a bare-knuckled fist fight, a talent that came in handy more than once in the diamond digging camps of Kimberley. Yet humble origins and Jewish heritage hadn't held him back in the new frontier. His was one of the many stories promoting the parable that mining created a land of opportunity – save up a little money digging, buy up some mining rights, find a few diamonds through hard work and luck, plow funds back into buying more claims, and own more mines. Within ten years Barnato had metamorphosed from a nobody, just another Jew escaping oblivion, to an immensely wealthy baron powerful enough to challenge the legendary Cecil Rhodes. Rhodes in return cleverly sponsored Barnato joining the exclusive Kimberley Club, then backed Barnato's election to the Cape Parliament for Kimberley. Jacob had re-read many times the tale of Barnato's rise, akin to a biblical Joseph, searching for lessons. Now by sheer chance Jacob found himself proximate to the great man himself.

I must talk to him, he thought. How to get close? Then he remembered what he carried in his pocket. Jacob strode brashly towards the clutch of men.

"Mr. Barnato, I am an admirer," Jacob strode up to the three men, placing himself squarely in front of Barnato.

"Who are you?" Barnato half-scowled.

Jacob flourished the distinctive medallion, holding up Kruger's likeness facing Barnato. "I am a Hebrew befriended by President Kruger, one who hopes to follow your path to fortune."

Barnato absorbed the cocksure young man's speech and audacity in flashing the Kruger trinket at him, then broke out into a guffaw.

"Well, friend of Kruger, do you have a name?"

"Itzkowitz, Jacob Itzkowitz."

"Then, Mr. Itzkowitz, I wish you good fortune. You have the brass it takes to push to the top in this part of the world. We will enjoy very different levels of this ship, but perhaps we shall meet again in the future," Barnato said with the air of a man bemused by a precocious child. With that, he turned his back on the interloper and resumed conversing with his companions.

Jacob understood he was being dismissed like a servant, but nonetheless remained elated. He had met the great man, had talked to him like an equal. So what if Barnato abruptly terminated the conversation? The encounter was enough to buoy Jacob's spirits for the fortnight crossing.

Hours later the SS Scot slipped her moorings and edged into Cape Town's majestic Table Bay Harbour. Passengers lined the decks, waving emotional farewells to loved ones on shore. The Scot's tall central funnels discharged billows of black coal smoke, horns blasting in salute to the onlookers as the steamer headed for open sea. As they passed Table Mountain, Jacob imagined the journey ahead. Weeks at sea up the continental coast, landing in Southampton, a shorter crossing to Hamburg, and finally the last leg landward home to reunite with Leah. Then would come the hard part, persuading her father to let them marry and return to the Rand. The voyage would furnish time to compose his best arguments to win the prize he sought.

In the meantime, he determined to enjoy the passage on the Scot. On this crossing he was avoiding the hard straw mattress and heavy rough blanket assigned to single men in cramped dormitories on the lower steerage decks. He and a hundred others had paid extra for middle deck berths, sleeping just below the cabins of the wealthier passengers. That made it easier for him take the air on deck and stretch his legs whenever weather permitted.

The voyage was largely unremarkable. There were rough seas a few days out, but Jacob managed to not get overly seasick. The shipboard monotony gave him plenty of time to imagine what awaited him in Shavlan. For the last three years, he and his cousin Leah had been exchanging letters. Their correspondence had begun lightheartedly, Leah sharing small bits of local news, he telling her tales of frontier characters. Over time, however, they shared increasingly intense, personal thoughts and feeling. Leah, only sixteen when he left, now was very much of marrying age. By all indications, also of marrying intentions. His fondness for her had grown stronger during the lonely times in the Rand. Her writings indicated she'd grown into a sensible young woman, containing hints that their common Aunt Sora had portrayed for Leah the challenging life of a married woman in the Rand. Nonetheless, Leah insisted she was undeterred by the rougher edges of mining town life. Encouraged, here he was, journeying thousands of miles to ask for her hand. Mental images of his bride-to-be proved an excellent antidote to the boredom of the passage.

Ten days out of Cape Town, the Scot was nearing the Island of Madeira off the coast of Morocco. The excitement of the passage to England was waning for Jacob, boredom and impatience waxing. The allure of spotting an exotic isle had drawn him out of his berth for a stroll.

Looking across the white caps, he recalled his prior voyage along the African coast, escaping a bleak future if he remained in Shavlan. I've come up in the world since then, he complimented himself, dwelling on how he'd become so confident he could brashly approach the world famous Barnato and make the man's acquaintance.

Suddenly the ship's bell began clanging loudly. Jacob lurched towards the railing as the steamer came about. Shouting from the opposite side of the ship grew louder, drawing him to the stern and back up the port side to see what was afoot. The chaotic scene defied comprehension at first. A man in uniform was thrashing about in the waves, hauling a life preserver. A limp body 50 yards further to the rear floated face down. Other crew were launching a life boat, and a crowd was gathering on deck.

He gravitated into the mass of passengers peering over the side as if watching a rowing match, but their commentary indicated otherwise. Jacob could hear a lively debate, punctuated by murmurs of "pushed, I tell you" and "the rich cannot take it when they lose their money, they're cowards" and "poor Mr. Barnato, I hear he had three small children." Barnato? Was he the one bobbing lifelessly in the sea? Within a remarkably short time, the rescue boat was hauled back to deck level. He gaped along with hundreds of others as four sailors carried a human form wrapped in canvas through the furthest first class doorway. Speculation in multiple languages grew raucous all around him.

Eventually the crowds dispersed, so he headed below deck to his berth. Falling in with a smattering of second class passengers spinning out theories, he caught sight of another passenger pointing a uniformed man in his direction.

"Excuse me sir, are you Mr. Itzkowitz?" A crewman loomed in front of Jacob, eyes expressionless.

"Yes. What's this about?" Jacob replied guardedly.

"Nothing troubling sir. The Captain wants a word with you, if you don't mind sir."

What could the Captain want with him? Was he accused of something? He'd been nowhere near where Barnato must have plunged overboard. A chill ran down his spine. Was someone misconstruing his dockside conversation with the diamond baron as a threat?

"All right, lead the way," Jacob said, determined to act nonchalant.

The Captain's door opened promptly in response to the crewman's knock. "You must be Mr. Itzkowitz, come in sir." The Captain seemed at ease, but Jacob remained wary.

"I have a request for you from the Barnato family, sir," the Captain began. "I understand that it is Hebrew custom for a Jewish man to guard the body of a deceased."

"Yes, that's right. I was part of the *chèvre Kadisha* in the Rand," he responded.

"Mr. Joel has asked for you to perform that task. Might I tell him your reply?"

Jacob exhaled. He felt relief that there was no accusation. But acting as a *shomer* would mean solitude, forgoing mingling with fellow third-class passengers, any one of whom might prove to be the connection that made his future. He would mourn the pleasures of the passage, his daily walks, the open-air meals with other strivers dreaming of bright futures. Trade that for the vigil, locked alone with a dead body? It wasn't fear – he had stood *shomer* for a miner killed in a collapse. He felt trapped. Maybe that observant Jew he'd met, Epstein, should watch the body? He indulged this yearning for escape briefly until a pang of guilt won out. He couldn't shirk his duty to the grieving family.

"Let me talk to this Mr. Joel," he replied firmly.

Escorted by a crewman, he ascended through levels of increasingly opulent materials and furnishings. Suits were of a finer cut, dresses more resplendent. Finally he was ushered into the first class smoking room, with its leather benches and dark mahogany paneling. A room of wealth. He knew he'd made the right choice. Always better to go with the richest friend you can make.

A short man sat with a cigarette at a far table, appearing lost in thought. Jacob recognized him from Barnato's entourage before embarkation.

"Ah, Itzkowitz," Joel remained seated, waving a hand at a chair. "Good of you to come. Did the Captain tell you why we've asked you here?"

"Mr. Barnato needs a *shomer*. But why me? There must be other religious Jews on board," replied Jacob evenly.

"Well, you demonstrated confidence in yourself, marching up to him on the dock. I was there, you may remember. A man as self-possessed as you is right for the task. My poor uncle was out of his mind when he jumped. You undoubtedly know that under Jewish law he nevertheless gets the usual burial rites. His body must be watched constantly until we land," Joel looked him in the eye, seeming to try to discern something.

"I know what's customary. But we are four days out, I believe. Isn't there someone to relieve me?"

"I'm afraid this is a job for one man," Joel said with finality.

He sensed Joel meant more than he was saying, but decided to keep still and wait. Silence hung for a moment.

"We know that guarding a body for four days is an arduous task. Would twenty-one Guineas be a fair compensation?" Joel said casually.

Jacob could not avoid a start. That's a fortune, he thought. He must want something more than just the body washed and watched. "Why yes, more than fair. Is that all there is to it, I follow the rituals, recites the psalms, stay with Mr. Barnato's body?" he ventured tentatively.

"You are a perceptive fellow, as I intuited," Joel said. "Let me be candid. Mr. Barnato was, well, quite famous. His widow and I are worried about rumors floating around. You can imagine, Itzkowitz, the speculation about the circumstances of his death. We don't want the odd person going in and out of where his body will be kept. We want a strong man who will respect the family and keep all this private. Can you do that, Mr. Itzkowitz?"

"He deserves that respect. All Jews in the Rand admire the way Mr. Barnato made his fortune. He went from being like the rest of us, nothing in our pockets, to the top of society." He choose his words carefully.

"Good, then it is settled. Please follow the crewman and begin right away. We will have your belongings and food brought to the room." With that, Joel stubbed out his cigarette, turned and strode out of the ornate room.

Within the hour, Jacob was alone in an elegant cabin with the corpse. Barnato's body lay covered by a sheet on one of two beds. Jacob set to the task. A body without its soul must be treated with respect, thoroughly cleaned and purified for the burial. With a basin of water and a pile of washcloths, he began the ritual, toe to head. Each portion of the body was uncovered slowly and carefully. Jacob worked steadily for hours.

As the cleansing reached Barnato's chest, Jacob noticed something odd. Two areas on either side of the sternum, each the size of a large coin, were bruised. Had the man struck something solid that was floating by when he landed in the water? The discolorations were maybe eight or ten inches apart, just below each breast. Strange, Jacob said to himself. I guess if someone jumps overboard there is no predicting how he will land.

After completing his labor on the front of the lifeless form, Jacob rolled the body over to attend to the rear. Another curious marking caught his eye. A black and blue stripe across the lower back, a single neat slash as if drawn with a straight edge. This is even stranger, thought Jacob. How could he hit debris on both his front and his back?

Jacob resumed his chore, but could not let go of the puzzle of these markings. Had Barnato been in a fight aboard ship? It was common knowledge that he was an ardent pugilist in his younger days, but certainly not now that he was nearly 50 years old and among the wealthiest men in Africa? And with whom would he have been fighting on the Scot?

Maybe the bruises have nothing to do with his death. Perhaps an accident somewhere, fallen down stairs? If he'd hit his head in a fall, that might explain why people were saying Barnato had been in an unstable state. The common wisdom aboard ship was that he went insane and jumped. Yet the markings didn't match up with where bruising from falling down stairs would appear, and they appeared fresh. Jacob reconstructed the layout of the deck area where Barnato had gone overboard. Like other passengers, Jacob was drawn there out of morbid curiosity, baffled by why such a rich and powerful man would choose to leave this world. In his mind's eye, Jacob took a mental tour of the row of deck chairs along the wall, the promenade that was narrower near the front of the ship than aft, and the sturdy wooden railing atop its iron frame.

The railing! Straight, with a narrow sharply rounded edge. About the height of a man's lower back. Could that be it? Certainly the railing made the most sense as the source of the straight line of bruising on Barnato's back. Still, to cause an injury as vivid and elongated as the one Jacob saw on the corpse, the man must have been moving with great force. And stumbling against the railing could not explain bruises on his chest. Those looked more like the results of being punched from the front. What if he had been punched or pushed hard, then hit his back on the railing? He would have....

Jacob caught himself. These are dangerous thoughts. The nephew's report was that his uncle jumped. But no one has seen what I have seen, he realized. Nor would they. Due to Joel's arrangements only he, Jacob, would be examining the body so immediately after death. Would bruises fade away by the time they reached port, he wondered? He searched nervously around the bare room, as if someone might be spying on his thoughts. It took him a few minutes to feel settled enough to resume fulfilling his duty to the deceased. Jacob continued methodically until the body was thoroughly cleansed. He continued the *taharah*, the ritual purification of the body. As a baby he entered this world cleansed and pure, so will he depart. Carefully Jacob poured three buckets of water over the corpse, from head to toe, right side then left side, then patted what remained of Barnato dry with freshly laundered towels. After that, there was nothing more to do but rest and await the end of the voyage.

Rest eluded him during the lonely vigil. Jacob found himself constantly turning over the clues, wrestling with all possible explanations for his observations. Troubled, he slipped out late one evening to examine the scene of the incident. Heavy rain pelting down, he assumed no passengers would be abroad, and he was right. Jacob slowly placed a hand on the railing at the approximate location where Barnato went overboard, then carefully turned round while keeping a tight grip. He felt the thin edge press sharply into his back. The height matched.

On the fourth day next, the Scot docked in Southampton just after nine in the morning. Jacob was reciting the morning prayers beside the body, properly shrouded in a plain white *kittel* sewn by the widow from sheets. Three short knocks at the door interrupted *shacharit*. Joel entered followed by two men with a stretcher. The pair moved quickly, hoisted the body onto the conveyance, and silently left. Joel turned to Jacob: "You've performed your task well, Mr. Itzkowitz. Do you have any questions for me?"

Jacob looked Joel in the eye, unsure what to say. "No sir," Jacob finally answered, returning Joel's gaze. "Do you have anything to tell me?"

Joel's eyes narrowed, as he appeared to catch just the slightest hint of implication in Jacob's manner.

"Here are your twenty one guineas, Mr. Itzkowitz," Joel said, as if all that was being discussed was the conclusion of a simple bargain. "We trust that you remember our initial conversation. Mr. Barnato's death has already caused a great stir in the global newspapers. Foolish people are fostering all kinds of speculation. I know you will keep your role in this entirely between us."

"Of course, Mr. Joel," Jacob said, clutching the proffered purse.

"We are a large family with connections throughout the world, Mr. Itzkowitz, with lots of resources. Please remember that," Joel said, his voice rising just a hint. At that, he turned his back and exited the stateroom. Jacob stood, mind racing.

Jubilee
London 1897

Posters proclaimed the grand celebration. "Queen's Diamond Jubilee!" shouted at Jacob from wall after wall as he walked away from the Southampton docks. His original plan was to book the first available passage to Hamburg, then on to home. Alone aboard the Scot, guarding the body, his longing to get back to Shavlan had grown in intensity. Although Jacob didn't regard himself as the least bit sentimental, watching over a dead body conjured up memories of lost relatives and a desire to reunite with the living. But a chance to see this Queen the English constantly talked about, maybe that was worth spending a few extra days in this country amidst the bustle of festivity. After all, the English seem poised to take control of South Africa away from the Boer. Maybe he should get to know them better. The ones he knew from the Rand were not as friendly as the Boer. If I am going to settle back there with my bride, Jacob told himself, it might help to know more about them. Maybe even make a few friends here in

England. With the reward from Barnato's family on top of his pay from Kruger, he could certainly afford lodgings for a few extra days. Stay he would.

The train to London delighted him. Having only traveled previously in third class on rough rails in Africa, the two hour journey across the English countryside to Waterloo station was another burst of opulence. Like glimpsing the upper class areas of the Scot, this exposure to the benefits of having a few pounds in his pocket spurred Jacob's imagination. He spent much of the trip gazing at the rolling landscape while considering various possible futures. Arriving in London, he set about wandering the streets in search of rooms. The city was mobbed – undoubtedly the attraction of the great Jubilee. After a few failed attempts, Jacob found a landlady in the East End with a modest room willing to let it for a few days at a steep premium.

The next day Jacob rose early, partook of the landlady's fare, and inquired of the other boarders what they knew of the celebratory agenda for the day. Fortified with food and information, he headed off to find a good spot from which to watch the promised procession. Jacob determined to position himself among the hundreds of thousands crowding the London sidewalks at a point near St. Paul's Cathedral, where he might get the best view. Along the winding streets of the City, vendors hawked every kind of souvenir. Flags, mugs and any number of other objects that could bear the likeness of Her Royal Highness were on display. Tourists seemed all too willing to hand over a few pence for a bauble marking the day. The air of festivity was intense, although offset by the presence of a continuous phalanx of soldiers, bayonets pointing skyward along the six-mile procession route. Jacob was unsure whether the massive military presence was prompted by fear of an unruly crowd getting out of control, or simply illustrated the English propensity to put the power of the Queen's warriors on display.

Hours and hours passed as Jacob waited among the sea of English. Mixed in were some obvious foreigners, subjects from the far reaches of the Empire, among them Malays, Sikhs and even a few Africans. As the sun reached midday, the regal procession began to appear along the route. Over a dozen grand carriages, gilded with the wealth harvested from India, Africa, Occania and the New World, led the way bearing members of the extended royal family, . Then, finally, the eight cream-colored horses with the Queen's open carriage came into view. There she was, the elderly Victoria, all in black —her mourning color for husband Albert and two of her children. All around Jacob delirious subjects of all ages cheered wildly, at one point breaking into spontaneous verses of "God Save the Queen." As Victoria's carriage turned past Jacob to round a corner leading to St. Paul's for a thanksgiving service, he could swear he saw the Queen Mother wiping tears from her cheek.

Jacob was surprised to discover himself feeling moved by the display, but not in the way of her adoring subjects. This Victoria is just another Czar, he thought. In fact, her granddaughter was married to Czar Nicholas. Other grandchildren sat on other thrones throughout Europe. Nicholas had been Czar only a short time, but Jacob expected him to be as brutal as had been his father Alexander, at least towards the Jews. Would Victoria's heirs be any better? The people here seemed to love her, but many of the peasants back in Russia cheered loudly for the Czar as well. Sometimes it seemed that the worse he treated them, the more the serfs loved him. Not the Jews, though. We have no love for Czars, that's why so many of us ran away on ships to Africa, or America. In America, at least, there are no Czars. His thoughts drifted to his oldest sister, who had written him saying that life was good in America for her and her husband. Maybe I could get rich there, he mused. Uncle Helman needs me for his horses. Can he get along without me? Then again, he recalled, Helman is the one who has been saying that the way the Boer and the English treat the Kaffir is troubling. If that's how they treat the blacks they rely on to do all the backbreaking work for them, how long before they turn on the Jews next? Already they have taken to calling us Peruvians, falsely blaming us for the collapse of their mining shares.

As he walked back to his lodging house, this reverie kept running through his head. He decided to focus on one thing – returning to Shavlan to marry his dear cousin. After that, he would weigh his options.

In the meantime, Jacob had one more destination in London before his ship sailed the next day. He carefully removed the tissue paper letter from his pocket, examining the address scrawled under the signature in familiar handwriting. He would get directions from the landlady, who seemed to possess encyclopedic knowledge of all the back alleys of the East End. He calculated that arriving at Moishe's at the dinner hour was the best strategy. His visit would be a complete surprise, given that Jacob had not himself expected to be in London until forty-eight hours earlier.

They had been inseparable since they were little boys, from the day Moishe became part of the family. For Jacob it had been almost like having a twin. Many in town mistook them for biological brothers given their familial resemblance. While Jacob loved his siblings, since his mother's death he'd also harbored an ever-present feeling of distance from them. With Moishe it was different. He was the one member of the *mishpocha* with whom Jacob felt

completely natural, safe even. When at age 17 Jacob decided it was time to leave Shavlan to make his fortune, he
assumed Moishe would join him. They would be a team,
protecting each other along the difficult journey that lay
ahead. He thought back to the day Moishe revealed a different vision of his future.

"Moishe, I've saved up enough for passage to Cape
Town," Jacob had said brightly as they pitchforked hay for
winter feed.

"Cape Town? You're still serious about working
in the gold fields?" Moishe had replied, wiping his
brow.

"We'll get rich together! They're still finding plenty of
new strikes. It's hard work for a few years, but we'll strike it
rich," Jacob had pressed.

"Jacob, you're strong as an ox. You could live that life,"
Moishe had answered gently. "Me, I'm better at using my
head than my back."

"What are you talking about, Moishe? You're plenty
strong. You work the fields sunrise to sundown during the
harvest, just like the peasants."

"That's just it, Jacob," Moishe had said firmly. "I'm
leaving Shavlan so I don't have to break my back laboring
like a peasant."

"Moishe, I need you! You want me to go alone?" he'd
pleaded.

"Jacob, I'd just be more a burden than a help," Moishe
had said, his hands clasped in front of him as if praying.

"Where will you go instead?" Jacob had asked eventually.

"Lots of Jews are going to London. Maybe that's my future."

Now as Jacob sat on a hard mattress in the decrepit lodging house re-reading Moishe's most recent letter, the bitterness came rushing back. Moishe had been the one family member on whom Jacob had counted to always be honest with him, yet even Moishe had not been forthcoming. He'd never mentioned having separate plans until Jacob had forced the issue. That had troubled Jacob greatly, reviving the pain of the secret his family had kept from him as a child. Yet Jacob could never stay angry with Moishe for long.

Moishe's occasional letters over the last few years had detailed the life he'd built for himself in London. The growing Jewish diaspora flooding into London from Kovno province embraced Moishe. He was surrounded by *landsmen,* a community of like-minded strivers all rejoicing in their freedom from the privations of the Czar's empire. While his first reports to Jacob were filled with awe at the grandeur of London, over time Moishe admitted that adjusting to the new country was difficult, finding a path to fortune even more challenging. After a year of odd jobs and subsistence living, he'd gotten a lucky chance. Striking up an acquaintance with a well-dressed young man his own age at the Great Synagogue had led to being taken on as a junior clerk in a small bank connected to the man's father, who came from one of the older Jewish merchant families in London. While this position kept him out of poverty, Moishe described how it instead drenched him in drudgery. The hours were long, the tasks repetitive and boring. As junior clerk he was at the beck and call of every other soul in the establishment. Worse yet was the stultifying insistence of the bank's President on a rigid code of conduct. To maintain an essential veneer of propriety, the banker regulated not just dress and decorum during the work day, but the life Moishe could lead outside the bank's gilded walls. He could not frequent any establishment the banker deemed unseemly, limiting the delights of which a young man could partake in the glittering city.

Jacob therefore was unsure in what spirits he would find Moishe, if he found Moishe at all. Armed with his landlady's directions for navigating through the winding streets, Jacob headed down Whitechapel, turned off onto Commercial Street, and sought out the alley in which he was supposed to find Moishe's lodgings. Wending down Brick Lane, Jacob passed row after row of dilapidated residences. At the number indicated in the letter, seeing not the worst of slum buildings but hardly the grandest, Jacob entered the foyer then knocked. Spotting an older woman dressed entirely in black sweeping the hallway, he said simply "Moishe Mazaroff?" "Top floor, back room on the right," she called back without looking up.

Jacob bounded up the stairs. Exhilaration saved him from feeling out of breath as he rounded the third flight, headed to the designated door, and pounded loudly. "Who's there?" came a tired sounding voice. "Moishe, open up, it's Jacob!"

The door flew open wide, revealing a thinner but well dressed Moishe staring in disbelief at his surprise guest. "Jacob? Jacob, you're here?" was all he managed to utter before Jacob encircled him in a tight embrace. Moishe clamped back hard, the pair remaining entangled for close to a minute. Finally Moishe stepped back, held Jacob on both shoulders, and examined him up and down. "You're really here. How is that possible? You look weathered, but stronger. It's so good to see you. Come in!"

For the next hour each recounted to the other the details of their lives during the three year gap since last they were together. Moishe painted a more detailed picture of the life of a young Russian Jew in London than the constraints of a letter had allowed, conceding that he was adjusting to the demands of banking as time wore on, but still determined to somehow rise much higher. Jacob for his part regaled Moishe with what must have seemed fanciful tales of frontier life, drawing out the story of his dangerous errand for Kruger and the rewards that brought, ending on the chance encounter with the Barnato death that resulted in his coming to see the Queen's Jubilee.

"Barnato's death was in all the papers!" Moishe exclaimed. "I was just reading that the coroner's inquest determined he was temporarily insane when he jumped overboard."

"Let me see that," Jacob said, reaching for the newspaper lying on a bedside table. He scanned the short article, eyes lighting on passages that quoted testimony.

The deceased's nephew, Mr. Solomon Joel, testified that he and Barnato were strolling just before the incident. "Barney asked me 'What is the time?' Then I saw him dash by. I had not time, in fact, to even to lift my eyes, when he gave a spring. I threw out my hands to catch him, but only caught the back of his trousers. He jumped over the side. I screamed 'murder,' and saw the fourth officer, who was sitting dozing, and said, 'For God's sake save him'.

The other witness was fourth officer Clifford: "On the 14th, I saw him leap overboard. Mr. Joel said something I don't remember, and I said "I'll go," and jumped in after him. I saw the body floating face down some way off. I was subsequently picked up by the ship's boat."

Jacob furled his brow. If Clifford was dozing, how could he say he saw Barnato jump? And why would Joel shout "murder" instead of "man overboard"?

"You were on the ship, Jacob! What did you see? The tabloids are full of speculation about the mysterious drowning."

"I didn't see a thing," Jacob replied, eliding around Moishe's probing questions propounding the various theories floating around. He decided it was time to change the subject.

"Moishe, I'm going back to Shavlan, to marry," Jacob declared.

"Have you a match?"

"I will marry Leah," Jacob said, as if announcing a settled fact of nature.

"Leah? Your cousin? She must be quite a beauty by now," Moishe said with a wink.

"We've been writing letters. She's ready to leave Shavlan," Jacob added.

"We are all scattering. Soon there will be no one left to tend to the cemetery. Who will visit our loved ones when everyone has run away to another country?" Moishe said wistfully.

"It's a terrible thing, Moishe. There is little I miss about Shavlan, but it has been hard not to visit her grave," Jacob said, his eyes slightly misting. "I guess that's why the rabbis invented *yahrzeit*."

Mama
Shavlan 1882

The two chubby boys lay in the tall grass listening to frogs croaking. Tall birch trees lining the Susve riverbanks arched overhead, guarding them as they pretended to be spies tracking a band of Cossacks. The occasional encounter with a fox or porcupine transformed the pair into expert hunters. The honking of a vast flock of geese overhead during fall migration snapped their eyes upward, setting Jacob to wondering what might draw these noisy birds south like a magnet. He cherished these hours with Moishe in their secret fortress, a small untended meadow formed where the slow Susve waters reached the bottom of a u-shape bend and began turning north and west. There the companions could pass an afternoon undisturbed, telling each other the stories little boys share, or marveling at an unbroken trail of ants marching from log to decaying log.

It would be dinner time soon. Knowing they must be home in time for the evening milking, the pair were storing up last lazy moments. It did not take both of them to do the chore – Jacob had been the milking helper since he could walk, and doing it on his own the last few years. But since Moishe had begun living with them, they did everything together. At first Moishe was tentative – his shopkeeper parents had not owned a cow, only chickens. Reaching under the huge bovine bulk made him nervous. Over the past year he'd become sure of hand, seeming to love squeezing out the warm sweet stream into a pail. In the same way, Jacob had at first been tentative at having another boy in the house. He loved being the youngest boy of the family and the bounty of time that gave him with Mama. He was the one she would milk with when he was littler. Later, when he could fill half a pail himself, her joyous exclamation "What a big boy to produce so much milk!" would fill him with a sense of power. When Moishe suddenly arrived, he feared his special time with Mama would be stolen from him. Gradually that fear gave way to the camaraderie of having an almost brother his own age.

That evening the boys produced an abundance of milk, deftly managing not to spill any while lugging the pail into the house. They proudly presented the bounty to Mama Rochel (at first Moishe had called her Aunt Rochel, but over time her gentle coaxing brought him around to calling her Mama.) Normally she would have beamed her warmest smile, wrapping them in enormous hugs. Her hugs always left Jacob infused with joy, feeling safer and calmer. Not that he was overly fearful of anything particular during most days. But the other boys at school had started teasing him more and more, calling him a "fatty." Sometimes he could hear the Russian boys, especially the older ones, talking about "yids" in menacing sounding ways. When he reported this at dinner one night, his father had told him to ignore them, "they're just dumb peasants who talk to hear themselves talk." He wasn't sure Papa was right about that. What about that Jewish boy in another town, around bar mitzvah age, badly beaten by half a dozen Russian teens after he called them stupid oxen? None of his friends knew if the story were true, but nevertheless it made him uneasy. An embrace from Mama was like being girded in a suit of armor, one that would protect him from any evil.

So when Mama merely half-smiled and meekly told the boys "Good job, put the milk down in the corner" without the customary hug, his face fell. Had they done something wrong? Was Mama annoyed with him? He stepped towards her, arms outstretched towards her waist. "Ah, Jacob, come here, I'm just a little tired today," she said, stooping a bit to lay hands on his head while he clung tightly. "You too, Moishe," she turned, offering the same soothing touch to her poor sister's son. "Now boys, go wash up. We will have dinner as soon as Papa gets home."

The boys dutifully headed to the well behind the house with their wash basin. As Moishe pumped, Jacob held the the basin, letting his thoughts swirl. Out loud he said, "Moishe did Mama seem different to you?"

"She said she was tired, Jacob."

"But Mama never gets tired!" he nearly shouted at Moishe, the full basin sloshing as his hands shook.

"Everybody gets tired, Jacob. Don't get so crazy. It's probably nothing," Moishe replied evenly while they carried the white bowl to the tiny bathroom shared by the family.

Over the coming days, he noticed things to which he'd been oblivious before. At night, when he had trouble falling asleep, he would catch whispering voices. Hearing Moishe's light snoring, he'd sneak out of bed to put his ear to their bedroom door, straining to hear Mama and Papa. He could not make out their words, but he'd swear they sounded different than normal. After school, before he and Moishe wandered off seeking adventure, he began studying Mama's face and movements closely. Is she a little thinner, or am I imagining? Was she moving a little slower? Turning these worries over in his head at night, he could convince himself it must be imagination. Surely Papa or Fayga would tell me if anything were wrong, he assured himself. With that comforting mantra he could fall into a peaceful sleep.

Waking one morning from a disturbing dream, he got the notion to visit Uncle Oreh. It would be a long walk, as most fall days Uncle Oreh tended the flax fields of great-grandfather Israel a mile south of town. Hoping to be back in time to not be missed, he stuffed a hunk of brown bread into his pocket and set out briskly. If any adult in the family would reveal the secret of Mama's health, it would be Uncle Oreh. Oreh was the elder brother, the one his father and their other siblings looked to for guidance in important matters. At Pesach it was Oreh who easily assumed the role of family leader after great-grandfather had passed. It was Oreh to whom Jacob's oldest brother Hersch had gone for advice when considering what trade to take up. Uncle Oreh was the family oracle. Jacob trusted his Uncle to enlighten him even if no one else would.

After what seemed like half a day, Jacob reached the flax fields, finding Oreh hard at work alongside three helpers. "Jacob, you are a long way from the schoolhouse, are you lost?" Oreh called out in a jovial manner, head cocked to one side.

"No Uncle Oreh. I came with something important to ask you."

"It must be very important, my son, for you to come all this way on your own. Tell me," he said with an earnest look down at the boy, "what is this matter of such urgency?"

Jacob clasped his hands, wringing his wrists. His cheeks got red. Suddenly he felt foolish for coming, but he had to ask. "Mama" he stammered.

Oreh put down his scythe, stepped a little closer to Jacob. "What about Mama?" he asked, his eyes closely searching Jacob's face.

"Mama seems – different. She was lying down last week. Mama never does that. Everyone says it's nothing, but I think something is wrong. I am worried Uncle Oreh!"

Oreh knelt down, face now at Jacob's level, and touched one shoulder with his calloused hand. "Listen to me, Jacob. Your Mama Rochel, my sister-in-law, she is a strong woman. Even strong women get tired sometimes. Strong men get tired sometimes. You will grow up to be a strong man, and even you will get tired sometimes. That is all part of life. Now go back to your school before they send out a search party for you." He leapt forward, threw his arms around Oreh's neck and squeezed as hard as he could. Reassured, he ran back with a light heart, out of breath by the time he reached the schoolhouse.

Weeks went by. What was scary at first became routine over time. Maybe Mama was always this way and I just never noticed, he hypothesized. Maybe Mama and Papa always talk at night after we go to bed, I just never listened. Still uncertain, one afternoon he mustered the courage to question his oldest brother. "Hersch, is Mama, is she all right?" he inquired, holding up Hersch's delivery of a horse for their father. Hersch pursed his lips, halted a moment, then pronounced, "Jacob, stop asking questions. Everything is fine" before continuing on with the mare. Jacob soothed himself with his brother's certitude. Moishe doesn't seem to notice anything, and Fayga hasn't said anything, so maybe everything is normal, he repeated often to himself. Each night while reciting the *Shema* before bed he added an extra prayer asking God to keep Mama safe. Otherwise he assured himself all was fine.

Then came the day he arrived home from school to find Mama laying down in bed in the middle of the afternoon, breath rasping. His body reacted before his mind registered the panic. Dropping his book, he ran out of the house, legs carrying him to the secret meadow by the river bank. There Moishe found him, flung on the ground curled up with hands covering his face, shoulders heaving as if unable to catch his breath. Moishe too was panicking, mimicking his surrogate brother's surging emotions. Moishe dropped to his knees and put a hand on Jacob's shoulder, but he shook it off. "Go away", he sobbed. Moishe stayed put. As the hours passed, the frogs began their song. It became time for the evening milking, but both remained connected to the ground, absorbing its stability. Finally they heard Fayga's voice calling in the distance. "Jacob, Moishe, come home, it's time for dinner and Papa wants to talk to you." Gently pulling on his shoulders, Moishe managed to get him on his feet. They trudged home as if under a spell.

"Jacob, Moishe, sit with me at the table," Papa said as the pair came in following Fayga. Spent, they both sat, slumped. Papa leaned towards them, putting a hand on an arm of each. "I'm sure it was a shock to see Mama in bed today," he began. "She is never sick, never one to be in bed during the day. But something is happening inside Mama's body. The doctor says she just needs more rest. You are good boys, you help Mama with the work around the house. For a little while Mama will need to rest as much as possible. You will need to help more around the house. Fayga will need your help too. Can you do that?"

Jacob's hand twitched. His eyes rose up to meet his father's. He opened his mouth. At first no sound came out. Then, louder than he meant to, he cried out "Why didn't you tell me Mama was sick? Why did everyone keep it a secret?"

Gently, his father said, "We just weren't sure what was happening, so we didn't want to say anything to worry you."

"No, you all lied! You all pretended everything was OK. It's not!" Shaking off his father's hand, he bolted for his bedroom.

The six weeks that followed were a horror. Each day's waking brought terror of what he would find as Mama grew thinner and paler. When he brought her hot milk in the morning, she would gather up her warmest smile for him. For an instant Jacob would convince himself that she was getting better. Mama would thank him for being a special boy, for bringing her milk, as she took a sip and made a pronounced smack of her lips. After a few days he realized that she wasn't drinking his offering anymore, just putting it down on the side table as soon as he stepped away. Her hugs, once a cocoon warming his whole body, now felt like wires binding him. As the weeks passed, her soft moans became random shrieks of pain. Slapping his hands over his ears failed to block out his mother's suffering. Then Papa sent him to stay with Uncle Oreh. "It's just until Mama gets better, Jacob," Papa had said as they walked together to Oreh's. "I'll come get you when the time is right."

Ten days later Papa came for him. Seeing his father's face, he froze. Papa's eyes were red in a way he had never seen them. His father's burly shoulders sagged, his feet nearly dragged on the ground. Was Papa sick too, he wondered with growing terror? Running forward, he wrapped his arms tightly around Papa's waist, comforted by his sturdiness. Papa stopped and looked absently down at him. "Come home, Yankele, we have to put Mama to rest."

Shira's World
Shavlan 1897

The wisp of reddish whiskers suited him. Eliyahu had been a spindly child, easy to miss among the gaggle of boys spilling out of school each day. She had known him since she was little – in tiny Shavlan you would have to be a hermit to not know a little something about every other Jewish child. Now watching Eliyahu out of the corner of her eye, Shira took inventory: Two years older than her. The only son of Oreh, the flax farmer. Brother to her friend Leah. Always a book in hand, a quiet studious boy. Precocious in matters of the Talmud. A favorite of the Rabbi. Year before last, she recalled, Eliyahu left Shavlan for serious studies in a Vilna yeshiva. Now here he was, back to help his father with the fall harvest. Eliyahu's body, she noted in particular, had morphed from skinny teen into sturdy young man since last year's High Holidays.

Covertly stealing glimpses of Eliyahu while he toiled in the field, feelings rushed through her that were scary and exhilarating all at once. She'd had crushes and yearnings from time to time since her body had begun changing a few years earlier. The store keeper's son had smitten her for a while. They had even secretly stolen kisses on the rare occasions when they were alone. Last year she was swept up with the notion that Bentzi, who limped a bit, was very cute. Unfortunately Bentzi didn't seem interested in much beyond getting chores done for families that hired him for odd jobs.

The topic of boys and how they made her feel was one she spoke about only with her closest friend, Channah. Channah was older, more shapely, and attracted more attention from the local fellows. But like Shira, Channah thought most of them dull, with limited ambitions beyond someday taking over whatever it was their father or uncle did to feed the family. The two girls yearned to see the world, although exactly where to go and how to get there they had not worked out. Both were avid readers, and had ferreted out which adults in their village possessed books portraying life in exotic locales like Paris or New York or London. They discovered the furniture maker Spektor ventured twice a year to Kovno to trade, and during each trip he visited the Jewish free library for a pile of books. The girls talked the jovial old man into bringing a selection for each, which they would savor and share until his next journey.

Going about her daily routine, Shira often caught herself drifting to distraction with mental images of Eliyahu. Sometimes he was smiling at her from a distance, other times they were strolling in a garden. At first, when catching a daydream floating into her mind, she would gently reprimand herself with a slightly audible "that's silly". Such images, though, gave her a sliver of joy in otherwise dull days. Soon she was succumbing more and more to a sensual enjoyment of them. As the days expanded since last spotting Eliyahu, the small brief fantasies felt insufficient. She began weaving plans to encounter him in the flesh. What time does he head to the fields? When does he return home after a day's work? She knew the routines of the village and could make educated guesses as to his rhythms. She constructed a routine for herself to increase the odds of an apparently chance crossing of paths. Channah's house was down the street from Oreh's, so it became necessary to visit Channah in late afternoon to discuss their latest book. Her mother's brother's farm lay to the south, maybe there was something to be baked and delivered there? She concocted a dozen different interception options woven into her daily chores.

Soon her timing on the way to Channah's paid off. As she strolled slowly along the dusty street heading east, a tired looking Eliyahu came trudging from the fields. Adjusting her pace, Shira managed to pass in front of him a few houses before his destination. Holding her breath waiting to see if he would speak first, she felt an inordinate thrill when from behind she heard a hearty "Good afternoon, Shira". She glanced backwards, deliberately slowing her reply. "Good afternoon to you, Eliyahu. How goes the harvest?"

Nearer to his house they briefly fell in step while keeping a distance respectable in the ways of Shavlan. Now at her side, he answered, "The days are long, the work hard, but I take joy in helping my father. It is a wonderful change from the yeshiva." With that, they reached his door. Eliyahu smiled broadly and turned up his stoop, Shira merely nodding goodbye before continuing on her contrived errand. Intense feelings rushed through her again as she hurried away. *Karenina* sprang to mind, a volume she and Channah had read to each other much of last year.

Memories of its characters flooded back, frightening and intoxicating her as she reached Channah's house.

Over the next two weeks, she achieved four more accidental planned encounters. One was an early morning crossing of paths as she delivered eggs to a family friend's home. Another was truly by chance, when Eliyahu happened to be shopping for potatoes at the market on a rare day off from fieldwork. Each such meeting produced a few words of greeting, smiles, sometimes an awkward silence punctuated by blushes. Each left an aura of ending all too soon. Shira suspected that Eliyahu had feelings for her, but what those feelings were her senses could not quite discern. More unsettling, she could not quite interpret her own feelings. Her only certainty was an intense desire to spend more time alone with him. She just needed a plan.

Shira methodically set about contemplating the geography of the area, plotting out his likely daily circuit to and from the flax fields. Some of his route would be along town roads, where many villagers passed to and fro. At the flax fields others would be working: local hired men and even Oreh himself. Neither setting would offer any chance of privacy. In her mind's eye she traced his route and considered more options. Open fields also would not do; it would seem strange for her to stalk him across a wide expanse. Mentally walking further along his path, she realized that his route required crossing the small wooden bridge over the Susve. Just before that, to the west, was a dense stand of trees. The birches blocked from view a lush field of wild flowers and grasses along the banks where the Susve curved sharply back north. As a girl she had picked flowers there with friends during short intervals away from school and chores. That oasis was generally deserted. Perhaps she could entice Eliyahu to walk with her there?

Two days later she chanced upon her opportunity. Her mother had preserved pears from a particularly abundant crop. With an excess beyond the capacity of their storage area, her mother wanted to gift several jars of fruit to her brother. Shira quickly offered to be the emissary. Her mother, happy to not make the long trek herself, quickly accepted. Shira then waited patiently for the moment Mama departed to buy a chicken for the next night's Shabbos dinner. With Mama not looking on, she changed into a nicer frock and brushed her hair. Luckily, the timing worked well. She had already calculated when he would likely be leaving the fields and reaching the river crossing, and Mama's shopping excursion provided a cushion of time. She set off, basket of pear jars in hand. As she left town and crossed into the fields descending to the Susve, anticipation grew. She felt suffused with an urge to be held by Eliyahu. Her earlier fear of such urges had receded, she realized, while the thrill of imagining had blossomed.

Once the weathered footbridge came into sight, Shira slowed her gait almost to the point of being stationary. Nonchalance, she told herself, was the demeanor to achieve. She began paying close attention to any plant of slightest beauty, and strained to see any rabbits or rodents scurrying in her vicinity. For nearly fifteen minutes she preoccupied herself with the flora and fauna along the path, inching along towards the bridge. Finally she spied Eliyahu in the distance, scythe on shoulder. He seemed lost in thought, never looking up from his path until he was nearly to the bridge. To her extreme delight, when Eliyahu finally seemed to notice another person ahead, he broke out into a beaming grin and excitedly called "Shira!"

"Oh, hello Eliyahu," she replied, adopting a tone to convey at most mild enthusiasm.

"What are you doing here?" Eliyahu said, advancing quickly across the river and closing the gap between them.

"Delivering Mama's pear preserves to my uncle. You know, he has the farm a little to the south," she said as he came to a stop directly in front of her. "It's a lovely afternoon. I would love to stroll a bit before going there. Are you in a hurry?"

Eliyahu's eyes widened a bit. "Why, no! It would be a pleasure to accompany you."

"Wonderful! I know a lovely field close by. Few in town even know it exists. Would you like to see it?"

"Sure. Lead the way!"

She pointed towards the woods to her right and set off, Eliyahu walking in silence at her side. It suddenly dawned on her that she had not planned out this part. What to talk about? She became nervous, worrying Eliyahu would find her dull. "How goes the harvest?" she asked, exhaling.

"Oh, it goes well. The crop is good this year, which means a lot more work before Rosh Hashonah," Eliyahu replied, taking evident pride in his work. He added nothing more, and the silence returned. When they reached the stand of trees, she concentrated on finding the narrow trail she and Channah used to admit themselves into the serene pasture beyond. For a few minutes their entire exchange consisted of "this way" and "watch out for the low branch" punctuated by "I see" and "oh thank you."

They penetrated the thicket, emerging into an expanse of wildflowers stretching a quarter mile down to the Susve below. As they passed from the shadows of forest into the late afternoon golden glow bathing the field, Eliyahu gawked. "You didn't tell me how beautiful this would be!"

"I'd forgotten myself how wonderful it is," Shira replied, feeling herself aglow. "I haven't been here for years. There are more flowers than I remember. I love it!"

They stepped forward in unison, scanning across the colorful field, enchanted.

"Let's go sit down by the river," she suggested. Eliyahu fell in close behind her as she aimed for a bend of low bushes along the banks where a wild patch of rue burst forth. Arriving at the gentle slope bordering the so-called herbs of repentance, she turned back to Eliyahu, reached out a hand and gestured to the bed of grass. "Here, let's sit." Eliyahu carefully tossed his scythe off to the side. She arranged herself, reclining on elbows, face turned towards the last afternoon rays of the sun. Eliyahu did his best to follow her lead, clumsily sprawling on his back and landing by her side.

They remained in that repose for many minutes, soaking in the feel of falling summer, that liminal time when the shortening days remain warm as August, but the verdant trees hint at what comes next by shedding their first few gold and brown leaves. Only half consciously, she became acutely aware of his breathing. Her mind was racing: Finally we are alone. No one comes to this field. We have some time before we are missed. When will this be possible again? She inhaled a mix of sweet boy and sweaty man alongside her. How do I smell to him, she wondered.

Almost without realizing what she was doing, she turned towards Eliyahu. Pivoting on one elbow, her other hand reached out to touch his. He twitched, and she instinctively drew back. To her surprise he reached towards her, covering her hand with his broad palm. Eliyahu sat up, turning even closer to Shira. Their eyes met, each leaned forward. Lightly touching Eliyahu's face, she deliberately but gently guided him to her until they were kissing. She felt the return of the exhilaration she had experienced each time she had seen him. Only this time the sensation was more intense. She wanted more, to satisfy overwhelming desire, to experience the fullness of being a woman. Part of her resisted, knowing the traditions of Shavlan would never permit such things without marriage. In that moment, though, the intensity of her body was more immediate than intricate rules of courting and betrothal. She wanted Eliyahu, and sensed his desire rising.

"We're alone," she whispered between kisses. "We can be together." Eliyahu drew his face back a few inches, his eyes revealing excitement mixed with fear. He said nothing, gazing as if seeing her for the first time. She held her breath, examining his features for anything that would tip her one way or another. It was the tenderness that she saw, or thought she saw, that moved her. Ever so slightly, she nodded. Then moved a hand to his waist. He did the same. They fumbled out of their clothes, neither with any experience in the attire of the other.

Afterwards, they lay listening to birdsong, neither knowing what to say. She lay on the grass staring off at the yellow rue flowers, replaying in her mind's eye what they had just done. The sensations still pulsing through her were both delicious and frightening.

As the sun slipped lower, Eliyahu finally broke the stillness. "Shira, we should get back." His words pulled her out of the reverie. Glancing around she suddenly felt a wave of panic. "Yes, let's go, I still have to get to my uncle's and then home before dinner. Too much time has passed!" Propelled by the force of imagined gossip and intruding thoughts of dire consequences, they quickly brushed down clothes to remove brambles and grasses, making sure everything was tucked and buttoned. As if on a military march, they quickly retraced their steps through the woods. Emerging from the trees, having scouted to be sure no passersby could see them, they turned towards each over, wavering as to whether to embrace. A moment's hesitation and the time for one more intimacy passed. Shira said simply "Goodbye, Eliyahu, I hope to see you tomorrow." With that she turned to cross the Susve, while Eliyahu turned north, scythe over shoulder, walking with a lighter step than one would expect from someone who had completed a backbreaking shift in the flax fields.

The days following were agony. The weather turned rainy, foreclosing the possibility of contriving another chance meeting. Her thoughts might carry her back to the magical afternoon with Eliyahu in the field, but reality precluded seeing him, let alone arranging to spend time with him. As time wore on, a new emotion crept in, silently stealing through dark cracks in her moods. A hint of shame began playing on her emotions. By the end of the week shame was mingling with its companions, remorse and doubt. Why had she been so quick to give herself to Eliyahu? Did he have real feelings for her, or just a boy's willingness to indulge himself? What if someone found out? They had no understanding between them. Daydreams of a future together was her own foolishness, she berated herself. I'm turning into one of those silly girls in the books Channa and I devoured. And then her breasts began to itch.

She felt the unfamiliar sensation on the seventh day after laying with Eliyahu. Waking and stretching on a gray morning, she detected a discomfort she had not known before. Focusing on her body, Shira perceived her breasts feeling slightly swollen and tender. Never having experienced anything like it, her mind raced to possible explanations. Panic set in when she ruled out all possibilities except one. She recalled something grandmother had said years earlier to an older cousin, around when Shira was starting to bleed. It had barely registered with her at the time, something remote and unpleasant, certainly not connected to her life. But now Bubbe's words flooded back. "A woman knows first in her breasts."

Pregnant? Could she possibly be pregnant from the one time? How could that be; she had been with Eliyahu only a few days after her last blood. She was not really sure exactly how many days. Her periods were never very heavy and often slowed to a trickle after only a day or two. She had not paid much attention to the timing of her cycle, it had never mattered. Was she really far enough along to get pregnant? She must consult Channah, who knew more about such things. It would be embarrassing, but she had no choice. She had to know.

Late that afternoon, the dark gray skies lightened a bit and the driving rain eased to a drizzle. Shira threw an old shawl around her shoulders and set out with determination the four blocks to Channah's house. Striding along the muddy lane, her breathing sped up while her mind conjured troubling scenarios. To be unwed and with child was unthinkable, shame she could not imagine inflicting on her family. Yet confronting Eliyahu and demanding they marry would be its own horrible embarrassment. Angrily she dwelled on the fact that Eliyahu had not come by, nor even tried to see her. He must not have any feelings for her. She had been foolish to ever think he might. Another of Bubbe's expressions popped into her thoughts. "A woman is like a dishrag, a man wipes his hands with her and tosses her away." That's just Bubbe, she had thought at the time, someone prone to a dark view of the world. Now the old woman's pearls of wisdom sparkled with bitter truth for Shira.

She reached Channah's door, knocked, but no one answered. Waiting nearly a minute, heart pounding through her chest, she knocked again louder. Still no response. Where could Channah be? She needed desperately to talk to her, to talk to someone, to unburden herself. She peered through the front window, hoping Channah was merely asleep in a chair so she could wake her. Only shadows from the late afternoon haze filled the room. She tried calming herself, forcing deep breaths to make her heart stop its drumbeat. Her hands clenched and unclenched, her weight shifted from foot to foot. She felt incapable of deciding what to do next, where to go, until a familiar figure hurrying on the opposite side of the street caught her eye.

Aunt Chaya! Her father's sister was a clever woman, the village's unofficial *shadchante*. Aunt Chaya knew everything about marriages, a human ledger of who was eligible, who was difficult to match, who was "damaged goods", and how to make the most of anyone's attributes. Mainly she took to arranging betrothals among her extended family, which encompassed seemingly half of the Jews of Shavlan when you counted the multitude of Singers and Lipmans and Wolfs to whom Chaya was related to one degree or another. Aunt Chaya had aquired even more *mishpocha* when she married the widower Itzkowitz a few years back. Her Aunt must know all about childbearing, and could diagnose whether she was truly at risk. Chaya had always shown a special affection for me, she thought, surely she will help.

Regaining control of her feet, she dashed after her Aunt, intercepting her a half block farther on. "Tante!" she called to the briskly moving older woman. Chaya wheeled around and, seeing who it was, flung open her arms. "My darling Shira! Come to your old aunt," she sang out, arms encircling her niece. Bending forward, Shira embraced the stocky older woman fiercely, feeling calm flow into her just by being held with love. She clung fast a few beats longer than usual, finally stepping back. "I am so glad I ran into you, Tante. Can we go somewhere and, uh, talk a bit?"

Chaya looked quizzically into her face. "Of course, of course, come home with me. I will make us tea. We can talk, no one is there." They reached Chaya's modest house in no time, shook the rain drops off their outer coverings, and stepped into a comfortable, well worn sitting room. She had been here before, but now noticed as if for the first time how much of the room resembled a photographer's gallery. Chaya collected portraits of family members far and wide. Before she could inspect closely the myriad faces staring out unsmilingly in stiff poses, Chaya took her hand and led her to the kitchen. While lighting the stove and putting up a kettle of water to heat, Chaya kept up a patter involving the latest stories from relatives who had scattered from Shavlan across the world. Pausing to pour steaming water over chai leaves in a pot, Chaya cleared her throat and said, "Now, Shira, sit and tell me why you've come."

She obeyed, finding a wooden chair beside her Aunt's high backed throne at one end of the main room. Where do I start, she asked herself. Feeling lost, eyes reddening, swallowing a few times, she remained mute. Aunt Chaya sat patiently, holding her hand while she squirmed in the chair. Finally she found words.

"I think I'm in trouble, Tante Chaya."

"Trouble my dear? What sort of trouble could a wonderful girl like you have?"

Shira hesitated again, eyes focused on the floor. "I did something foolish, Tante."

"We all do foolish things, Shira. There's no shame in that."

Hearing the word shame brought sobs. Chaya squeezed her hand, leaned closer. "What is it my Shirele? You can tell your aunt anything."

Her nose began to run. Reflexively wiping it with her sleeve, she croaked out, "I lay with a boy, and now I think I'm pregnant." Tears welled back into her eyes, her shoulders heaved.

"Oh my, my darling, that is trouble. But you are not the first girl in this village to have done so and you will not be the last. Together we'll figure something out," Chaya said soothingly, gathering up her other hand, holding on tightly until the tears came no more.

Her cheeks pale, she recounted in nearly a whisper her unexpected joy after the first chance encounter with Eliyahu. As if retelling a story she had heard about someone else, Shira catalogued carefully tracking his patterns, excuses made to be out of her house on some errand, and the culmination of her plan. As she inched closer to the intimate details of the afternoon alone with him by the river that now brought her to Chaya's sitting room, she faltered. Tears welled up again, her voice caught in her throat.

"It's all right, Shirele," Chaya cooed. "No need to tell me everything, I understand."

Throwing her arms again around the solid woman's neck, she held on tightly as if afraid of being swept away by a rushing current.

After a few moments she sat back, breathed deeply, and asked tentatively "So am I?"

"Am I?" Chaya echoed. "Because of an itch in your bosom?"

"Yes, Tante, that's what Bubbe used to say was the first sign."

"Your Bubbe said a lot of things, dear girl, and not all of them made sense. I've heard of itching as a sign, that's true. It never was for me. All I can say my dear is maybe yes, maybe no. From what you've told me, we won't really know for sure for three or four more weeks. By the time you know for sure, unfortunately, it is too late. We need to take action now."

"What sort of action, Tante? I don't know what to do."

"We must get you married, of course," Chaya said, as if declaring a law of nature.

"But I haven't seen or heard from Eliyahu since, since that day," she said disconsolately. "What if he says no?"

"Oh, not him dear," Chaya stated firmly. "That boy is married to the Talmud."

"What do you mean?" she cried anxiously.

"I've already tried and tried to get my brother-in-law to let me make a nice match for the boy. They tell me that Eliyahu just wants to study in the Vilna yeshiva. He would rather sit all day with his books and the other yeshiva buchers. No time for a wife and family. Unless we tell Oreh what happened ..."

"No!" Shira sharply cut her off. "I'd be so ashamed. Anyway I don't want to be a yeshiva bride. That sounds worse than being stuck in this village."

She noticed the grimace passing swiftly over Chaya's face before her perpetual smile resumed. "Shavlan has been a wonderful place to grow up. But I dream of seeing other places, of living in a more, uh, modern world."

Chaya sat back and studied her niece. "That's a good thing, my dear. Because we might have another option for you."

"Another option?"

"Yes, my girl. One that might just fix this, this problem."

Shira held her breath, waiting for Chaya to continue.

"Do you remember the Itzkowitz boy, Jacob? My stepson, the one who went off after his brothers in South Africa? Well, he's back. I just spotted him getting out of a wagon."

"Jacob? We played together sometimes when we were little. Then his mother died and he became, well, more serious. Sad in some way. I remember him going to the gold mines a few years ago."

"That's the one! The rumor is that he's come back with the idea in his head to get a wife. That's where you come in, my dear Shira."

"Me?"

"Yes. We have to plant a seed, dear girl. That seed is you. We must let the idea grow in his mind that you're the bride for him."

"But Tante, I haven't seen Jacob in years. He'll barely remember me. Why in the world would he ever think of marrying me?"

"Oh Shira, you've already proven yourself clever at showing up at the right time. You have everything a girl needs to turn a boy's head. We'll come up with something."

Shira's cheeks flushed at hearing this. Chaya ignored the blush as she unveiled the intricate dance of matchmaking, the artistry that made Chaya a *shadchante* with no equal for miles around.

Return
Shavlan 1897

The marketplace in the town center was still round. The road to Tzitovian still ran to the west, the one to Radvilishok always to the north, and the third south towards Shidlova still took you to a shrine to the Christians' virgin mother. He knew those roads well, had delivered goods and flax and horses along each of them. Shavlan looked much the same even after three years absence.

But it felt different. Never a bustling town, yet neither was it sleepy while he was growing up. The thousand or so townspeople sustained a constant commotion of daily life. The synagogue anchored spiritual and social life for his half of town, the tavern and church for the other half. Farmers came each week from the surrounding country-side to sell their produce and livestock, returning home with supplies and a few extra coins. As long as the Czar's men stayed away, life back then went on much as it had for generations. Yet now that he was back, he could sense a change. Maybe it was the scarcity of young men like himself and his brothers, who had crossed oceans escaping conscription and seeking wealth. Or the nascent agitation of the intelligentsia's emissaries coming to spread revolutionary calls for an uprising against the Czar. Whatever it was, he knew that Shavlan was not his future.

He arrived with a mission. Finally he would have a bride, like any man building a life for himself must have. If all went as planned, he would not need to stay long. Leah's intentions were clear, they just needed to go through the formalities. First, though, he would seek Uncle Oreh's blessing. With both parents gone, Jacob looked to Uncle Oreh for a father's guidance. After his father's sudden death it was Oreh, eldest of that generation, who'd encouraged him to follow his brothers to the frontier. It was Oreh who gave him the money for passage. It was Oreh who beseeched Sora and Helman to take him in as a boarder, vouching for him as a hard worker. He owed many debts to Oreh. Personally asking for Oreh's approval of the marriage was the respectful way. Of course, he never doubted the answer would be yes. Would Leah have encouraged him to come so far if she thought her father would refuse? No sense in delaying, he told himself.

Jacob walked the quarter mile from the marketplace to their house. Pulling his hat brim down to shade his eyes, turning his collar up, he avoided passing gentiles on the street as best he could. Jacob feared word about his return spreading, as he was of conscription age and could be dragooned into the Czar's army if the authorities knew he was back. Unannounced, he rapped on the door of a modest one story wooden house. When she opened for him, he beamed and she gasped. "Jacob!" Leah's arms flinched upwards, then quickly returned to her sides. Physical displays would be inappropriate, he understood, now that she was grown.

"Who's there, Leyele?" came a deep voice from the other room.

"A special traveler, Papa! It's Jacob!"

"Yankele, you're back," Oreh said, entering the front room. "Come here my boy, give your uncle a hug." They embraced, then sat around the one table in the room. Oreh commenced quizzing him about every aspect of life in the Rand. Though never formally educated beyond age nine, Oreh had learned to read and voraciously kept abreast of the wider world. His questions were insightful, peppering Jacob for details of the ongoing tensions between the English and Boer. Rivalry for domination of southern Africa's rich mining areas had deepened after the fiasco of the Jameson Raid. "Will there be war?" Oreh asked.

He nodded assent. "Not soon, but eventually it will come to that again. The Boer are stubborn, proud and good with guns. They want the wealth in the ground for themselves. The Boer and the English both treat the *kaffir* like dogs. Each year they make their lives more miserable, worse than serfs."

Impatient to broach the topic most dear to him, Jacob saw his opening when talk of world affairs dwindled.

"Uncle, you've been like my own father to me these last few years. While I toiled far away, all I could think about was my longing to be united with the family."

"Yes, Yankele, we missed you. Are you coming back?"

"No Uncle, Shavlan is not the future for any young person." He slipped a glance towards the other room, where Leah would be listening in. "That is what I want to talk about with you Uncle. The future is not here for Leah either. Her future should be with me," he said, his voice rising more than intended.

"With you, Yankele?" Oreh said, sitting up attentively. "You're her cousin. I love you dearly, but that would be a *shonda*. I cannot bless this."

He was stunned. Hadn't it all been arranged? They had exchanged many letters, each inching halfway to a declaration of betrothal. Hadn't Leah written many times how her father looked forward to having Jacob as a true son?

"But Uncle, it is not forbidden," Jacob stammered. "I consulted the Rabbi in Johannesburg. The Talmud does not prohibit cousins marrying. Such marriages happen often in the Torah."

"Well, Yankele, we are not in the time of the Torah anymore," said Oreh gently. "It is wrong. Some believe it is not healthy. Every farmer sees what happens from close breeding among livestock."

Jacob swung his head around, hoping to catch Leah's eye. Had she gone out?

His search for Leah was cut short by rapping on the door. "Halloo, halloo, Oreh, Leah, are you home?"

He knew that distinctive female voice. Mumma Chaya, his father's second wife. A hard woman with a strong will, who dosed out discipline in place of love. Jacob appreciated her, though, for treating him no differently than her own children.

Chaya had merged into his family three years after his beloved mother had died. She was a help to his father, keeping their house and raising the children still at home, including then twelve-year-old Jacob. The arrangement benefited both adults, particularly Chaya after her dear Menashe was felled by a lightning bolt years before. He thought back to the story of that tragedy. Mumma Chaya and her husband were returning from market with their youngest two children when a summer squall suddenly overtook them. They took shelter under a large tree (a fatal choice that always left Jacob wondering, as any fool knows not to shelter under a tree during a thunder storm). After the storm had passed, a passing group of locals found four bodies sprawled under the blasted trunk, all apparently dead. Luckily, someone thought to check each presumed corpse and perceived a flicker of life in the mother. Another quick thinker organized the rescuers to dig a deep, narrow hole. Applying the local folk remedy, they inserted her limp body upright, piled around dirt up to her neck, and prayed while the earth drew off the lightning. Miraculously, Chaya revived, sadly waking to discover her family decimated. Her cry of anguish was said to be heard in the village a mile away. No surprise, he thought, that such tragedy would harden her.

"Chaya, come in, come in. See who is here!" Oreh welcomed his sister-in-law.

Dressed in black, the squat woman stepped inside, putting hand to mouth upon seeing the seated figure.

"Jacob, what are you doing here? The Czar's men will get you! They're always patrolling the villages."

"Hello, Mumma Chaya. If no one tells them, I'll stay out of sight and be fine."

"What brings you by, Chaya?" Oreh asked, steering away from talk of danger.

"My lovely niece, Shira. It's time for her to have a husband."

"The twin?" noted Oreh. "She seems like a lovely girl. She will make someone a perfect wife. You're always matchmaking, Chaya, you should become an official *shadchante* and charge for it."

"It's for the *mishpocha*, Oreh, you know that. And you're *mishpocha*."

"What are you talking about, Chaya, I don't need a wife!" Oreh grinned.

"Not you, *schlemiel*. Your Eliyahu, he should be married already."

"You're right, my son should take a wife. But he wants to go back to Vilna and continue studying to be a Rebbe."

"A Rebbe also needs a wife," Chaya protested.

"When the Rebbe is ready, you can find him a wife!" Oreh said with finality. "Now come have a cup of tea."

Jacob watched this banter intently, hoping to discern how to change Oreh's mind about Leah. With Oreh resisting marital overtures, retreat seemed the best path for the moment. He had hoped to lodge under Oreh's roof, but with his uncle's opposition to the engagement that would hardly be the best way to raise his fortunes. Instead, he took his leave to find a room for let down the street, and settled in to consider his strategy.

For a week, daily he strolled to Oreh's house in the early evening, on each visit bringing a different offering. One night some schnapps, another night some carrots from the market, and for Shabbos a chicken. Oreh had a powerful appetite and appreciated good food and drink. He accepted each token with delight, thanked Jacob profusely, invited him to stay for dinner, and offered lively conversation in return. Not once did Oreh budge on the topic of betrothal. No amount of Jacob painting a rosy and successful portrait of his future as a mining king in South Africa moved Oreh. On the contrary, Oreh became increasingly effective at painting his own, darker picture of all the ills ahead in that land. The more he attempted to convince Oreh, the more confused he became himself.

Maybe Oreh's right, he thought. Going back to the Rand is risky, the possibility of war too real. He'd wrestled with these doubts during the voyage to Southampton, and Oreh was magnifying them. Kruger could not be trusted to be good to the Jews, he knew that firsthand from the sentiments out of the mouth of his former cargo. Even if the Boer won, his personal connection to the President might not protect him. Troubled, his mind turned to letters from his oldest sister Fayga over the past few years.

"The life is good here in America", she had written last year. "We lack for nothing, the farmland is rich and we grow whatever we need for our kitchen in our garden. Our little store does good business, and the *goyim* treat us kindly, not like at home. Come and be our partner, Yankele! This is a land of opportunity. You needn't break your back in a mine or live among the blacks like you do there. Your place waits for you here, my brother. Harry is a smart businessman. We can grow wealthy working together."

He kept this letter with him during his travels, but had not given it much of thought in a while. Fayga had been like a mother to him after his Mama Rochel died. Already in her early 20s, after the funeral Fayga took charge of raising the younger ones – Avram, Jacob, cousin Moishe, and their little sister Pearl – putting off her own chances to marry. Fayga's sacrifice continued until their father remarried Chaya. Finally Fayga was ready to accept a long-standing proposal from Tsvi Mazaroff, a man with great ambitions to make his fortune in America. Tsvi always seemed destined to be somebody and somewhere else, not a small-timer in a shtetl. Off to the new promised land went Fayga and Tsvi (who now called himself Harry) within a month of Chaya marrying their widowed father.

Jacob had his own marriage riddle to solve. He had barely seen Leah since his return to Shavlan. Remaining inconspicuous, out of sight of Russian authorities who might tip off the army that a young Jew was back, limited his movements. Leah had her responsibilities around the house, tending to the daily routine for herself and her father. It would be unseemly for them to be alone together while Oreh was out working the land that provided their sustenance. The one time he had been able to see Leah alone was the evening mid-week when he'd come by for his nightly conversation with Oreh, who was delayed by a thrown horseshoe. Leah greeted him with a wide smile but her eyes betrayed something else, he perceived. Apprehension? Seconds thoughts? Was her father's opposition to the marriage undermining the eagerness to be with him?

"I'm so glad to see just you, Leah," he said when informed that Oreh was still not home.

"Jacob, it brings me joy to have you back here," she replied. "Come wait for Papa. Would you like tea?"

Her body radiated tension. Leah smoothed her apron and touched her hair absently. She wore it pulled back, under a kerchief, but Jacob could see that her curls were long and full. He stopped himself from imagining more.

"No thank you. But it's lucky your father is not home. We need to talk, Leah. Our plans, what are we going to do?" He remained standing, and began pacing around the living room.

"I'm trying, Jacob. I remind Papa that other cousins in the family have married," Leah said quietly.

"That's true. Uncle Shmuel's daughter, the cross-eyed one, didn't she marry a first cousin on her mother's side?" he said excitedly.

"That's one example. There are others," she agreed. "But Papa hasn't budged. He says the more he reads about it, the more science tells him we shouldn't do it."

"Science? Now your father's a scientist?" He turned to her.

"Jacob, you know how Papa reads everything. He talks about someone named Mendel proving it's a bad idea."

"I don't care what he reads, Leah!" he said loudly. "I came back to get you, so we could start a life in the new land. I thought from your letters he was in favor of our marriage!"

Her smile faded, hands dropping to her sides, gaze fixed on the floor. "I told you, I've tried to bring him around. I've told him how happy I would be if we could start a life together. You know Papa loves you, he already thinks of you as a son. That's another reason for him to feel it is wrong for us to be together."

He felt his stomach clench. "We can still be married."

"No!" Leah burst out. She looked horrified at his words. "I cannot defy Papa, Jacob. I'd never forgive myself."

He was losing her, and he didn't like to lose. "I will talk sense to him, Leah! Don't give up. I know that I can make him see it my way. Give me a few more days." As he spoke, her head remained bent. She seemed incapable of bringing her eyes up to meet his.

They both started at the sound of a horse and wagon outside. Each instinctively took a step back. He moved quickly to take up his usual chair, Leah retreated to the kitchen to put on water for tea. Oreh soon entered, saw Jacob, and opened his arms wide. "My boy, I am glad you are here, I didn't know if you would wait. Problems with our mare in the fields delayed me. I am famished. Leyele, is there dinner?"

"Yes, Papa," she called from the kitchen gaily. "Just a few minutes."

The next day he lay on his back staring upwards, hoping to devise a new strategy. All week he had kept largely confined to the small shed behind widow Logowitz's house, sleeping on a low pallet with dry straw for a mattress. The smells of her cows wafted through the gaps in the wide wallboards shared by the shed and her barn. In exchange for the shelter he performed chores, including the morning milking and mucking. To his surprise, he found himself contented by the familiar shtetl life and the rhythms of his childhood. The Rand teemed with dirty miners and choking dust, crowded with horses and ox-drawn wagons. Shavlan was peaceful; he could hear the rooster crowing in the morning and chickens clucking during the day. Maybe life here wasn't so bad? Should he stay longer? Should he stop trying to persuade Oreh with arguments, just take it slowly until Oreh got used to the idea? Staying in Shavlan was dangerous, though, he might be caught. The unease of confusion was seeping into his bones, he sensed.

That evening he strolled once again towards Oreh's house, determined to make another attempt at persuading his uncle. Lost in thought, he nearly crashed into a girl carrying a laundry basket. She veered at the last minute, snapping out "pay attention" in a peeved voice. When he looked up, he realized he had almost collided with Shira Moscowitz, Chaya's niece. The sight of her took him aback. The scrawny girl had blossomed into a handsome young woman with bright blue eyes while he was away. He felt a slight blush fill his cheeks as he took in the transformations since last he'd seen her. He also noticed her piercing eyes cycling through multiple expressions in the seconds since they avoided impact: He read first anger at the absent minded body nearly stepping on her, relief when the collision was averted, recognition when she apparently remembered him, and finally amusement betrayed by the crinkles around her eyes.

"So," she said, breaking the awkward pause. "The great explorer is back home."

"Pleased to see you again, Shira," he replied with a slight bow, as if they were meeting at the opera.

"My aunt said you were back, but hiding away," Shira continued in a soft but confident voice. "How long are you staying?"

He paused, wondering what was the right answer. "Until I settle some affairs," he said, unsure even to himself what that meant.

"Tell me, do you like the miner's life? Others who have gone to conquer the Transvaal tell of a hard life among hard men." She looked at him intently, seemingly thirsty for knowledge of the wider world.

"Liking the life is not why we go there. There is money to be made, a fortune if one is hardworking and lucky. I met a man on board a ship who was both, but then he died mysteriously."

"Maybe he wasn't so lucky," she interjected with a small laugh. "Anyway, I must get home. Someday you must tell me more of your travels. I too want to travel, to find a better life away from here. But the miner's life – it sounds worse than being trapped in Shavlan."

With that, Shira stepped briskly along her intended path and left him with an unexpected desire to continue the conversation.

Shidduch
Shavlan 1897

It all happened so fast. Oreh steadfastly continued refusing Leah's hand to him. He despaired of achieving his goal of finding a bride. Then Chaya swooped in.

"Oreh, if your son the Rebbe won't marry, maybe the businessman you treat like a son wants to make a match?" Chaya, sitting with steaming tea at Oreh's table, spoke as if Jacob wasn't across the room hearing every word.

"Ask him yourself, Chaya. As far as I know his ears still work. You're his stepmother, you talk to him." Oreh flicked a hand in his direction. Jacob detected a sly look passing between Oreh and Chaya, almost a wink. Or was he imagining it?

She shifted her bulk around to face him, while he balanced on the front edge of a wooden chair, right leg jiggling rapidly. Her heavy brows, like those adorning many Moscowitzes, shot up and down as Chaya spoke. She had the remarkable ability to appear to be smiling while still looking terrifyingly stern. He found her manner compelling even without hearing her words.

"Yankele, you have great plans. You're an ambitious young man. You want to be a diamond merchant or some such? Impressive! Well, apparently you made a great impression on my niece the other day. She came to me and asked for a complete update about you, whether you were betrothed. Questions, questions, she was full of questions. You knew Shira when she was younger. She's grown into a fine young woman, a quick mind with nimble hands around the house."

"I didn't know her very well, Mumma Chaya," he said, leaning forward. "She was always with a bundle of girls back then."

"Take my word for it, Yankele, she's a gem. You know I have your best interests at heart. When I married your father I tried being the best mother I could. I know you missed your real mother terribly, may her memory be a blessing." He detected the slightest glistening of her eyes as she said this.

"You and your brothers left us behind in Shavlan. You struck out far away to make your lives. That's ok, we will be just fine. But always stay connected to where you come from. Wherever you go, remember your home," Chaya said, taking Jacob's hand in both of hers. "To make a new life, you need a strong partner. It's my duty to help you with that. There is no better blessing I can give my stepsons than to make a *shidduch* for each, the Itzkowitz boys with my wonderful Moscowitz nieces. For you, Shira is the perfect match."

He let out a long breath. She'd said the words out loud, releasing into the air the inchoate desires that were trapped

inside him since the chance encounter with his step-cous-
in. His craving for a wife remained strong. If Oreh would
not permit him to be with Leah, maybe this match was
bashert? He didn't believe in fate, that was something the
goyim made up to excuse their failures. You make your own
luck, your own future. Still, he had to admit, there was
something all too coincidental about running into a possible bride just as you are searching for one.

"Mumma Chaya, Shira seems like a wonderful girl. But
when we spoke she disdained the life of a miner's wife in
South Africa. Are you sure she wants to leave here for a
new life? Maybe she'd be happier staying in Shavlan," Jacob
said, getting to something nagging at him the past week.

"Yankele, Shira doesn't fear leaving here for something
better. She does wonder why you would want to go back
to a rough and tumble mining camp. Wouldn't you have
greater opportunities someplace else? " Chaya cajoled.

Jacob felt as if Chaya had thrown a switch, a jolt of
electricity coursing through him. Her question illuminated
a foreboding flickering at the edges of his mind for weeks,
every time thoughts drifted to the inevitable clash between
the Boer and the British. His stop in London had rein-
forced his revulsion at the thought of letting anyone rule
over him, whether Czar or Queen. He declared firmly,
"America."

"America would be good," said Chaya, forcing her stiff
face to smile. "Then we have a deal!" A deal, he thought.
That's what Papa always said when the farmer agreed to
his price for a horse. Is that what marriage is? If this is
what it takes to get a wife in a new land, fine by me, he
thought.

Just then a soft sob emanated from the other room.
Leah had been listening, he realized. His face contorted

from the shame of forgetting all about her. Before he could move, Oreh leapt up, turning to the doorway. "Leyele, my dear Leyele." The pain in Oreh's voice was palpable as he hurried, arms wide open, into the adjacent room where her sobbing was growing louder. "Papa," he heard her gasping, "Papa will I ever get out of this place? I don't want to leave you, Papa, but everyone is going to something better. What will happen to me?"

Chaya approached the crying girl. "Don't worry, dear" she cooed in a comforting voice. "Aunt Chaya will find someone."

Jacob remained frozen in his chair, elbows on knees, hands clasped. Unable to find words of comfort that didn't sound foolish, he felt a violent urge to escape. I was cruel, he thought, as he bolted out of Oreh's house, sprinting back to the solitude of the spare shed.

The next day rumors reached Shavlan that the Czar's men were scouring towns in the north, grabbing young Jews as army conscripts. Hearing this, Jacob knew there was little time to dwell on the hurt he caused Leah. If he didn't leave soon, he might never leave except as cannon fodder for the Czar's army. Nor was there time to entertain second thoughts about the deal struck with Chaya. His marriage must happen as soon as the Rabbi could perform it. They were still within the Ten Days of Awe, so the *chuppah* would have to wait a few days until after Yom Kippur.

Chaya took charge of all arrangements, as was her custom. The ceremony would be simple, just immediate family as witnesses. A larger gathering could call attention to Jacob being back in the area. The Rabbi was consulted about the unusual situation. He agreed that after the last shofar blast and a few bites of bread and fish to break fast, they would remain at the synagogue for the wedding. Shira would wear a dress borrowed from a cousin. No need for one of her own; it would be impractical to take a fine gown on their journey to a new country. The newlyweds would have to pack as lightly as possible to make haste on their voyage.

The October evening was cool, the fall racing towards winter that year. The Jews of Shavlan were gathered for the Day of Atonement in the pride of their community, their centuries-old synagogue. The sturdy wooden structure was one of the largest buildings in the region, almost as large as the church. From the outside, a stranger would be hard-pressed to identify its function. Its multiple stories, high-set latticed windows, rear turret and gently sloping gables gave it the air of a minor nobleman's manor house. A closer look disclosed the absence of lower level windows and an off-center main doorway, leaving one hunting for a grander entrance. The planking on one side stood vertically, on another horizontally, as if the builders were unsure which pattern evinced holiness. Unlike many local structures, the synagogue was meticulously maintained, not a single shingle missing. Even a casual inspection would convince a passerby that this house of worship was special to the community.

The building dated from before the birth of great-grandfather Israel, a giant who stood nearly a head taller than most village men and lived for nearly a century. Jacob had always marveled at Israel's massive boots, which he and his siblings would see during their weekly ritual visit to the ancient man's farmhouse a mile outside the village. Israel had been an early patron of adding a further adornment for the synagogue, insisting that they bring a craftsman from Vilna to create a work of art. "We may live in a tiny corner of Russia, but we should have a house for our Torah as grand as any in the country" he was said to have insisted. So the farmers and shop owners pooled their money to adorn their synagogue with the massive but delicately carved centerpiece in front of which now stood the Rabbi.

This *bimah* rose 15 feet high, pulling one's gaze upwards towards the vaulted central ceiling. The open-sided octagon was supported by eight matched columns of oak, carved to highlight intricate grains and whorls. On top of open arches was a magnificent crown, rising in three layers. The first was a set of inward sloping arches letting light filter down to the center, then the crown rose with intricately carved interlacing lattice work. Finally it was topped off by a rounded uppermost delicate covering, like a *kippah* worn by an observant Jew to show humility before the Holy One. It was said the artist toiled a full year, from one High Holy Days to the next, seeking just the right woods and rejecting any flawed choices. Over a half a century later, the wood had breathed in the prayers of thousands upon thousands seeking the solace of their rituals from the hardships of life. The *bimah* glowed as the last light of day was falling.

Concluding the moving Ne'ilah prayer, the congregation once again expressed relief and exhaustion from the annual day of fasting and introspection. Together they proclaimed "Next year in Jerusalem!", *tekiah gedolah* sounded on a curved ram's horn, and congregants shuffled home to break their fasts. Only Jacob, Chaya, Shira and her parents, and Oreh stayed behind with the Rabbi. Leah was pointedly absent, he noted with a momentary stab of guilt. Reminding himself that time had come to move his life forward another step, he focused all his attention on the ceremony ahead.

The wedding party assembled at the steps of the monumental *bimah*. "Now we go up," commanded the Rabbi, and the group ascended to the platform under the crown. The ceremony proceeded swiftly, the Rabbi respecting Jacob's urgent need to depart with his new bride a few steps ahead of conscription. The wedding contract, a simple *ketubah*, was signed and witnessed. Next Jacob covered Shira's face with the *bedeken* veil, bringing to mind the traditional story of the patriarch with whom he shared a name: the biblical Jacob who was tricked into marrying Leah instead of his true love, her sister Rachel.

As the ancient tale echoed in his thoughts, a disturbing notion took hold. What if Oreh is scheming like the Yaakov of Genesis? That glance with Chaya, was that real? Was it probable Chaya appeared at precisely the right instant with a match, just not a match for Eliyahu? Jacob's face grew red, his head swiveled to inspect Oreh's face. Nothing he could read. The Rabbi's voice broke into his racing thoughts. "Who has the ring?"

They sped through the rituals of the bride circling the groom, him placing a ring on Shira's index finger, and the seven blessings. Oreh produced a delicate wineglass wrapped in a cloth, which he stamped on with extra force. A hearty Mazel Tov from the small assembly, and Jacob and Shira were led off to a tiny back room for a few moments of seclusion. Silence hung between them, as each absorbed the change in their lives the rituals had brought about. Then Shira spoke.

"Jacob, you are now my husband," she said. "We are making a life together. I am ready. Are you?"

He gazed at her tenderly, in some ways seeing her for the first time. "Living is easy. Making a life takes hard work. We cannot stay here, you know that. We will make a life in America."

"In America, so you've decided," she said. "Good, I was afraid you might change your mind and want to go back to the mines."

"My sister Fayga has a place for us. I've written her to say we are coming. In the mining camps I saw how the Boer and the English want to fight each other over who rules the blacks. I don't want to be part of their war. America offers a better life."

Then the wisp of uncertainty that had distracted him during the ceremony fluttered back into his thoughts. His broad grin faded as intense memories from childhood overwhelmed Jacob. *My own father lied to me when Mama was dying*, he brooded. *All the adults pretended she was just tired, even Oreh. What if Oreh has lied to me again?* He nearly gagged, the taste in his mouth foul. Shira looked at him quizzically, with even a hint of fear in her eyes. "Jacob, what is it? What's wrong?"

"Nothing, nothing, dear wife!" he replied, forcing the corners of his mouth to mimic a smile. "Just a little tired, thinking of the long journey ahead. We need to leave right away."

America
Tuckerton 1897

Disembarking at the Hudson River pier in the bustling city on a late October morning had brought him ela-
tion. Arrival in mid-afternoon at the final railway station,
a small wooden structure with bright peach trim colors,
brought relief. We're finally here, he said to himself, then
recited a *shehecheyanu*. The weary pair stepped down briskly
from their coach and began eagerly searching for a familiar
face. It wasn't until the steam engine blasted its horn and
pulled away that they spotted Harry, bearded and dressed
like a farmer, across the tracks smiling expectantly at them.
"Welcome, welcome, Jacob! Shira!" he called out.

Jacob was jubilant to see his brother-in-law, as much for
the prospect of finishing the long day's journey as for the
family reunion. He had not seen his sister or her husband
for over a decade, not since their wedding and departure
for their new life in the New World. "Tsvi!" he boomed,

arms wide for an embrace. "Sorry! I know you're Harry now," he corrected pleasantly.

"Call me whatever, Jacob," replied his brother-in-law. "Shira, you were just a child when last I saw you, now you're a grown woman, a wife! Welcome sister!" Shira took her turn exchanging hugs, barely stifling a yawn as she stepped back.

"Ach, you're both tired of course. You've been traveling all day. Were my instructions helpful?" Harry looked to Jacob for affirmation.

"Yes, excellent, thank you," he replied. "You are right, the journey has been a bit tiring." With that, Harry set to bringing the horse and wagon around to where their steamers were stacked up, and together they loaded it all into the back of the rig.

"It's about ten minutes to the house," Harry informed them, flicking the reins to spur on his handsome chestnut draft horse. Harry began a travel banter, punctuating their journey past farmhouses with detailed descriptions of the occupants. As his brother-in-law's wagon rounded a curve and clusters of buildings came into view, Jacob found himself oddly annoyed by the narration. Perhaps I'm just tired and hungry, he wondered to himself, then realized something else was nagging at him. On the train leg south of Bay Head, he'd studied the farmhouses strewn along the railroad route, most appearing to him in various states of decline. Some were barely larger than the farmers' shacks dotting the environs of Shavlan, while others seemed almost grand. Whatever their scale, all evoked an air of decay to his eye. Occasionally they passed through a sad little town, a concentration of more of the same. None of the houses he saw along the way appeared new. "Decrepit" sprang to mind, perhaps worse than what he'd left behind.

It's another *shtetl*, he groaned inwardly. Did we cross the ocean, journey thousands of miles, leave everything behind, just to end up back in the same place? He glanced at Shira, who seemed entranced by the seaside village. Her gleaming eyes calmed him a bit, but still his hand twitched. Absentmindedly he reached down to the pocket carrying the token. Would its aura carry across the sea? He forced himself to continue absorbing his new surroundings.

Entering little Tuckerton, he noticed tidy homes with hints of more prosperity than he'd seen along the railway. Not that these would be suitable for the wealthy, but certainly the dwellings in this community were more substantial than those of most of the Christian shopkeepers of his hometown. Harry prattled on, explaining that this village began as an early port of the young United States, becoming a ship-building hub for the new nation. Fishing and clamming abounded in the area. Since the extension of the rail spur some years back the Great Bay region had become quite popular with summer tourists seeking a seashore break from city heat. Harry pointed out that their dry goods establishment depended on these seasonal outsiders for half their annual sales. Like most locals, they welcomed the dollars of the tourists while delighting in deriding their coarse manners and clothes unsuited for the outdoors. Then again, if city folk arrived with bathing suits and the like there would be nothing to sell them.

Taking in the sights and Harry's travelogue, Jacob was gripped by a sense of familiarity. Roads were not paved in gold or any material for that matter, and the dust of America was no different than Russian dust. Trees he recognized lined the path from the train depot to their destination, a modest two-family house on a narrow street overlooking a creek.

A square-faced woman in a blue gingham dress overlain with a white cotton apron stood expectantly on the porch. Her hair was pulled tightly back, almost entirely covered by a kerchief. As the wagon pulled up, she ran to greet them. "Yankele! It's really you. Little brother, finally you're here!"

He blinked a few times getting a closer look at her face. Feeling as if he had discovered a lost photo of his mother, a lump swelled in his throat. An instant later he snapped back to the present and beamed at his sister. Fayga had been the one caring for and comforting him after their mother died. Here she was, doing so again, welcoming him to a new life. A peace and joy he had not known for a decade washed over him. He held her in a tight embrace, then stood back and assessed his older sister. She had filled out. Perhaps because she was released from the burdens of surrogate motherhood, he wondered? Or maybe life here was less harsh? He was delighted to see her looking healthy, putting to rest a deep fear he had not consciously harbored. Then, as if remembering a forgotten item, he turned back to the wagon: "Fayga, do you remember my Shira Frayda?"

"Of course I do!" Fayga replied, holding out strong arms to greet her new sister-in-law. "Oh my goodness, Shira, how you've grown! Such a beautiful bride! Harry, take their things in for them and let them wash up."

Harry had already hoisted their steamer trunks down from the wagon and loaded one onto his back before Jacob called out "Tsvi, I can do that." Harry, striding forward and up the several steps, waved him away.

"Nonsense, Jacob, you just finished a long trek. I can handle it," Harry said, pushing open the right side front door and hauling the crate inside. His brother-in-law had wobbled a bit under the load, he noticed. Not wanting to embarrass Harry, he took hold of their smaller satchels and left the second trunk. Shira fell in behind, following the pair into the dimly lit apartment. After Harry had lugged the second steamer into the front room, given them both warm hugs and basic instructions, then taken his leave, Jacob set about examining their lodgings while Shira started to unpack.

"It is very plain," he pronounced after scanning the sparsely furnished front room of the three that formed their accommodations. "What did you expect, the Waldorf?" Shira sang out brightly from the bedroom. "Be thankful we have a place to put our heads tonight." He smiled at her cheerfulness, remembering his apprehension aboard ship. He had wondered how his new bride would react when the reality of being uprooted from family and familiar surroundings set in. He had recalled his own sense of disorientation when first setting foot in Cape Town years earlier, weary from the uncomfortable voyage and assaulted by unfamiliar smells and sounds. He had been miserable for nearly a week back then before beginning to feel somewhat at ease. Perhaps, he thought approvingly, Shira is more adaptable than I gave her credit for. His musings were interrupted by her call for a hand with unpacking the trunks, setting him to work on the welcome chore of settling into a new home.

Hours later, seated around Fayga's table, a roasted chicken and mound of potatoes beguiled them. Their hosts took turns plying Shira with questions about various old friends from Shavlan. Bentzi was courting Rebbe Zilbershtein's daughter down the road in Sakot, but the Rebbe wasn't ready to give his blessing. Velvel, Shira's brother, was living in Philadelphia, working for a kosher butcher. This news brought laughter from Fayga. She recalled Velvel as a little boy always fearful around her family's cows. "Maybe Velvel's getting back at the animals for scaring him!" she chortled, almost giddy at reports evoking a parade of characters from her far away past life.

Then it was his turn to be interrogated. Harry and Fayga posed a steady stream of questions about his adventures of the past several years. Between mouthfuls of chicken legs he described the arduous life of the mining camps teeming with immigrants from around the world, all gambling on striking it rich. He took delight in recounting the tale of the mission he accomplished for Kruger, embellishing the danger until the two bandits had become an entire platoon. Harry and Fayga marveled even further when he spun out the details of his fateful voyage encountering the Barnato family, exclaiming in amazement upon learning of the family's generous reward for Jacob's service. Tales of the sea voyage from Hamburg to New York were told. He elaborated on the wonders of traveling second class, dwelling on his joy in avoiding the indignities visited upon steerage class Russians, who were forced to line up like cattle for inspection to enter America. Fayga exchanged a glance with Harry.

"It's good you come with a stake, Jacob," Harry began, as Fayga cleared dishes. "You'll need it to get yourself launched."

"Launched, Harry?" He was confused.

"Yes, of course, you'll need something to support yourself and Shira."

"Of course, it's my duty to support my wife," he replied, slightly indignant. "I'm not a freeloader."

"No one said any such thing," Harry said smoothly. "It's just good you have some capital, it will make things so much easier. You'll be able to fit out a wagon. Most peddlers start out with everything on their back."

"I don't understand, *Harry*," he said, emphasizing the anglicized name.

"What's not to understand, brother? There's great opportunity awaiting you."

"Fayga told me I would be working with you, in your business. In a store, not out wandering on roads I've never seen before." He cocked his head to one side.

"Jacob, Jacob, we had every intention of taking you into the store. Unfortunately the dry goods business in Tuckerton is not Bloomingdale's. We need you to go far afield," Harry said, plaintively.

"What are you saying? Fayga wrote me. She said your business was good, we would be partners!" His cheeks flushed.

"That was true last year, when she wrote. Lately, not so good. Shipyards are closing up, men are losing jobs. We've lost customers." Harry stared down at his food as he said this.

"Maybe I can bring in new customers, Harry. In the mining camps, you learn to deal with a lot of different people. I was good at trading horses for Uncle Helman. Selling dry goods can't be any harder." He delivered this offer with a piercing look in his blue eyes, shifting his gaze back and forth between Fayga and Harry.

Harry lifted his head, a plaintive look in his eyes. "We barely keep ourselves fed. For now we only need a local girl to help around the store, and then just in the summer tourist season. No, brother, you will make your fortune from a wagon!" Voice growing firmer, Harry spoke with an air of finality, as if he were a judge pronouncing sentence.

Jacob gaped at his brother-in-law. His entire face turned red, the color rising through his temples. Breathing heavily, he raised an outstretched arm. Finger aimed at Harry's forehead, he barked out an angry "You lied!" Harry merely sat stonily, holding the edge of the dinner table as if to keep from being pushed back by the force of the accusation.

His arm chopped to the right, pinpointing Fayga as he lashed out "And you, sister, you deceived me too! 'We can both grow wealthy', that's what you wrote."

"Yankele, calm down," Fayga pleaded. "Nobody lied to you. Why would I do that? We had a setback, that's all. Don't be this way."

"I'll be however I want! I made a foolish mistake, believing someone in my family," he said, chest heaving as if he were having difficulty taking in air.

"You're exhausted from the travel. You don't know what you're saying!" Fayga protested.

"I'm not too tired to see what's going on. You all lied to me about Mama. I see nothing's changed."

"Yankele, that's not true! You were just a little boy. Papa, *olev ha'sholom*, didn't want to worry you. He made us swear not to tell you all the details. What good would it have done? You would have just been miserable for months, and that would have made Mama feel worse. Seeing you happy and smiling gave her strength." Fayga's eyes were watering.

"You should have told me the truth!" he bellowed, pounding the table. "Well I don't need you, I don't need anyone. I'll make my own fortune. Then you'll come begging to me for help!"

"Jacob, please," Harry spoke up, turning his palms upwards in supplication. "You're worn out. I know this must come as a surprise. We can work this out. Our situation, it's just temporary. Get some rest, we can talk tomorrow."

"Talk?" he growled. "I've heard enough talk. You think you're clever, tricking me into coming here and then sending me out on a wagon to make you rich?"

"No, no," Harry said, clasping his hands together. "That's not it at all. We'll make a deal that's fair for both of us."

"I don't make deals with people I can't trust," he sneered.

"Jacob," Shira spoke in an even tone. "We must go." She placed a hand on his tightened fist, gently pulling his arm down to his side while he continued to glower at his sister. Harry and Fayga remained mute, appearing dazed by the sudden surge of rage. Only the ticking of the clock on the mantle filled the silence. He stood stiffly, jaw set. Shira persisted in guiding him away from the table.

"I'm sorry, brother." Fayga finally eked out in a choked voice. "What else could we do? We can grow wealthy together, but we need help."

He merely turned his back, putting his arm around Shira. Without a word they walked briskly out, banging the door loudly behind them. They crossed a few steps on the porch, then entered the side apartment that shared a wall with his sister's house. Shira set about making up the bedding on the hard mattress atop a simple metal frame. He fetched a bucket of water, filled a wash basin, then took to the one chair in the front room. After a few minutes, Shira, attired in her night clothes and hair brushed out, stepped into the front room. "Jacob?" she said softly.

"Tomorrow" he responded after a long interlude "I will begin. They can't piss on my head and tell me it's raining. They need me, I don't need them."

Sisters
Tuckerton 1897

Shira rose with the sun the next morning, having barely slept. Dark thoughts had flooded her mind during long
interludes of staring at the unfamiliar ceiling punctuated
by fits of disturbed sleep. Is this what Jacob is truly like, she
wondered? She'd been charmed by his actions until now.
Gentle on their first night together, despite his gruff daytime
manner. Genuinely admiring her for all the books she had
read, something most young men of Shavlan would have
dismissed as frivolous. When she'd calculated a budget for
them during the Atlantic voyage, he'd been quite complimentary about her facility with numbers. This growing list
of Jacob's good qualities rendered last evening's emotional
outburst all the more unsettling. How could he explode in
a flash at his sister and brother-in-law over a misunder-
standing rather than a deception, she pondered. If such a
thing could ignite his anger, would he also be a powder keg
towards her?

Compounding these anxieties were the changes taking over her body. She was certain her stomach was ever so slightly bumping out, although nothing was visibly different. The pangs there were distinct from any aches or cramps in her experience. She had awakened to a wave of nausea, a more frequent sensation in recent weeks. It had been easy aboard the steamer to attribute the occasional urge to vomit to seasickness. Now that they were on land, what could she pretend was the cause? How could she hide it from Jacob? So far he'd shown no suspicion she was pregnant, and she wanted to keep it that way for as long as possible. Mumma Chaya's advice was to wait two months from their first night of intimacy before hinting at pregnancy, to avoid sowing any seeds of doubt. She must plan carefully to keep Jacob oblivious to these signals of new life, signals blindingly obvious to the person carrying that life.

As if his simmering temper and her secret were not enough burden, Shira fretted over the possibility that soon they could be destitute. She knew they were starting out better off than her cousin Labe, who had emigrated to South Jersey the year before. His letters back home told of arriving virtually penniless, having spent his meager savings on passage. Labe's lucky break was that another cousin let him lodge in a spare room, but otherwise he earned his bread trudging dirt roads schlepping a massive peddler's pack on his shoulders. In his missives Labe envied their *landsmen* who arrived with sufficient funds to afford a wagon, and those few even more blessed with sufficient capital to open a shop and skip life on the road. Labe never said so directly, but among the *mishpocha* in Shavlan who passed around his letters it was gospel that even after a year of backbreaking work her cousin must barely be able to feed himself. Why else hadn't he sent money home to his young wife patiently waiting in Shavlan to cross the ocean and join him?

It had comforted Shira before they boarded ship in Hamburg that Jacob had amassed a sizable stake with which to launch their life in America. A healthy nest egg would cushion them from Cousin Labe's fate. At the time, she had not worried of consequences from the splurge when Jacob insisted on upgrading them to second class passage. Instead, she had luxuriated in the relative splendor of their accommodations, vastly superior to the privations most of their fellow Russian Jews endured down below. How wonderful of Jacob to make their travel as newlyweds almost magical! They both reveled when dining among the better class of passengers in the grand saloon, furnished almost as elegantly as first-class, with solid oak paneling, mahogany tables, and a groaning sideboard. She felt regal alongside Jacob as he strutted through the dining room, puffing out his chest like a preening rooster. And what an extra benefit, she recalled, that their second class ticket permitted them to land dockside in New York and get on with their journey, rather than being deposited on Ellis Island to suffer the slow and humiliating poking and prodding that Labe and other immigrant relatives traveling steerage reported as the price of entry into America.

The memory of their sophisticated shipboard travel produced only anxiety for Shira that morning, as she began calculating how much those extravagances had drained from Jacob's funds. What had seemed justified in the moment when expecting him to arrive to a profitable situation with a steady salary now was revealed as silly profligacy. Their prospects had deteriorated overnight. She comprehended that they would be gambling their remaining funds on Jacob quickly finding a new talent: Could her husband spin goods peddled from a horse and wagon into enough gold to keep food on the table? Jacob, a stranger in a strange land? The all too likely possibility of failure brought on a nausea more intense than anything produced by her pregnancy.

Shira forced a deep slow breath to steady her nerves when she heard Jacob stirring. She splashed cold water from the basin on her face and built a fire in the small cast iron stove. Fayga had thoughtfully left butter and milk in the icebox and eggs on the kitchen table alongside half a loaf of bread. Turning attention to getting breakfast for Jacob, she composed herself, sorting out what she would say to him. Act as if nothing untoward had transpired with Fayga and Harry? Find way to express worry that there might be a different Jacob lurking inside her new husband? She recalled an interlude aboard ship when she joined a circle of women taking afternoon tea. An American woman dominated the conversation, holding forth about a fascinating novel making the rounds. The well-dressed matron recounted the intricate story of a kindly doctor Jekyll who battled secret vile urges, intermittently succumbing. A potion transformed the good doctor into an evil version of himself called Hyde. The ladies had been simultaneously transfixed and horrified at this tale of depravity lurking inside an otherwise reputable person, until one of them lightened the mood with a mocking declaration, "Why, that sounds just like my husband!"

Jacob entered the kitchen wiping sleep from his eyes. "Good morning," he said flatly. "Shira, is there coffee?"

"The stove is almost hot, I'm putting water on now," she replied as cheerily as she could muster. "We have eggs! I'll scramble you some."

"Fine, fine," he said absently. "There's a lot to do today. I want to get an early start."

"I'm sure there is. I'll have breakfast for you in a minute," she said while grinding coffee beans. Paused a moment, she ventured, "What do you have planned?"

"Planned? There's only one thing I can do, now that my *lignerisher shvester* and her *farshtunken* husband have tossed us out."

"Jacob," She sat down across from him and put her hand on his arm. "Fayga's your sister. I can see she loves you."

"Loves me? Do you lie to someone you love?"

"Husband, maybe she was bending the truth a little," she responded, voice slightly quavering. "Maybe for a good reason. I'm sure she was looking out for your best interests."

"Then she should have told me the truth," Jacob began pulling his arm away, then relented, allowing her touch to linger.

" You can't really think she meant to hurt you. You're the one who told me it was Fayga who hugged and cared for you after, when your father was sad and busy with the farm."

"I'm not a mind reader. I'm tired of my family keeping secrets. If business was bad, she should have told me!" Jacob said loudly. "Now can I have my breakfast? I've got to find a rig and prepare to go out on my own."

Seeing that his hurt was still too raw to repair the breach, Shira resumed preparing a simple meal for Jacob. Silence hung in the air as he wolfed down the eggs. Finished, he pushed back his chair and started to leave. Turned around abruptly, he said gruffly, "I'm not speaking again to Fayga or Harry. I want nothing to do with them."

116

"Jacob!"

"And that goes for you too," he continued, ignoring her pleading tone. "Husband and wife must stand together. I don't want you having anything to do with them. I'll be damned if they can lie to me and expect me to act like nothing happened."

From that morning on, a silent barrier separated the two households as solidly as the wall between their apartments. At first, when Fayga or Harry passed one of Jacob or Shira coming or going, they would nod, smile and call "hello" as naturally as if the dinner incident had never happened. In return the Itzkowitzes would look past the Mazaroffs, uttering no reply. The first few times this happened, Fayga and Harry were clearly bewildered, bruised feelings paining their expressions. Undaunted, they continued probing for a response, their greetings gradually shifting from pleasant to terse. By the third week of rebuffed pleasantries, they adopted the same demeanor, seeing but not seeing Jacob and Shira. The two couples soon mastered the awkward art of stepping around the others on the shared porch as if their bodies were as lifeless as fence posts.

Jacob threw himself into readying for his first voyage into the scrub pine backwater in search of customers. Shira marveled at his industriousness, his single-minded ability to plunge into remaking himself as a peddler. Each morning Jacob set off on foot in a quest to outfit himself with all the elements necessary for success as a wandering merchant. Each evening he reported his conversations with various strangers. She admired his apparent talent for putting them at ease and keeping the dialogue going until gleaning a beneficial tidbit. In this manner he assembled the necessaries: A strong horse and sturdy wagon, an initial inventory of items likely to appeal to isolated farm families, and most important of all the rough whereabouts of a dozen or so farm-wives the locals considered dissatisfied with their current peddler. For her part, Shira set about transforming her shipboard budgets into ledgers, tracking Jacob's expenditures and creating columns where she hoped to enter revenues sooner rather than later.

Early one Monday morning, holding in hand the basket of food she had prepared, Jacob said simply "I'm off. Wish me luck." She stepped close to him, embracing him briefly. "Husband, be safe," she gave as her simple blessing. To herself she said, "our fate is in his hands." She took an appraising look as her husband gave a silent nod then walked briskly out the front door to begin his new profession.

As soon as the door closed, she ran to the kitchen sink and vomited. Relief washed through her. It had taken all her will power to hold off until he'd left, especially as she nearly gagged from the smell of his strong coffee. Waves of nausea had washed over her at random times these last few days, forcing her to contrive excuses to duck outside the few times Jacob reappeared during the afternoon. He apparently had noticed nothing unusual, completely absorbed into his own challenges as he was. Even when around, Jacob was nattering about the high cost of pots and pans, or poring over maps plotting routes through the rutted roads. Under other circumstances, his preoccupation to the point of ignoring her would have annoyed the new bride. Now she considered it a blessing. Let him remain lost in his plans, she thought, it helps my little ruses achieve their results.

Shortly after Jacob had gone on the road, however, a different mood set in. Even when Jacob was engrossed in his work, his companionship and occasional conversation warmed her. Now she was almost constantly alone, feeling isolated. The infrequent errand, buying meat from the butcher or walking to the dairy farm for milk and eggs, provided the veneer of human relationship that accompanies marketplace transactions. Most shopkeepers were pleasant enough, willing to smile at her as if she were a long time regular. They're better than the *goyim* back home, she thought, recalling the brusque, dismissive treatment Jewish girls endured entering gentile shops in Shavlan. While she'd rarely needed to venture beyond the Jewish proprietors selling kosher meat, produce or ritual objects, there were items like cloth and shoes sold almost exclusively by Christian merchants. The more hold the *goyim* had over a product, she hypothesized, the worse they treated us. Being treated with polite attention like any other customer quickly endeared her to life in Tuckerton.

Excursions to local shops, however, filled only a tiny portion of her life. She felt guilty shopping, reminding herself to hoard their money; who knows what success he will have on the road? To offset guilt, she undertook devising strategies to stretch their funds as far as possible. First was purchasing several laying hens to provide fresh eggs. Parting with precious dollars was hard, but she anticipated yielding a quick return. Next was tackling the decaying chicken coop out back behind their portion of the house. Having helped repair such structures on her family's farm, she set about the task undaunted.

As she twisted the last loop of wire around a post, securing the coop against foxes and other predators, Shira heard a door loudly slap against its frame. Glancing sideways, she spied Fayga carrying a basket of wash to the clothesline behind their half of the house. The thin rope lattice rack on which clothes were dried was barely ten feet from where Shira stood. Her heart began racing, an urge welling up to turn and greet to her sister-in-law. Immediately Jacob's edict rang in her ears, freezing her in place. Obedience won out over desire. Her eyes bored into the structure she was repairing. Even without shifting her focus, Shira sensed she was being surreptitiously examined. The occasional sharp crack of a wet towel being shaken out called to her, heightening Shira's struggle to repress a yearning to speak. When finally there was quiet, slowly she swiveled around, confirming Fayga was gone. She relaxed, safe to walk back inside.

Over the ensuing weeks such encounters became ever more frequent. Gradually Shira perceived that within minutes of her stepping into the back yard, Fayga would automatically appear. Sometimes Fayga emptied a chamberpot, other times she tended the small vegetable garden supplying herbs for her kitchen, all without directly engaging Shira. With each episode, Shira felt herself slightly more at ease in Fayga's presence. As time wore on, she chafed more and more at abiding by Jacob's commandment against speaking to his sister and brother-in-law. Maybe he can stand being on his own day after day, she thought angrily. He has customers to talk to, I'm alone. Her urge to rebel was heightened by her sense that during each seemingly chance backyard rendezvous, Fayga's gaze was more an assessment than a glance.

One bright December morning, as she began the weekly ritual of hanging wash on the line, Fayga appeared similarly burdened and marched purposefully to their wash line held up by the y-shaped beams. As her sister-in-law proceeded snapping each item in place with wooden clothes pins, Shira took a deep breath and composed her thoughts. Before any words could form into sentences, she heard Fayga clear her throat. Shira looked over at Fayga inquisitively, their eyes meeting for the first time in a month.

"Shira," Fayga said hesitantly. "As you feeling OK?"

She stood up straight, smoothing the apron she was wearing over her belly. She closed her eyes while her lips moved just a fraction, as if she were praying on a matter. After a few seconds she blinked, looked steadily at Fayga, and said evenly "I'm fine."

"Good, good," said Fayga. "It's just, well, you just seem a bit different."

"Different?" She asked guardedly. "How so?"

"Well, it's hard to say. Your face is a little redder. Maybe you look a bit, fuller."

Shira put her hands to her cheeks, giving no reply.

"It's as if, well. It's not my place, but other girls begin looking this way when they are with child."

She felt suddenly terrified. "Why would you say something like that?"

"Shira, sister," Fayga began gently. "I've lost two babies. I know what a woman's body goes through."

"Jacob never told me that."

"He didn't know. I didn't even tell Harry the first time, it happened so early on."

"Oh, Fayga, I'm sorry, that must have been hard."

"Like I said," Fayga pressed on. "I know what you're going through. I've seen you back here, retching. That feels terrible but they say it's a good sign."

Tears began to run down Shira's face, slowly at first. Then sobs. Fayga stood still for a moment, then Shira felt herself being enveloped in a hug. She succumbed, leaning her head on Fayga's shoulder, muffling the sounds of her weeping.

Feeling relief as the sobs abated, Shira pulled back, wiping her eyes with her apron. "It's just so hard being alone."

"Have you told Jacob?" Fayga asked.

"No, not yet," she said meekly. "I wanted to be sure first. He returns exhausted from the road, I didn't want him to worry if it wasn't real."

"Oh Shira," Fayga said brightly. "Don't be silly! Jacob will be thrilled that you're expecting."

"How can you be sure, Fayga? Maybe he's not ready. Maybe with all the *tzuris* of having to become a peddler he'll resent another burden."

Fayga's face fell. "He made his choice."

"Oh Fayga, I didn't mean it that way," she said quickly.

Fayga put a hand on her shoulder. "I truly believe Jacob will be happy."

She smoothed her apron. "Fayga, can I ask you a question?" A quizzical look crossed Fayga's face.

"Jacob is my husband. But I've only known him for a short time. His, uh, reaction when we came, his temper. It surprised me. Was he, was he imagining things?" she asked this as evenly as she could. Without intending to an edge of bitterness crept into her voice.

Fayga turned back to her basket, picked up a damp shirt, flapped it smooth, then pegged it to the line. "Shira, my dear, listen to me. I raised my brother when our mother died. He was only 8, and something of a Mama's boy. Our dear Mama Rochel doted on him, and he clung to her. Then, horribly, she withered and died in front of our eyes. Poor Jacob, he couldn't understand it. He kept asking why she was gone, why didn't anyone stop her from leaving us. He kept looking for clues, thinking that maybe his father or I or one of our brothers had kept secrets from him. In his little boy mind, he believed grownups had lied to him, that if the grownups had told him the truth he could have saved Mama. He couldn't conceive of Mama's life slipping away without a cure. After that, Jacob was different. Less loving, more distant, more suspicious." Fayga paused, locking eyes with her.

"You told me a lot. But you didn't really answer my question."

"I am just saying, dear sister, that sadly Jacob sees darkness in people. My brother always tends to look for the deception in their words."

She bit her lip. "Didn't you write him things that weren't true?"

Fayga sighed. "Did we tell him this could be a good life? Yes, because it can, it will be. Did we say we could get wealthy together? We did, because if family sticks together we do better than any of us can do alone. We invite mishpocha to join us here because we still believe that. We offered you a roof over your heads. Sadly your husband misunderstood our words, he believed we promised to give him wealth – we really offered an opportunity to take charge and create it together. I just hope he comes to his senses and stops seeing us as his enemy. We will be patient. You can live here as long as you want even with his wall of silence. We will wait for him to turn back to his family. Please help him come around."

With that, Fayga turned, not waiting for a response, leaned over her basket, and resumed clipping wash to the rope line.

Peddler
Tuckerton 1898

"You need a horse and wagon?" the post office clerk responded, parroting his inquiry. Jacob figured that the person keeping track of everyone's mail likely knew who was coming and going, so he'd routinely found excuses to drop for a chat with Postmaster Lippincott. The reward for his ingenuity was the tip received one Tuesday morning. "Try Breunig, the dairyman out on Bass River Road. He's heading to Philadelphia to work for his wife's father. Fella stopped in with the forwarding address".

Armed with this intelligence, he wasted no time, setting off on foot after Breunig. Along the way, he dwelled on the man's choice to go from farmer to employee. Is that a better life, he wondered, trading the whim of nature and *Ha Shem* for the whim of a father-in law? Ready to be his own boss, Jacob prayed that the dairyman, no longer in need of his equipment, would sell the lot to him at a fair price.

A mile out of town a farmhouse and pasture enclosing half a dozen milling cows came into view, with a milking barn off to the right. Hitched in front stood a sturdy chestnut mare yoked to a wagon laden with metal milk jugs. He was surprised to see the unattended cargo. What might have befallen the dairyman, he wondered? Just then the outhouse door swung wide and a short, bearded man with a white shirt and black vest emerged.

"Are you Breunig?"

"Who's asking?" the man responded gruffly. Registering that he might be moving too abruptly, Jacob smiled and held his hands wide.

"I'm new in town. Asking around for the best dairyman, everyone said to talk to Breunig!" He spoke as ingratiatingly as he could.

Breunig visibly eased. "Yeah, that's true, I am the best. But not for much longer. I'm moving away soon."

"Oh, too bad," he said, attempting surprise. "I hope for something good."

"It'll make my wife happy," Breunig answered with a wry smile. "Her father's done well for himself. There's a place for me in his business. The wife's been nagging me for years she wants to live near her mother. But that's probably more than you wanted to know, mister."

"Well, I hope it's all for the best." He paused, putting hand on chin as if suddenly struck by an idea. "Say, if you're leaving, what's going to happen to your horse and wagon?"

"Daisy here is a good horse. I'm sad to see her go, but the rig's no use to me in the city. Why?" Breunig's eyes narrowed just a bit, appearing to take a close look at Jacob for the first time.

"Just so happens I'm in need of a horse and wagon. For my new business," he answered, then waited. He watched Breunig absorb this information then make a quick calculation. The dairyman tossed out an exorbitant price for the outfit. He responded with half as much, a lively negotiation ensuing until they'd reached a mid-point. He happily parted with more of the nest egg earned aboard the Scot, but no more than he could afford. "Come by Sunday with the cash and she's yours," Breunig concluded as they shook on the bargain.

Taking possession of the rig on the appointed morning, Jacob climbed aboard for the first time. For a long moment he merely sat savoring the view from the buckboard perch. He had always loved that feeling now flooding through him, seated above pedestrians like royalty on a throne. High up once again, a sense of optimism permeated his body. I'll never be beholden to Fayga and Harry, he thought smugly. It's almost a blessing that they dealt with me highhandedly, he said to himself. "I've made my own way before, and I'll do it again," he uttered as he shook the reins, urging Daisy forward.

The wagon was in good repair and sturdy, easily adapted for use as a traveling dry goods emporium. A local wagonsmith carried out his instructions to enclose the sides, adding a leather top for protection against rain and snow, and hinging the rear doors. Jacob designed a clever locking device to automatically hold the rear doors open whenever he dropped the back flap, creating an instant display area for customers. The idea had sprung from a conversation with a shopkeeper in Tuckerton, one of the many locals he'd politely interrogated while formulating plans for his venture. Applegate was the man's name, a gray haired bespectacled fellow with something of a hunchback. He'd dropped into Applegate's store just after the blow-up with Fayga and Harry on the pretext of wanting to buy a good cigar. Delighted to find no one else in the shop, it was easy to strike up conversation. Soon he learned that Applegate for many years made a little money on the side supplying goods to the itinerant peddlers of southern Jersey, and was more than forthcoming with observations about success.

What separated the prosperous from the *schlemiels* who never seemed to make a dime out on their routes and came back time and again begging Applegate for more and more credit? "Presentation, my good man," Applegate told him. "The peddler who looks disheveled can hardly convince a farmer's wife he's giving her his best. If I were you, I'd make sure to display your wares as grandly as if you were one of those New York Fifth Avenue department stores. Your customers will love that." Jacob thanked him by buying two of the older man's best cigars.

Heeding the advice gleaned from Applegate and other locals pumped for information, he set about burnishing his appearance. At the haberdashers he acquired a bowler hat. Shira insisted the fashionable headgear would present a more distinguished look than his typical cloth cap, and after one look in the mirror he had to admit she was right. He gave equal care to the appearance of his wagon. A fresh coat of red paint added a festive look, while providing the practical touch of visibility from a distance. No sense surprising customers who might be nervous if a stranger suddenly loomed up on their doorstep. The final touch was stenciling in bold black letters with a gilded outline "J. Itzkowitz, Dry Goods" atop each side panel. Finally, he thought with satisfaction, I'm ready to take to the road.

Early on a crisp November morning, he bade Shira a simple "I'm off, wish me luck", threw back his shoulders and strode out the door. Hauling himself on to the driver's bench, flicking Daisy's reins, he beamed a broad grin at Shira while she stood on the front porch waving. Heading west, horse and driver navigated across the Mill Creek dam and down the dusty road leading into the Pine Barrens. He began whistling an old Yiddish folk tune, stopping in mid-melody when a fork in the road ground him to a halt. Despite having considered every minute detail of outfitting his rolling shop, suddenly he was unsure which way to go. A shiver of panic seized him as he sat staring at seemingly identical options, the maps he had pored over evaporating from his memory. Absentmindedly reaching into his vest pocket, he fished out the Kruger coin and rubbed his thumb back and forth across the profile of the far off Oom Paul. The familiar sensation served to calm, and the many tidbits he had gleaned over the last few weeks condensed back into focus.

To the left lay New Gretna, more a cluster of small farms radiating out from an old church than a town. Several sources had urged trying his hand in that direction, arguing that those settlers lacked nearby stores and were too tired after tending to their animals and crops to ride into Tuckerton for provisions. Moreover, many New Gretnians worked the nearby cranberry bogs, yielding them extra cash from the recently completed harvest. An equal number of his new acquaintances argued the opposite. They were convinced his best luck would arise from heading more northerly towards Philadelphia, to the Harrisville paper mill. Begun as a bog iron smelting center, Harrisville for decades was known for producing paper from a stew of old rags, rope, scrap paper, and salt hay. The laborious alchemy employed an army of workers shredding raw materials into pulp, cooking the pulp, then spreading, drying and rolling the resulting slush into coarse brown paper. Boosters of the Harrisville option asserted that the

arduous grind of mill work would make its inhabitants sus-
ceptible to desire for a few bright objects around the house.
After twenty minutes of near paralysis brought on by an
unfamiliar fear of making the foolish choice, he settled on
tossing the coin. Heads led him to the right.

Two miles down the road, as the maple trees of town
receded and the way was lined with scrub pines, Jacob
overtook a peddler on foot. Assuming this stranger to be
a *landsman,* he called out a greeting in Yiddish. The man
instantly spun around, surprise mixed with joy on his face,
and replied in turn. Conversation revealed that the fellow
was seventeen years old, had recently crossed from War-
saw expecting to stay with a cousin in New York, only to
find the cousin succumbing to tuberculosis. The young immigrant found himself shipped south to a different cousin
living a few miles north of Tuckerton, in a village called
Parkertown. With no other prospects, his cousin assigned
him to earn his way as a peddler, a profession learned simply by doing it for the last five months. Listening to the
lad's travails, he imagined Shira's cousin Labe relegated to
his comparable fate, stumbling along a desolate road. Taking pity on the skinny fellow struggling under the weight
of his pack, Jacob offered a ride to the turnoff ahead for
a crossroads called Munion Field. There the young man
thanked him profusely, shimmied back into his load, and
trudged north, Jacob watching his back until the man faded into the scrub pines.

Resuming his journey solo, he mumbled a prayer of
thanks for his good fortune. Having a wagon gave him
an advantage over the myriad foot peddlers throughout
southern Jersey. Poor souls who started out with next to
nothing, they carried everything on their back. Even the
sturdiest young immigrant laden with a trunk stuffed with
goods could only cover a mile or two per hour, needing

more frequent rest stops than a horse. Speed was only one portion of the edge he enjoyed. A wagon merchant offered customers a larger stock and variety of goods, making for more instant sales. And as he learned to tell his customers, whatever he might not stock he could get and bring next time, having more room than a foot peddler to deliver future orders. Covering ground faster and promising swift merchandise delivery gave the man with wheels an edge.

In time, Jacob would learn to exploit these strengths. On this first foray as a wanderer in a strange land, he was learning lessons the hard way. An hour on from discharging his passenger he spied a whitewashed farm house set back from the road. "A customer!" he exclaimed, steering Daisy down a rutted path to the residence, anticipating a potential first sale. In his excitement, he failed to spot a black and white dog sleeping under a tree. No sooner had his wheels entered the farmer's property than the hound leapt up, barking furiously while bounding directly for Jacob. The dog's unexpected assault startled Daisy, who suddenly leapt ahead to avoid the danger, causing the wagon to jolt sharply forward. Off balance from instinctively reaching under the seat for his whip as a weapon, he was nearly thrown. Disaster was averted when a blonde young man stepped out from behind the house, put two fingers into his mouth to produce a sharp whistle, then called out "Jack". As if reaching the end of an invisible rope, the yapping pointer braked abruptly, its jaws just short of Jacob's leg.

"Who are you?" the dog's master asked in a manner neither friendly nor unfriendly. The shotgun he held may or may not have been pointed at Jacob's head; he was too shaken at the time to later recollect clearly. What he did notice, besides the weapon, was an unsmiling dough-faced *schlub* in farmer's garb confronting him. He's like the dumb *muzhiks* from home, Jacob thought, admonishing himself for not anticipating a need for his own gun while making his rounds. Conscious of a very real threat if he said the wrong thing and provoked the fellow, he raised his hands very slowly.

"I'm Jacob," he answered, summoning as much non-chalance as possible. "I have, uh, all kinds of things to sell. Is the wife, the woman of the house at home?" He'd practiced this opening over and over in his head while Daisy had ambled along the stage road, but now found himself stumbling over his words when speaking to a stranger wielding a menacing weapon.

"Mister, you talk funny." A drip of sweat formed on his brow as he watched the fellow's eyes narrow to slits.

"My English is not so good yet," he enunciated slowly, recalling a time in Shavlan when he'd crossed path with a juvenile bear and had spoken soothingly while inching away from the menace. "Maybe you'll tell me if I say a word wrong."

To Jacob's relief, the barrel of the gun tipped skyward as the man set the butt end down on the ground. "I understood ya. You just sound strange. You wanted to know if Ma's home, right?"

"That's right. Is she around?"

"Nope. Ma's over at Aunt Mae's, she's not feeling well."

"Will she, uh, be back any time soon?" he asked.

"Dunno."

Now calmer, he studied the blonde fellow carefully. He determined him younger than at first thought, maybe thirteen at most. The boy wore a grey heavy cotton shirt buttoned to his neck, frayed around the collar but looking other in decent shape. His pants, however, though of a heavy coarse fabric, possibly wool, were so patched that the wearer appeared to be a walking checkerboard. He wore boots so muddy it was difficult to determine their condition. Regardless of the tattered clothing, the boy was not the customer at this homestead. Frustrated by the misfortune of the mother being away, Jacob sighed and started to say goodbye. Then a thought occurred.

"Your Aunt Mae, where does she live?"

"Down the road a piece." The boy nodded in the direction Jacob was traveling.

"Thank you, young man. I've told you my name, what's yours?"

The boy hesitated. "Luke," he said finally.

"Luke, I am sorry I surprised your dog. He's a good guard for you."

Luke broke into a toothy smile. "Jack watches out for us, that's for sure."

Having acquired a nugget of intelligence, he steered Daisy back on course and set off evolving a plan. Another mile and half along a house larger and better maintained than the previous farmhouse came into view. Before pulling into its driveway, he halted Daisy, making a point of standing up to scout for a dog. I can't make the same foolish mistake twice, he said to himself. Seeing no immediate threat, he proceeded cautiously, scanning constantly for a sleeping sentry.

Jacob stepped as confidently as he could on to the small porch of the two story saltbox. Noting a recent coat of white paint, he rapped on the front door. Remember to smile, he silently instructed himself. A round-faced woman in a blue muslin dress pulled back a lacy cloth and peered through the door's glass panes, looking him up and down. "Who are you?" she said in voice that echoed Luke's.

"Good morning, Ma'am," Jacob began, taking off his hat. "I am Jacob, a merchant, and I met your son Luke earlier. He said you would be here attending to your sister Mae. I hope she is feeling better."

"Luke told you that?" she said suspiciously. "Why'd he go blabbing on like that?"

"I hope you don't mind, Ma'am. We fell into polite conversation. I'd stopped by your house to display the wares on my wagon, he didn't want you to miss the opportunity. Might you care to take a look? I'm well stocked for all your needs. Perhaps even some medicine for your sister?"

Focusing on her face, he hoped to discern any reaction registering at the mention of medicinal items. The woman's eyebrows flickered, eyes darting towards a rear room. Slowly the front door opened. "I suppose it can't hurt to look at what you've got," she said, emerging onto the porch. "Mae's head is all stuffed up, she's dripping and sneezing and blowing her nose constantly. I've been boiling water non-stop so she can breath steam, but that's not doing much good."

"Ah, I have just the thing. Dr. Sage's Catarrh Remedy! Comes highly recommended," he explained, leading her to his wagon. Throwing the latch he had designed, the rear upper panels flew open, dropping the lower panel into place and revealing his heavily stocked interior with a flourish. He smiled as the woman's eyes flitted from item to item, widening as she took in the full array on offer. Just as I hoped, he thought. While the prospective customer gazed at his goods, he leaned and snatched up a tall greenish bottle. "Only fifty cents," he said, holding the patent medicine close to her face.

"What did you say your name was, fella?" the woman asked, appearing enchanted by the wonders in his wagon.

"My name is Jacob, Ma'am. I didn't catch yours," he said.

"Applegate," she answered, snatching the bottle from his hand.

"That's a familiar name," he replied, lifting an eyebrow. "Say, by any chance are you related to the Ulysses Applegate who runs a shop in Tuckerton?"

"You know him?" she asked equivocally.

"I bought something in his store." He wondered if he'd unwittingly ventured into dangerous territory.

"Well if you see him again, tell him it wouldn't kill him to visit his niece Betty once in a while," she said, now grinning.

"I certainly will!" he answered, relieved. More comfortable from her reaction, he decided to plow ahead with his plan.

"Mrs. Applegate," he began, noticing her attention drifting back towards his goods. "Perhaps there is something else for you or your family I could supply? If you don't mind me mentioning it, I noticed that Luke is a growing boy. Does he do lots of work around the farm? I have with me the latest in quality work clothes. These are what they are calling 'overalls', heavy denim pants combined with a bib, all in one." In one graceful motion he shook out a specimen of this new fashion, holding it up for his prospect to examine.

"Luke sure could use something sturdy for working with his father. I've patched his pants so many times I can hardly find a scrap to stitch on a new piece," she said, rubbing her calloused hands across the heavy cloth. She pressed hard on the rivets, apparently inspecting whether they would hold up under her thumb. "How much?"

"A mere dollar thirty. A bargain, as these will last him till he's grown," he said, showing her the rolled up cuffs.

"I'll need credit," she said matter of factly. "The last peddler who came through this way, that fella was unreliable. He only turned up every other month. Are you comin' back this way soon?"

"For a good customer like you, Mrs. Applegate? Certainly," he said with a slight bow, pleased to see a slight blush in her cheeks.

If I can land one customer, I can land many more, became his mantra while Daisy carried him further along his route. Confidence bolstered by this first victory, over the ensuing months Jacob threw himself into becoming ever more adept at his new trade. He discovered that his smattering of Afrikaans combined with fluent Yiddish yielded a common tongue with German settlers. When calling on a farm-wife named Van Something, he could even comprehend enough Dutch to sell a pot. The English he'd acquired in the Transvaal was passable enough then, and during passage on the Scot and his stint at the Jubilee he'd routinely forced himself to repeat unfamiliar words silently. Criss-crossing South Jersey his facility with English improved still more rapidly. Communication meant customers.

Like peddlers before and after him, he built his business along back roads, knocking on doors, smiling, and introducing himself. If a door opened, his immediate goal was to cross the threshold and gain time to win over the woman of the house. More and more he became a merchant anthropologist, learning local dialects and cultural knowledge. In order to sell, he had to know his prospective customers. What were their aspirations? Were their needs merely practical, or did they desire some trinket to liven up a dull existence? He meticulously tracked birthdays and anniversaries. He memorized who had a sweet tooth, what farm implement might be worn out, and when a farmer's child had an upcoming special occasion calling for a special outfit. A very satisfied customer could offer another prize -- a recommendation to a new neighbor. Soon he would pay a visit, and the wooing would begin all over again.

Over time, a growing list of loyal patrons welcomed him into their homes during a cycle of several weeks. Some relationships grew so warm that Jacob was invited to bed down for the night in a barn, occasionally even inside the customer's house. Where to lay his head each night was a constant challenge. If need be, he could squeeze into the rear of his wagon, but doing so wasted valuable time rearranging goods. When in the vicinity of Toms River, he could count on a night's rest with Shira's cousin Labe and his wife Stella. Stella would lay blankets on the floor in the main room near their fireplace so he could warm himself during the cold months. He delighted in these visits over the years, growing especially fond of Labe's youngest, Charlie, an inquisitive toddler who shrieked with joy when Jacob lifted up the child to show him all the wonders of the wagon. The brief respite of a night with mishpocha was often followed by a day of melancholy. Will I always be a nomad, doomed to wander alone away from my own family, he would ask himself.

At the end of each circuit, Jacob returned home to Shira for a day of Shabbos rest. Then all too soon, Shabbos was over, he was on a day trip by train to Philadelphia to replenish his stocks, followed by a half day at home, and then back on the road. It was a grueling pattern, with little time for levity. The rare occasion for an amusing tale, even at his own expense, was to be cherished. Over one Shabbos dinner, he recounted to Shira a bitter cold night when Daisy was navigating the wagon homeward through a snowstorm. Spying a light still lit in a general store near Eagleswood, he thought, ah, a few swigs of whiskey will warm me. Covered in flakes, he entered the establishment and asked the proprietress for 'a little Schnapps, please'. To his surprise, she proffered a bag filled with ginger snaps. Flustered, he sheepishly paid her the stated price and trundled back to the wagon. Oy, he thought while recalling the blonde boy's comment from his first outing, maybe my English is still not so good. Shira laughed heartily with him at the mix-up. After that, he practiced even harder sounding more like the locals.

When at home, he steadfastly refused to speak to his sister and brother-in-law. On the road, however, during long lonely gaps between farmhouses and villages, he had more than ample time to brood over the situation. She betrayed me, he would regurgitate with renewed feelings of outrage. But as time wore on, the outrage became more muted. He found himself more often missing the sister he had crossed an ocean to see. Time and again during solitary treks along back roads, he lapsed into a sulking monologue, replaying the same lines in his head like one of those repeating gramophone disks he had listened to in a shop in Toms River: "Fayga was right about one thing, she was like a mother to me after Mama died. She's even grown to look like Mama. Shira thinks my sister would never have intended to mislead me. Maybe she's right, maybe Fayga was telling the truth this time. But Shira doesn't know how I felt, seeing one thing with my eyes while all the grown ups were telling me the opposite. Fayga never said a word about Mama's sickness, and she must have known. My whole family knew Mama was dying and nobody told me the truth. I can't go though that again, my own family hiding things from me. It's time to get away, be my own man."

Incrementally these jumbled thoughts resolved into tangible actions. Although no rental terms had actually been discussed with Harry, Jacob always paid a fair rent and then some, slipping bills under his brother-in-law's door the first of each month. Doing so gave him a surge of pride, signifying that he could earn his own way. He had done so in South Africa, and now he was achieving independence in America. On the road, he began carefully assessing each hamlet and crossroads. Was there a school? Were there children playing? Previously he'd only focused on each locale's potential for adding new customers. Now he searched for more subtle indications of suitability for resettlement.

Approaching the village of Manahawkin one Friday afternoon, he stumbled across a tidy two-story house with a picket fence and a fresh coast of paint. Catching his eye were three young children playing together in the front yard, while a woman of Shira's age rocked on the front porch knitting furiously. A moment later a bearded man emerged from the house, stooping to pick up the littlest of the trio, then hoisting her overhead while she squealed in delight. An unfamiliar pang of longing struck Jacob. Weeks earlier Shira had told him the marvelous news that she was carrying their child. He was joyful enough at the time, hugging Shira and reciting the *shehecheyanu* blessing of thanksgiving. Seeing this vision of quiet domestic harmony galvanized him, made it real. Soon I will be a father! It's time to really provide for my family, he thought. Slowing Daisy to a crawl, he tried not staring too obviously as he drank in a long absent sense of contentment.

Arriving that evening, greeted by the aroma of roasting chicken, he *kvelled* upon seeing Shira in her apron. That small bulge in front, he marveled, is our child growing in her belly. The sight brought both joy and determination. Wrapping Shira in a firm embrace, he felt her warmth against him. Releasing her, he placed both hands gently on her shoulders.

"It's time we have our own home," he announced. "We are moving to Manahawkin."

A Store
Point Pleasant 1904

Daisy loped along the wide gravel road, avoiding trolley tracks neatly snaking down Arnold Avenue while he surveyed storefronts admiringly. I could prosper here, he told himself, taking note of several newer buildings lining the street, two more under construction, and numerous shoppers out strolling on a Tuesday morning. This lovely little town is growing, the railroad brings tourists, my dry goods store will thrive here.

Making the move from Manahawkin to Point Pleasant had become his mission. At first the life of a peddler had suited him, was even somewhat thrilling. He relished being a free spirit rambling the back country with Daisy. The work was hard and strange, but it forced him to adapt in ways he now appreciated. It was lonely to be away from Shira, but they made up the separation when he returned each Friday. After all, the Rabbis taught that Shabbos sex is a mitzvah. As they grew to know each other better, both looked forward to Friday night. As the *goyim* say, he'd tell Shira, absence makes the heart grow fonder. At least for him it made the urges of the flesh grow fiercer.

As time wore on, the realities of the peddler's life began to feel more like a sentence than a blessing. More and more he asked himself: Can this be my future, to make my "living" plodding through uncertain country, depending on farmers for my nightly rest? Will my children know me as anything more than a phantom who disappears almost as quickly as I reappear? The fonder I've grown of Shira, the more separation pains me. Worse, her burdens only multiply when I am on the road, alone tending house and children. He was determined to change all that, and a store was the key. Manahawkin was stagnant, no place to invest. Point Pleasant, that was the future.

For the fiftieth time during the trek to Point Pleasant, he rehearsed his appeal to the banker. I've worked tirelessly since coming to America six years earlier, venturing alone on back roads three weeks out of every four. Starting out, I was just another greenhorn with an accent, but little by little I taught myself to smile more and schmooze with the farmwives and shopkeepers. They appreciated someone interested in hearing about their lives. I have an instinct for what will delight each prospective customer, getting them to buy something extra to brighten up an otherwise dull existence. They always appreciate me remembering a child's birthday or asking after a sick husband, and caring can seal a deal. My hard work and talent have paid off with one of the largest customer bases in Ocean County, over a hundred regulars and many more occasionals along the way. Selling from a wagon means time lost meandering from farm to farm, village to village, with long gaps between customers. Lost time means lost sales. I'm certain business will triple selling from a store. As he recited his arguments in his head, Jacob absentmindedly fiddled the Kruger coin in his watch pocket.

Further down Arnold the ornate two-story brick façade came into view. It evoked both wealth and sturdiness. As Daisy pulled up closer, through grand windows he saw marble counter-tops between tellers, an extravagance enhancing the message to all who entered that this was a place in which money belonged. Atlantic Building and Loan was merely five years old, yet already established at the center of commerce for the seaside resort. Eager to arrive on time, he briskly hitched Daisy to a post near the filigreed front door of the bank.   Dusting off his one suit and best hat he'd worn to give himself an extra dose of confidence, he thought of Shira home with the children. She'd fallen in love with this town during last year's visit, he remembered, prompting one last pep talk to himself "I must get this loan. Enough with the peddler's life, Shira deserves having me home."

Inhaling deeply, he walked determinedly into the open cashiers' area. Spotting a young man bent over a ledger at an oak desk to the rear, he approached the clerk, cleared his throat, and said formally, "I am Mr. Itzkowitz, here for my appointment with Mr. VanNort. I wrote to him last week, about a loan."

The clerk slowly raised his eyes off the page of figures,squinting up at Jacob. In a bland voice he responded, "Please have a seat sir. I will tell *Vice President* VanNort that you are here and see if he is available."

Choosing the nearest of several unoccupied heavy wooden chairs along the wall, he sat. The clerk had disappeared briefly and then resumed his perch behind the oak desk without a word. As the minutes ticked on, Jacob removed his bowler, holding it in his lap with a firm two-handed grip. He willed himself to sit still, resisting the urge to consult the clock on the wall behind him. To pass the time, he kneaded the hat brim with his thumb and forefinger. A further ten minutes ticked by with no indication that anyone cared he was waiting. His right hand moved to the arm of the chair, squeezing the carved scroll at the end. When a full twenty minutes had passed, as doubt about why he'd bothered coming clenched his stomach, a tall bald man with a stiff collar and a dark pinstripe suit approached. "Mr. Itzkowitz, I am Vice President VanNort. Follow me."

Jacob stood to extend his hand, but saw the man already rounding the clerk's desk and striding into an office tucked into the rear right corner of the floor. All he could do was follow a few paces behind. Entering the dark paneled room, he found VanNort already seated behind a massive mahogany desk shuffling papers. Realizing no polite invitation to sit would be proffered, he took the high-backed chair opposite, noticing immediately that the seat was not designed for comfort.

"Mr. VanNort, thank you for seeing me, I wanted...."

"Mr. Itzkowitz," VanNort began, ignoring that Jacob was speaking as he lifted a letter. "I understand that you are here seeking a loan of $750 to capitalize a dry goods establishment in our town."

"Yes, sir, and ...."

"A peddler for the past 6 years or so, living in the southern part of the county, married with three small children. Is that all correct?"

"Yes, and business has been very good, I have some savings..."

"Where are you from, Mr. Itzkowitz?" VanNort peered over his glasses.

"From? You already said, I live in Manahawkin."

"No, Mr. Itzkowitz. Where are you *really* from?"

He swallowed, looking down at his hands. "I was born in Russia, grew up there. I worked in the gold fields in Africa for a few years. Now I'm an American."

"Hmmm. Russia, of course." VanNort placed the letter face down and sat back into his leather seat. "Mr. Itzkowitz, what collateral do you have besides your horse and wagon? Their salvage value would hardly be worth half the loan amount you seek."

"Well, Mr. VanNort, as I was trying to say, I'm your best collateral. You see, I'm a very accomplished businessman and seller of dry goods. I know how to size up any customer, win them over and provide them with quality merchandise. My method builds loyalty going door to door. With a location in this lovely town I would be very successful. You just need to stake me with a modest loan to get started. You'll be winning a loyal successful customer for decades. In fact…"

"Mr. Itzkowitz," VanNort abruptly lifted his right hand, palm facing Jacob, and cut in sharply. "All well and good. Your high opinion of yourself, however, is not collateral. We are a prudent financial institution. We do not make loans without tangible assets as back-up. Moreover, if I may say so, you overestimate your prospects. We already have two Hebrew establishments in our community, Gottfried's Dry Goods and Zwiback's store. That is more than enough of your kind for the good people of this area. I highly doubt a third such enterprise would be well received. Pity you have traveled all this way, but we are a bank and not a speculative institution." With that, VanNort stood, walked to his office door and extended an arm towards Arnold Avenue.

Jacob felt the blood drain from his face. His gut contracted as if an invisible fist had landed a blow. Springing to his feet, one hand pressing down on the chair's arm, he faced VanNort.

"More than enough of *my* kind? In Russia I heard this kind of talk. But here? I came to the land of the free to get away from all that. This is America!" He expelled the last words so loudly he startled himself. Rage filled, he stomped past a smirking VanNort and bellowed, "I'll find money and start my store. You won't stop me!" As he stormed out the ornate doors he overhead VanNort instruct the clerk in full voice "Don't ever let that Jew back in my bank."

He sat motionless on the wagon seat. Elbows on knees, forehead in palms, he struggled to regain composure, finally sitting up straight, fists clenched. "What will I tell Shira?" he whispered, despairingly. She has her heart set on moving here, he agonized silently, I have to make it happen. Absentmindedly he reached into his watch pocket, letting the knot in his stomach dissipate before being ready to set off.

The journey home felt interminable. Normally he delighted in spotting gulls and other shore birds on the return loop south after a spell on the road. His preferred route ducked in and out from the Barnegat Bay shoreline, carrying him through grassy fields reminiscent of his boyhood. On summer's eves he was blissful hearing bullfrogs. The occasional low red flash of fur in the corner of his eye signaled a fox nearby, and a deer's white tail was not uncommon. On this journey home bitterness crowded out beauty. All focus was on the disastrous turn of events. He'd been certain his industriousness and talent would sway any banker. Instead, he was returning with nothing but the sour taste of scorn. Worse yet, he felt foolish.

To a passerby the wagon driver would appear fixated on the road ahead, as if anticipating imminent danger coming at him headlong. In fact, he was lost in a fog, a soupy mix of dread and disappointment, sorting out what next. Another bank was not an option, as no other bank served that market now that the Building and Loan operated there. He considered the mishpocha, but none were prosperous enough to have $750 to loan. Fayga and Harry were doing better than when he first came to them, but he'd vowed never to be beholden to them. Besides, they had their own mouths to feed. Cousin Moishe, who was like a brother to him and was Harry's actual brother, had come over from London. Moishe was building his own import business, and was nowhere close to having surplus to lend. Only one *landsmanshaft* in the region helped Jews from Russia, mainly those from Vilna. Even if they would welcome an immigrant from Shavlan, that mutual aid society, like most, primarily served to aid the needy with charity for medical emergencies, alms for the impoverished, burial for the destitute. While recently they'd begun making business loans, he'd heard the amounts were $50 at most. Each life preserver he mentally grasped for on the trek home quickly disintegrated once he concentrated on it, like trying to hold beach sand in your hands.

More viscerally, he dreaded admitting the setback to Shira. His return loop home had always filled him with pride, heading back to wife and children with a lighter wagon and a heavier purse. On this trip, however, it was his heart that was heavier. Lost in a disquieting internal soliloquy, he let Daisy lead them home as she trundled along roads familiar to her after many passages.

As their trim cottage in Manahawkin came into view, he stirred from his trance, shifting from a slump to his more usual erect posture. Noticing his vest soiled by crumbs -- that must have happened while I gnawed on black bread without even tasting it, he realized -- he flicked those away and made himself ready to face his family with a smile. No sense in saying anything to Shira until I have a plan, he thought. Bad news can wait, when with a little more time and creativity he could present a happy alternative.

"Papa," shouted Ann, the oldest, who'd been reading on the front porch. She was a precocious six year old, like her mother apt to have a book in her hands when no task occupied them. Her cry alerted the others. Out of the house poured younger sister Esther and the toddler Lew, Shira following. Jacob grinned at the sight of his brood, troubles momentarily fading from his consciousness. He gathered the quartet into outstretched arms. Warm embraces enveloped him from shoulders down to knees, each touch imparting a measure of love he needed more than he'd realized. This, he thought, is why I will succeed.

By the time he'd washed up and joined the family for dinner, the anxious thoughts had reemerged. Holding them at bay, he carefully avoided any commentary leading to questions about Point Pleasant, instead holding forth with tales spun around the lives of customers. The Wagners of Waretown, their son married a Toms River girl and moved away from their farm. Such migrations were happening often along his route, as opportunities for young people in the smaller cities were burgeoning in the new century. The Oliphants of Cedar Creek welcomed baby Cordelia, who would be needing a crib, guaranteeing a sale for him on his next trip. Mr. Curtis the Barnegat surfman nearly drowned saving passengers on a schooner run aground off Little Egg Harbor. Thankfully Curtis was recovering at home quite nicely. He delighted in sharing with the children these glimpses into the lives of their neighbors, recounted through their Papa's encounters. Shabbos dinner was his hour to bring home the world one met from a wagon bench.

The meal only held off the inevitable for so long. When, dishes washed and children tucked in, he was finally alone with Shira, Jacob sensed the question she'd waited to ask. He let the silence in their bedroom linger. Putting down her hair brush, Shira turned to him. "*Nu?*"

"Nu? What's new with you?" he tried to sound jovial.

"No jokes! Jacob, I've thought of little else while you were away. I've been biting my tongue all evening." She wasn't angry, he could tell from her tone. He also knew her well enough to know that her patience for evasions was thinning rapidly.

"It's under consideration," he said, steadily returning her gaze. Maybe they are having second thoughts about turning me down, he imagined, as if convincing himself that reconsideration was a remote possibility.

Shira picked her brush back up, resuming carefully stroking her curls. "When did they say you will you hear?" She looked into her mirror, talking to Jacob only in reflection.

"It's a busy time for the bank," he said. "I'll give them a few weeks. Maybe I'll stop there on my route. It's best to do these things in person."

Her grooming finished, Shira came over to him and lay her head on his chest. She held tightly, saying, "I know you will make it happen, my dear husband. You have a way of making things turn out for the better."

He awoke at dawn, not on account of the rooster welcoming the morning, nor due to the neighbor's dog growling at a passing scavenger. A memory had stirred him, woven into a dream. Barnato. Jacob saw himself back aboard the Scot, only now he stood on an upper deck peering down as Barnato and his nephew neared the fateful spot. They floated rather than walked, moving half normal speed in the way dreams often unfold. Barnato suddenly rotated seaward, attention captured by a bird diving for prey. Just as abruptly Barnato turned back, looking at Joel as if suddenly realizing he'd neglected to say something vital to his nephew. In the same instant a man in uniform, one he didn't recognize, charged Barnato. Joel retreated several steps, perhaps avoiding the inevitable collision of the other two, but with the effect of leaving his uncle fully exposed. The faceless seaman then rammed Barnato full on, propelling the startled diamond magnate backwards into the railing with such force that he toppled overboard into the cold gray waters. Jacob felt more than heard a wailing force emit "murder" as the vision swirled and became the stateroom where he'd stood *shomer*. He shivered at seeing the familiar naked body hovering, as if caught in limbo.

Passing from twilight sleep to full wakening, Jacob lay still while a plan blossomed. He had followed from afar Joel's ascendancy after Barnato's death, the nephew first taking control of Barnato Brothers enterprises then consolidating an ever-larger fortune in mining. Jacob's friends and relatives in South Africa, still bemused by his unlikely shipboard encounter with the unfortunate Jewish magnate, forwarded along news of the nephew from time to time. Solly Joel was now quite rich, and rich meant powerful. He must tread lightly and artfully if this scheme were to work.

Later that morning, with Ann in school and Shira off to market with the younger two, he took out a sheet of writing paper. Filling his Waterman's fountain pen with ink, he began slowly composing a letter, working it over and over to perfect the tone:

My Dear Sir Solomon Joel,

You will no doubt have forgotten me by now. You came to know me under difficult circumstances for only a brief few days. I am the man whom you entrusted with the sacred duty of all Jews to the departed when your esteemed Uncle Barney Barnato met his early death aboard the Scot. It was a great honor for me to be asked by such an important family to be the shomer, to tend to the body of the great man. I performed the rituals until we reached London where he could find a proper Jewish burial.

You treated me very fairly and compensated me very well for that service. I recall your words when we met. You said Mr. Barnato's death would cause speculation. You asked if I would respect the family's privacy and keep the matter private. I have done so, sir, for these past 7 years. It would be my intention to continue to do so.

You also mentioned that your family is one with worldwide connections and business ventures. I write because of that. You see, I have done well since coming to America not long after we made our acquaintance. My dry goods business has prospered, producing a modest amount of savings. Now I seek to establish a permanent location for my business in a growing town served by the railroad from New York. It is a very desirable location sure to prosper in the coming years. But the local bankers harbor prejudices against Hebrews like ourselves. They will not lend me the $750 needed to provide initial capital for the venture. Because of that, I humbly turn to you, sir, as a generous businessman.

You have knowledge of my character from your time of need. You know I have kept all confidences regarding anything I might have

*observed surrounding the tragedy aboard the Scot. I therefore hope that
you will grant this request. I ask only for standard commercial terms,
not charity.*

*If you would favor me with a reply to the address above at your
earliest convenience, I would be most grateful.*

Yours very sincerely,

Jacob Itzkowitz

He stared at his words on the page as if parsing a Tal-
mudic text. Would it produce the desired effect? Would
Joel react with interest or anger? A few years earlier, newspaper reports recounted that Joel's own brother was murdered by a con man under circumstances that were never
clear. The culprit was somehow involved in a fantastical
scheme to kidnap Kruger, although the details contained
in the tabloid articles sent by South African friends were
fuzzy. Would Joel be colored by that tragedy and view me
as a threat, he wondered. Sending this letter is dangerous.
Would a man who would harm his flesh and blood for
money hesitate to do something drastic to me, a nobody, if
he believed I might reveal his crime?

Despite these fears, he convinced himself it was
worth chancing it. He fixated on owning a store of his
own, on giving Shira the life she'd dreamed of when she
first suggested settling in America. He could not turn
back. Without money, there would be no store. Without
a store, he was condemned to the vagrant wanderings of
a peddler, or worse yet to working for someone else. Ap-
pealing to this titan he barely knew was a long shot, but
he'd taken chances before that had paid off. Jacob folded the letter tightly, fitted it into an envelope, and walked
with determination to the tiny Manahawkin Post Office.

Affixing a George Washington two-cent stamp with a steady hand, he dispatched his lottery ticket on its way.

The following days passed with distractions, as Jacob put all his attention into preparing for the familiar routine of the road. He spent an extra day home repairing the wagon, tending to Daisy, sorting through scraps of paper written in half a dozen languages on which customers specified orders for his next return, and compiling his own shopping list for Philadelphia. At breakfast on the third morning, he cleared his throat. "Shira," he said casually. "Today I must be off to market." His eyes darted to her, over to the children, then out the window to a cloudy sky.

Shira, for her part, had projected a routine outward demeanor since his return from Point Pleasant. She had washed the family's clothes, mended a hole in Jacob's work pants, gathered his receipts, updated the books, stashed some of the cash in the small strongbox they hid under the floorboards, and deposited the rest in the bank. As usual, she handled all this while tending to the ubiquitous needs of the children. If she was a little quicker to demand a stop to the inevitable bickering between sisters, or to scold Jacob a bit harshly for extending more credit to the Johnsons of Bayville, this time because their horse was lame, then Jacob for his part willed himself to not notice. After all, he thought, she is counting the days until my return trip to the bank, eager to receive better news. As long as she believes in that possibility, he assured himself, he would buy time for his audacious gamble to hit the jackpot.

And so it went for a fortnight after posting the letter. Pulling up to their house once again on Friday afternoon after still another week serving customers, his mood lightened as always from the ritual of returning. As usual Ann spotted him first, yelping happily and alerting the younger ones, all three scrambling to smother their father in hugs. The customary greeting completed, the children scampered back to the house, passing their mother walking purposefully towards the wagon for her turn.

Midway through their hug, Shira straightened her back abruptly, reaching into her apron pocket to produce a yellow envelope. "Who sends you telegrams, dear husband?"

His gut clenched. The missive could only be from Joel. A bead of sweat formed at the edge of his thinning hairline. "Some business to attend to, I suppose. Here, let me have it, I will read it later. First we must get ready for Shabbos."

Shira's hand wavered, as she perhaps considered ripping open the Western Union envelope right there. Placing the telegram in Jacob's outstretched hand, she echoed, "Yes, let's get ready for Shabbos. Business will wait." Quickly he folded the envelope, tucking it into his watch pocket. Taking Shira's arm to escort her towards the savory roast chicken aroma, he silently admonished himself "I will just have to restrain myself until I can read it alone." Despite his intentions, he felt as if an electric current were coursing through him all during the ritual meal. Only Shabbos intimacy with Shira managed to drain the anxiety and let him fall into a deep sleep.

Waking with the dawn, he slipped silently out of bed and padded over to where he'd draped his coat and vest. His hand trembled as he retrieved the message and considered the possibilities. Carefully placing each bare foot firmly on the floorboards precisely where they were least likely to creak, he tiptoed noiselessly to his chair at the head of the dining room table. Without even realizing it, he took a deep breath before slowly opening the packet and removing its contents.

"Letter received. Meet my men at your house Tuesday next, noon. SJ"

He blinked, then re-read the dozen words. His men? Coming here? To what end? He parsed the text for any hidden meaning, as if studying a passage from the Torah. Joel had received his letter and was acknowledging it, that's good. These words are neutral, not angry, also good. He is sending his people to me, taking me seriously. They must be coming from New York or Philadelphia, worth a major effort. "His men" means more than one. Is that a threat? Do they plan to intimidate me? Would they come to my house, in front of my family, to do me harm? So lost in thought examining every nuance of the message, he failed to notice Shira standing in the doorway.

"Now will you tell me who is sending you important messages?" Shira's mouth turned down at the edges, last evening's smile faded into a look of impatience. His neck twitched. He looked around to locate the voice which had broken his concentration.

"An old business acquaintance from my time in the Rand. He has associates in America now. He wants to discuss something, but the telegram doesn't give the details," he said quickly.

"Uh huh," Shira uttered, clearly not satisfied.

"We have a meeting here on Tuesday. Who knows, Shira, this may be another opportunity!"

"You never told me about any business acquaintances from the Rand, other than Uncle Helman and the man with the bar," she said, cocking her head slightly.

He let her words hang in the air, face reddening just slightly. Shira seemed to sense his discomfort. "Well, if this businessman is in touch after all these years, I hope it turns into something good," she replied in a manner indicating the topic was finished. Nothing more was spoken between them on the subject, a welcome respite from further inquiries. He turned his energies to plotting out every detail of how to deal with Joel's men.

On the morning appointed for their visit, Jacob recited his list of preparations with the intention usually saved for High Holiday prayers. Unsure of Joel's objective, he maneuvered Shira and the children out of the house. Telling her he wanted no disturbances for his business meeting was insufficient. Her obvious skepticism at his tale of a mysterious reappearance of someone from the Rand willing to travel all the way to Tuckerton left him worrying she might linger nearby. To thwart her curiosity, he implored Shira to make an important delivery to a customer at the far end of town, tossing in extra money to buy the children Coca-Cola ice cream floats at the soda fountain. He reckoned that with three young ones in tow, she would be gone at least two hours. Precisely at half-past eleven, though her expression betrayed displeasure at the banishment, Shira set off as requested with the children at her side.

With the house to himself, he turned to arranging the front porch according to a layout giving him the greatest advantage were something untoward to arise. Setting a pistol on the lower ledge of a side table placed next to his chair, he covered it with a cloth napkin. I can reach the weapon in a single motion if the need arises, he assured himself -- they'll figure out what's under the cloth without me having to wave it in their faces. Just enough of a signal that he can defend himself, in case Joel's men are hostile. He felt more secure with a gun within reach. Jacob practiced snatching it with eyes fixed on the chairs set across the porch for visitors; on the third try he was armed and ready without looking away. It was still only quarter to noon, time for a few more tries to improve the speed of this maneuver.

Just after the hour, Jacob heard an unfamiliar growling far down the street. Leaning forward, he saw coming into view something so out of place that he didn't recognize it at first. As the noise grew closer he realized his visitors were traveling in an automobile. He'd seen this new breed of machine on his last trip to the city, motorized small trucks near the market. But this was a touring car, with two men in black suits perched on a dark red leather bench above a green metallic body. He grew entranced by the motion of the contraption horselessly gliding down the street.

The automobile smoothly arrived across from his front stoop, and the stockier of the two men called out. "You must be Mr. Itzkowitz," he said, climbing down from the bench while swatting off dust. "I'm Goldstein, this is Markowitz. I see you got our employer's telegram."

Jacob stood up to better assess the two. Both wore similar dark suits, although Goldstein's clung too tightly around the waist and shoulders. If I had fitted him, Jacob mused, he wouldn't look as if he'd been squeezed into a sausage casing. Markowitz was leaner and muscular. His eyes darted around, seeming to scan the area for information, as if looking out for threats. He's here if things get rough. As he formed this thought, Jacob resumed a seated position with the pistol close at hand.

"Come on up," he called back. "I have chairs for you." Before heeding, Goldstein reached into a back compartment and hauled out a good-sized briefcase. The pair walked briskly side by side in lockstep up the three steps to the porch. Goldstein extended his right hand, offering with it a forced smile. Jacob felt no choice but to extend his own, engaging in a brief, firm handshake. Markowitz mainly stood to one side.

"Sit, sit," he said. "You've come a long way. Can I offer you any water or lemonade, gentlemen?"

"Thank you, it was a long trip from Philadelphia. We would like to get right to the point."

Glancing furtively at his side table, Jacob quickly refocused on Goldstein and waited.

"Our employer was quite surprised to receive your letter. He asked us to convey that he had not forgotten of your existence. However, he had not expected to hear from you again. In fact, at first he was rather offended by your presumptuousness. He considered all interaction fully terminated when the ship docked. And of course, you were paid handsomely for your services." Goldstein seemed to be reciting these words from memory, as if he were repeating a script practiced dozens of times en route to Manahawkin.

"He has reason to suspect the motives of any individual making claims of connections, as you may be aware." Jacob tensed. He had worried whether the tragedy that had befallen Joel's murdered brother would color his reaction. He'd counted on his letter being subtle, suggesting only obliquely possible menace to Joel while leaving him an easy way to avoid it. Soon I'll find out if I've miscalculated, he thought, as his heart raced faster.

"After thinking it over, however, he saw certain advantages that could flow from expanding connections to other Hebrew businessmen in new regions of America. He was also admittedly taken by your *chutzpah* in seeking him out. Accordingly, he decided to take a chance on you, Mr. Itzkowitz. You must apprehend that our employer does not do so lightly." Goldstein leaned forward, as if waiting for a reply. Markowitz remained stone-faced, continuing to patrol the surroundings. Jacob held his breath.

"If we are to proceed, Mr. Itzkowitz, you must understand the terms. Our employer is prepared to advance you the requested financing and then some, authorizing us to loan you $1,000 dollars." Jacob inhaled sharply, unsure he had heard correctly. Goldstein plunged ahead, ignoring the reaction. "The precise terms will be in documents I have in my brief case. We ask that you sign those before we leave if you are prepared to accept this. Typical interest rate and payment schedule."

"That's very generous, Mr. Goldstein. I was not expecting, uh, such an offer right off," he said, trying not to sound too eager.

"My employer doesn't waste time," Goldstein broke in. "Most important is what is *not* in the legal documents, Mr. Itzkowitz. I am sure you will understand that in return for our employer placing his trust in you, you must be prepared to honor him in return. What form that takes, we do not know precisely today. There may be nothing additional required of you for quite some time. However, as our employer's activities expand in this country, we may need to call upon you for assistance. When and what, we don't know. But if asked, you shall help. Is all this clear Mr. Itzkowitz?"

He could feel his chest tightening, uncertainty capturing his thoughts. I fancied myself clever, reaching out to Joel with hints of secrets revealed if a loan were not forthcoming. I expected to hear nothing, figured he'd take me for a yapping dog with no bite. Why would a powerful man on the other side of the globe bother? I just had no other options. It was worth the risk, even of provoking a hostile response. I never thought it through, never anticipated Joel might demand much more in return. They want me to swear an allegiance to do who knows what. I can pay the interest on the loan. Can I afford whatever other obligation might be called in some day? What if I say no?

He felt trapped in his own scheme. Having come this far, knowing how much opening the store and moving to Point Pleasant meant to Shira and to him, he had only one answer.

"Yes, Mr. Goldstein, it is all clear. Let me have the papers. I am ready to sign."

Reunion
Philadelphia 1972

They were half an hour down Route 70 before Jake broke the silence. Until they passed the gargantuan hangars in Lakehurst, he'd just been enjoying the novelty of a long car adventure with his father in their new Olds 88. It was almost always Mom behind the wheel for any trip out of their tiny town, like drives to the synagogue in Bricktown for teen gatherings, or when she'd drag him along to Delicious Orchards to buy pies for some occasion. If Pop was driving any distance it was inevitably a full family outing to a simcha with relatives up north.   A long drive alone with Pop took some getting used to.

Crossing Route 9, he saw a sign for Lakewood that triggered memories of visiting the cemetery there, the one that seemed full of Itzkowitz and Moscowitz headstones. His grandparents were buried there, on a little hill near some shade trees. When he was younger, he used to go with his father for each *yahrzeit*, following Pop's lead and placing a pebble on the headstone of the grandparents who'd died before he was conceived. No one ever explained why they left a rock behind, but that was true of a lot of Jewish customs, so he just did it too. After his bar mitzvah it started feeling creepy to him to visit the graveyard, so he'd stop going.

The proximity to those graves now tugged at his thoughts. He'd heard stories of Grandpop's adventures in South Africa, but didn't really know much about him as a person. Except the angry stuff that Mom says about him, he thought. Her most recent tirade was still ringing in his ears. Earlier that week Pop mentioned at dinner that he'd called the roofer about a leak, and that had set her off again. "When I married your father, I thought I was marrying a man of means. A big shot, the owner of a department store! Naturally I expected we'd have our own house. Boy, was I a schnook. 'We can't leave my father alone' he'd tell me. The old man could damn well afford a housekeeper, but instead demanded his son and the new bride live with him."

He'd heard variations on her grievance rants before, and tried to head her off with a bland "I know, Mom." Undeterred, she'd barreled right ahead, holding forth about Grandpop always acting like royalty, wanting someone to wait on him hand and foot. How she always kept her mouth shut and was the good daughter-in-law, cleaning, cooking, driving 20 miles to the kosher butcher because Grandpop insisted on kosher meat. She'd tossed in one of her zingers, "Making me keep a kosher home didn't stop the hypocrite from eating shrimp cocktails when we went out to a restaurant." She wrapped up her diatribe with a frequent refrain, that Grandpop had set up the Estate to spite her and spit on his children.

As usual, during Mom's monologues, Pop sat mute. Was that because everything she said was true? Or was

Pop tired of arguing? Alone with his father, maybe he could glean some truth.

"Pop," he said. "Tell me about your father. I know the South Africa stories, but that's about it. Except for the stuff that Mom says."

Lew cast a sideways glance at him while keeping both hands firmly on the steering wheel. "Hmm, well, I don't really know what to compare him too. I guess I'd just say Pop was a self-made man. He came to this country with nothing, just a few cents in his pocket. He started out here as a peddler."

That's not telling me much, Jake thought.

"Right, but I didn't think peddlers made much money. How did he get the Store?" Maybe at least I can get some blanks filled in, he said to himself, deciding to be more concrete in his line of questions.

"Like I said, he was self-made. He worked hard, saved up. Little by little he accumulated enough money to build the Store," Lew explained. "Have you read Shakespeare? In Hamlet the father tells his son 'neither a borrower nor a lender be.' Pop followed half that advice, he hated being a borrower, insisted on doing it all on his own."

He waited to see if his father had any more to offer. When nothing came, he figured he needed to probe a little deeper.

"Pop, why does Mom always call Grandpop Jacob 'the old bastard'?" He gazed out the passenger side window, watching the scrub pines speed by.

"Your mother met my Pop when he was pretty old," Lew began slowly. "He and I lived together, just the two of us, for a few years before Mom and I got married. Old people get set in their ways and don't like change."

"From what she says, sounds like he was mean to her," he pressed.

"Your grandfather could be pretty stubborn. So can your mother. Two stubborn people end up butting heads a lot, especially when they're like oil and water," Lew said, eyes set on the road ahead.

This fell far short of explaining the vehemence with which his mother spoke of her father-in-law, but he gathered Pop was saying no more on the topic. She had strong opinions on just about everything, that was for sure. The TV news blared away nightly during dinner. If Huntley and Brinkley reported the latest Viet Nam protest, Mom would yell back that they're all a bunch of hippies and spoiled brats. To reports that some guy shot his whole family and then killed himself, she would admonish the TV "the sicko got it in the wrong order, he should have started with himself." He remembered that when Muhammad Ali refused the draft, she cursed at the screen, mocking him as a big shot in a boxing ring but too much of a coward to go fight for his country.

After a few minutes he decided music was the way to pass the time. Flipping on the radio, he turned the dial away from his father's news station and over to WABC pop radio, eager to catch Dan Ingram's top 40 rundown. Cat Stevens flowed into Elton John, the Rolling Stones wafted through, and Roberta Flack closed out the hour. It wasn't counterculture like the Nightbird on WNEW, but the signal was strong and he was enjoying the variety until his father interrupted.

"We'll be at the reunion soon. I haven't been to one in 30 years, not sure who will even be there. It's funny," Lew said, mostly to himself. "Nobody knows I got married or have kids."

"Anything at this reunion for me to do?" Jake asked, drumming his fingers on the passenger's armrest.

"Might be. But I want to show you off, Jake. I'm hoping the old boys I knew will get a kick out of it." Lew stole a peek at his passenger and smiled.

"Pop, why'd you go there for college?" he asked. In just a year he'd be applying to college, and his father had never said a word on the topic.

"Actually, I really wanted to go to Princeton. Mr. Cash, our principal, said that's where I should apply. He even wrote me a recommendation. My father got the Mayor or some politician to write one too. But they turned me down. Nobody said why at the time. I found out later it was the quota."

"They had a quota?" Jake was taken aback. It wasn't like he was clueless about anti-Semitism, growing up in a gentile town had seen to that, but an actual quota?

"Back then they had an unwritten rule that we could only be three percent of the class," Lew answered matter of factly. "Things worked out. Luckily Penn didn't have a quota. I got a great education and met some terrific guys there. And later on I even got back at those snobs. I pulled a helluva prank on some Princeton boys."

A prank? This was more startling than the quota. He had friends whose dads played practical jokes. Not Pop, he was all business.

"What kind of prank, Pop?"

"Summer after my freshman year I was working at the Store. One day a couple of fellas came in. I knew right away they were Princeton men. One was wearing a silly belt with tigers on it. Another was the Harris kid from

Bay Head, his grandfather was some big shot at Princeton. Anyway, they were shopping for shirts. I overheard them talking about being more careful when drinking beer, how they kept slopping foam all over their clothes. That's when I got a bright idea. 'Gentlemen,' I said. 'I couldn't help overhearing that you need a way to keep neat when imbibing.' They gave me a funny look, like 'who are you' but they listened. 'We have just the thing for you,' I said. Took them over to the work clothes and spread out a canvas painter's jacket. Those boys had never done any real work and didn't know what it was. I told them it was a beer jacket, and we sell lots of them. Their eyes lit up!"

"Did they buy them?" he asked, intrigued to see his father so animated.

"I sold four right off," his father said proudly.

"Wow, Pop, you really fooled them."

"I got a huge kick out of it," Lew continued. "Then a funny thing happened. The next weekend a bunch of their buddies were coming down for a stay at one of fancy Bay Head oceanfront cottages. They came straight from the train station to the store, demanding to get their beer jackets! I guess word spread. Later on I'd see some of those fellas at a local tavern sporting their jackets all decorated with stencils, lots of orange and black. I enjoyed taking money from Princeton men who'd pay extra for a workman's jacket if we called it a beer jacket. Pop was impressed with how I'd come up with that on the spot."

"Do we still sell those? I haven't seen them around the Store," he asked, adjusting to his father as practical joker.

"I wish we did, Jake. Years later, while I was recovering out in Arizona, one of their alumni saw an opportunity. He started selling 'authentic Tiger' beer jackets and we lost the business. I still got a tickle out of fooling them all those years." Lew was chuckling, something he rarely saw his father do, as they pulled up to the Gothic campus.

At the registration desk, they acquired an assortment of paraphernalia for the gathering. The most distinctive items were fake straws boater hats trimmed in bright blue and red, and a big sash for Lew proclaiming "Old Guard." Properly attired, Lew led him to a tent with a huge "50th" banner above the entrance. The space was crammed with old men in animated conversation. Some men had women of the same age by their side, others draped an arm around a woman more his Mom's vintage. He scanned around hoping to spy other teens, spotting only a handful.

As they entered the tent, a portly fellow with a flushed face strode up to them. "Itzy!" he boomed in a deep bass, a glass filled to the brim with brown liquid and ice in his wobbly hand. "Great to see you after all these years!" The big man extended his free hand, grabbing and pumping Lew's rapidly.

"Hiya, Snooky," he heard his father respond. Looking quickly back and forth at the two old men in silly hats, one familiar, the other a stranger, Jake was baffled by the transformation he was witnessing. They were acting like teenagers despite their gray hair.

"And who's this fine fellow?" the big man bellowed, mussing Jake's hair. "This must be your grandson!"

"This is Jake," replied Lew, beaming. "Actually, Snooky, Jake's my son, not my grandson."

"Your son! You old devil, siring an heir at your age," the other man said with a lascivious wink. "You must have robbed the cradle for your bride."

"You could say that, Snooky. His mom, Toots, was born right about when we were graduating," Lew said, a note of pride in his reply.

"How about that! Well Jake, you look like a smart boy," the beefy man remarked, guzzling down a swig of the brown liquid. He peered down at Jake. "Your Pa was a smart cookie back in the day, a physics whiz. Did he tell you he was also fluent in German, French and Latin? Why, we always said that Itzy was quite the cunning linguist!"

Jake snorted, biting his lip. Lew suddenly coughed loudly. "Snooky. Cut it out!"

"Ok, ok, Itzy. But hey, is Toots your second wife? Did you end up marrying that blonde you were having all that fun with senior year?" the portly one said with a leer. Lew just shook his head in a vigorous no. Even through his haze, Snooky seemed to sense it was time for a new subject. He turned to Jake. "Are you following in your Pa's footsteps, Jake? Going to study at his alma mater?"

"No idea, this is the first college I've visited," he answered, looking over at his father.

Lew amiably steered the conversation to Snooky's life story, recalling him once being on Madison Avenue. This opened up a torrent of anecdotes, some risque, that seemed to make his father uncomfortable but only bored Jake. When the big man finally took a breath and a gulp of his cocktail, Jake quickly said he was hungry and hurried off to scour the buffet table.

At first, he amused himself with as much fried chicken as his stomach would hold. Stuffed, he took to wandering among the sea of wrinkled faces. Looking around, he wondered about his father's life. At home, Pop was just Pop. Jake had never given thought to how old Pop was, he just was. It's not as if he'd never noticed that some friends' dads played sports with them, while Pop never tossed a ball around. Plenty of his friends had dads who went fishing by themselves, hung out in bars, or worked all the time. Saturday morning at the bowling alley was more Pop's style. So what? There were all kinds of dads. Now, surrounded by the remnants of the Class of '22, it hit him just how old they all looked. And Pop was one of them, another old guy.

Could it be that he'd known his father his whole life, yet he'd never really wondered what Pop was like when he was younger? That presented a mystery, and Jake was partial to solving them. He loved detective stories, especially Sherlock Holmes. Here he was among a whole clutch of people who knew the young Pop. Should he interrogate some of them? He crossed Snooky off the list as too obnoxious and drunk. As he was formulating his strategy, a thin man with glasses and salt and pepper hair stopped and turned towards him.

"Itzkowitz?" the man said pleasantly, leaning forward to read Jake's name badge. "Related to Lewis?"

"Yes sir, I'm his son," he replied. Everyone called his father Lew back home, so it was curious to hear this stranger use his full name.

"His son! Well nice to meet you," the man put out a hand. "I'm Morton Edelstein. I knew your father back in our day. In the Menorah Society."

"Menorah Society? What's that?" he asked.

"I see Lewis hasn't mentioned it," Edelstein began. "The Menorah was for Jewish men of all backgrounds who desired serious intellectual discussions alongside Hebraic values. Back then, there weren't a lot of Jews on campus, so we needed to stick together."

"It was like a club for Jews? A fraternity?"

"A club, yes. A fraternity, no," replied Edelstein. "It was for more than just having fun. After the war, a lot of fellas just wanted to have a good time. Who can blame them? We all wanted to forget about the death from war and then the scourge of the Spanish flu. A lot of fraternities started popping up just then, including ones for Jews. We Menorah men, we fancied ourselves more serious. We were scholars who read books in foreign languages and wrote poetry, while also embracing Jewish history and culture. We had a saying, 'Menorah men discuss the classics and we light Shabbos candles'".

"My dad was active in this Menorah group?" he asked.

"Your father was one of our brightest lights. He was great at recruiting, too, especially boys from Russian families. My grandparents had come from Germany decades ago, so I grew up very assimilated, in a Reform temple. But your dad, his parents were Litvaks, with thick accents. I remember him saying they were traditional Jews living in a gentile world. I guess that's why Lewis was good at reaching out to the other first-generation men from similar backgrounds, getting them involved in Menorah."

"I never knew my grandparents. They both died before I was born," Jake replied.

"Ah, I'm sorry to hear that. I was lucky to know mine. A connection to your past is very important," Edelstein observed. "Do you think you'll want to come here for college like your father?"

"People keep asking me that, but I have no idea," he responded with a shrug. "They also keep asking what I want to be when I grow up. A lot of adults say I should become a lawyer. I guess that's because I'm good at arguing."

"That's very interesting," Edelstein pulled at his chin. "We all thought your father was going to be a scientist, probably a professor. He was enamored of physics and talked of going on to get his Ph.D. I remember at graduation, though, Lewis saying that he had go work in the family business for a while. I recall your father lamenting that your grandfather told Lewis he owed four years to him, because your grandfather had paid for Lewis' college. Your father seemed torn and a little upset by the subject. I never knew what ended up happening, we lost touch."

"Gee, I didn't know that," he replied. "He's never said anything about wanting to study science. My dad runs the Store."

"Do you think you will go into the business with him then?" Edelstein asked.

"Me? Actually, I really want to be a detective," he said enthusiastically.

"A detective? What makes you say that?" Edelstein raised an eyebrow.

"I notice things. Like your shoes. Your pants and jacket look nice and new, like you just bought them. But your shoes are all scuffed and the leather is cracked. Like you wanted to dress up for everybody but then ran out of money." He looked at Edelstein expectantly, waiting for confirmation.

"Very observant!" Edelstein chuckled. "The truth, however, is much simpler. The forecast said there might be rain this evening and tomorrow morning. I remembered that these courtyards can get very muddy. Hence my choice of an older pair of shoes that I don't mind getting a little wet."

"Darn, I didn't think of that," he said, stroking his chin. "But I'm still in training to be a detective. "

"Well, young man," Edelstein said wistfully. "Our lives don't always work out the way we hope they will when we are young. If there's something you want to do, sometimes you just have to go your own way. And speaking of going your own way, it was very nice meeting you, but I have to meet up with some other classmates. When you see your father, give him regards from Mortie."

He reunited with his father, finding him off to one side in the big tent. Lew had been chatting with another gray-haired man, who was now ambling away leaning on a cane.

"Pop, when do we go to sleep?"

"I think I'm about ready for that, Jake," Lew answered. "There are not that many fellas I know here. Not many left I guess. I'm running out of things to say to the ones I do know. After going over the same ground half a dozen times, I'm a little tired of hearing myself talk. Let's go turn in."

Later, as they lay on the hard mattresses in a sparse Upper Quad dorm room, the sour smell of beer wafting in from the hall, he stared at the ceiling. After a day of strange experiences and small revelations about his family, sleep was eluding him. Jake turned over what seemed like a torrent of new information in his mind. One detail kept nagging at him. Listening carefully, he could hear that his father's light breathing had not yet metamorphosed into his sleeping snore.

"Pop?" he ventured in a whisper. "Can I ask you something?"

"Hmm?" Lew responded, sounding groggy. "What's that, Jake?"

"When you were here, at college, were you planning to be a professor?"

"Who told you that, Jake?" Lew asked, sounding more awake.

"This man came up and saw my name and started talking to me, Pop. He said his name was Mortie."

"Edelstein? I haven't head from him in a thousand years. He was here?"

"Yeah. He seemed nice, told me all about the Menorah Society."

"Mortie was the one who got me into Menorah," Lew said, now fully engaged. "We met in German class."

"Well, he said that you planned to study physics, but your father made you work in the Store."

"It's not that simple, Jake. Your Grandpa Jacob needed my help right then. The Store was growing, he was planning to build his own building, my sisters were married. I figured I would help him out for a little while, until he got the new building built, and then it would be time to decide if I still wanted to pursue science."

"So why didn't you, Pop?"

"I don't know, Jake," Lew began, then paused. "Remember earlier I said your Grandpa could be stubborn? Well, every time I thought things were under control in the Store and I could get my Ph.D, he'd say, 'Lew, not yet, I just need you another year'. There was always some this or that he needed my help with. It was hard to say no to him. One year slipped to the next, and then I got sick. Pop paid for everything until I got better. At that point, I couldn't abandon him."

"Do you wish you'd become a professor, Pop?"

"I don't think much about it, Jake. Some things you just have to do for your family. Now get some sleep."

The March
Point Pleasant 1924

He stood across Arnold Avenue, arms folded, intently watching the workman hoist an eight-foot plank into place. It spanned the gap between the corner of the new building and the telephone pole at the intersection of Bay and Arnold. Nestled 14 feet above the sidewalk, the heavily shellacked oak board proclaimed "J. Itzkowitz Dept. Store" in ornate black and gold lettering. Pleased with this declaration of his presence in the center of town, he shouted to the sweating worker, "Good job. I have a little extra for you." Crossing over to Jacob, the workman plucked a shiny new dime out of his patron's palm. "Just like Mr. Rockefeller," the craftsman quipped under his breath, pocketing the coin.

Jacob proudly contemplated the imposing structure that now bore his name. He thought back over how much he'd accomplished these last two decades. He'd risked his life writing to the South African magnate, he told himself, now savoring how handsomely that gamble had paid off. His audacity had yielded the funds needed to launch his first store, enabling him to relocate the family to a town with a future. The loan was long since paid back, at least the terms that were written down. Even while relishing all this, unease at the unwritten debt to Joel hung over him. Once again he found himself pushing to the edge of consciousness lingering fears that Goldstein and Markowitz might someday return to collect. He took solace that so far, on the few infrequent occasions over the years that pair had come round, they seemed to merely be verifying that his business was intact and solvent.

He thought back to when he'd first arrived in town and rented a vacant storefront owned by a shady local named Bassinger. Throwing himself into the new locale with all the energy he'd poured into peddling, Jacob had quickly acquired a niche among the town's merchants. He'd specialized in catering to the surge in summer tourists arriving on increasingly frequent trains from newly prosperous north Jersey cities. Essex and Hudson counties had nearly doubled in population since 1890, bursting with immigrants pouring into America through New York harbor. Many crossed the Hudson seeking better opportunities in growing metropolises: Newark, Elizabeth, and Jersey City. For them, a day at the beach was a wonderful escape, a weekend in a bungalow even better. Some among the mass of immigrants were successful enough to afford a whole week or even two at the shore. They arrived needing bathing suits for the whole family, the women shopping for the right cap and footwear. Men with a few extra dollars splurged on an outfit of summer whites or knickers. Catering to their desire for status, Jacob stocked his shelves with the most famous labels. Soon Itzkowitz's became the frequent first stop for tourists departing the train station. Speaking Yiddish, or Russian, or the smattering of other languages acquired during his peddling years, Jacob took pleasure in turning several small advantages he enjoyed over his merchant rivals in town into tactics for growing a loyal customer base.

He developed a knack for learning from his customers of other opportunities. One day a farmer with wife and daughter in tow was shopping for a work shirt. Jacob overheard the mother badgering her husband to hurry up so they could catch the train north to Asbury Park in time for a motion picture. The daughter began complaining that her hose were full of holes, wailing that she needed new stockings right away. Suddenly the mother smacked the teen across her cheek and dragged her out the door, saying "Stop it! The money is for the the movies!" After they left, he observed to himself, "So movies are more important than stockings?" The next day, he struck a deal to rent a vacant lot adjacent to the store, then built a high fence at the back of the lot. Within a few weeks, he'd obtained a movie projector, installed outdoor benches, and hauled in a piano under a tent. With the showing of the popular new film Dr. Jekyll and Mr. Hyde the first cinema in Point Pleasant was born.

Lost in reminiscences of his path to owning the largest building in town, Jacob was roused by a familiar voice. "Pop, it's tonight." He turned to see his son, who'd been at the old store helping his mother and several employees pack up merchandise.

"What did you say, Lew?"

"Tonight. People are saying they march tonight. Right down Arnold Avenue."

"The bastards. Worse than the Cossacks. At least you could see their faces. These cowards with their hoods...."

"Pop, the windows. Shouldn't we board up the windows?"

"The windows? They wouldn't dare. Maybe I'll bring my pistol in case any of them try something."

"Uh, Pop, there will be a lot of them."

"I know their type. Talk big but they back down when you stand up to them…"

"Pop, look, maybe we should wait until tomorrow to move the merchandise. Just in case."

"Good thinking, Lew. I knew I sent you to that fancy college for something. OK, tell your mother and the rest of them, pack it all up but leave the goods in the Bay Avenue store. We can wait another day to open."

As Lew hurried off to relay the orders, Jacob looked after him with pride. He'd had only a grade school education, but there was his son, a graduate of what people called the Ivy League for reasons he didn't understand. Lew's acceptance to the University of Pennsylvania was a big deal with the locals, who took pride in one of their own going off to one of the country's best colleges. Like his older sisters, Lew had been the valedictorian of his class. They all take after their mother, he thought. She's the one with her nose always in a book, and good at math too. Yet a frown emerged as he watched Lew stride away. Is he shrewd enough to be a businessman, he wondered? I had to use my wits at every turn, even back in the Rand. Kruger would have cheated me if I hadn't thought ahead. The *goyim* will always take advantage of you if you let them. Maybe Lew's too soft. That's my fault, he chastised himself. I was probably too soft on all of them, made life a little too easy. They'll get eaten up in this world.

He shifted his worries to the more immediate threat. The Ku Klux Klan was rising up all over New Jersey, descending on small towns. The white-robed haters were especially active in Ocean County. Just a month earlier, carloads of robed vigilantes carrying torches had burst into Lakewood without warning, burning a Catholic church. That had confused him – aren't they all Christians? They all believe Jesus was the Messiah, so why are they killing each other, he wondered. It seemed strange to him that their prejudice extended beyond Negroes and Jews, raging at other *goyim* they considered "un-American." Klan leaders spouted a jumbled creed that made little sense to him. On the one hand, they despised any mixing of races and were clearly behind the lynchings and beatings of Negroes. Yet they spoke up for women's rights, supported giving them the vote. And Klansmen had propelled the prohibition movement that swept the country. Above all else, they waved the flag and thumped the Bible, blaming anything bad in America on the flood of immigrants coming after the Great War. They made him sick. Worse, if he were to admit it, they scared him. He was a Jew succeeding in a gentile town. That made him a natural target. He had to be prepared for tonight.

He walked to the old store, where the half dozen figures inside were busily loading dresses and suits and shoes into packing crates. Nodding approvingly, he sought out his son and son-in-law Marvin, Ann's husband. Marvin was a squat young man with a prize-fighter's build, a furniture mover before marrying Ann. Now and then Marvin helped in the store when a schlepper was needed, but his real plan was to open his own furniture business. He knew that Marvin was hoping for a loan to stake the venture, but Jacob's money was tied up in the new store building. Marvin apparently was savvy enough to bide his time, in the meantime ingratiating himself to his father-in-law. So there he was on a Saturday, working alongside the rest of the family.

"Lew, Marvin, look. We need a show of force when those cross-burning bastards march tonight. You each need to bring friends. Some strong looking guys. Maybe Gottfried's kid? Lew, call your cousin Charlie, tell him to get up here if he can. Make sure everyone brings a baseball bat or a big stick. I'll pay a dollar for each man who stands guard."

"Pop, no gun, OK?"

"Lew, just go find some big guys with big sticks."

"What good are a couple of us with sticks? There might be hundreds of them."

"Lew, Lew, we have to show them. They're just bullies. They see a man ready to fight back, they pick on someone else."

Marvin spoke up. "I will get our friend McKendry to join us. He's a Catholic. He hates those Klan rubes as much anyone."

"McKendry, shmeckendry, I don't care who you bring, as long as he's big and won't pee in his pants when they march by." With that, Jacob walked out of the store.

Lew turned to Marvin. "My father is big on being tough. Tough isn't always smart."

Marvin just smiled, not meeting Lew's gaze. "He's the boss," he muttered, and turned back to loading crates.

Leaving the others to pack, Jacob plodded the four blocks home. The weather had turned spring-like, with early buds on the trees lining each side of Arnold Avenue. He was fond of this time of the year, when life re-emerged and the winter gray brightened into stretches of blue skies. Townspeople were re-emerging as well, many out shopping on a Saturday, though nothing like the throngs of a summer's day.

He passed the firehouse where he still volunteered. Despite being considerably older than most of the dozen or so firefighters, over the decades he'd kept himself strong and fit. He prided himself on keeping up when the firebell rang out and the men all came running or, in his case, bicycling to the fire station. Joining the volunteer firefighters had been a smart move. Men from the influential families belonged to the fire house crowd, something he had noticed soon after settling in town. He was the first Jew to join, and it had taken a while for the others to size him up. A few fires allowed him to demonstrate he could pull his weight without fear, taking first position on a hose. Eventually they accepted him. Just as he'd hoped, facing another danger had paid off. When he needed a favor from the building inspector, the firemen's brotherhood delivered.

Continuing north on River Avenue, well-kept homes lined his path. He recollected the financial stretch he'd endured relocating the family to this upscale neighborhood back in '16, when business was slow. He'd been saving up cash by cramming his family into the small apartment above the store, with the girls sharing a bedroom. Shira never complained directly, but she had her ways of letting him know that she expected a reward for working her fingers to the bone, tending the home and doing the books for the store without pay. For several years he quietly sized up different parts of the Beach. When his friend Cramer, the realtor, mentioned that Parson Connors was ill and might need to sell, Jacob swooped in with the first offer. Buying an expensive grand home was a statement that Jacob Itzkowitz was now somebody in town. As he crossed McLean and his three story Victorian came into view, his pride swelled.

At dusk, he and Lew wolfed down the supper Shira had prepared as if it were just another Saturday evening. Jacob pushed back from the table, said matter-of-factly "Shira, the boy and I have more to do tonight," and signaled Lew it was time. Minutes later, father and son were striding back towards the downtown, each wielding a menacing club. Lew, who wasn't much for sports, brandished a baseball bat borrowed from the Carpenters next door. It looked awkward in his hand. Jacob gripped a short length of iron pipe left over from the recent upgrade of their well. What he did not display was something he had slipped into an inner pocket of his overcoat. Marvin was off rousting McKendry from the tavern, while Ann arrived to play piano and keep their mother company. Halfway to Arnold Avenue, father and son turned up the front steps of a modest house with a wide porch. They knocked loudly and waited until Max Gottfried emerged. Gottfried, a few years behind Lew in high school, had not been the brightest pupil but was a popular athlete. He carried a tire iron with a grim set to his features. "Lew, Mr. Itzkowitz," he acknowledged them simply.

The trio marched silently towards main street. As they rounded the corner, clumps of men appeared at intervals, spread along the avenue under the yellowish street lamps. They recognized other shopkeepers and assumed them to be there for the same purpose – to defend their property against the mob soon to appear. Or maybe they were there to root them on? Hard to tell. Jacob had no doubt why he was there. He'd be damned if he would let anything happen to what he'd built with years of blood, sweat and tears, he told himself. As that thought passed, other images — uniformed men on horseback riding galloping down the main street of Shavlan — flashed by, sending a chill of fear through him. Their kind are everywhere, he said to himself. Same evil, just different uniforms.

When the three arrived in front of the large plate glass windows flanking the "J. Itzkowitz Dept. Store" sign, they found Marvin and McKendry waiting. Each carried a thick, sturdy club fashioned from a tree branch. Nods were exchanged. A few minutes later, Charlie Moscowitz drove up in a Model T and pulled into the store's parking lot. He hopped out, turning back to grab a billy club from behind the seat. Rounding the corner of the building, Charlie called out cheerily "Wouldn't miss it for the world!" as if he was meeting up with Jacob and Lew at a family picnic. They all clapped Shira's cousin on the back as he joined the cluster of men assembled to stand guard.

With the sun down the evening air grew chillier, and they could see their breath as several vehicles crammed with hooded figures drove past. The could also tell that the 7:05 southbound train was depositing an unusually large flock of passengers. Klansmen must be arriving by train, Jacob figured, and the large parking area near the station made a good marshaling area. Soon he heard a low drumming sound coming from the direction of the ocean. Peering down the street, he realized that the march must have begun. What must be hundreds of hooded and robed figures were marching towards them. As the parade neared he could discern crosses covering every heart, American flags fluttering above the marchers, and a truck bearing their signature burning cross leading the throng along Arnold Avenue. He hissed at his guard, "Spread out." Each hastily moved into pre-arranged positions, standing six feet apart to line the storefront. Seeing his platoon in formation, Jacob turned back eastward to assess the approaching phalanx of white and gasped.

Coming around the corner, barely 150 feet ahead of the river of Klansmen, was Shira. He blinked. It really was his wife, in her knee-length, fur trimmed surplice coat, sporting a stylish wool cloche. She briskly crossed the street and hurried to his side. "It's my store too, I'm not going to let those scum do anything to harm it." He was speechless. Then he noticed that she was holding a broom handle close to her side. Shira walked along the storefront, past her son and the other sentries, and took up a position near the far end of the building.

His bewilderment at his wife's arrival was quickly disrupted by the approach of the throngs of marching Klansmen. They filled the avenue in wavy rows five abreast. They made no pretense of military precision, walking more like men out for a Sunday stroll. Their parade was made even eerier by its silence. They neither sang nor chanted, instead intimidating onlookers by sheer numbers and the ghostly appearance produced by medieval hoods and ankle-length robes. As row after row started passing in front of him, Jacob clenched his iron club ever more tightly, his shoulders tensing. Then he heard Lew whisper "Pop!" Lew grabbed his shoulder and leaned in close. "Pop, it's VanNort. The man one row in, it's VanNort, the banker."

Keeping eyes fixed on the marcher Lew had gestured at, he whispered back, "How do you know?"

"The two-tone wing tips. I sold them to him a month ago. He's the only guy in this mob with dressy shoes like a banker. He's even got the same build as VanNort under those robes. I'm sure it's him."

Jacob's jaw set tighter. He seethed at the realization that the supposedly respectable banker, who was now also a Town Council member, was just another bigot in a robe. "I'll deal with him later," he whispered back.

"Who you staring at, kike?" The epithet emanated from a booming, angry voice belonging to a large marcher a few rows back. As Jacob looked towards the voice, Marvin came running to his side brandishing the stout branch like a knight with a longsword. Catching sight of his son-in-law, he reached out an arm to restrain him. Just then a rock came whistling past Jacob's ear and hit the building, denting the stucco but thankfully missing the display window. He wheeled around, straining to see who had cast the stone.

"You bastard, come over here and say that," Marvin shrieked at the hooded assailant. Another rock flew from a different sector of the Klan assembly, this one hitting Marvin's left arm. Seeing the assault, the other men guarding the store clumped together around Marvin and Jacob. They eyed the Klansmen warily, holding their various armaments up menacingly, but being careful not to advance. They all instinctively understood that now was not the time to provoke the mob. Already some of the Klansmen had broken ranks and were crossing to their side of the street, nearing where Jacob and his men stood their ground. Cooler heads in the KKK cluster called their fellows to return to the march, to no avail. Nearly a dozen, including the hulking Klansman who had prompted the melee with his offensive remark, were closing in, about to descend violently upon the five Jews and McKendry. Just before the two gangs collided, a shot rang out.

All froze. Heads turned towards the puff of smoke swirling away from the end of the pistol. Shira called out to the silent throng, "Get away from my family or the next shot won't be in the air."

No one could see the expressions of the Klansmen, but their postures betrayed a mix of fear and resignation. After a moment of indecision, as if some still considered resuming the attack, the mob retreated. They were easily absorbed back into the ranks of white robes. The driver of the truck bearing their burning cross, who had jammed on his brakes upon hearing the bang, slowly accelerated. The rally resumed down Arnold Avenue towards Clark's Landing and a rendezvous with a crowd awaiting them.

As the Klansmen moved away, Jacob walked to Shira, a look of astonishment still on his face. "You brought my gun?" he sputtered, then he threw his arms around his wife, who by this time had returned the pistol to the inner pocket of her stylish overcoat. He felt her heart pounding as she leaned against him and relaxed. They remained entwined for a few extra seconds. Released from his embrace, Shira shook her head as if to shake off a spell, noticing that Lew and the others had formed a loose semi-circle behind her husband. "Mama, what were you thinking?" her son asked in an almost scolding tone. "Those Klansman are dangerous. Someone might have shot back. They're thugs, they could have killed you!"

"Nobody was going to kill me, certainly not those cowards," she waved her hand as if shooing away a fly. "It's cold, let's go home. I have soup. You other boys, you come too." With the Klavern already a quarter mile away, Shira led the exhausted crew back to the house. As they walked back, Jacob idly thrust his hand into one of his pockets and felt around. The Kruger coin was there, and he fingered it reassuringly.

The next day's headline in the Press shouted, "Shots Fired at Klan Melee." The small item continued:

186

A gunfight broke out on main street in Point Pleasant as shots were exchanged between marching Klansmen and onlookers. According to eyewitnesses, a hooded Klansman brandished a gun at the proprietor of the newly built Itzkowitz store. While it is unclear who shot first, witnesses said Mr. Itzkowitz fired several rounds over the heads of the 20 or so Klansmen descending on him. No one was reported injured. The main group of over a thousand KKK members finished their march with a ceremony inducting dozens of new members at the fair grounds on the edge of town.

Jacob put down the paper on the breakfast table and thought to himself, better they all believe it was me. Especially if anyone comes looking for more trouble.

The Candidate
Point Pleasant 1924

Jacob sat stewing in his high-backed green rocking chair. He'd been ruminating on VanNort ever since Lew had spotted the wing tips. He despised the banker. For a moment he savored recalling his joy in locating his new edifice directly across from the Atlantic Building and Loan, forcing the anti-Semite to daily observe a monument to the Jew's success. He really *had* shown him, exactly as he'd vowed that humiliating morning twenty years ago.

Now smug satisfaction came with a sour aftertaste, the recognition that most in town considered the Klansman banker a pillar of the community. All the Jews in town knew better, that the man was a bigot, although among Hebrew businessmen there was tacit agreement to avoid speaking much of the slights and indignities they all endured. None wanted to let down their guard, to appear weak or bitter. Nevertheless, it was well-known among their congregation that to VanNort, if your name ended in -witz or -stein your money was never as good as that from any poor Christian soul barely scraping by. Only Gottfried still banked at Atlantic, perhaps because he opened accounts there well before VanNort's arrival. The others all banked at the newer Jersey Shore National, where Jacob had taken delicious pleasure in becoming a founding shareholder when the rival bank first sought investors. Another way to bring the racist down a notch.

As he rocked away lost in this train of thought, Shira joined him, shawl over her shoulders. The months since the Klan confrontation had been a whirlwind. Stocking their new store and greeting the influx of curious customers kept them all working from morning to dusk six days a week. Shira handled the bookkeeping, tracking increased inventory and payroll for the additional store clerks needed for the larger selling space. Jacob appreciated her expert juggling of it all, only vaguely aware in his obsession with VanNort that he'd failed to acknowledge her efforts.

Stepping past him, Shira dropped into her low-backed oaken rocker.

"You look like you ate a rotten egg," she said, scanning his face.

Jacob sat mute. She waited. After many years of conversation, she knew he'd eventually fill the silence.

"VanNort is an anti-Semite," he finally blurted out.

"And the sky is blue. Tell me something I don't know."

"He's got no business being on the Council. Just because he's a banker people think he's good for the town? Don't they realize he's rotten to the core? I don't like his type running the show. "

"Some people like that type running the show."

"Well, I don't. I've seen what happens when hate-filled men get power. Now it's happening here."

Shira stopped rocking, turning to look directly at Jacob. "If it bothers you so much, get rid of him."

He grew still. "What are you saying?"

"You think I'm going to use your gun again?" she chuckled to herself. "If you think he shouldn't be on town council, replace him."

"Replace him? How?"

"They have elections in this country. It's an election year. If he shouldn't be there, go get rid of him yourself. Run for council," she said, resuming rocking.

Days passed without either mentioning the subject. Every morning Jacob headed off to work early, returning home as usual for lunch and dinner. Only now he began deviating from his routine, taking more circuitous routes. The extra blocks yielded time to cogitate on Shira's preposterous suggestion. Run for office? He wasn't a politician, not one to give flowery speeches. Wandering into neighborhoods he rarely frequented, Jacob wondered what did matter to voters. In some neighborhoods, he discovered, many streets needed sidewalks. In others, particularly near the railroad coal yards, houses were shockingly run down. Were those voters happy with VanNort and his crowd on the council? Maybe, he considered, I could offer them an honest voice instead of fancy oratory.

His deliberations on these meanderings began subtly shifting. What's the worst that can happen, he asked himself one evening en route to dinner. It's not like I'd lose the store if I lose the election. It would be humiliating to lose to that anti-Semite. But how good would it feel to beat him! Walking past the firehouse brought a smile. Maybe the fire company guys would support me, I'm one of them. More and more, he dwelled on his strengths. Given his knack for charming tourists into buying things, surely he could charm voters too. He picked up his pace home, whistling.

Making his rounds the next day, he felt more confident but chided himself for not analyzing his opponent. Something popped to mind, written by the scientist Albert Einstein after visiting America. Even anti-Semitic newspaper editors gushed over theories they did not understand, judging by how extensively newspapers quoted Einstein's observations about America. Lew, who was smitten with Einstein, read them aloud over breakfast. One passage stuck with Jacob: "The over-estimation of money is still greater in this country than in Europe, but appears to me to be on the decrease. It is at last beginning to be realized that great wealth is not necessary for a happy and satisfactory life." Einstein might be a genius, but Jacob thought he was wrong about America. Wealth mattered more and more each year. A person like VanNort who controlled money was put on a pedestal. He resolved to use his own growing wealth to knock VanNort off that perch and hoist himself up there instead.

VanNort's stature in town had risen over the last twenty years. While Jacob and the others could avoid banking with him, with VanNort being a prominent councilman anyone doing business locally would inevitably confront his influence one way or another. A Klansman holding a position of honor in his town; that was a bitter pill to swallow. Like many immigrants flocking to the new world, Jacob was a believer in American democracy. He'd fled living under the whim of the Czar, and disdained second class status under the ostensibly democratic rule of the Boer.

Every American was equal, newcomer and descendants of the Mayflower alike. Or so he'd believed.

Yet looking around he saw the Klan surging, their power extending even into his little village. It revolted him that Klansmen saw themselves as true Americans, superior to Jews, Negroes, Catholics, anyone who wasn't a "real American." Georgia's Governor even preached to a Klan convention that America should "build a wall of steel, a wall as high as Heaven" to blockade immigrants. He couldn't let that *shtick drek* VanNort run his town.

To beat the sonofabitch, he brooded, would they need to expose the banker? Could Lew simply write a letter to the editor saying he recognized a pair of shoes? That would be absurd. Lew surely was right, and just as surely publicly accusing VanNort of Klan membership would fall flat on its face. The man would just deny the accusation, or laugh it off. They had no hard proof. Worse yet, it might backfire. What if being a race-baiter might not offend as many voters as he wanted to believe? It was time to plan his own campaign.

The following Monday, as Lew and Jacob were locking up the store, Jacob said casually, "All right, I've decided."

"Decided what, Pop?"

"I'm running," he said.

"Running?" Lew looked perplexed.

"For town council,"

"What's gotten into you, Pop?" Lew said with a wry smile. "You're always criticizing politicians as full of hot air."

"Exactly! We deserve someone who tells the truth!" He jabbed a finger towards the sky.

"Not sure that wins elections," Lew grinned.

"Well that's how your father talks to people," he said. "Not like that snake VanNort."

"VanNort?" Lew said. "You're running against him? Now I get it."

"Never mind that," he waved dismissively. "It's time someone stood up for the taxpayers, the property owners. We're the ones who foot the bill for everything."

"You're against the working guy?" Lew said.

"The working guy benefits if this town is well run. If his children go to a decent school, if the roads are paved so he can get to work. There're too many slackers around town hall, too much patronage. Now VanNort's pushing for a golf course. How does that help the working man?"

"Golf's pretty popular, Pop," said Lew. "Lots of working guys play a round or two now and then. McKendry's a working stiff, invites me to golf with him all the time."

"Enough about golf! You're missing the point," he said, exasperated.

"Lots of people probably think VanNort's Mr. Upright Citizen," Lew said as they headed for home.

"I'm not asking your advice. I need you to round up some of your friends to help the campaign."

Engrossed in their conversation, neither noticed Shira reading a book on the porch. They both started when she spoke up. "Finally you've made up your mind! If you're doing this, do it right."

"What, you think I plan to do it wrong?" he said brusquely.

"Don't forget the women," Shira continued, ignoring his tone. "We run the households, shop for food, send the kids to school. Women know what needs fixing. We have the vote too, now."

"I've been thinking about that," he said, more contemplatively. "Most of our customers are women. If we can get them on our side, maybe some will bring along their husbands."

"I can help you there, Pop!" Lew said with a grin. Jacob scowled. At college his son had turned into quite the ladies' man. Now Lew was stepping out on dates with what seemed like a different blonde each weekend.

"I don't need you spending more time with your *shik-sas*, thank you very much," he spat out. "Find a nice Jewish girl and settle down already!"

"Don't worry Pop. I'm just having fun. No gentile grandchildren for you," Lew replied lightly.

"Nu," Shira interrupted. "Enough about Lew's girl-friends. Jacob, what's your plan?" She set down her book and followed them into the house.

For ninety minutes they huddled in their living room as Jacob spun an elaborate battle strategy. Out tumbled ideas percolating ever since Shira challenged him to run. He assessed various constituencies with the same instincts honed over decades sizing up potential customers. Who had what needs, what would appeal to them, how to get them over their natural reluctance to make a purchase. Voters were no different than prospective customers, he theorized. They don't always tell you up front what they need, you have to get to know them a bit to figure out their motivations. Then you can sell.

Take the Methodists, for example. Most likely Methodists would side with VanNort, who was some kind of church lay leader. He had no clue how Christian churches operated, but it was plain as his nose Methodists consider VanNort a big shot. Perhaps more importantly, his bank had loaned the congregation money to build the church. Congregants would feel gratitude. Still, the Methodists also knew him up close. Maybe some resented his imperious manner. How to suss out more about how the Methodists felt about VanNort from someone on the inside? Lew mentioned a Methodist friend from his high school class. Maybe that source would disclose some inside information. "Worth pursuing, Lew, just do it without raising suspicion," was his conclusion.

Catholics, they're a different story. There had long been Irish settlers at the shore, and more trickled in before the war. But Catholics' numbers in town had grown rapidly over the past decade, mainly first generation North Jersey Italian immigrants moving down, looking for a better life for their children. Swinging their votes his way might be the key to a majority. He'd observed that Catholics tended to follow authority. Could they get some prominent Catholic to endorse him? There was no one obvious, no one he knew well enough. Two of the store's shopgirls were Catholic, so was Lew's friend McKendry, and many customers belonged to St. Peter's Church. Maybe one of them could advise who to win over. Surely if the Catholics got wind of VanNort's Klan affiliations they would turn against him and towards Jacob. How to invisibly set that in motion, the trio was unsure.

Then there were the Jews in town. The two other merchants, Gottfried and Bromley, had maybe a dozen votes between them counting their sons and daughters-in-law. (Bromley, he mused to himself, thinks because he Americanized his name nobody knows he's Jewish.) There are other Jewish voters, like Rosenblatt, the lawyer he'd engaged to handle all legal work for the new store building. He assumed he could count on his fellow Jews for their votes. Or could he? Gottfried was still a customer at Van-Nort's bank. Would that undermine his loyalty to a fellow member of the tribe? Would Bromley be jealous of a rival businessman? All told there were few Jewish voters in town. He could take no vote for granted.

He also knew that, just like in any old country village, word travels fast in a small town. Sharing with anyone his intention to run, saying "keep this just between us", was as good as plastering a sign across one of his display windows. Within hours the confidante would tell the barber or the druggist (in confidence, of course), who would whisper it to a friend (on the QT), who would spread the tidbit to the bartender (on the down low). Likely as not, by next morning the news would come full circle, a customer revealing to Jacob with a wink that she knew his secret, as if letting him in on the latest gossip. To avoid tipping his hand, Jacob and Lew spent evenings in the store basement workroom hunkered over their new typeset printing press. He'd bought the machine originally for creating signs blaring "SALE" and "25% OFF". The press was converted into an essential piece of campaign equipment. By week's end over one hundred large placards shouting "ITZKOWITZ FOR TOWN COUNCIL" and "ITZKOWITZ: YOUR WATCHDOG" were piled high. His campaign was ready to launch.

The day after Memorial Day, Jacob's candidacy burst into the bright sunshine concurrently with the summer tourist season kickoff. As employees turned up for work, he personally informed each one of his candidacy and asked for their support. All but one responded with genuine enthusiasm. Jacob wisely refrained from pressing the recalcitrant shopgirl after her lukewarm reaction. Employees were given fifteen extra minutes at lunchtime to fan out to designated locations carefully chosen for visibility, tacking up campaign posters on telephone poles. Lew rounded up friends with cars, deploying them to the further reaches of the municipal limits where they plastered those areas with Itzkowitz placards. By day's end, the whole town knew Jacob was running. Including VanNort.

It took VanNort the better part of two weeks to mount his counteroffensive, apparently sparing no expense in doing so. On a mid-June Monday, some two hundred professionally printed posters appeared, one for nearly every street corner. In vivid red, white and blue, each proclaimed "Vote VanNort: He's One of Us."

When Jacob saw the theme, he was livid. "That sonafabitch!" he thundered to Lew, specks of spittle flying. "He's saying Jacob Itzkowitz is not 'one of us'? After all I've done for this town?"

"Calm down, Pop," Lew said soothingly. "This could help us. Lots of folks are like you, born somewhere else. Or like me, the kid whose parents came to America and worked hard. Let's just bide our time. See how people react."

"I hope you're right," he said, a bit more calmly. "It still galls me. Some *schlemiels* will fall for his garbage. You read the papers. Politicians want to shut the doors to America. If we came today, they wouldn't let in me or your mother."

With campaign battle lines drawn, politicking continued over the summer unabated. Most residents' attention was far more on making money off the tourist trade than the future of town government. Jacob bent the ear of any-one who came into the store. He cast himself as the pru-dent businessman who would be the eyes and ears of the average citizen, pledging to prevent the rest of the Town Council from spending their tax dollars wastefully.

Most of his regular customers liked Jacob and were only too pleased to have his attention, although a few with-ered under his vigorous manner of holding forth. Some simply kept their mouths shut as he campaigned, leaving him wondering if they were VanNort voters. His bombast lost only one customer for sure, a middle-aged widow from one of the oldest families in town. Barely a minute into his pitch, the woman cut him short, calling him "full of hot air". Muttering that VanNort had a point about "newcom-ers", she exited in a huff. He was left stammering, though by evening he'd regained his equilibrium. Recounting the incident to Shira, he ended with "Good riddance, she buys on credit. And she's always late anyway."

Shira wagged a finger at Jacob, "If you drive away every credit customer who pays late, we better cut our in-ventory in half." After that, he practiced more restraint when promoting his candidacy to any shopper he did not already know well.

The Proposition
Point Pleasant 1924

The late August morning sun warmed Jacob as he stood on the sidewalk. Midway through his daily ritual, hand-cranking down the green and white striped awnings that prevented clothing inside the massive plate glass display windows from fading, a Western Union delivery boy suddenly appeared. Hastily signing for the telegram, he stuffed the envelope into a pants pocket, tipped the boy and resumed his routine. With customer entrances unlocked, sales help accounted for, and Lew dispatched to the bank for rolls of quarters, he could finally retreat to his oak desk. Settled in the backroom office to tackle the day's paperwork, he remembered the unopened telegram and fished the yellow missive from his pocket.

"Dear Mr. Itzkowitz. Have followed your successes. Wish to talk business with you. Will arrive Monday next 11 am. Goldstein, for S. Joel."

He felt the blood drain from his face, hand tremble every so slightly. Them, he thought. What could they possibly want now? I already paid them back in full with interest fifteen years ago. They should have forgotten about me, I should be nothing to them. But when you make a deal with the devil, he's got you until you're in the grave. Nothing I can do until Monday, he told himself, except focus on the correspondence piled on my desk.

Walking to the store on the appointed morning, he recalled Lew's attempt to explain Einstein's relativity. Maybe this is what that fellow means by time slowing down. The days had dragged on endlessly since receiving the telegram. His consuming schedule that normally energized him from morning until night, running the business and talking up his candidacy, had deteriorated into an extended exercise in self-control. He found himself watching the clock every ten minutes, losing concentration, pacing nervously behind his desk, or going outside to check up and down the street. Pay attention to this customer, he had to remind himself multiple times a day. Each customer is a voter. All attempts at self-discipline, however, failed at keeping him from conjuring a parade of unpleasant images, as if he were bound to a chair and forced to stare through a Kinetoscope at scenes of disaster.

At night, his body betrayed the stress hidden during the day. Falling asleep was a struggle, when he tossed and turned to an uncommon degree. He sensed Shira watching him with concern, although so far she had said nothing directly. Feeling the burden of her scrutiny, he resolved to keep the impending return of Joel's men to himself, despite recognizing that was a fraught choice. He'd paid dearly twenty years earlier when Shira, as his bookkeeper, had noticed an additional $1,000 in their accounts and forced him to reveal exactly who had supplied their seed money. So great was her anger at his deception that, after a withering tirade, she refused to talk to him for a week. Gradually she'd calmed down, eventually coming around to grudging acceptance that unlocking a source for funding their new life merited a modicum of forgiveness. Despite the risk of reigniting her fury, he reasoned it was better sparing her from angst until he knew what they were after.

Two hours before their scheduled arrival he tried calming himself. Maybe all they want is something simple? Maybe. Today, he instructed himself, just stick to your routine. If they come, they come. He unlocked the Arnold Avenue doors, fetched the awning crank, and proceeded with his daily protection of precious inventory from the sun's rays. Awnings lowered, as usual he relocked the front doors (no customers inside until half past nine), then unlocked the rear staff entrance, permitting sales girls to drift in. Next he visited the two bulky brass National Cash Registers, each strategically placed to allow salespeople to watch over an entrance while ringing up sales. Once again he personally confirmed that the morning cash count matched exactly to last night's final tally; never chance someone finagling a duplicate key or hiding in a dressing room pilfering his money undetected. Lastly, he checked that the miniature paper roll was properly loaded. His registers produced receipts imprinted on the back with the inked image of a lady's high button shoe, a signature touch he'd added. Itzkowitz Department Store merited a special identity, which also worked especially well for the less literate customers to keep track of where they purchased an item.

Opening routine accomplished, it was time to climb the flight of stairs leading to the balcony running the length of the back wall. He'd insisted his architect add this feature, even though it wasted storage space, asserting it would create an open and elegant look, which was true. Unspoken was his other motive: a perch on high from where, like a hawk in search of prey, he could easily scan the expanse below him. The right rear corner was where he nested behind a metal roll-top desk, with multiple pigeon hole filing cabinets arrayed behind him. Settling in on his swivel chair that morning, he absorbed himself in the stack of fall merchandise orders he needed to review.

The distraction lasted only so long. By quarter to eleven, his concentration had evaporated into repetitive checking of the wall clock, as if the slowly ticking second hand could be forced to turn faster by an anxious stare. He took to catching glimpses of various automobiles trundling by on Arnold Avenue, pondering which make was his visitors' this time. Through the store's tall glass front doors he spotted mostly the normal parade of popular Model T Fords. Sometimes a stalwart still employing horse and wagon mixed in among the automobiles. The occasional Nashes, Buicks and Chryslers glided by. Amidst the familiar river of brands a black swan suddenly appeared, a bright red Studebaker Big Six, as out of place on a backwater main street as would have been a gilded royal carriage. They're here, he registered with a jolt, instinctively thrusting his hand into has vest pocket for a reassuring touch of his charm.

From his vantage pointed he watched the pair of suited men barge through the front door into the women's department, then stand blinking as their eyes adjusted. The taller, leaner one scanned rapidly the faces of the half dozen customers and smattering of sales help milling about. His suit jacket and vest hung even more loosely than before, as if the body underneath had become more bones than flesh. A narrow face with taut skin and a sharp nose gave him the appearance of a bird of prey. The shorter, heavy-set man assumed a square stance, arms crossed, like someone waiting for an answer to a question that had not been asked. He was more fashionable this visit, sporting a white fedora and a dark bow tie which nicely accented his tan linen suit. The outfit was completed by two-toned spats wrapping his wingtips, rendering his appearance more like that of a man out for a society evening than one arriving for a business meeting. His gaze landed on the stairs, slowly following their upward ascent. Jacob saw the man's head swivel like a searchlight as his focus swept along the balcony. Finally the man's eyes locked on Jacob; a wry smile spread across his face, and the dandy nodded.

Jacob flinched. Placing both hands on his desk, palms down, he forced himself to resume idly watching cars pass by instead of leaping up to run as his body wanted him to do. The stockier man signaled his companion with an index finger, pointing up to the balcony with his hand forming an imaginary pistol shape. Jacob heard heavy footsteps crossing the balcony until finally the two men entered his field of vision, taking up positions directly in front of his desk. Looking up he said flatly, "Goldstein, Markowitz. I hoped never to see you again."

The sharp-nosed one stared intently at Jacob's mouth, lips curling to a sneer as his right hand slowly inched towards his hip. But the nattily dressed of the two quickly put up his left hand, causing the taller one to relax his arm, letting it hanging loosely. His fingers, however, continued twitching.

"Mr. Markowitz may be deaf, but he can read lips. I suspect he was hoping for a warmer greeting after so many years. Aren't you going to offer us chairs, Mr. Itzkowitz?" said Goldstein.

"Chairs are for my customers," he said brusquely. Waiting for their arrival, he'd willed himself into the frame of mind that he'd be having just another business meeting, nothing more. That had been his morning mantra. Now with these apparitions breathing in front of him, eying him as if he were quarry, he experienced a wave of trepidation. Swallowing hard, he rebuked himself for snapping. Bide your time, he told himself. Collecting himself, his tone turned neutral. "Of course, of course, bring over the ones against the wall."

"Thank you, it is much easier to discuss business when everyone is comfortable. Are you comfortable, Mr. Itzkowitz? I don't see any firearms within reach this visit."

"Should I have brought one?" He stared directly into Goldstein's eyes.

"You didn't need a weapon then, you don't need a weapon now," Goldstein replied brightly, slowly extracting a miniature mother-of-pearl handled pocket knife from his vest pocket.

"Good. Then I am comfortable. What brings you here?"

"We have come here, Mr. Itzkowitz, to renew our, hmm, relationship." As he spoke, Goldstein flicked open one blade, more of a pick, and began absently scraping under his nails

He said nothing. Goldstein kept a half smile on his face, yet his eyes looked cold and dead to Jacob. The effect was unsettling.

"Your success opening this store and establishing yourself in this town was, shall we say, mildly intriguing to Mr. Joel. He sensed you have a good head for opportunity."

"I'm honored he thinks so."

"We were instructed to keep an eye on you. I must say, your ability to turn a profit as a newcomer in town, paying back your loan ahead of schedule was, well, most impressive," Goldstein paused, as if waiting for a thank you. Jacob merely nodded.

"Let's just say we took it as a good sign. A sign that there is money to be made at the shore."

"I've done just fine," he interrupted. "I built this store on my own, you know"

"So you did," Goldstein continued. "We take a long view on Mr. Joel's behalf. We took our time, sizing you up. Then came the war, and the inevitable market disruptions. The war had a substantial impact on Mr. Joel's holdings throughout the British Empire. This required us to be more, umm, selective with our investments. Happily, since Armistice Day Mr. Joel has come to see the United States as the land of greatest opportunity."

"Then he's a smart fellow."

"Very smart. Anyway, on his behalf, we've been scouting investments in this area for some time. It might surprise you to learn that we have already made an initial purchase. A small beach front parcel bordering Bay Head."

He frowned. He prided himself on keeping up with all the property activity in town. Did I miss something, he wondered.

"The land records said the buyer was that *shicker*, Macklin. People figured he was buying a lot to build himself a new house," Jacob interjected, trying to sound nonchalant. Inwardly he berated himself for not taking a closer look at that transaction. He knew Macklin well enough. With his uneven business dealings he would have been hard pressed to have the capital to build on the lot.

"Ah, well, you are correct. It is Mr. Macklin's only on paper. Title appears in that name. He was our, let's say, 'representative.' We hoped to do more business with him, until he proved to be unsuitable for the task." Goldstein paused, arms spread wide and palms upwards, shrugging his shoulders.

"Unsuitable?"

"As I was saying, we invested in beach front property to test the waters, so to speak. With the improved rail service, with even working men owning automobiles, we anticipate growth in people taking their leisure at the shore. We see a good future here. Very good, in fact. Mr. Joel wishes us to expand along the coast sooner rather than later. That is where you come in, Mr. Itzkowitz. We need someone local, someone we can rely on. Truth be told, we would rather do business with a *landsman* like you than with *goyim* like Macklin," Goldstein flashed his forced half-smile again.

"Go on, I'm listening."

"Here's the deal. You will be the face of our investments. We supply the capital. And we will deal fairly with you, Mr. Itzkowitz."

"'Fairly' could mean many things. You want I should just trust you?"

"Your share will be ten percent, net. After the return of Mr. Joel's capital, of course," Goldstein paused, observing his reaction. Stay silent, he told himself.

"Oh, and another thing, Mr. Itzkowitz. We know of your race for the local borough council. You could well be elected. In that case, you'd be ideally positioned to enhance the value of our investments. It could be very lucrative all around."

He reflected on the options. Ten percent of profits without putting up a dime was a fair offer. At the same time, he was averse to relying on partners. With partners you lost control. Especially if your partner employed muscle men with guns. Partners were like family: supposedly on your side, people you could trust, until they showed you otherwise. On the other hand, teaming up with a very deep pocket into which he could reach held enormous appeal. Most of his own funds were already tied up, having bought the house and purchased several small lots on his own. The rest of his capital was sunk into buying the land and building the store. His bank lent only half the money for that project, forcing him to invest years of savings into his dream of owning his own building. Eventually, he was certain, doubling his inventory and sales would more than refill his coffers and then some. How long was "eventually", that was the question.

Goldstein had a point. The town was on the cusp of an economic boom, Jacob could see it and smell it. The moment would pass him by if he sat on the sidelines until his own personal war chest were refilled. He was sorely tempted to accept, but showing eagerness would betray weakness.

"What makes you think I want to be in business with you?" He leaned back in his chair.

"You do remember our original conversation, Mr. Itzkowitz, don't you? I recall talking to a rather desperate man back then. You were in need of someone willing to take a very big chance on you. No collateral, no prior history actually running a store. A risky gamble, it was."

"Not such a big gamble. Your boss already knew the sort of man I am. My prospects were good. The banker was an anti-Semite, but I would have found the money elsewhere. I just gave Mr. Joel the first opportunity. Anyway, I repaid my debt in full, he got all that was due. Ahead of time at that."

"The loan was repaid, that's true. But you're forgetting something." Goldstein rubbed the handle of his pocket knife between thumb and index finger as he spoke. "I personally informed you quite clearly. A day might come when further assistance would be needed. As a condition of Mr. Joel making that big bet, you would render future assistance. You do remember *all* the conditions of the loan, Mr. Itzkowitz, do you not?"

He clenched his teeth. They are not coming to me as business partners. They think they have a hold over me. Well, he thought, you cannot make a good deal if you have to make a deal. Panic began to grip him, as if he'd stepped into a trap. Suddenly he leaned forward, hands squeezing the edges of his desk, shifting his weight as if readying to pounce on Goldstein. Markowitz instantly reached towards his pocket. But Goldstein again snapped his left hand up into the air, and Markowitz sat back like a dog called to heel. Jacob stayed still.

"Speaking of big bets, Mr. Itzkowitz, there's something more you should consider. Someone in your family is fond of gambling, betting on horse races."

"What the hell are you talking about?" he said, taken aback.

"Ah, we thought you might not be aware. Your son is quite the avid player at the race track."

"My son has nothing to do with this. I thought you were discussing a business deal."

"He's run up quite a debt, nearly $2,000 dollars, counting interest owed. Coincidentally, he owes it to a bookie who happens to have a strong relationship with us. Although your son – Lew, is it? – would have no way of knowing that."

"So Lew's playing the horses, so what?" He fidgeted with the coin in his vest pocket.

"He seems to have a unique betting system. Perhaps it's quite good, but our system is better. In any event, your boy is just about past due with repayment. Or course, if we can come to a business arrangement today, Mr. Itzkowitz, we can make your son's debts part of the bargain."

"I don't need you, I can pay it off ." He seethed, enraged they were involving his family.

"Well, it might not be that simple Mr. Itzkowitz. It's not about the money. A few thousand dollars in the scheme of things is not a big amount to us. Consider that the public disdains people who cannot pay their own debts. We would hate for young Mr. Itzkowitz's shiftless character to become public knowledge. The timing would be unfortunate, just as you're gaining ground in your election bid. It might, well, cast a pall over your chances."

He laughed. "Lew's a young man. People around here know him. Sure he's a bit of a ladies man. But times have changed, even in a small town like Point Pleasant. Maybe some folks still think gambling is a big sin. Most won't care a whit he's been betting on horses."

"Maybe yes, maybe no, Mr. Itzkowitz. Is that a bet you really want to make?"

His demeanor shifted. "The bet I'll make, Goldstein, is that you need me more than I need you. You understand the *mamaloshen*, Goldstein? I don't like dealing with *goniffs*."

The smile dissolved from Goldstein's face, but he said nothing.

"You show up here out of the blue and act like I still owe your big-shot boss something? And on top of that try to blackmail me? Drag my son into this? I ought to throw you out on your ear," he said, shaking his fist. Seeing heads in the aisles below turning upwards, drawn by the commotion, he realized he'd been shouting.

Goldstein nodded to Markowitz, and both stood. He gestured to his silent companion, who stepped away, stopping at the top of the staircase to watch. Goldstein then said in a calm, quiet voice, "I can see you're upset, Mr. Itzkowitz. Perhaps it was my mistake to insert your son's, umm, entanglements into our arrangements. Before that I perceived you were intrigued by the possibility of expanding your holdings. I hope you will focus on that aspect of our visit here today."

Taking a few paces towards Markowitz, Goldstein stopped and turned half round to Jacob, as if forgetting something. "Oh, and perhaps there are ways we can be helpful to your political career. After all, that would be mutually beneficial. So please, do not make any hasty decisions out of anger. Take a few days. I will be in touch again, in a week."

With a tip of his hat, the stocky man rejoined his sidekick at the top of the staircase. Jacob glared at the pair until they had descended the stairs and exited his store. Then, feeling drained, he lowered himself back into his chair, slumped forward, and rested his forehead in his palms.

A Choice
Point Pleasant 1924

Subdued and feeling vaguely disoriented after the emissaries departed, Jacob moved as if in a fog through the
balance of his day. Mid-afternoon he was attempting to
woo a customer's vote, only to recall sheepishly that she
lived across the river in Manasquan and couldn't vote for
him. By day's end he was all too ready to close up shop.
Stepping out into the warm late summer breezes, he felt
propelled to follow a circuitous route home, soon finding
himself walking east towards the ocean. He'd managed to
shove the morning's encounter into a dark mental closet
for the rest of the day, but now that memory was bash-
ing against the door demanding to be let free. Goldstein's
threats, direct and implied, tumbled out. His rage surged
again, mingled with fear. Had he really indentured himself years ago to men who wore a veneer of respectability
covering their true thuggish nature? Could he still be in-
debted to Joel? After all was said and done, that man was
just another Jewish immigrant to South Africa who'd been

lucky to arrive a decade earlier than Jacob, in time to make millions from diamond mining. Jacob was overcome with bitterness at the unfairness of the situation, tinged with self-recrimination for allowing them power over him.

The rhythm of walking gradually calmed him. He'd marched nearly a half-mile so immersed in brooding that he had failed to notice his surroundings. As the fog of emotions lifted, Jacob began logging in evidence of Point Pleasant's evolution visible to any careful observer. Like a geologist envisioning the rise and fall of a landscape from outcroppings and glacial markings meaningless to the untrained eye, he discerned the flow of economic forces reshaping the town. He interpreted construction underway on a three-story rooming house with a prominent turret merely blocks from the beach dunes as a harbinger of the future influx of vacationers. The dozen Victorian-style homes dotting the landscape, each harboring multiple parked automobiles, were portents of a surging tourist trade carried south in affordable transportation wrought by Mr. Ford's assembly lines. The shingled steeple of the newly expanded St. Peter's church dominating the skyline to the west he understood as a welcome beacon to the state's burgeoning Catholic population seeking enclaves in which to settle and thrive.

Reaching the eastern terminus of Arnold Avenue he tramped onto the recently expanded stretch of boardwalk. The growing demand of visitors for a wider promenade on which to appreciate an ocean view prompted town fathers to replace the deteriorating snake-way of portable planks with sturdy railroad ties raised on pilings. Clusters of strollers filed past him enjoying the sounds of waves rolling in with the tide, wandering in a constant north/south circular flow. "Bursting at the seams" sprang to mind as he foresaw the inevitable pressure to extend the boardwalk the full length of the borough's oceanfront. A mile-long wooden avenue beckoning visitors with money in their pockets, he knew to a certainty, would attract a rush of businesses hawking every type of refreshment and amusement craftily designed to separate that money from those pockets. Empty sand dunes would skyrocket in value before too long.

Turning seaward, he saw stretched out before him the fishing club's pier, jutting nearly three football fields into the Atlantic. A massive deck on telephone pole stilts defying the constant battering of waves, the pier proclaimed the determination of the locals to extend their dominion over the ocean. The fishing club organizers first launched their project in the waning days of the World War, erecting a more modest structure only to have it washed away by brutal fall storms the following year. Undaunted, they pooled resources and tripled the scale of their monument to the fishing hobbyist, embellishing the pier with a bait and tackle shop at one end and a restaurant at the other. Passing the foot of the pier, he saw dotting its railings dozens of men casting their bait, hoping to reel in a blue, a striper or maybe a fluke. Club membership topped one thousand souls, each paying substantial dues for the rarefied privilege of standing above the ocean to fish, despite fishing being free in the beachfront surf below. People seemed inevitably drawn to the status of belonging to an exclusive club, he considered. It's hard to feel important on your own. For some it is fishing, for others their church denomination, for still others their political party. Maybe Klansman flock to robes and race hatred to find their club, a concept that filled him with disgust.

Meandering further north, he reached boardwalk's end at the foot of the Active Club headquarters. The Active Club was populated by members of the Newark

Sailors baseball team, who delighted in the manly culture of physical prowess through sport. Years back these health-conscious athletes scoured the shore in search of a summer home where they could breathe fresh sea air. A small bungalow served as their base of operations, the location providing easy access to a beachfront playground for all manner of sports competition. Their marathon ball games and weight lifting competitions drew curious crowds. The Actives returned year after year in greater numbers, bringing growing families and friends in tow, filling up lodging houses. As he stood sizing up their clubhouse, it was obvious to him that soon they would need a larger facility to accommodate their swelling ranks. This observation corroborated his growing list of clues signaling inexorable pressure for rapid development in the area.

It's just the beginning, he was certain after ruminating on the evidence. As if fitting jigsaw pieces together, he was finally bringing an image into focus. He could see not just what was already there, but what someday would be: A wider, sturdier boardwalk stretching from the Manasquan River inlet in the north all the way south to the Bay Head border. A boardwalk that would magnetically attract more hotels and amusements, each addition increasing the desirability of vacationing there, bringing the next incarnation of the Actives seeking summer relief. More attractions would bring thousands daily to the area, filling up bungalows and inns for blocks and blocks. Demand would prompt construction of myriad boarding options on the vacant lots littering the east half of town. All this generating throngs of customers for his store and the other downtown merchants. As puzzle pieces clicked into place, his conviction hardened: Whoever first seizes control of the beachfront, he prophesied, controls the future of this town.

Rousing from this reverie, Jacob reversed course and set off for home so as not to be late for the dinner Shira was undoubtedly preparing. He still suffered dread brought on by the reappearance of the distant Mr. Joel, though his rage had mostly subsided. Part of him was livid at Lew's foolishness for falling into debt to bookies. Not that the amount in question was crushing, he could afford it. A reputation was harder to ransom. Despite what he'd said to Goldstein's face, he knew the *mamzer* was right: many good church-going citizens would look askance at a businessman who could not control his own gambling urges. Gossip could ruin Lew's ability to head up the store. He'd always imagined bestowing his growing empire on his son when the time came, but now a shadow was falling across that vision of the future. He had to get this situation under control. Worse yet, if it became public knowledge before the election, it might even cast the candidate in a bad light. The apple doesn't fall far from the tree, his neighbors were fond of saying.

These dark thoughts only rekindled Jacob's anxiety as he approached home. He recoiled at being blackmailed into a business deal. For every pull towards yielding to Goldstein's pressure, his stubborn obsession with independence pushed him to resist. That brought to mind something Lew had once tried to explain. His son the college student had felt compelled to give him a lesson in Newton's laws of motion, then proclaim that Einstein had turned Newton on his head. Einstein may be a genius, Jacob thought, but Newton's laws make more visceral sense. He could feel in his bones how pressure to do one thing provoked an equally powerful reaction to do just the opposite. He felt old, worn out from struggling with forces tearing him in conflicting directions.

215

On the porch he found Shira, motionless in her rocking chair, seemingly engrossed in a crossword puzzle. She'd taken up the fad sweeping across the Atlantic from Great Britain. Most evenings lately he'd arrive home to be greeted by Shira humming to herself, brows knitted, pen in hand, staring intently at a back page of the Asbury Park Press. Tonight she was not humming, and her eyes flickered ever so slightly in his direction as he reached the final step of their porch. A pitcher of iced tea was sweating on the side table that lived between their rockers, and a glass for each. He knew the familiar signs. She was waiting for him, waiting to have a talk. Nervously he took his appointed seat.

"*Nu*, you had visitors today," Shira declared without looking up from her puzzle.

"Who told you that?" he replied quickly, a touch defensively.

"It's a secret? I need spies to tell me when big city goons in a fancy car come round to see my husband?" Shira had set down her paper and was now looking at him intently.

"I'm just wondering who's gossiping behind my back," he said, adopting nonchalance.

"Oh, only four different people I ran into just going to the grocery store. It's not like their type shows up every Monday around here. They stood out like a sore thumb. Quite a pair, I'm told. One of them looking like a squat gorilla in fancy clothes. The other a tall skinny ostrich with his head bobbing around."

He couldn't help snickering at such apt descriptions. The momentary amusement quickly faded as the memory of their mission flooded back.

"They were the same two *goniffs* who came to Tuckerton years ago, weren't they," she said, reminding him of how his lawyer cross-examined defendants in court. "You paid back their loan in full. I know that much from doing the books. But you never told me the whole story, did you?"

He winced at the steely edge in her voice. She'd always been strong-willed, a quality he'd admired from the onset of Mumma Chaya's matchmaking. It was Shira who'd insisted that America was the right destination, he recalled. Her determination had strengthened his own resolve to head into the unknown. She'd always been a vital part of the business, handling the books when he was still a peddler, and keeping the growing dry goods business well accounted for, all while raising the children. But she was still his wife, a woman. He was the head of the household. His duty was to shield her from the burdens of building a business, he told himself. And yet, she was right. There was more to the bargain struck with the Joel syndicate than he had ever let on. It was a weight on his shoulders, one he had carried alone for a long, long time. He sighed.

"Look, I was desperate back then. I was tired of forever being on the road. You were tired of it too. We needed money to settle down, to open the store. I deserved to get a loan. You remember, the bank had turned me down, all because of that SOB VanNort and his…"

"Enough about VanNort, I know all about him," Shira cut in. "Get to the point. What did you promise these money men?"

"I'm getting to that. It was a long shot the rich Mr. Joel would even read my letter, let alone send his agents to talk terms. It was like manna from heaven. We struck a deal for the loan. Then the mouthpiece, Goldstein, kept hinting at other conditions. It was nothing definite, just some vague talk that above and beyond the loan, there was a catch."

"A catch? What sort of a 'catch'?"

"Like I said, it was vague. Someday I might need to do them a favor of some kind."

"You said yes to this? Without knowing what sort of favor? Is anything written down?" She stopped rocking.

"I did what any businessman would have done!" His face flushed.

"Oh really? And what was that?" Shira asked, staring back at him.

"I took the loan. We needed the money, so I told myself it was just a bluff. What could they want with a Jew in the *schmata* business in a small town? I figured they just talk tough, to make sure they got paid back."

"Do you always tell yourself *bubbemeises*?" Shira scoffed.

"It wasn't nonsense! I just didn't take it very seriously," he protested.

"And yet here they are, come to collect," she said, almost to herself. Pouring a glass of iced tea, she took a long sip. "Well, what exactly do they want?"

He paused, emitting a deep sigh. "They want me to buy up property, along the ocean. They want me to be their front man. They put up cash, I get ten percent."

Shira put down her glass and resumed rocking. After nearly a minute, she asked, "And that's bad?"

Jacob looked at Shira as if she were an oracle who had just uttered a Delphic prophesy.

"You think it's good?" he said quizzically.

"Look, husband, I do the books. I know how little cash we have in the bank right now, and how much profit we are making. Numbers are numbers. We won't build up enough for you to buy oceanfront property for years. By then the opportunity may slip away. So I figure, if they are offering a better deal, listen to them. Negotiate. That is, if you can trust them."

"Well, there's another catch," he said tentatively.

"Ha, I knew it. Another favor they will need some-day?"

"I don't like blackmail," he said, scowling.

"Blackmail? They're blackmailing you? What have you done? What are you not telling me?"

"Not me." He took a deep breath. "Lew. He's gotten wild, with all the girls he chases, but I had no idea."

"Lew? Our Lew? What are they saying?" Shira was now getting flushed herself.

"Bookies. Lew's been playing the horses and borrow-ing heavily from bookies. Now he owes them nearly two thousand," Jacob said with agitation.

"Two thousand? I said we don't have much in the bank, but we're not broke," Shira said, idly smoothing her dress.

"I can pay it off, but that's not the point. The bookies he went to, they're in business with Joel's guys. They have the evidence."

"Evidence of what? So he's borrowed some money. Since when is that a crime?" She shifted in her rocking chair.

"That's what I said. I laughed in their faces. I put on a show of not caring. 'Nobody gives a damn what a young fella does at the racetrack,' I said. The truth is, they'll ex-pose him if I don't go along," he said, dejected.

"But you were right, weren't you? Who's going to care?"

"All the busybodies. Maybe it'll be nothing, but why take the chance? Lew doesn't need a black mark."

"So you'll kill two birds with one stone," she said firmly.

"It still sticks in my craw. If I go along with their deal, they own me." He pounded the arm of his chair.

Shira went very still, hands tightly gripping the mushroom carvings capping the rocker's arms.

"Don't get distracted," she spoke as if scolding a child. "They offered you a good deal. Take their money, buy up land. Now is the time. Don't let your pride get in the way. You don't always have to do everything on your own."

He frowned at Shira as if she had just pinched his ear. "I've done just fine on my own," he said defiantly.

"You have! Shira reached out, patting his arm gently. "Now you can do even better with their money. Look, husband, you've always outsmarted the other guy. You'll do that again with these hoodlums. Let them think they've got you. When the time comes, you'll turn the tables on them. I know you will." She pressed her hand down and held it there.

Silently he looked down at her touch.

She slowly let go and got to her feet. As she reached their front door, she called over her shoulder, "I've got dinner to make" and disappeard into the house. He remained, rocking away, deep in thought.

Garden Club
Point Pleasant 1924

Leaving Jacob on the porch, Shira gently closed the screen door behind her. She halted in the foyer, putting a hand to the wall to steady herself. Her heart pounded wildly. Pausing to hear if Jacob would come after her, she let out a relieved breath to the faint sound of slow rhythmic rocking.

Shira peeled her hand from the wall and walked steadily through their dining room to the rear of the house. Entering the kitchen, she immediately felt calmer in her familiar domain. She had overseen the modernization of everything in this space, junking the bulky coal oven in favor of an enameled gas stove with five burners, two ovens and a bread warming drawer. The old wooden ice house remained outside, but for most daily needs she turned to her indoor icebox. Best of all, she'd insisted on completely updating the plumbing. Hot and cold water ran to her large freestanding porcelain sink. Most everything in my life has changed, she contemplated, except maybe my husband. "Stubborn mule, he has to be the boss all the time" she muttered to herself, tying a floral apron around her middle.

The ritual of creating a thousand past meals allowed her to robotically prepare dinner while her thoughts meandered. He doesn't need to know every little thing that goes on around here, she assured herself while retrieving a large roasting pan. Potatoes and carrots were piled onto a wooden butcher's block, next to a large pullet. Working methodically, she washed, chopped and measured a meal she could prepare in her sleep. As she neared the last step in the process, the back door burst open. Lew swept in, flashing a broad smile. "Hiya, Ma! What's cookin'?"

"Lew, you startled me!"

"You'll be more startled when I tell you the news, Ma," Lew said, plopping into a chair.

"News?"

"You won't believe it!"

"Stop telling me what I won't believe. What happened?"

"Your longshot, in the third race? It paid off!" Lew waved a stack of greenbacks at her.

She dropped the chicken she'd been seasoning into the pan and stared at her son.

"20 to 1, Ma. You made $400 today!"

"Shh! Quiet down, we don't want your father to hear," Shira whispered, giving Lew a quick hug.

"My lips are sealed," Lew whispered back, smiling broadly.

"Lew, hide the money. Here," she said, handing him an empty storage tin, "put it all in here for tonight. To-morrow, you go back and pay $400 to the bookies."

"Why Ma? Your system is starting to pick winners. You should take this and spread it over more bets."

"I'll explain later. Now's not the time, just do it. Not a word to your father. Go sit with him on the porch, talk about the weather or something."

"Sure, Ma, your secret is safe with me."

My secret, she repeated silently. If he only knew. Well, I'm good with secrets. For twenty five years I've kept his father in the dark about something much more important. I had to. Mumma Chaya was right, it solved everything. Where would I be now if I hadn't heeded her wisdom? I can't imagine. It was the right thing, a *mitzvah* to spare him. But this? Betting on horses, debts to bookies, and not telling him?

It all started with the garden, she recalled. Years earli-er they'd bought this house, with its expansive yard. A few days after moving in, while hanging wash on the line, she had noticed her neighbor snipping flowers in a small for-mal backyard garden. "How beautiful!" she'd exclaimed at the sight. Mrs. Carlson, adorned with a wide brimmed white hat, had looked up smiling and waved her over. "Come take a look," and Shira had obeyed. The younger woman, at most thirty, proudly introduced a dozen flower varieties as if pointing out old friends. Shira found their fragrance and vivid colors almost intoxicating. "You have plenty of room to create your own lovely garden," Mrs. Carlson had said. "Come to the Garden Club meeting, I'll introduce you around."

She was hesitant at first. She had passed on multiple solicitations to join one of the growing number of women's societies in town, begging off as preoccupied with children and helping Jacob establish the store. Now those priorities rang hollow, more excuses than explanations. Ann and Esther were both married, Ann with her own baby Evelyn. Only Lew was still home, and he was always out and about. If she were honest, her afternoons were tinged with loneliness. Shira succumbed to the allure of the invitation.

Of the dozen or so women at her first Garden Club meeting, most were like Agnes Carlson, a decade or more her junior. It soon became apparent that flowers and shrubs were merely a fraction of the conversation at club meetings. Each member she met revealed herself as much more than a housewife and mother. They were accomplishing things she'd never dreamed of women doing. Even more mesmerizing was the manner in which they spoke of their activities, so matter-of-factly, as if women had been driving cars and selling real estate since the time of Moses and Aaron.

Some, like Katie Ferguson, had husbands who'd shipped off to Europe to fight the Kaiser. Mrs. Ferguson headed the family grocery business while he was overseas. Then Mr. Ferguson returned with lungs burned by mustard gas, too weak to work. "The bank cut off my credit when Billy came back," she told Shira as they arranged bouquets. "The banker scolded I should be home taking care of my man, not running a shop."

"What did you do?" Shira asked, panic-stricken as it dawned on her she had no plan on how to get by if Jacob ever fell ill, or worse.

"I told him, 'You listen to me. I am taking care of my man, I'm putting food on my family's table!' I wouldn't leave his bank until he agreed to give me another year, and lo and behold, he gave in! Now I'm my own boss," Mrs.

Ferguson said with a grin. "That smug banker is nice to me now. Guess he doesn't want to lose a good customer."

There was Hazel Clayton, a whiz at cultivating roses, who was also leader of the local Suffrage Association chapter. Active in the National Woman's Party, Hazel was locally admired for traveling to Washington a few years earlier to represent the chapter in the grand Suffrage Procession. She had even returned to Washington to join in boisterous picketing of President Wilson when he dithered over backing the vote for women.

"You know, Mrs. Itzkowitz, they laughed at us when we announced that women's rally in Washington demanding the vote," she recounted over tea at a Club meeting one day. "Even some of the older women in the party proclaimed us 'unladylike' for marching, raining on Mr. Wilson's grand inauguration parade."

"It must have taken courage," Shira had replied, thinking back to newspaper accounts of women getting banged up by onlookers while police stood idle, with hundreds of protesters ending up going to the hospital.

"Courage? Maybe. To me it just made common sense. Like Alice Paul would say to us, 'there is nothing complicated about ordinary equality,'" Hazel laughed heartily. "Now we have the vote, and the sky hasn't fallen."

At first, the free-thinking ideas and self-reliance of these women shocked her. Back in Russia, a girl was raised to be a wife and mother, never a shopkeeper or a politician. Even in the books that she and Channah had delighted in, brimming with tales of far-off cities, women aspired to marry wealthy men, not to be their equals. Now she was among young women with radical notions. They were up on the latest ideas, infused with a spirit of possibility that both unnerved and inspired her.

Her new companions were so modern, so American. Tradition didn't matter much to them. What was new and exciting mattered. Shira found herself comparing her own daughters to these garden club ladies. Though Ann and Esther were younger than most of these women, she considered, they might as well be a generation older. We may have raised our daughters here, but we must have brought the old country with us and passed it along to them. They speak Yiddish with us, they know the rituals, they're not expecting to fly airplanes or go drinking in jazz clubs. That was tradition, she'd always told herself.

Yet when listening to the garden club women, their stories and their desires, she felt unsettled. Maybe Hazel Clayton and that Paul woman had a point. She was as smart as any man she knew, and she worked just as hard. Despite that, everyone in town saw only Jacob as the businessman, even Jacob. She was the invisible woman. As time wore on, she tried on a few of the Garden Club ideas in her imagination, like a woman modeling a whole new wardrobe. Some fit, some didn't. She liked the ones that bedecked her in a garb of independence. Recognition of her worth and intelligence was a modern fashion she was drawn to.

As Shira sat alone in her kitchen considering whether to reveal to Jacob who really was in debt to the bookies, she felt her back straightening and her jaw setting. Maybe I was a bit foolish, getting in debt to bookies, she chided herself as she peeled carrots. So what? Jacob went into debt to start the department store and that was called good business. Why are my bets less worthy? Anyway, it's none of his business if I want to have a little fun, she told herself. Women do all kinds of things these days without getting their husbands' approval, she muttered, as if trying to convince the chicken of the rightness of her actions before shoving it into the oven.

Like Hazel said, she reminded herself, we have the vote now, and the country's better off for it. We vote however we want. He doesn't know who I vote for, she thought with mischievous satisfaction. There's even that Mott Amendment to fix the Constitution and give women equal rights. I deserve the right to bet on the horses, she assured herself, shutting the blue and white enameled oven door with a louder than usual bang. I'm only gambling with my money, or at least it should be mine. I've worked just as hard as he has. It wasn't easy being at home alone with the children, keeping the house up on my own, feeding, washing, cleaning, and then doing his books and paying the bills. Did he notice? True, she admitted, Jacob had it plenty hard doing what he did for the family, out on the road sometimes weeks at a time. I'll give him that, my husband works as hard as any man I know. But I pulled my weight for the family too, she declared to the mound of potatoes she had peeled by rote.

Shira sighed. Alright, she confessed, it got easier when we moved here and he stopped peddling. He helped with chopping wood and other heavy chores I used to do on my own in Tuckerton. More than that, just having his company was a blessing. I never complained, but he had no idea how hard it was to be alone with three little ones all the time. And Jacob was different, too, after we settled down. Gentler, more loving. I hadn't realized how much the loneliness of the road was taking out of him. He was always grumpy after returning home, she remembered, recollecting her growing fear at the time. She'd asked herself a thousand times if she had made a huge mistake marrying him, once his quick temper revealed itself. He was barely in America when he started that feud with his sister and her husband. Her visceral distress at the time came vividly back to her. She recognized the knot now tightening in the pit of her stomach. It was just like the anxiety that constantly gripped her while caught between her new husband's demand that she cut off contact with the Mazaroffs, and her deep yearning for a friendship with her sister-in-law.

My husband was like a scared little boy then, blustering to try to convince everyone including himself he wasn't afraid, she realized as she thought back on Jacob's reactions to unwelcome facts. She had barely known him then. How could she have, given the speed with which Mumma Chaya had arranged their marriage? She always worried it was her fault when his temper flared, imagining she was failing him as a wife in some way. Of course, she never said anything to him about her unease. At the time it was unthinkable to her to question him about his moods. The husband was the head of the family, that was the eleventh commandment. So she had endured his moods. Thank goodness Jacob mellowed and became more contented once he threw himself into the challenge of starting the store and building a life in town.

As she set water to boil, Shira strained to articulate the resurgence of old feelings, of growing distress, over the past year or two. It's like the early days when he was constantly on edge, she realized. The bluster is back. Did it stem from when we stretched finances to build the store, she wondered? She'd done the calculations, knew business was good and should only get better with the bigger store. True, Jacob hates being in debt; he likes being the lender holding the note. Is owing the bank plaguing him? Debt would give him some sleepless nights, she conceded, but this feels darker. There was also that business with the Klan. He must be more afraid than he's letting on, she concluded. Still, he doesn't have to take it out on me. She grew suddenly indignant, absentmindedly mashing the potatoes with extra force.

Election
Point Pleasant 1924

A week after their unpleasant meeting, Jacob wired Goldstein, "I accept your terms. J. Itzkowitz". Papers were drawn up by Joel's lawyers and blessed by Rosenblatt, Jacob's attorney. "Seems they respect you, Jacob," Rosenblatt remarked, noting approvingly the contract's even-handedness. Nonetheless, as Jacob scanned the documents arrayed for signature on the lawyer's desk, his pen hovered like a sparrow unsure where to land. Gulping a deep breath, he recited to himself *"Ha-shem,* guard me from making a terrible mistake" then scratched out his signature in quadruplicate, sealing the deal.

With that turmoil now put to one side, Jacob returned to his campaigning with renewed earnestness. Several crucial weeks had been lost. Luckily, in the interim, Lew had quietly transformed himself into the de facto campaign manager. Talking up his father's candidacy to friends, Lew coached a small group of volunteers on the art of injecting discussion of the council race into the circles in which they traveled. Jacob, preoccupied as he'd been, nevertheless marked his son's devotion to the effort. As Jacob and Lew took their usual morning walk to the store a few days later, Jacob offhandedly remarked "Maybe I should pay more attention to the voters the next few weeks."

"You're doing just fine, Pop" Lew responded reassuringly. "But we could do with a few special meetings."

"Meetings? What sort of meetings?"

"Well, Pop, we have to bring some more groups around. I've got my ear to the ground. The good news is VanNort's not that popular. Still, people tend to go along with the guy already in charge. It's the devil you know phenomenon," Lew explained.

"You think I don't know that? That's why I talk to everyone I meet on the street," he replied, defensively.

"That's important, Pop. People like being asked, but it's not always enough. Sometimes people need, say, permission from another guy in charge. Point Pleasant isn't so different from a feudal village where lords and clergy ruled."

"Stop talking in riddles, Lew," he was annoyed. "Who are we talking about?"

"I think it's time you met with Father Marchetti. He's the big guy in charge among the Catholics. My friend McKendry's talked to him. He thinks the Father already has his suspicions about Van Nort," Lew said.

"Me? Meet with a priest? Sure, I want Catholic votes. Going begging to a priest…"

"Not begging. Just discussing, Pop," Lew interrupted. "Seems they were as rattled about the noisy Klan march in town as we were. Right after, the Father started quietly asking around, trying to figure out which locals are with those goons."

"Ok, I see your point. You think he'll try to convert me?" He gave Lew a sideways look.

Lew eyed his father. "Let me arrange it, Pop. This could make a real difference."

--

The darkened wood shingles and buttressed walls created a massiveness that impressed Jacob as they approached the church. He'd barely paid attention to the building over the years, never before having stepped inside any church. Not that he was opposed on any principle. He'd simply never had a reason to, and certainly no one had ever invited him in. Back in Shavlan, he mused wryly, we'd never have dared going inside the Russian church for fear of a mob beating us. The orthodox church at the other end of Shavlan, he recalled, resembled a palace with its gated wall and tall spires garlanded with gold. This St. Peter's looks more like our old wooden *shtetl* synagogue. Maybe these Catholic *goyim* are not so different from us if they build their prayer house this plainly, he speculated.

Opening the sturdy wooden front door and stepping inside with Lew and McKendry, he immediately realized his error. The ornateness of the interior staggered him. The main seating area for prayers, though not large, assaulted his senses as garish. Every surface was adorned in bright colors, while the room was overflowing with life-sized carved figures. Colored glass windows, which appeared muted from the outside, shimmered and cast pink, blue and green beams across the high-backed benches. The ceiling, glowing an intense heavenly blue, was dotted with a welter of golden flowers. Do they paint with real gold, he wondered? Across the ceiling, massive intricate wooden arches supported two rows of guardian angels jutting out like figureheads from a ship's prow, hovering high above where congregants pray. Don't parishioners feel like they're being spied upon from heaven? Maybe that's how they want them to feel, he contemplated.

A massive floor to ceiling sculpture against the back wall awed him. Why display a white marble depiction of a church inside a church, he wondered. Ensconced within the sculpture's side niches stood several smaller robed figures. These tiny men appeared to be standing guard, arrayed on either side of a larger robed man with a mysterious smile, one whose hands spread in a gesture of welcome. That must be their Jesus, he registered. Thinking back to the grand synagogue of his youth, he marveled at the contrast. Our magnificent *bimah* was as large as their carving, he reminisced. A talented artist created it, and people came to see it from miles around. Yet displaying a statue of Moses would have been idolatry, he assured himself, as he struggled to make sense of the surroundings.

His contemplations were interrupted when a portly, round faced man with a fixed smile emerged from a door beside the altar. The entrant wore what looked to him like a black dress as approached, shuffling down the central aisle. "Welcome to St. Peter's, Mr. Itzkowitz."

McKendry touched his forehead, midriff and each shoulder, genuflecting. "Father Marchetti, thank you for meeting," he said. "This is my friend Lew, Mr. Itzkowitz's son."

"Bless you, Thomas, for bringing together people of good will," the priest said, placing a hand gently on McKendry's head. He extended a meaty hand first to Jacob, who shook it firmly, then to Lew who did likewise. "Come,

232

let us sit together in my office," he said, leading them back through the passageway from which he had emerged into a small room with white plastered walls. Jacob scanned the chamber, as if expecting to see gold hidden somewhere, but saw only a plain pine table and four wooden chairs. The simplicity of the priest's space surprised him after the grandeur of the main church.

"We lead a simple life as priests," Father Marchetti offered, as if sensing his bewilderment at the contrast. "Our nave is devoted to the glory of the Lord, while our work outside the sanctuary is done under a vow of poverty. Please, sit."

He shifted in his chair, unsure how to begin. Lew broke the momentary silence. "We are grateful for this meeting to discuss our common interests regarding the town."

"Thomas told me you have ideas along those lines. Mind you, the church stays out of politics. I'm afraid we cannot help with your father's campaign," the priest said, his smile now all but faded away.

"We're not asking for campaign help," Lew responded, glancing at Thomas, who sat quietly inspecting the floor. "We came because we understand that you have come to, well, similar conclusions regarding a prominent person."

The Father looked back intently, as if weighing his next words. "Let's say your understanding is well founded. That would be troubling, having someone with such hateful beliefs remaining in an important office. Yet we must consider, would the Church find in preferable if one of the Pharisees replaced such a person? Surely you see my dilemma."

"What does he mean 'farsees'?" Jacob turned to Lew, puzzled.

"He means Jews, Pop. It's an old term in their bible for Jews," Lew said, speaking through clenched teeth. He leaned closer, whispering into Jacob's ear, "He's spouting that nonsense that the Jews killed Jesus. Just ignore it."

The priest broke in, seeming to sense his lack of comprehension. "Mr. Itzkowitz, on Easter we celebration the resurrection of our Lord, and recall the deeds of the perfidious Jews, 'Judaicam perfidiam'. I cannot ignore the Church's teachings, even for some advantage locally by collaborating with you" the priest said, sighing.

"Pray however you people want. What happened thousands of years ago has nothing to do with me!" His voice rose. "Listen, I'm a businessman, not a politician. I wasn't planning to run until those hooligans marched down Arnold Avenue. I saw the hate in their eyes."

"We saw that too, Mr. Itzkowitz," the priest nodded. "Hate and ignorance, a terrible combination. False prophets lead weak minded people to do terrible things."

"Those men, they hate us both. They're out for your blood, too." He turned to his son. "Lew, read him what that woman wrote."

"This is the propaganda they spread around to get new members, Father," Lew said, unfolding a printed sheet from his pocket. "This woman right here in Jersey, the Methodists call her Bishop White, writes pamphlets like this: 'The unrepentant Hebrew is everywhere among us today as the strong ally of Roman Catholicism ... Roman Catholics have killed more Jews in the past than there are on the face of the whole earth today. To think of our Hebrew friends with their millions in gold and silver aiding the Pope in his aspirations for world supremacy, is almost beyond the grasp of the human mind. But there is abundant evidence that it is true.'"

Marchetti listened impassively to Lew's recitation. "It pains me to hear such blatant falsehoods. Deceivers like this poison the minds of average men and women. It is true, our new Pope has offered a certain renewed welcome to our Hebrew brethren. These people turn that into some sort of evil conspiracy," the priest said, face slightly flushed.

"What are we going to do about it? What are you going to do about it? These bums are right here in our town," Jacob said, locking eyes with the priest.

"Mr. Itzkowitz, as I said, the church does not get involved in politics. But your son was right. Our inquiries after the Klan march caused us concern that there are men in high office who carry hate in their hearts for both our congregations." The priest returned his gaze, raising his eyebrows and pausing.

"And as I said," Jacob spoke deliberately. "I wouldn't be running for Council if I didn't share your concern about a certain individual. Wringing your hands won't stop them. You still haven't said what you're going to do about it."

Father Marchetti pressed his palms together. "I will pray on what is in my power to do. You have my promise I'll keep our meeting in strictest confidence. As a priest I am bound never to reveal what is said in confession. My discretion can be counted on."

He glanced at Lew, confused. "Confession?"

Lew spoke up quickly, "We appreciate that, Father. Rest assured that we will not speak of this meeting either."

"Good. Now go in peace. With the Lord's blessing may our town be led by men of honor," Father Marchetti said. He spread his palms apart in a way that reminded Jacob of the statue in the sanctuary. "Oh, and Thomas?"

"Yes Father," the young man said nervously.

"Speaking of confession, you're long overdue."

"I'll be there this weekend, Father," Thomas said, his freckled face turning bright red.

--

The night of the election, Shira cooked a special meal, borscht to start with followed by the lamb chops he loved. He and Shira stayed home to await the outcome, dispatching Lew to Borough Hall. It would take hours to collect the ballot boxes and do the count. Despite the long wait, Lew wanted to be on hand.

As usual, it was only after Labor Day, when the vacationing lodgers and day trippers had dwindled to a trickle, that voters finally enjoyed enough leisure to pay attention to the upcoming election. In past campaigns, VanNort's style was merely to hold court at the bank. At most he would make a speech or two at the Rotary Club and the Chamber of Commerce, confidently presuming that the average citizen would naturally anoint him for another three years without him having to stoop to actually asking for votes.

That fall, VanNort's approach started off no differently, his manner indicating a confident dismissiveness towards Jacob's upstart candidacy. But as the leaves turned color, so did the nature of the contest. In the last three weeks before election day VanNort seemed finally to have noticed that his challenger was personally reaching out to voters in earnest. Lew had organized dozens of volunteers to pass out "Vote Itzkowitz, Put a Watchdog on the Council" handbills at strategic points around town every Saturday. Jacob set up a table and chairs outside the store on Thursday afternoons, inviting passersby to sit, share a glass of lemonade, and ask him whatever was on their mind. Few took him up on the offer at first, so odd was it to have a candidate willing to answer to people of any station. By early October, those chairs routinely filled with three or four workingmen, while housewives and more respectable men in suits stood listening in. Most in town already knew him as the prosperous merchant with the funny accent and hard to pronounce name, a purveyor of quality brand name merchandise at decent prices. Now they gathered to hear what he had to say about paving the dusty downtown roads with concrete, replacing the rickety bridge over the Manasquan River, or helping local fisherman compete with boats from neighboring ports now that the new canal was open. He warmed to holding forth, dispensing his opinions on the bread and butter issues in town. He had a pronouncement on every topic, and was never shy about sharing it. Not everyone liked what Jacob said, but most seemed to like the way he said it.

As the parade of citizens to Jacob's sidewalk campaign office grew, so too did the nasty rumors begin to percolate. In taverns and at church socials, a man here and a woman there was sure to be heard whispering to a companion "did you know he was run out of Tuckerton? I heard he cheated his customers." At the Odd Fellows clam bake, a few drinks into the evening local eccentric Darnell bent his lodge mates' ears, pontificating that "Itzkowitz ain't even an American! Been here twenty years and ain't bothered to become one of us. Never should have let that Russian in." Some were swayed by these libels, especially after hearing the same slander repeated multiple times. But most of the townspeople who heard such testimony against Jacob had shopped in his store, or knew him from the fire house. They'd bought on credit from him when a little short of funds. Familiarity generally inoculated them from the outlandish claims that had only recently begun circulating. Listening impassively to the rumor mongers such voters shrugged, inwardly maintaining their good opinion of him. Most also kept their opinions to themselves, not moved to speak up in his defense. In a small town, it didn't do much good to get into an argument with every loud mouth spouting off, especially if his friends might turn out to wear hooded robes.

Like in any other village, it took little time for the rumors to filter back to the Itzkowitzes. Jacob, hearing that lies were being spread about him, angrily vowed to Lew that he would find the *mamzer* ruining his good name and punch the guy in his face. Lew, apparently worried his father meant it literally, countered with, "The guy who you want to punch in the face, Pop, is VanNort. He's behind it all. Let's get even with votes, not with fists." He saw wisdom in his son's more thoughtful approach, but was hardly mollified. "Maybe I'll do both," was all he commented on the topic. The assault on his reputation served to galvanize him the last few weeks before Election Day. He lobbied voters morning to night.

Understandably, then, when Lew turned up at City Hall on election night, he was filled with apprehension. The Itzkowitzes believed they had run a strong campaign, unconventional for a town used to sleepy affairs with little drama. What they could not gauge was how the locals would react. One thing was for certain, more people than usual by far had turned out to vote. Over 1800 ballots had been cast, nearly half again the number from the last election. Some of that jump had to be more women voting, Lew figured as he took in the scene in the main council chamber at Borough Hall. The cherry wood semi-circle bench where the Council sat during formal business formed a marshaling area for the vote count. If all went well, Jacob would be sitting up there in a few weeks.

Inside the semi-circle stood the witness table, normally used for those offering testimony to the council. Tonight the sturdy table was pulled forward to create a counting station. Lew watched as a pair of men hauled in one of a half dozen ballot crates from an office adjoining the council chamber. The first crate landed with a thud on the counting table as Town Clerk Dan Mazzano removed a special key from his watch pocket. Working with focused energy as if he were unlocking a chest full of gold, Mazzano turned his key in the large iron padlock, gingerly lifting the lid of the first box. The Clerk personally set about sorting the paper ballots into neat piles. To his right Mazzano placed votes for Itzkowitz, to his left those for VanNort. When the crate was empty and all ballots assigned right or left, an assistant methodically counted the VanNort pile, while Mazzano counted the Itzkowitz pile. The Clerk then noted each result on a tally sheet bearing lines for each of the six wards in town. Mazzano and his assistant clerk moved through this choreography for all other contested offices, until all tallies were complete for the first crate and the container emptied. All ballots were then returned to their original box, Mazzano closed the lid with a loud thud, and the papers relocked for safe keeping. The final step was for Mazzano to chalk up tally sheet results from each ward count on a giant blackboard at one end of the room.

By the third crate it became clear the outcome would be decided by a razor thin margin. The first two wards broke for VanNort by modest margins. This was not surprising to Lew. He knew those wards housed many third and fourth generation families in town, those who considered themselves the real locals, different from the newer immigrants. When the numbers were posted, Lew stepped into an office in Town Hall with a telephone and called home. "Pop, it's going OK here. Wards 1 and 2 are in, he's up by 50. That's actually pretty good for us, considering who lives there," Lew growled into the handset, trying to avoid being overheard in the counting room. "Call me when they get to the last ward, Lew. Nothing more I can do about the votes now," Jacob replied, hanging up before Lew could add anything more.

Lew kept watch as the next ward crates underwent the same elaborate process. Ward 3, with its big swath of houses near the railroad yard, shifted strongly towards Jacob. Lew knew this ward encompassed the small but long-established community of black families, among them Clemson Morgan. A tall, affable man, Morgan performed odd jobs and handyman work around the store. Jacob once told Lew that Morgan reminded him of miners he'd known back in the Rand, hard working men beaten down by other men just because of their skin. One day a few years back Morgan had approached Jacob, telling his employer he was getting married Sunday next and politely indicating he needed Saturday off for the wedding. Jacob responded with congratulations and told Morgan he should take the entire next week off with pay, adding "you need time to take your bride for a honeymoon." Whether that small kindness had resulted in winning over votes in Ward 3 they would never know for sure, but as Lew heard the Ward count come in heavily for his father, he figured it certainly had not hurt.

The next two wards split fairly evenly. Wards 4 and 5 reflected the mix of old and new in Point Pleasant. Not many years earlier, those sectors were the blocks where workingmen lived. Those families were largely descended from the English, Dutch, Swedes and a few Finns who were the early settlers in the coastal area that eventually became Ocean County. Their forbears had come for the abundant fish to be found within the inlets and marshes of Barnegat Bay – named from the Dutch words barend-gat ("where the waters breaketh"). Finding teeming wildlife to hunt on land and sea, berries to harvest and bog iron to extract, many stayed. They settled an archipelago of tiny villages sprinkled up and down the shore. In recent years, the old settlement patterns were disturbed by the influx of Irish, Italians, and a smattering of Eastern Europeans into town. Seeking homes they could afford, these new settlers clustered in the more ramshackle neighborhoods, turning those quarters of town polyglot. For Jacob, these newer waves of citizens meant a more receptive crop of voters, citizens with little allegiance to an old time family and more of an affinity for a fellow immigrant. The running tally on the chalk board brought Jacob's total tantalizingly close, only seven votes shy of VanNort.

"Get down here, Pop," Lew barked into the phone, with uncharacteristic agitation. "It's close. Anything could happen when they count Ward 6!" Ten minutes later, Jacob strode into the counting room wearing his best suit, his outfit topped with a black bowler. The Clerk's key had already popped open the final lock. Another trove of ballots was being sorted out onto the counting table. A gaggle of men stood silently, arrayed in a semi-circle across from the Clerk's station, three observing on VanNort's behalf. VanNort himself, it seemed, still did not deign to leave his house. Next to the opponent's crew, Lew and a buddy named Bidwell kept watch for their candidate. Jacob silently fell in next to Lew, fiddling with a coin in his watch pocket. The election officials ignored the onlookers, plodding through the robotic tabulation of votes. As the ballot crate grew emptier, the room grew quieter. The watchers shifted forward on to their toes, craned their necks like herons stalking fish, and tried to guess the final tally. Mazzano, seemingly oblivious to the intent gazes, set down the last of the marked papers into the counted pile. Wordlessly he strolled to the chalk board, and with a flourish wrote into the Ward 6 row "147" under the VanNort column, "163" in the Itzkowitz column.

The two clutches of partisans stared for a fraction of a second as each man completed the mental addition, lips moving wordlessly. Then, as if a short fuse had been lit and a blast detonated, Lew and Bidwell whooped loudly, while Jacob emitted a loud *"gut in Himmel"*. Father and son spontaneously turned face to face, hugging and slapping each other on the back. The VanNort trio, for their part, sputtered sounds, apparently rendered unable to fully form words at such a shocking outcome. Their heads turned in unison, as if they were a cerberus and not three men. They gaped at the Clerk, their expressions imploring him to admit some error. Mazzano answered their disbelieving looks with a shrug of his shoulders, turning back to the chalk board to meticulously display the final count in large numbers. VanNort, 897. Itzkowitz, 906. With the official outcome glaring at them, the VanNort crew stamped out of the room, presumably to break the news to their candidate.

"Gentlemen, we have a winner," Mazzano proclaimed in a deep baritone to the remaining onlookers in the room. "The new Councilman at Large for the Borough of Point Pleasant Beach is Mr. Jacob Itzkowitz." He took a step towards Jacob and held out his hand. "Congratulations, sir. You will be sworn in on New Year's Day next."

Jacob, beaming, grabbed the outstretched hand with both of his. "Thank you, sir, for that wonderful news!" he said in full voice, pumping Mazzano's hand repeatedly. Mazzano, smiling back, leaned in close, put his mouth to the winner's ear, and whispered "Best wishes from the good Father. Oh, and also from a Mr. Goldstein."

Oasis-by-the-Sea
Point Pleasant 1928

Winning the competition for land was far harder than he'd expected in striking the deal with Goldstein. Jacob was hardly the only visionary to foresee the future of the little seaside town and quickly seize the opportunities. Despite his having Joel's money to play with, a soda fountain proprietor named Jorgenson had beaten him to the punch back in early '25. The upstart had swooped in and secretly outbid him for a large swath of land near the fishing pier. Within a few years, Jorgenson transformed his acquisition into an open-air pavilion boasting an oceanside candy shop, soda fountain and refreshment stand. Across the boardwalk he erected his crown jewel attraction, a giant sea water swimming pool. Not content, the intrepid entrepreneur soon launched a dance hall and a miniature golf course. Tourists loved these modern attractions.

Having let the central oceanfront location slip through his fingers, Jacob turned his attention to calculating the next best opportunity. He quickly reasoned that as his competitor created more and more amusements, summer crowds would burgeon, fueling demand for a grand hotel. Scouting out the best possible locations, he honed in on a vacant strip of land to the south, nearer to elegant Bay Head. There the beach widened out as Ocean Avenue veered slightly to the west. Studying the land records, he deduced that assembling these parcels would require a virtuoso performance, an application of all his business skills. The challenge excited him, whetting his appetite for making deals. Acquiring this land would enable him to build his dream, the Oasis-by-the-Sea resort. He devised a plan to coax four different owners to sell their land to him at discounted prices, all while keeping each in the dark as to his agreements with the others.

Macklin was the first, and the easiest. He merely needed to let Macklin know that he'd somehow found out that the old man was shilling for a dangerous out-of-town syndicate. Expressing sympathy for the man's precarious situation, he tipped off Macklin that "official sources" described the silent backers as armed and brutal to any confederate who failed them. The old man broke down quickly, unleashing a torrent of fears for his life eating away at him daily. Playing the public-spirited Councilman feeling sorry for his constituent, Jacob came up with an idea. What if Macklin signed over title to him, who was far better equipped to stand up to bullies? Macklin, his drinking on the upswing and health declining, was all too eager to escape through the proffered exit. A deed from Macklin to Itzkowitz was drawn up, signed and deposited with Jacob's lawyer. They would not put the deed in the public land records just yet, he explained to Macklin, to avoid arousing questions from the syndicate. That the private sale also avoided tipping off the other potential sellers to his scheme was left unmentioned.

The next two purchases were more challenging. He needed to acquire neighboring lots, owned by the children of two different old-time clam digger families. The current owners, both men in their thirties of little imagination, were cut of the same cloth. Both apparently saw no good use for their sand dunes other than as prime locations from which to surf cast from time to time. As is often the case with those who inherit something of value for which they never lifted a finger, neither had any plan to improve their property, but also no inclination to let go of it. To each, an oceanfront lot was merely a family heirloom to be held onto, something eventually to pass along to the eldest child. He knew both heirs well. One was a fellow volunteer fireman, the other a classmate of Esther's. Happily for his plan, neither could stand the other. These two members of the current generation had also inherited a tradition of bad blood between their fishing dynasties going back three generations. Like most such feuds, it sprang from some insult that nobody alive could remember, but one that everybody in both lineages was inculcated to avenge as a matter of familial honor.

Over the course of months he'd maneuvered to occasionally run into each titleholder. During the ensuing chitchat, he shared tidbits of the type of confidential information Councilmen are presumed privy to. To each owner he let slip that the other's family had suffered a financial setback, and now were quietly negotiating a sale for quick cash to a junk dealer. The prospect of an unsightly nuisance piling up next door to the hearer's fishing spot provoked the intended reactions. Each landowner angrily declared of the other's family, "it was just like those bastards to sell their birthright for a mess of porridge" when things got tough. After several more seemingly random encounters, Jacob knew that the seedlings of worry he'd sown had sprouted into vivid images of noxious mounds of garbage on the adjacent land, ruining for both owners any possible enjoyment of the ancestral beachfront. At the right moment, he offered up a friendly possibility. As part of his civic responsibilities, he would help them out by taking the plot of land off their hands at a "fair price". No need to suffer the coming unpleasantness, and naturally as an elected official he would be better equipped to deal with the junkman. Relieved, each heir was only too happy to shake on the deal, sign over title, and be done with the problem. Having connived to get three out of four parcels deeded over to him, he knew a more subtle plan was required to seize the final building block.

Parcel C was the linchpin. Without it, the northern lots extracted from the feuding fishermen were too small for a top-notch resort hotel. With it, in combination with Macklin's land to the south he would control nearly one thousand contiguous feet of prime ocean frontage.

But how to handle the *mishpocha*? He'd created his own dilemma by pursuing these lots, because Charlie Moscowitz stood between him and a small fortune. He'd known Charlie since the youngest child of Shira's cousin Labe Moscowitz was a toddler. Charlie, in turn, had long idolized him, admiring Jacob as a self-made man. While others in the second generation of Moscowitzes went off to college to become lawyers, teachers and managers, Charlie pursued business. An avid reader, Charlie devoured biographies of mythic figures like Franklin and Carnegie and the rags-to-riches stories of Horatio Alger. Growing up nearby in Toms River, Charlie revered Jacob as the man whose drive enabled him to rise from greenhorn peddler, to merchant, to real estate wheeler dealer, to respected elected official. Unlike many of the younger cousins who considered Sunday dinner at the Itzkowitzes as a ritual to be endured, Charlie reveled in the company of his hero, coming on his own to dine at their house long past the time when he was dragged along by his parents.

For Jacob's part, he basked in the admiration of the bright and charming young man who never ceased to pose intelligent questions about commerce. The contrast with his own son was stark. Lew more or less took the family enterprise for granted, demonstrating more interest in German literature and physics than in retail trends, while Charlie soaked up every business tidbit he doled out. By his teens Charlie was leading an organization of the newsboys, creating a lucrative delivery business that allowed him to build up a significant nest egg. At age twenty, Charlie invested those savings into a tobacco shop, betting that the rising popularity of smoking among women would propel rapid growth in that market. As revenues from newspapers and smokes poured in, Charlie decided to emulate his role model and buy real estate.

Over a Sunday dinner, Charlie had proudly recounted in minute detail to Jacob and Shira his clever negotiations resulting in his first real estate investment. One day a regular tobacco customer had come to the shop looking distraught. A few weeks earlier the man's father had died accidentally, and the deceased had left his family saddled with debts, obligations which the eldest son had no means of satisfying. Through gentle probing Charlie learned that the father had owned two vacant lots, both apparently bought on speculation. One parcel was located in Point Pleasant, the other in Mantoloking, further burdening the family with paying real estate taxes without revenue from the fallow land. At the mention of Point Pleasant, Charlie's ears had perked up, seeing his chance to own a piece of the town that his mentor so clearly believed in. Offering the customer a complimentary vintage Arturo Fuente cigar as a token of condolence, Charlie deftly played on the mourner's anxieties, agreeing that the last thing worth holding onto was empty land that would only cost money he didn't have. By the time the smoke was down to its last ashes, a deal had been struck at a price Charlie felt certain was a real bargain.

Finishing this tale of triumph, Charlie had thanked Jacob for teaching him that the best deals are to be had from a man who for his own peculiar reasons doesn't want what has fallen into his lap. Emitting a "Well done!", Jacob had briefly felt pride welling up that he had schooled Charlie in sizing up people and moving quickly when a favorable deal opportunity presents itself. More darkly, hearing the location of Charlie's find, Jacob had filed away the realization that soon, if his others maneuverings fell into place, he might have to finagle a way to relieve Charlie of the parcel.

What Charlie had no way of knowing was that Jacob had been scouting for some time the very same Parcel C. Indeed, he had contacted the father of Charlie's seller a few months before the man's untimely death. He'd been in his own process of sizing the man up, looking for the weak spot motivating a cheap sale, when the fatal accident upended all his plans. Undaunted in his determination to acquire the land, he'd directed his lawyer to examine the probate records, revealing that the deceased's property had been inherited by the son who also happened to be Charlie's tobacco aficionado. To Jacob's dismay, that son never responded to a feeler he'd put out through an intermediary. He'd been at wit's end over his inability to contact the man who now held the keystone to his resort plans, but now understood what had transpired. An incredible stroke of luck, he now shouted inwardly, upon hearing that his protege was the one who'd seized on the family's distress.

He took it as a positive omen that Charlie now possessed the very parcel he required to complete his assemblage.

But how to proceed? It was obvious that Charlie was too thrilled with the fruits of his business acumen to quickly part with the land. It would be only natural for the young man to want to hang on to his first major acquisition. From his own experience Jacob knew the magical attachment one gets from owning a piece of the earth. He also feared arousing suspicion if he suddenly offered Charlie a premium price for the parcel. Instead, as Shira brought a freshly baked blueberry pie to the table for their dessert, he contrived a more elaborate subterfuge. His best path, he conceived, lay through exercising the power he held arising from the younger man's adulation of his successful older cousin. And so after dinner, while Shira was in the kitchen washing up, as if initiating Charlie into a secret society, in a low voice he informed Charlie that he had something to share in deep confidence. Leaving the table, he beckoned his acolyte to join him outside where the two of them could be alone.

"Charlie, my boy, you've shown real savvy, mixed with a little *chutzpah*. You've impressed me," he began as they stood bathed in the setting sun, eliciting a beaming smile from Charlie. Looking all around as if to be sure no one was close by, Jacob continued in a near whisper, draping an arm over the young man's shoulders. "Would you like to join me in an enterprise that will make us both quite wealthy?"

Mesmerized, Charlie listened intently as he painted a picture of how together they could create the most elegant resort along the shore. "It will wow people, my boy. All the tycoons and their fancy ladies in furs will be dying to stay there," he prophesied. "A grand hotel requires a grand location". In a conspiratorial tone, he shared his deepest secret, that he already controlled the three adjacent parcels. What a stroke of incredible luck for both of them, he continued, that of all possible buyers, Charlie had been the one snapping up the final strip needed to properly site such a palace of pleasure.

"When you revealed that it was you, Charlie, that owned Parcel C, I knew it was *beshert!*" he exclaimed, gripping his cousin by the shoulders. All Charlie needed to do, he explained, was to sign over the deed for his recent acquisition to Oasis-By-the-Sea Corporation, the company Jacob had created to advance the project. In exchange, Charlie would get a ten percent share in the venture.

"What do you think, Charlie? Are you in or out?" he said, holding Charlie close in a near embrace. For a moment, Charlie looked rather stunned. Then, seeming to regain composure, the younger man mumbled a few words about being highly flattered by the prospect of being partners with the esteemed Jacob Itzkowitz. "Then it's a deal!" he burst out, Charlie nodding assent. Shaking his erstwhile partner's hand furiously, he glowed inside with the knowledge that the last piece of the land puzzle had fallen into place with remarkable ease.

The Gamble
Point Pleasant 1930

"Are you sure you want to do this, Councilman?" The banker asked, peering over his glasses.

"Enough with the Councilman, Olaf! We're old friends. I'm Jacob to you," he said warmly as he settled into the high-backed seat across from the banker's massive desk.

"You've earned the title, Jacob. You've done good things for the town. I just hope you're doing as well for yourself with this plan," said the dark-suited man, pressing his fingertips together as if in prayer.

"It's a good deal for both of us, Olaf." He leaned forward, wagging a finger. "The bank gets cash. You get a bad loan off the books. And I get, well, I get what I want."

"You'll be drawing down most of your cash reserves," Johanson replied, concern in his voice. "That's not very prudent if this economic slump gets worse."

"You're a good friend, Olaf. I appreciate you looking out for me. You're also the bank president. You need to look out for the bank first." Jacob eased back between the wings of the leather armchair.

"I am looking out for the bank, Jacob. You're import-ant to us. We both know that clothing sales are off, your customers are losing jobs and cutting back. The tourist season was horrible," the banker lectured, pausing as if to let his message sink in. "You're going to need your reserves to get through the coming year."

"I'll be fine. Besides, buying the hotel loan also serves my interests. I've got too much invested in your stock to let the bank fail," he said firmly.

"You're on the Board. You know the bank is not that close to the edge. At least not yet. I admit, it was a shock to see those Caldwell banks in the south fail. Can you imag-ine? Mobs beating down their doors, demanding their money," Johanson swallowed, pouring a glass of water from a crystal carafe on an ornate side table.

"Scared people run like a frightened herd. It's always dangerous to be the one standing in front of them."

"True. The last thing we want is to frighten our cus-tomers," Johanson said, turning a bit pale at the thought. "Luckily we never speculated in stocks like some of those banks. Still, you do have a point, Jacob. If a few large loans go bad and word gets around, that could really hurt us."

"Exactly! That's why you'll sell the bank's loan to the hotel corporation to me at seventy-five cents on the dol-lar. It's a good deal for both of us," he leaned forward, more animated. "Owning that loan gives me the hammer I need, something to hold over the heads of my partners. The bank gets cash, and all the risk of the loan going bad disappears off the bank's books. And I can afford to wait and see if the corporation can keep making the loan payments."

"Ok, I can see the point of that. How will you deal with your partners, the other shareholders in Oasis-by-the-Sea Corporation? They put in most of the original funding. What if the corporation can't keep paying? Won't they block you from ever foreclosing?"

"Ah, that's why this loan sale to me won't be public. Everything must remain confidential, just between me and the bank. In the public records it will look like the bank still holds the mortgage. My lawyer tells me that's kosher. The bank acts as my agent, but I call the shots."

"Hmmm. It's a bit unusual, but certainly something we could do. Still…" Johanson wavered.

"Good! Listen, Olaf, it's the smart thing to do. The bank takes a modest loss up front, but avoids a long run disaster. We both know the economy could get much worse. A half-built hotel will sit empty for years. If that happens, the bank will get next to nothing."

Johanson looked around his paneled office at his many mementos. A silver Tiffany clock from his distant cousins, given in gratitude for financing expansion of their boatyard. A framed photo of the Holtzman's market ribbon cutting, the first building his new bank had financed. A silver cup engraved with the phrase "to a good egg" from the Ratners, presented when they handed him a check paying off the loan that had launched their successful poultry farm. It had taken Johanson years to build Jersey Shore National into the dominant financial institution in the county. The odds were largely against the upstart at the outset when Johanson pulled together a group of prominent investors, Jacob among them, to launch a rival bank to VanNort's.

Over time, however, Johanson succeeded by catering to the myriad businesses popping up in the area, especially those that VanNort alienated with his imperious ways. Being nationally chartered also brought certain advantages over the Building and Loan, enabling Johanson to diversify the types of loans he could structure, bringing new connections and new customers. Yet despite all his hard work, the recent stock market crash and confused politicians in Washington threatened to undermine it all.

"In the end, it's your money Jacob. Lord knows you've managed it well over the years," Johanson said, wiping away a bead of sweat with an embroidered handkerchief. Suddenly he broke into a broad smile and extended his hand across the desk.

"Wonderful! I'm glad you've come around, Olaf!" He rose from the armchair and firmly gripped the banker's hand in return.

"I just hope we both won't come to regret this," Johanson said, hand on Jacob's shoulder as the pair walked to the office door.

--

The pieces are all falling into place, Jacob reveled inwardly as he emerged from the bank onto Arnold Avenue. His thoughts circled back to his reluctant acceptance of Goldstein's heavy-handed proposal years earlier. In that moment, in a weak position, he'd barely had a glimmer of an idea of how to extricate himself from Joel's grip. He'd only gone along with the deal Goldstein offered against his instincts to protect Lew's reputation. If Lew was exposed as a loser, in debt to underworld types, the good people of Point Pleasant could turn against his son. How could Lew ever take over the business with such a black mark against him? Keeping that shadow from spreading over his son, any father would do whatever it took. That's why he'd succumbed to Goldstein, he told Shira at the time. And himself.

Yet as he now sauntered past familiar storefronts, merchants and window-shoppers nodding to him and calling out a friendly "good day, Councilman", he finally admitted something to himself. It was a reality he'd largely kept at bay over the years, subconsciously avoiding the whole truth. If he were honest with himself, he must admit that protecting Lew was only a pretense, a byproduct of his ambition. Joel had actually offered him a prize far more valuable than a small cut of a land purchase. The South African's money enabled him, Jacob, to be the man shaping his town's future. Years earlier his eyes had opened to the inevitable attraction of the shore to the growing middle-class masses up north. As if called by a religious vision, ever since he'd been enthralled by the competition. All his energies would be devoted to racing ahead of the rest. He, Jacob, a peddler from the old country. The man with the accent children found funny. The Jew in a Christian town. Winning yielded power. And power brought acceptance.

Just look at how they treat me now when I walk down the street, he silently meditated. Accepting Joel's money let me build an empire, and people respect an emperor. Drunks used to spread rumors about me, slander me, claim I wasn't really an American. Sometimes worse. They thought I didn't hear what they were saying behind my back. I almost went after the bastards with my own fists, but thankfully Lew was level headed. "Get even first, Pop. Beat VanNort at his own game and that will shut them up" he told me. Turns out my son was right.

VanNort squawked a lot after I won, he recollected. The sonofabitch claimed the vote must have been rigged, how he couldn't have lost, so he demanded a recount. After the second counting was done Mazzano certified that my win turned out to be five votes more than his original count. VanNort sulked. Recalling this, he wondered: Was Mazzano doing someone's bidding? Did Goldstein have something to do with it? I never told anyone, not even Shira, what Mazzano whispered to me election night. It still sticks in my gorge, doesn't sit right. I campaigned hard, the voters chose me. They even elected me to a second term by a wide margin against that other fool, Staunton, who ran the next time. It wasn't a fluke, he insisted to himself. His cogitation came to an end as he arrived at his store building.

--

Six months later, a short news clipping arrived by post from Uncle Helman. Well into his seventies, the old horse dealer remained an excellent source of tidings from the land now called the Union of South Africa. Helman had shrewdly stayed neutral during the second Boer War with the English, quietly supplying horses to whichever side paid his price. He avoided the fate of the Boerjude who foolishly sided openly with the losers. Those poor souls ended up stripped of their citizenship rights after the British took full control. For Helman the war brought wealth, enough to move with Aunt Sora to a grand house near the Great Park Synagogue in Johannesburg. Helman corresponded sporadically with his nephew, heralding changes in the land from which Jacob had emigrated years earlier. This latest installment arrived in an airmail envelope, a signal that Uncle thought the news urgent enough to merit the extra cost. Jacob carefully opened the tissue envelope, revealing a short message in familiar Yiddish script: "We are well. This should be of interest." Enclosed was a terse clipping reporting that the renowned diamond magnate Solomon Joel and his related companies had lost a major lawsuit,

257

forcing them to pay the enormous sum of £350,000 to the aggrieved plaintiffs. The report mentioned that Joel was so worn down from the litigation that he had taken ill, perhaps succumbing to a stroke.

Setting the clipping down, Jacob tapped the worn oak desktop half a dozen times, as if sounding out a coded message. His hand grew still. Nervous energy coursed through him. He nodded multiple times, as if signaling agreement with some invisible figure seated across the desk. My moment has finally come, he thought with unbridled delight. He grabbed the phone, asked the operator to put him through to a familiar number, impatient for an answer. Hearing the click at the other end, he launched right in. "Olaf, it's time. Call the loan."

The banker quizzed him. Was Jacob certain about taking this step? Was the hotel construction really beyond salvaging? Might not the economy turn around later this year? Wouldn't foreclosure damage Jacob's reputation? Johanson argued that although the project was owned by Oasis-by-the-Sea Corporation, the public was unaware that Joel owned most of the corporation's stock. Everyone would assume that Jacob, its President and public face, had defaulted. To the average person, the bank would be foreclosing on an Itzkowitz project.

To each objection Jacob had a ready rebuttal. It made little sense to keep funding hotel construction in this downturn. Wishful thinkers might convince themselves the markets would improve quickly, but to Jacob that was just the kind of manic thinking that had pushed the stock market to ridiculous heights before the crash. Every day he heard from customers their travails of lost jobs. Their need to buy on credit would multiply the multitude of people overextended. In reaction, other business owners he knew were rapidly cutting back their future inventory, which would shrink jobs. He'd lived through panics before. This one felt immense. People had drowned out the bad memories of war and flu deaths with a frenzy of spending and silly optimism, but now everyone looked frightened all at once. Nothing would change in a few months, he told Johanson. As for his reputation, he foresaw a slew of prominent businessmen being foreclosed on in the years to come. He would be in good company. Anyway, he said to himself, one stain on his reputation was a small price to pay for the bigger prize he sought, freeing himself from Joel and his henchmen.

"All right, Jacob. As long as you're sure. I'll get the bank's lawyer going on the papers," Olaf said, acceding to the instructions.

When formal foreclosure notices were served on Jacob a week later, he played the part of poor landowner set back by the national collapse so well, he almost fooled himself into believing he was facing ruin. Reacting as would a man shocked by misfortune, he loudly complained into the phone within earshot of a few employees that "the bankers are making a terrible mistake!"

Not even to Shira did he let on the details of the scheme he had devised. How his wife felt while he was apparently battling a financial catastrophe, he never asked. He did notice, during the months the foreclosure process dragged on, that when he came home after a day's work she tended to linger with him on the porch a little longer than in calmer times. And more often than usual she baked the sweets he enjoyed, her rugelach and the special chocolate babka.

He missed having his son by his side during those months. Lew was off recovering in the dry heat of the desert, where the doctors had sent him after the first onset of consumption. He knew his son had adhered to a monotonous discipline for the last eighteen months, bedrest on his back for hours at a time, days on end. It was the standard therapy for everyone in the colony of fellow sufferers. Lew was well cared for at the Tucson sanatorium, at least that's what he reported in letters home, always striking an upbeat tone. Still, Jacob had read accounts of the regimen demanded of TB sufferers. Always surrounded by fellow patients who might appear heading for recovery one day, succumbing to the white plague of the lungs the next. The occasional photo only added to Jacob's worries. One snapshot in particular nagged at him. Lew and three other men stood shoulder to shoulder, arms draped over each other as if they were college fraternity brothers. To his eyes these men, Lew included, were frighteningly gaunt and somber looking. Dressed in pajamas, they resembled prisoners more than patients. He'd hidden that photo before handing the envelope over to Shira the evening it arrived, glad that Lew had made no reference to it in his letter. No need to worry his wife even more at a time like this, he told himself.

Lacking Lew's assistance, Jacob carried out the next step in his grand plan himself. Shortly after receiving the first foreclosure notice, he dispatched a telegram to Goldstein: "Bank has called the note. Foreclosure process begun. Please advise." The next move will be theirs. Will they have the cash to pay off the loan and stay the foreclosure? Will they be willing to hire expensive lawyers and fight? He knew he would just have to wait and see. Patience has rewarded me with this opportunity, and remaining patient is what is needed now, he reminded himself.

Goldstein called him at the store first thing the next morning.

"Itzkowitz, this is terrible. If the bank forecloses, we lose everything we've invested in the venture. You've got to stop this. Don't you have influence with the banker?" Goldstein sounded distraught. He doesn't have a clue that the bank is really my agent, Jacob thought, a smile crossing his face.

"I've pushed and pushed, Goldstein," he responded, adopting his own tone of desperation. "The bank has its own problems. They've already given us, me, more time than they would anyone else. But they have eyes. They're scared of a run on the bank, like what's happening all over. They can't shell out good money after bad."

"We need time, Itzkowitz," Goldstein pleaded. "There are, uh, circumstances that make it impossible for Mr. Joel to advance more funds. You need to work something out."

"I'm doing my best," he replied, feeling rising resentment at Goldstein's belligerent tone, and making no effort to hide that emotion from infusing his voice. "Everyone's panicking these days. I can only do so much."

"You better figure something out," Goldstein said coldly. "Don't let us down, or it could go very badly for you."

He heard the click as Goldstein abruptly ended the conversation. He had learned what he needed to know. Joel's legal troubles had drained the South African's coffers, leaving his American henchmen with no money to deploy to salvage the situation. All Goldstein had were his usual not-so-veiled threats. Is he bluffing, Jacob wondered. He sat back, reached into his watch pocket, and mused, "I'll find out soon enough."

--

The legal process ground along. More papers were served, foreclosure notices appeared in newspaper ads, an auction date was announced. He heard almost nothing from Goldstein after that initial call, just one telegram weeks later: "Have you stopped it yet? Don't fail." Goldstein didn't even bother to sign it. He didn't need to, Jacob knew full well who was lurking in the shadows. There was no turning back at this point, he constantly reminded himself. *My path out from under Joel and his minions is for the foreclosure to go through and wipe them out of the picture. No one but me and Olaf will know that I own the loan the bank is foreclosing,* he told himself for the hundredth time. *If my luck holds, Joel will chalk this loss up to the depression falling over this country, and be too preoccupied with his other troubles to make trouble. And if my luck fails, well, I'll deal with that when the time comes.*

Pruning
Point Pleasant 1931

He thinks he's so clever, she muttered under her breath while trimming away dead rose branches. Like I wouldn't know what he's up to just because he never said it out loud. After all these years, I can read his face like a book. And I'm not stupid; the ledgers tell a story. Of course I figured out what he's planning with this foreclosure business. Still, thought Shira as she wielded her shears, normally I wouldn't care. Not if this were just another in his endless parade of deals. With the business he can do whatever he pleases. But not with my family, she said barely audibly, tensing her jaw as she scoured the plant for thin, weak shoots to snip away.

The whole entanglement sprouted from a seed planted years earlier. Her cousin Labe, like many other Moscowitzes, fled the old country a few years before Shira came to America. Labe ended up lodging with still another cousin down in Toms River. Like Jacob, Labe started his new life in a strange country earning his way as a peddler. For Labe, though, lacking funds for a horse and wagon, the peddler's life began the hard way, with a rucksack on his back. A plucky young man, Labe carried his burden with good humor. He earned the trust of customers, increased his sales, and saved enough over a few years for his own buggy. Selling from a wagon enabled him to establish a bigger territory, one that spanned across the state from the Atlantic Ocean to the Delaware River. Knowing first-hand the skill and determination necessary to thrive as a peddler, Labe always looked up to Jacob. His cousin's husband's success served as a model to emulate. A frequent guest at their Sunday dinners, Labe always steered the conversation so as to get Jacob doling out tidbits of commercial advice. It was obvious to Shira that Labe delighted in this rapport with Jacob, enabling him to feel like an equal, businessman to businessman. Naturally Labe looked on proudly when his teenage son Charlie took an interest in these commercial conversations that bored his other children to tears.

When Labe finally had saved enough to consider opening his own store, he still had a gap. To launch his five and dime, Labe needed a loan. Before one Sunday dinner, Labe ducked out of the conversation in the living room, slipping to the back of the house to find Shira at work in her kitchen.

"Dear Cousin, may I interrupt?" he began cheerfully.

"Labe, for you I always have time," she answered while continuing to chop onions.

"I wanted to let you know something," he said, a bit haltingly. "I am going to ask Jacob for a loan. Not a gift! I'll pay back every penny. A loan. For my store."

Shira had put down her knife, wiped her hands on her apron, turned and looked directly at her younger cousin. "Shouldn't you go to a bank?"

"Banks are run by *goniffs*. I trust my *mishpocha*."

"Are you sure? *Very* sure?" she asked.

Labe, hearing Shira's words but not appreciating her meaning, nodded. "Yes!" he said enthusiastically. "If he'll be generous enough to lend me the money, it will mean a lot to me."

"Ok, Labe, *gey gezunt.* See what Jacob says." As Labe exited, leaving her alone in the kitchen, Shira picked up her knife. "Generous, eh. That's my Jacob," she murmured, resuming slicing onions.

After dishes were cleared and the men sat together, Labe floated his proposition. Jacob reacted with a broad smile, nearly a grin. He appeared tickled by the request, perhaps delighting that a family member recognized he was a man of sufficient means to afford bankrolling others. There followed a few easy back and forths about interest rate, term and timing of payments. The necessary *hondling* over, they shook on the deal. Oh, Jacob had said, of course there needs to be collateral for it to be kosher. Of course, Labe had quickly replied, although he hadn't anticipated this level of formality. Good, Jacob had continued, my lawyer will send you the papers.

The loan to Labe became the first in a series Jacob made over the course of a decade to various family members. Once word got around through the *mishpocha* grapevine that Jacob was a source of ready cash, a tad more expensive than a bank but much more pleasant to deal with, others relatives popped up with requests large and small. Some were Itzkowitzes, some Moscowitzes, all with a need. Each time, Shira thought back to what she'd said to Labe in her kitchen. Should she have been clearer about her reservations? What if she'd forewarned Labe that Jacob has a hard side, especially when it comes to "business"? She knew in her bones that if Labe ran into trouble, he would get no leniency from Jacob, maybe even less than he'd get from a real banker. Her husband would never let himself feel taken advantage of by anyone, family or stranger. That's how Jacob would view any plea for debt forgiveness. Labe, she wondered, should I have discouraged you? You wouldn't have listened to me anyway. None of them would have listened, including eventually Charlie. Still, she could not help blaming her silence about that first loan to Labe as the cause of Charlie's inexorable ensnarement in Jacob's scheme.

All these thoughts nagged at her as the foreclosure auction drew near. She had worked out Jacob's plan for herself, and dreaded it. Charlie would find out eventually that he had been played for a fool. Jacob had been clever, she had to admit, beguiling young Charlie with the allure of being an insider on a deal with the big *macher* the young man so greatly admired. Charlie must have been flattered when Jacob had offered him a share in the hotel deal in exchange for Charlie signing over the deed to his land. That part was not difficult for her to figure out, as Shira recalled one Sunday dinner over pot roast Charlie boasting of buying his first parcel of real estate for a song and owning a piece of the oceanfront. Later she'd picked up from doing the books that Jacob was buying up beachfront parcels with money from the Joel syndicate. It was then she simply put two and two together.

At first she felt *naches* that Jacob was taking Charlie under his wing. Her pride was tinged by a realization that Jacob adopting Charlie into real estate ventures meant he didn't see their own son blessed with the same head for business. Then it dawned on Shira that Jacob might have something more devious in mind. He'd never stopped fuming about being beholden to Joel and his thugs. Not that

Jacob ever shared his plans plainly, that just wasn't his way. Instead she knew his mind from little slips here and there. Like that time those two goons showed up unannounced in one of their fancy touring cars, just as Jacob was absorbed in closing the bank loan to start hotel construction. That evening over dinner he'd complained in a foul mood "I'm sick of seeing those two", adding without prompting "but before too long I'll be rid of them." It wasn't clear to her then whether or not he had an actual plan to sever the connection, or was just chafing at their hold over him. What was clear was that she had been wrong to believe that over time he would reconcile with the arrangement.

Months earlier, though, while reviewing the company accounts, Shira noticed a large sum transferred to the bank without a clear purpose entered. That puzzled her. The store had already made its usual January bank loan pay-down from cash built up during the Christmas rush. A few days later, while looking on Jacob's home desktop for an invoice, Shira found Helman's letter with the news clipping enclosed. Her mind raced as she absorbed the significance of Joel incapacitated, facing financial ruin. How would Jacob react, she pondered. Shira carefully replaced the correspondence it in its exact location and said nothing. When a few weeks later Jacob warned her somberly that a rough patch was coming, that the bank was calling the hotel loan, she studied his face. He's trying to look upset, to appear anxious. Yet his eyes hint at anticipation, not fear, she noted. She instantly understood what Jacob wasn't telling her, that he'd secretly bought the mortgage loan. That explained the mysterious money transfer. The sudden aggressive action by the bank was actually her husband's doing, part of some grand scheme to free himself. She'd grasped that a foreclosure would not only terminate the corporation's ownership, wiping out Joel's investment; foreclosure would wipe out her cousin's stake as well.

Now as Shira trimmed back the thicket of thorny branches, each snap of the shears brought her closer to the moment when she could no longer put off making a choice. Deciphering Jacob's scheme was like receiving a letter likely bearing disturbing news. Her first impulse was to shove bad tidings into a drawer unread rather than confirm the worst. As the days went on, though, the injustice to her cousin loomed larger in her thoughts. Mentally she opened the drawer, slit open the envelope, and stared directly at the troubling options. If she said nothing, Charlie would be ruined, losing his investment due to the foreclosure, while Jacob would secretly come out the lone winner. Yet if she spoke up, she would be confronting Jacob with her knowledge of his subterfuge, essentially accusing her husband of swindling a family member. He would be enraged, and her bold move would be unlikely to change the outcome. Jacob, she knew, had come too far with his plot, was too close to ridding himself of Joel, to turn back now. Even if proceeding meant hurting Charlie.

Shira longed to talk to Chaya, her wise Aunt. Chaya had guided her at the most agonizing time in her life. Only Chaya knew the truth of her marriage. She alone would understand the enormity of Shira taking a step that threatened to undermine the life she had built. For the first twenty years after Shira had left Shavlan for a new life in America, Chaya remained an ocean away. Nevertheless, despite time and distance, Shira's closeness to Mumma Chaya had not diminished. To her joy, a few years back her Aunt had finally come to the United States, settling with cousins in Ocean County. Each time Shira made the pilgrimage to visit the now frail woman of nearly 80 she found solace. On her last visit, unburdening herself to Mumma Chaya, Shira shared the secret of her surreptitious gambling hobby and the deception she'd pulled off with Lew's aid. In typical fashion, Chaya relieved her of that guilt with a single sentence. "Nu, my lovely one, a wife who doesn't have secrets from her husband is a very dull wife."

Sadly, Chaya had died the year before. Remembering her Aunt revived the searing grief of the funeral. Chaya's passing was a double loss. Shira mourned Chaya the wonderful caring person herself, and also the breaking of the one link back to the most crucial moment of her youth. Churning over what step to take, Shira felt adrift. She cast about for who else to turn to, overwhelmed with loneliness. There was not another soul to whom she could bare her worries. As Shira struggled to push aside despair and refocus on pruning her roses, past conversations with the Garden Club ladies bubbled up to fill the void.

She recalled one gathering where Hazel Clayton held forth on a "situation" with her husband. "He was getting ready to fire a perfectly good woman. An employee who'd been with his business for years. Worse, he was going to replace her with some kid, the son of a golfing buddy. 'Why on earth would you do that?' I asked him during our cocktail hour. 'Well, the boy needs a start in his career. Anyway, she has a husband. He should provide for his family.' Well, ladies, I nearly clobbered him with the gin bottle, I was so mad. 'That woman has every right to make her own living!' I barked at him. I gave him an earful. It was the first time I ever stood up to Wendell about anything to do with the business. I could see he was burning mad, I was talking way out of my place. Still, I just stared him down. And you know what? Something got through his thick skull. In the end he didn't fire her. Instead, he took the boy on as a junior clerk. I'm sure it cost him a pretty penny to pay both, but he did it. Sometimes you just have to stand up to your man."

Shira teetered back and forth. At first she was sure Hazel was right, she should stand up for Charlie. Immediately she felt guilty, flipping to equal certainty that she wasn't like these rebellious young women, it was her duty as a wife to stand by her husband. She'd been taught from birth that family is family, your first loyalty is to *mishpocha*. But what if family turns on family? How do you choose sides? She had largely stood by Jacob when they first came to America and he quickly found reasons to feud with his sister and brother-in-law. Even then, she recalled, the pull of fondness for her new sister-in-law, her need for connection in a strange new country, had diluted her devotion to Jacob's hard stance. At least back in Tuckerton she could blur the lines of loyalty without her husband knowing. This would be different. Taking Charlie's side is outright defiance, a slap in the face to Jacob. She shuddered at the thought of his reaction, oblivious to what her hands were unconsciously doing until she pricked her finger on a thorn. The pain snapped her out of the haze. Sucking away the blood on her finger, she realized what she would do.

--

"Nu, so how does it work? With the bank?" she broached to Jacob as they sat side by side, settled into their customary porch rocking chairs. She kept her eyes focused on the challah cover she was embroidering for Esther, pretending just mild curiousity. Jacob did not answer at first, his attention seemingly rapt by an article in the Sunday paper.

"How does it work?" he said after a silence so long she'd begun to wonder if he'd heard her. "It's an auction. Friday."

"I know the date, and I know it's called an auction. That's not what I'm asking," she responded.

"So what are you asking?" Jacob turned a page.

"What actually happens. Who shows up at this auction. What do you do. Will those hooligans from Philadelphia be there. That sort of thing," she said, banishing vexation from her voice as much as she could control it.

"Why are you so curious all of a sudden?" Jacob looked over at her.

"What all of a sudden? This is a big deal, your big project. I just want to know how it all works. Anyway, I need to keep the books the right way. I need to understand what's going on, don't I?" she replied, meeting his gaze.

"I guess so," he said after a pause. "It's like this. Foreclosure auctions have become pretty routine since the crash. A bank officer shows up at the property, the borrower shows up, and whoever else plans to bid. Most of the time there are no other bidders. There's an auctioneer. He reads out the notice that's been published in the papers. Then he takes bids. Usually the auction itself is over pretty quickly."

"You mean anyone can just show up and bid on your property? Someone can just buy it for ten dollars?" She made herself sound shocked by this possibility, as if she did not know the answer to her question.

"The bank never lets that happen. If someone shows up and makes a lowball bid, the banker just puts in a higher bid. If the other guy bids again, the bank responds with a higher bid." Jacob spoke like a teacher lecturing a dull student.

"How high can the bidding go? Isn't the hotel property worth a lot?" she asked.

"Times like these, no one is sure what anything is worth. Sure, if things bounce back quickly and tourists come back to the shore, a hotel will be worth a lot. Right now jobs aren't coming back so fast. I was just reading in the paper what the President says about handouts the Congress wants to give. Hoover said, 'If we break down this sense of responsibility of individual generosity to individual and mutual self-help in the country in times of national difficulty ... we are faced with the abyss of reliance in future upon Government charity in some form or other.' He's right, we can't have a cure that's worse than the disease."

"That doesn't sound very charitable to me. Lots of people are hungry. We give money for *tzedakah* but that's not nearly enough to feed everyone who needs it," Shira said, unable to let his comment go, but wanting to get back on topic. "But I was asking about the bidding. What if someone comes along prepared to pay a lot for the hotel, and keeps outbidding the bank?"

"The banker will keep going higher until he gets the bidding up to the amount of money owed the bank. If there's a sucker out there with cash who wants to pay more than the full amount of the loan, the bank will let him win the bidding. But that never happens. At foreclosures the bank's always the highest bidder," Jacob replied. Then, seeming a bit nervous, as if a new thought had just occurred to him, he said, "I suppose if some speculator comes along and thinks he can make money buying a half-built hotel, he might outbid the bank. Not likely. It's too risky to take over a project in the middle. But I suppose it's possible."

"Well, what if it did happen. Who gets the money if the bids go sky high?"

Jacob sat back and thought for a moment. "Well, first the bank gets back everything owed, including interest and all costs of the auction. If the buyer pays more than all that combined, any extra money goes to the borrower."

"That would be a good thing, no? Someone else pays off the loan, you'd get out from under the bank and get some money out of it. Shouldn't you be looking for a speculator? Won't those *schlubs* from Philadelphia want that too?"

"I'm not worrying about those *mamzers* anymore," Jacob spat out. "They've had some setbacks lately. There's not much they can do. I don't even know if they'll show up."

"I thought they were dangerous, gangsters. How can you be so sure?"

"You're asking a lot of questions. I'm dealing with this, isn't that enough?" his voice was rising.

He must still be scared of them, she thought to herself. "This is all new to me. I just don't want to see anything bad happen to anyone."

"I'm not going to let anything bad happen, OK?" Jacob was still clearly annoyed, but her answer seemed to mollify him.

"I know you're not. You always take care of people," she said, putting her hand on his arm. "I still have a few questions about the whole foreclosure thing."

"Now what?" he said, this time sounding more like the pupil caught having not done his homework than the impatient teacher.

"Well, you told me what happens if someone comes and bids a lot. But what if no one but the bank shows up and bids?"

"Oh, right," said Jacob, sounding relieved. "That's most likely what will happen. Then the bank is the winning bidder. The auctioneer declares the bank the new owner."

"You're saying the bank has to pay out more money? Aren't they throwing good money after bad? Why would they do that?"

"The bank is not actually shelling out more money," Jacob replied, now comfortably back in his area of expertise. "Think of it as if the bank is wearing two hats, is if it is actually two different people. The bank is both the buyer of the property, and the seller of the property. Say the balance of the loan was ten dollars, but at the auction the bank's winning bid is only three dollars. The bank as seller sells the property for three dollars. But the bank as buyer doesn't pay in cash. Instead if pays the three dollars by writing off part of the debt. That is, on its books the bank gives the borrower credit for what it bid at the auction, in this case it reduces the loan by three dollars."

"Then what happens to the rest of the ten dollars that was owed? The seven dollar balance?" she asked, her head for numbers finding the flow of finances interesting.

"The original borrower has lost the mortgage property, but it still owes the bank the seven dollars. What happens next is up to the bank. The bank can sue the borrower and go after anything else the borrower owns," Jacob said, matter of factly.

"That's terrible, isn't it? The bank can come after you for the rest?" She put extra emphasis on 'come after', sounding aghast.

"Well, they could, but I don't think they will," Jacob answered, again calmly.

"You don't think they will?" she began, then paused. Shira took a breath. "Could that be because you're in control?"

"What do you mean, 'in control'?" Jacob again shifted his attention fully back to observing Shira's face.

"You paid the bank fifty thousand dollars a few months back. Did you think I wouldn't notice?" Her voice trembled slightly.

"You're spying on me?" Jacob pulled his arm away from her hand. "My wife is spying on me?"

"What are you talking about, spying!" she snapped back. "I do your books. I'm not deaf and dumb. You make the decisions, but I see what's going on. I'm entitled to know what you're up to, aren't I?"

"The bookkeeper doesn't talk to the boss like that!" the color had risen to the top of his bald head, his voice following.

"So that's what I am to you, just the bookkeeper?" Her cheeks reddened from a hurt more painful than a slap. She felt herself stumbling away from the path she'd intended to follow, as if possessed by a *dybbuk*.

"I didn't say that!" Jacob protested, seemingly struggling to regain composure.

"It sure sounded like that's what you meant," she plowed ahead. "Anyway, it's my money too you're gambling with, I have a right to know what's going on."

"'My money'?" Jacob looked at her the way he would look at a cat that had just asked him the time of day. "Since when is it your money?"

"Since I've been slaving away in the store for years and years. You never paid me a dime. I've earned that money ten times over." Her tone clearly startled Jacob as much as if she'd dumped a pitcher of ice water on his head. He looked directly at her, appearing more bewildered than offended.

Her mouth curled down, jaw clenched. "Don't try to fool me, Jacob. You've schemed to get the bank to foreclose. I know you secretly bought the loan yourself. That's how you're getting rid of Joel and his thugs. Good riddance to them. But somebody else is getting hurt by your very clever plan. Someone innocent. It's not right."

"What are you talking about? Who's getting hurt?" he asked.

All of a sudden Shira stood, pulled herself to her full five foot two inch height, and looked down on Jacob. "Have you forgotten Charlie, my cousin? That boy looks up to you, puts his trust in you. And you're ready to flush him down the toilet!"

Jacob's shoulders twitched at her mention of Charlie. He looked down at his hands, as if they would reveal some wisdom to him. When he looked up, she was glaring at him with fierceness, as if she were seeing Abraham about to sacrifice their son.

"No, I haven't forgotten Charlie. I've been losing sleep over what to do about him. I can't tell him the plan, I can't risk word getting around. I know he'll be crushed, it's his first big deal. He's going to lose his investment. But I'll make it up to him someday, I promise, I will," the pleading in his eyes even more desperate than the dejected tone of his voice.

For an instant, she found herself softening, seeing Jacob suffering his own internal turmoil over the crushing blow to Charlie. Maybe his conscience bothers him more than he ever lets on, she thought briefly. Then her empathy quickly dissolved as his attitude towards her came back to mind. He kept all this from me, thinks of me as just the bookkeeper. He deceived Charlie, treats him like a minor casualty in his war with the syndicate. Who knows what else he's not telling me. His actions speak louder than anything he says. He's not the man I thought he was. Or maybe not the man I wanted him to be.

Shira showed her back to Jacob, stepping towards the front door of the house. "Shira wait!" Jacob called after her, half command and half plea. "It's the only way. I've tried to think of another way to get us out from under those goons. Nothing else will work. I have to do this for the family!"

She wheeled around. "For the family? That's what you tell yourself?" Suddenly she spat on the porch, turned around slowly, and wordlessly disappeared into their house.

Upheaval
Point Pleasant 1938

"Look at this," Lew rattled the newspaper, anguish straining his voice. "On the front page of the Asbury Park Press. 'Nazis predicted today a restoration of the Ghetto for Jews under new restrictive decrees promised after the Thursday upsurge of anti-Jewish sentiment.'"

"They're animals," Jacob said with palpable disgust, wielding a spoon to attack a soft-boiled egg. "Hitler is worse than the Czar. And those fools in Europe, they're all too afraid to stand up to him."

"They're not afraid, Pop, they just don't care," Lew's hands were shaking from uncharacteristic rage. "They want to believe this will all just blow over. Listen to this: 'The Nazis are confident the new decrees will mark the final liquidation of the Jewish issue in Germany, and that there will be no more anti-Jewish outbreaks like those yesterday in which millions of dollars of damage was done in the smashing of Jewish store windows, the looting of shops and the burning of synagogues in a dozen cities.'"

"What did you expect?" Shira said through a rasping cough. "It gets worse and worse, and what do they do? They send Chamberlain to make deals with the devil."

Jacob scowled at Shira. "That's what I'm saying. Chamberlain is weak, the English are scared. Maybe it's a smart strategy, just buying time. Sometimes in negotiating you bide your time to get the upper hand."

"This isn't one of your business deals!" Shira snapped, returning Jacob's look with a piercing one of her own. "The longer they wait, the stronger that anti-Semite bastard gets."

"Well, maybe the Ghettos will help," Jacob said, renewing his assault on the egg. "Back in Russia, the more we stayed to ourselves, the less chance there was for some drunken peasant to start a fight."

"I can't believe you've gotten this old but turned this foolish," Shira said gruffly, pausing to catch her breath. "You think they're crowding Jews into Ghettos is doing us a favor? They're stealing our homes, our businesses. Those goniffs will strip us of everything before they're done."

Lew shifted uncomfortably in his chair. It was plain to him that his parents' relationship had soured while he was away in Arizona recovering. What must have triggered these ongoing hostilities, he wondered. She can hardly breathe, but she finds the strength to argue. And his father argues back, as if his wife were not wasting away in front of him.

It was bad enough that he'd returned from Tucson to find his mother racked by a deep, dry, lingering cough. Her spasms dredged up for Lew his own exposures to the waves of death that flow from failing lungs. He'd gone off to college in the fall of 1918, just as influenza, the invisible killer, was spreading across the country. Philadelphia had been particularly hard hit, with hundreds dying daily. Although his campus remained a relatively safe haven, he and his classmates had been terrified. Students were quarantined, fraternity houses were commandeered as field hospitals, and vigorous young people his age mysteriously sickened rapidly and died horribly. The epidemic burned out and faded away, but the scar of fear stayed with him.

Then a decade later in a cruel twist, having survived one plague unscathed, Lew's own lungs turned against him. It appeared as a seasonal cough, some fever, night sweats, symptoms common to a host of ailments. He felt weak at times, but that impairment ebbed and flowed. They consulted their usual physician, Dr. Karlsen. The genial general practitioner trundled up to Lew's bedroom, opened his black Gladstone bag, and performed the standard array of diagnostic devices: checking heartbeat and lungs with his stethoscope, poking into both ears with his otoscope, depressing Lew's tongue with his flat metal probe. Having cycled through his routine, Karlsen opined authoritatively that Lew had pneumonia. Time for bed rest and letting the malady just "run its course", the doctor intoned.

When the symptoms persisted many weeks and even worsened, his mother grew frightened. She'd marched to the physician's office and demanded he do more.

Karlsen returned to Lew's bedside and was aghast at how emaciated his patient had become. The doctor ordered serum therapy to begin immediately, injections with some sort of activated horse blood. When that therapy also failed to quell his symptoms, Karlsen finally realized he'd been grossly mistaken, having confused the ravages of tuberculosis with those of pneumonia. Knowing no drug that could cure the young man, Doc Karlsen prescribed the only available treatment of the day, advising his parents to send Lew immediately to a desert sanatorium. Fearful that so much time had already been wasted, within days Jacob and Shira had finalized all arrangements, shipping him off by train to the epicenter of recovery facilities in southern Arizona.

All during his convalescence, his parents' letters revealed no hint of strife at home. Yet strife there was. Sometimes the tension in the house was subtle, so veiled it was nearly impossible for him to discern if it were real or if he was imagining it. Today was more typical, when a topic which should have produced unity instead turned into a contest with points scored by finding fault. He was ready for a lighter topic.

"Pop, Mama, cousin Evelyn sends her regards," Lew tossed out casually.

"Evelyn was at the wedding?" Jacob asked, ignoring his wife's last comment.

"Yeah, she and Herbert ended up sitting next to me and Charlie. Evelyn had her usual 'I'm better than you' expression, and Herbert was pedantic as always," Lew replied. "But how they got there was actually the damnedest thing."

"What's that supposed to mean?" Shira cut in, still sounding peeved.

"Well, they seated me and Charlie together at a table with some other relatives. Next to me was a woman named Harriet. I was trying to place her, and then she reminded me that her grandfather is Moishe Mazaroff."

"Moishe? My Moishe?" Jacob said with interest.

"Exactly," he replied.

"You know we grew up together like brothers. After his mother died we took him in. I haven't talked to Moishe in ages. He got rich importing feathers, of all things," Jacob said.

"I remembered Moishe, Pop, as soon as she said his name," Lew said. "Anyway, Harriet and I got schmoozing away. Then another vaguely familiar couple sits across the table. I introduce myself, and they say they're Julius and Rebecca. I didn't catch the last name at first."

"Rebecca? My sister Pearl's daughter?"

"The very one, Pop. I haven't seen her since she was maybe ten. We chatted, then they turned towards Harriet. The same routine starts, nice to meet you, blah blah blah, bride's side or groom's? They're happily gabbing away, pulling on the family history thread. Suddenly it comes out that Harriet is descended from Mr. Ostrich Feathers and his wife Lottie. Rebecca turns white as a sheet, like she's seen a ghost. Harriet goes stony silent. I'm watching, not a damn clue what's going on," Lew said.

"What happened?"

"Rebecca whispers into Julius's ear, and suddenly both storm off in a huff. They march over to the bride's mother, obviously agitated, fingers pointing back at our table. Next thing I know, Rebecca and Julius are seated at the other end of the banquet hall, and Evelyn and Herbert are plunked down with us looking flustered."

"What was that all about?" Jacob asked, entranced.

"That's what I wanted to know! So I turned to Harriet and said 'What the hell was that all about?' At first she's reticent. But I wasn't going to let her get away without an explanation."

"Don't keep me in suspense," Jacob chided.

"Here's what she tells me. You remember that about fifteen years ago Moishe sold his store in Barnegat to Aunt Pearl and her husband Myron?" Lew paused.

"Sure," replied Jacob. "After the war Moishe was heavy into the ostrich feather business, spending lots of time in New York. You know he got the idea from one of the South African mishpocha who was getting rich exporting ostrich feathers to London. Moishe was clever, he figured out that fashions here follow London. So he persuaded the cousin in Cape Town to make him Northeast distributor for their plumes. I was surprised, though. Moishe always was smart, but never that ambitious."

"To listen to Harriet, Lottie was the ambitious one, always pushing Moishe," Lew interjected. "Her dream was to be the wife of a rich man. Moishe was a softie, but Lottie drove him to make a killing in ostrich feathers."

"What does this have to do with Rebecca?" Jacob asked impatiently.

"I'm getting to that. It was Lottie who demanded that Moishe sell the Barnegat business. She couldn't stand being a shopkeeper, she wanted a fancy New York life. That's why Moishe made the deal to sell the store to his cousin and take Lottie to New York."

"That's the last time I spoke to him, when they moved to a fancy building in Manhattan," Jacob interrupted.

"Sounds like Moishe, being a mensch, must have given Pearl and Myron a good price. Anyway, in New York Moishe becomes even richer and Lottie spends her way into fancy society. A few years go by, and Lottie begins to become 'strange'. That's the word Harriet uses about her grandmother. She remembers visiting Bubbie Lottie and hearing her grandmother rambling on about people out to steal from her. Seems Lottie got into her head that Pearl and Myron swindled her Moishie."

"My sister Pearl would never cheat Moishe!" Jacob protested.

"Of course not. But Lottie just raved that she'd get revenge."

"Did she actually do something?" Jacob asked.

"Oh, in grand style. Next thing you know, Lottie has their chauffeur drive her to Barnegat in their big silver roadster. She scouts the tiny main street, sees a vacant storefront, tracks down the owner, and that very day buys a building a block down from Pearl and Myron's store."

"That's meshugenneh!" Jacob looked aghast.

"It's just the beginning. Next she heads up to Waretown and visits a guy named Rebscher who owns a general store. Knew him from back when she and Moishe ran their shop. Lottie makes the guy an incredible offer – free rent for five years if he opens up a satellite store in her Barnegat building. Rebscher's job is to undercut Pearl and Myron and drive them out of business!"

"Did she – did it work?" Jacob asked tentatively.

"At first her scheme worked well. You know, it's a small town, there isn't room for two stores selling pretty much the same goods. Pearl and Myron lost lots of customers, it looked like they might go under. Then little by little, things swing back in their favor. Turns out not too long after Lottie made this deal, Rebscher's wife left him for another man. Rebscher takes to drinking, ignores the Barnegat operation. Eventually the guy simply disappears."

"Serves Lottie right!" Jacob said with glee.

"The good news is Pearl and Myron got their customers back. Harriet told me that she rode by Lottie's building a few years ago and it was still abandoned, with a bunch of mannequins in 1920s fashions still in the display windows."

"I can't believe Lottie did that. Pearl and Myron! They did nothing wrong to her. How could someone be so rotten to their own family?" Jacob said.

Shira, who'd been listening intently, began coughing loudly. Lew took note of a strange, almost malicious expression on her face.

Lew fell silent as he watched his mother spasming to bring air to her failing lungs. When Shira's dry cough had begun last year and persisted, he thought back to his own misdiagnosis. He'd been the one to brush aside her protestations that "it was nothing", insisting that she bypass Doc Karlsen and consult experts at the University Hospital. A phalanx of doctors had poked and prodded her before coming to their common verdict: Shira was dying of lung cancer. They pronounced this sentence with certainty and finality. They were sorry. They had nothing to offer, no reprieve, no hope. When pressed for details, they were vague. She had a year, maybe two. If pain became severe, they could offer her options to ease it. Her condition had no cure. They told her she was part of what seemed like an epidemic, a statistic that offered no solace. Other doctors around the country were reporting an uptick in lung cancers. There was no obvious common cause, nothing that would lead to a vaccine or a miracle drug on the horizon. She should rest as comfortably as possible, and get her affairs in order, was all they could prescribe.

Yet there his mother sat, doing anything but resting. Instead, she seemed to him determined to do just the opposite, quarreling more and more with his father. And his father, in turn, struck Lew as acting oblivious to his mother's fate. It's as if the closer she gets to death, the more they pretend nothing out of the ordinary is happening. Meanwhile, the ordinary has a bitter tinge to it.

He felt unmoored by the ebb and flow of anger in his house. Growing up, he'd perceived his parents as an old fashioned couple. Their manner of marriage was not unlike that of the parents of many of his friends, those born in the last century and raised under harsher conditions than Lew and his generation. Husbands and wives of that vintage showed few signs of adoration and love, instead relating to each other more like a well-matched team. Each spouse had an assigned role; when such marriages were working well both team members were yoked and pulling in the same direction. Throughout his youth, Lew's sense of the matter was that his parents regarded each other with mutual respect and some degree of affection, occasionally displaying playfulness in a word or a touch. Now as an adult back in his childhood home after a considerable absence, he was witnessing a vastly different dynamic. He questioned whether his youthful perception of their marriage had been just the naive perspective of a child, or if the bond between wife and husband had indeed only recently become badly frayed. Was he seeing the inevitable disintegration of any relationship when the union is built without the proper foundation?

Preparations
Point Pleasant 1939

Where am I, she wondered as she floated up to wakefulness. Blinking, she scanned the small room, confused. Hadn't she just been home in Shavlan, talking to her mother? Her mother? As Shira's mind began to clear, she became agitated. This makes no sense, she scolded herself. How could I be talking to *Mamme,* she died when I was twelve? Still, it had been so vivid. Closing her eyes, she revived the scene. A smile came to her pale lips. She saw herself next to her mother by the fire, sewing together a dress for some upcoming occasion. Her *Mamme's* voice is soothing, like the warm milk with honey she gives to ward off chest colds. Yet although she strained to do so, Shira could not retrieve their words, only the feeling of being suffused with peace.

A sharp pain in her side sliced through the reverie. Her momentary peace was shattered as she reawakened to the relentless reality of her waning days. She heard herself wheezing, gasping for full breaths that never quite came as her mind reabsorbed the truth. She lay in the same bed, in the same bedroom, in the same house, she had barely left for months. They had moved her to the little bedroom on the north side of the house, where the light was diffuse, never too bright to bother her eyes or disturb her day-time dozing. No carpet covered the wide pine flooring in this room. The doctors had them remove fabrics to avoid capturing dust that might irritate her fragile lungs. The formerly bare walls of what was normally a spare bed-room were now hung with cheerful nature paintings. Shira had requested pastorals to adorn the room when she was moved in to the chamber. At first the naturalistic scenes prompted her mind to roam around in the rural beauty that had always lain just outside of the towns she'd inhab-ited. Lately these landscapes taunted her, reminding her of fields and forests in which she would never again walk.

As she wrestled with retrieving a picture of her moth-er's face, other long gone relatives flitted at the edge of awareness, more sensations than image. There was *Feter* and Chaya, her childhood friend Channah, and that *yeshi-va bucher*, handsome Eliyahu. She had not thought of him in years, at least not for more than a fleeting instant here and there. Now that he had returned to her, she could not shake free of wondering. What had Eliyahu become? Was he a Rabbi? Had he married? Children? Did he ever think of her? What if he knew he had a daughter in America?

Her Ann. Her first born, the eldest. Her precocious child, an early reader always with her nose in a book. The musical one, who played piano effortlessly and lyr-ically with barely a lesson. They had seen little of Ann in the years after she married Marvin. The young couple moved fifteen miles south to where her ambitious husband founded his furniture store. Furniture was sold mostly on weekends, so the pair rarely came to Sunday dinners in the early years of their business. Then Ann gave birth to Evelyn, followed two years later by Janice. Asserting that raising two little ones took up all her time, Ann begged off making the hour's drive despite Shira's repeated invitations. Finally, when the girls got a little older, Ann relented, dropping by with the grandchildren now and then. Every rare visit was a special delight for Shira. Years earlier Shira had insisted to Jacob that they must keep their old piano in the front parlor, even though neither of them played. As a child Ann had spent hours daily calling forth rich tones from that upright, crafted with quarter-sawn oak panels and Tiffany-like lamps topping posts at each end of the keyboard. Jacob, always on the lookout for a bargain, had bought it for a pittance from a funeral parlor operator who was relocating his business. The delight of reuniting with her childhood piano helped lure Ann to visit more often. A routine developed, with Ann taking to the piano bench to play pieces from memory while Shira schooled her Evelyn and Janice in one old country recipe or another.

Thinking of Ann pushed away the physical pain while bringing on a pang in Shira's heart. She had never told Ann the truth. Of course not, she told herself. Ann might be grown, a mother herself, but she's still my child. Ann didn't need to know, she repeated to herself for the thousandth time. It could only cause strife. Would Ann hate her if she knew? Would Ann change how she felt about Jacob? Pull away, stop loving him as her father? She knew in her soul she'd done the right thing, keeping the secret. To do otherwise would have been foolish, as misguided as bringing the evil eye on yourself. Even so, doing the right thing can gnaw at you. Not with any immediacy, not every day, but the gnawing persists, deeply and silently. Years, sometimes decades, had slipped by for her with barely a moment's anguish about whether to reveal the secret, but the anguish always returned. Now the luxury of oblivion was running up against the hard reality of her lungs. Would she die deceiving her flesh and blood? She swallowed, took another gulp of air, and resolved to unburden herself.

Slowly, struggling, Shira propped herself up on pillows, then reached for the writing board she kept on her side table. Methodically opening the cherrywood top hatch and slipping out two sheets of paper and a carbon, she took up her pen. Shira hesitated, bit her lip, and began to write.

My dearest daughter Ann,

As I think back on the happiest moments of my life, the first image that springs to mind is holding you as a newborn infant. You are special to me in so many ways. When I close my eyes, I see you as a little girl eagerly acting the mature big sister to Esther and Lewis. I hear your lovely fingers creating magical music on the piano in the parlor. I kvell as you walk across the stage to get your high school diploma, first in your class. Thinking of you growing up gives me joy.

Other thoughts also come to mind. Now that the cancer is eating away at me I do not have long to live. I need to tell you something that I have not shared with anyone. I cannot bring myself to talk about this out loud or face to face with you, so instead I am writing this down as I near the end.

What I am about to tell you may be a shock. But it will not change anything that really matters. You are our daughter in every way and Papa has never thought of you as anything but his daughter. My darling Ann, the truth however is that your actual father is a boy I knew many many years ago, back in the village. He was a special boy, very learned. He probably became a highly respected Rabbi. I cannot say that I truly loved him. I was just a girl. But I thought I did and that's where I made a mistake. Only not a mistake, because out of those feelings for him came you, my very special firstborn.

As far as Papa knows, you are his special firstborn too. He knows nothing of the boy. There was no reason to tell him. I know telling him could not change his love for you my child, but it might hurt him. So I will meet Ha-Shem without telling him. But I could not leave this earth without letting you know the truth. I hope it will not hurt you or change how you feel about me or about Papa. As for the boy, do not try to look for him. I thought about him from time to time in the years since. If he lives, he surely has a life long gone from me and our moments together. You will not be able to know him, because our homeland is now ruled by Stalin, the new Czar.

I am sorry I am not strong enough to tell you this face to face. Now that you are a mother, maybe you will understand how much we long to be perfect for our children. I was not a perfect woman, not a perfect mother. But writing this letter to you, it gives me peace.

With all my love,

Mama'

Through tears she read over her confession. She scratched out a word here, added a word there. Finally satisfied, she took out two envelopes, put the original letter in one and wrote her daughter's name on the outside. The other, the copy, she put in the second envelope. She then sealed both and slid them under her pillow for safekeeping. Laying back, exhausted by effort, she pondered a practical dilemma: How to pass her letter to Ann? She could not just leave instructions for someone else to deliver an envelope upon her death, that would cause too much curiosity. Drifting in and out half in a daze, a solution came to her. Ann is the oldest and has two daughters. Esther is pregnant, but so far only has her boy Norman. Esther will understand that it is only natural for Ann and her daughters to inherit most of my jewelry. I'll put aside one special item for Esther, maybe my mother's ring, so she isn't too hurt, she decided.

The next morning, when Lew came in with breakfast, she told him to haul to her room the small wooden crate in which she kept her "souvenirs", along with her jewelry box. Lew looked surprised, as for months his mother had not worn any jewelry other than her wedding band. "I just want to have a look," she told him. Lew complied, depositing both next to her bed before leaving for work.

When she was sure she was quite alone in the house, Shira took out a key from her side table drawer. With an audible click of the tumbler, she opened her souvenir crate. Rummaging inside, she lifted up a tattered book she'd brought with her from Shavlan. In its vacated space she carefully placed the envelope containing the copy, then set the small volume back in its spot, covering the envelope. When the crate was relocked, her attention turned to a sky blue jewelry box with gold filigree decoration. Flipping open the solid lid, she removed the top inset, with three distinct compartments for separating earrings, rings, and charms. "Charms", she half-smiled upon seeing the label, sardonically musing "if only I had some charms with the power to cure me".

Below the inset was a bottom cavity for larger pieces, such as her tortoise shell comb. Wistfully she took note of how minimal was her collection of treasures. Just the few earrings she'd tucked away before leaving Shavlan, some silver and turquoise pieces Lew had brought from the southwest as gifts, her mother's silver ring (the one she never wore so as to keep it safe), and one simple but elegant pearl necklace from Jacob on their twenty-fifth anniversary. Removing her mother's ring to set it aside for Esther, she pushed the other trinkets to one side, delicately laid the envelope on the red velvet lining, then arrayed the assorted pieces to cover the stationery. Replacing the top inset, she firmly closed the lid and closed her eyes. No turning back now, she said to herself, as she placed the casket-shaped container on her side table.

That evening, following his mother's instructions, Lew returned the crate to the attic. The jewelry box he placed on his mother's dressing table in the master bedroom. There it sat untouched for three months, until after the reading of Shira's last will and testament. Then Lew delivered it to his eldest sister, as his mother had specified.

The Fiancé
Point Pleasant 1944

The table was set for seven. He'd chosen his favorite private room for the occasion, the one with floor to ceiling windows closest to the river. The Ved Elva boasted a dozen such rooms where one could cut a business deal, dine discreetly with a lover, or celebrate a milestone. An inn of one sort or another had occupied its verdant location for nearly a century, the last incarnation falling into disrepair during the Great War. Then a Norwegian immigrant chanced upon the ruin. Struck by the stunning wooded setting that reminded him of home, Abrahamsen bought it for a song and set about restoring its grandeur. The Norwegian had also chosen the foreign but apt name for the stately resort at the water's edge. Business was booming, as prosperous businesspeople considered its restaurant the premier dining spot in the area. The food, however, was not why Jacob frequently chose it for special meals. Rather the view overlooking the bend in the river was what brought him back time after time. A vista of a slow-moving river with lush vegetation along its banks evoked in him warm childhood feelings for reasons he could not quite articulate.

Besides, he thought, sitting alone waiting for the others, meeting Lew's girl over Sunday dinner at the house would not feel right. If Shira were alive it would be different. She loved to have *die ganze mishpocha* in her house once a week, all the grandchildren plus nieces and the nephew gathered around. He relished presiding over those occasions from his armchair at the head of their long mahogany table. He took pride that his offspring followed the fifth commandment, honoring their father and mother with their weekly presence together. The ritual set them apart from some of the other Jewish families in town. Take Gottfried for example. The son fell out with the father years ago. Probably over money, he assumed, it always is. The Gottfrieds weren't on speaking terms for years, he'd heard. How could a child turn his back on a parent like the wicked son in the Haggadah, he wondered.

Closing his eyes, he pictured Shira in her kitchen creating her distinctive mix of old country *tzimmes* with conventional American meat loaf. She did not fancy herself much of a baker, but the extended family always made short work of her babka, to which she added a heavy dose of cinnamon. He remembered her joy seeing them all, especially the younger ones, devouring her cooking. How many times had she declared, "I don't go around saying 'I love you' to *der kinderlach*, I cook for them. Food is love." Judging by the vast amounts typical of her Sunday dinners, Shira was fond of showering immense quantities of love on the family.

Now she's four years gone, leaving me and Lew to fend for ourselves. The Sunday dinner rituals had dwindled, he recalled wistfully. During the first months after Shira's passing, we adopted a bachelors' routine, cooking for each other. One or the other could fry an egg well enough in the morning, or roast a chicken for dinner, but there was little variety to the repertoire. Neither showed any inclination towards learning new menus. Sunday gatherings involved largely store-bought items, anything they could simply re-heat. The grandchildren, already saddened by the loss of their *bubbeh*, could taste the absence of a loving hand in the kitchen and begged their parents to skip the increasingly somber meal. More and more over the past two years it was just he and Lew of a Sunday evening, with the occasional sibling or cousin dropping by.

Then one day Lew returned from his typical long winter vacation out west and announced unceremoniously that he'd found a bride. At first he thought Lew was joking. After all, Lew had only been gone two months. How could he have found a girl to marry in eight weeks? But Lew wasn't joking, leaving him wondering about the bride-to-be. What kind of girl would agree to marry a middle-aged bachelor in such a short time? Was she a gold digger? Was something wrong with her? He'd interrogated Lew, asking every question he could think of to try to understand why his son would be leaving him. "I'm not leaving you, Pop. Toots will move in with us. I told her all about you," Lew had reassured him.

Tonight he would finally meet this girl. Lew had dropped him at the restaurant before heading back to meet the fiancée's train when it arrived from Penn Station. That gave him solitary time to position himself at the head of the table and ruminate. From his perch he could enjoy the dance of the gulls over the river, circling around each other until one would dive. Just as the intrepid gull emerged with a fish in its beak, it was surrounded by several of its kin jostling to tear away a hunk for themselves. Birds and people are not so different, he observed, as this competition for dominance repeated itself over and over.

His contemplation of nature was interrupted by the arrival of Esther and Bernie. "Hello, Pop," Esther said, planting a dry kiss on her father's cheek. "Pop," added Bernie, offering a brief handshake to his father-in-law. The pair sat down to Jacob's right.

Esther had married Bernie Mettler in the early 20s, a year after each graduated college. Back then Bernie was making a go of it as an artist: a painter and sculptor. He was talented enough to be hired on by a graphic designer in New Brunswick, and paid enough to cover their rent. The day job left him free to pursue his own more avant-garde creations nights and weekends. Esther, with her sharp mind and love of art, thrived on Bernie's entrée to the creative community. With a practical side instilled by her upbringing, Esther supplemented household earnings through freelance editing at the nearby university. The newlyweds were happy living independently of the center of family gravity. Bernie sensed that his free-spirited passion for the bohemian life might not flourish in the orbit of his decidedly bourgeois father-in-law. Esther too was pleased by their choice of lifestyle. She'd always felt stifled growing up in Point Pleasant, where the most absorbing topic of conversation among locals centered on how well the summer season would enrich their coffers in any given year. As the middle child she'd chafed at the sibling competition for their father's affections, wedged between her strong-willed older sister and her baby-of-the-family younger brother. New Brunswick was just far enough away, or just close enough, to Pop's home as it needed to be.

Then came Black Thursday's stock market roller coaster, the downward economic spiral, and the slide into Depression. National turmoil crashed against their independent life, upending the joy they felt when their first-born Norman arrived. Esther and Bernie limped along, scraping together enough for rent and food and baby necessities for another eighteen months. Eventually it became clear that their options were limited. Swallowing their pride, unsure of what reception they would get, they drove down to Jacob and Shira's house to join in one of the Sunday family gatherings. To Esther's relief, that particular Sunday only brother Lew was in attendance. After dinner she stole a few minutes alone with her father, while Bernie entertained their toddler with Uncle Lew. Jacob had anticipated their reason for coming – "It's not like you two drop in all the time for the good food" he'd remarked when she finished unburdening herself. To her apparent surprise, he was pleased that they were ready to come work for him. She couldn't know that he'd been dwelling on his own reversal of fortunes. The ripple effects of the crash were hardly as dire for him as that facing the young couple, but he'd realized he needed to cut back on store payroll. Welcoming Esther and Bernie as workers in exchange for room and board would save him money, he calculated. The new arrangements worked well for all involved. The young couple and their child moved into his house the next week.

Once they'd settled into the life of shopkeepers that the younger Bernie had fought so desperately to avoid, the new routine soon became familiar. Over time the familiar became normal. Before long they'd become fixtures in the family business, attuned to the rhythms of commerce as if born with natural mercantile talent. Jacob and Lew schooled them in all aspects of the dry goods sector. After Shira's demise, he'd begun retiring from overseeing the day-to-day decisions, creating a void which allowed the Mettlers to evolve into partners with Lew in running the store. They were partners, however, only in a sense: He still owned the great majority of stock in the enterprise, and had no intention of turning his stock over any time soon. Happily for Esther and Bernie, over time business had improved enough to pay them each decent salaries. Increasing prosperity enabled the couple to buy their own three-bedroom house on a lovely street for their family, which had grown in the interim to give Norman a younger sister Shirley.

Hearing Esther's greeting, he shifted attention from seagulls fighting over scraps to his daughter. "How are the children?" he asked.

"Good, good. Norman just won a math prize. Top one percent in the state," Esther said with evident pride.

"Math, yes. I could only do simple figures in my head, but he gets it from your mother, rest her soul. She had a mind for math. It will help Norman when he goes into the business," he said.

Esther flashed a brief, knowing smile at Bernie, then turned back to her father.

"College, Pop. After Norman graduates he'll go to college."

"Sure, sure. Just like you and the others, children in this country go to college to get educated. Then what?"

"You're right, Pop," Bernie spoke up. "Norman should go into the business. You've taught him a lot over the years. He'll be ready when the time comes. It's just…."

"Just what? He's got some notion in his head?" Jacob was drumming his fingers on the table.

"No, nothing like that," Esther cut back in. "We just, well, Lew has no kids and Ann is off with Marv running their own store. But with Lew now getting married…"

"So he's getting married. What's that got to do with anything? We haven't even met this girl."

As he finished this remark, another couple entered the room.

"Pop, sorry we're late! The bridge was up over the canal. Who expects boat traffic this time of year? It took forever for this charming little schooner to pass through." The woman was practically breathless by the time she took a pause. Leaning down, she gave her father a hearty hug. "You look great, Pop!"

"Channah, come, sit next to me," he said, smiling broadly as he called her by her Hebrew name. "Marvin, you too!"

His mood brightened when Ann stepped through the door, husband Marvin in tow. Ann was taller than her sister by several inches, yielding a look more like a model than a matron. She dressed the part, too, bedecked in a floral print dress. Her hourglass shape accented a trim figure, a point of pride as she neared fifty. Ann had always been popular among classmates, particularly at Trenton Normal School. That's where a handsome Marvin Friedman had spotted her one Saturday evening when his gaggle of Rutgers lads had dropped down for one of the regular socials hosted by the sororities. A war veteran, Marvin was several years older than many of his companions and carried himself with a brash air that caught Ann's eye. By the end of the evening neither was dancing with anyone else. Their romance continued all semester, until Marvin finally popped the question. "First I'll finish college," Ann had answered, "and then we can be married."

True to her word, Ann wedded Marvin a year later, swapping her cap and gown on a Tuesday for a bridal gown the following Sunday. At her insistence they moved back to the shore to be near her family. Putting her teaching diploma to good use she found an elementary school position in nearby Bay Head, while Marvin had a notion to start his own business. "I want to be my own boss, like your dad" he was fond of telling Ann. But with a recession gripping the country after the war, Marvin settled for earning a living with his labor. Jacob had offered work in the department store – with his planned expansion he thought his capable son-in-law might be a good addition. But Marvin was elusive, taking instead a job as a furniture mover and telling him that manual labor better suited his inclination towards keeping his muscles taut. Jacob had been miffed at first, thinking his new son-in-law ungrateful. Over time his attitude morphed into a grudging admiration. When Ann and Marvin came around for Sunday dinners, he became cognizant that Marvin was not just hauling around other people's possessions, he was studying the furniture industry. Marvin would hold forth about marketing and product quality. It became clear that Marvin had decided his future lay in that arena. When Marvin's boss took ill a few years later and needed to retire, Jacob floated his son-in-law a loan to buy the furniture store. I have to hand it to him, he thought while greeting Marvin, the kid had gumption: On his own the young man had built a nice little operation for his family.

"Pop, you look good!" Ann said as she sat. "Esther, Bernie, so do you."

"Nice dress, Ann," Esther commented, plucking a Parker House roll from the heaping basket in the center of the table.

"Thanks Sis. Just a little something Marv picked up on his last New York buying trip," Ann replied with a pert grin. "When will Lew and his girl get here?"

Before Esther could answer, Lew stepped through the doorway with a woman on his arm. All heads turned, assessing the newcomer with laser-like intensity. Most obvious was that she was at least an inch taller than Lew, even wearing low heeled shoes. Her peplum suit was a muted coral, flaring at the hip and accentuating her long legs. Dark voluminous hair curled tightly down her neck nearly to her shoulders, a hint of victory rolls on top. Something of a taut smile spread across the Mediterranean complexion of her face, her eyes darting brightly around the table to take in each of the guests. On her left wrist she sported a silver bracelet with large turquoise inset stones. She's quite striking, Jacob judged, having given Lew's fiancée an appraising look. Lew's pictures didn't do her justice.

"Everybody, meet Ruth Fisher!" Lew announced with a flourish. "Actually, only her mother calls her Ruth. She's Toots!"

Ann leapt up and hurried over, wrapping Toots in a hug. Marvin followed, offering her a hearty handshake. "Great to meet you, Toots!" the pair said, almost in unison. "Likewise, I've been looking forward to it!" Toots replied, her face relaxing.

Esther and Bernie strolled over with more reserve. Esther ventured a polite peck on the cheek, Bernie lightly brushing Toots' arm in greeting. "Welcome to the Itzkowitzes," Esther said in a monotone.

"Thank you, very happy to meet everyone," Toots responded quickly, her voice a touch gravelly.

"I love your suit," Ann said. "Very stylish."

"Oh, thanks. It's been in my closet from when I worked in Washington," Toots answered a touch sheepishly.

"Yes, bold choice," Esther chimed in, affectless. Toots shifted her gaze to Esther, looking perplexed as she pursed her lips. Before Toots could formulate a reply, Jacob stood up and caught Lew's eye.

As if summoned to the throne, Lew immediately stepped into the scrum hovering around his betrothed, gently took Toots' arm and led her over to his father.

"Pop, here she is. This is the girl I'm going to marry. Meet Toots!" Lew beamed.

Jacob reached out two hands, taking the young woman's right hand just as she was awkwardly starting to lean forward, seemingly expecting a hug. Toots wobbled a fraction of a second, regaining her balance as he pumped her hand between his. "So lovely to meet you, Lew has told me so much about you," Toots said.

"Sit down, sit down, let's get to know you." He released and dropped back into his seat. Lew and Toots reversed course, slipping into the two remaining chairs at the opposite end of the table. Toots reached for her water glass. A short silence hung in the air.

"So, I hear your parents are like me, from the old country," he declared, more like he was repeating something he'd read in the newspaper than posing a question.

"Yes, that's right. From Poland, or what's now Poland but used to be Russia. They met here, in New York."

"I came from Russia. For a while it was Lithuania. Now its Russia again, only they call it the Soviet Union under that murderer Stalin. We're all lucky, your parents, me, anyone who got out before it all turned horrible. Some of our family were not so lucky," he said, melancholy tinging his voice. "But enough of that. Tell me about them. What do they do?"

"Pop, I told you all that," Lew interjected.

"Let the girl talk, Lew!"

Toots looked back and forth between son and father. "My parents? They work hard," she began. "Papa's a bookbinder, he does beautiful work. Mama takes in laundry. She turned my older sister's bedroom into a whole little operation after Bessie moved out."

"They work with their hands, charming," Esther commented. "Are they active in the labor movement?"

Toots stole a quick glance at Lew. "Uh, I wouldn't say active. Papa belongs to the bookbinders' union."

"The unions will kill this country if they don't wise up," Jacob interjected. "One of our shopgirls started talking up the unions a while back. I put a stop to it."

Toots folded her hands in her lap, then said deliberately, "Well Papa says that without the union he'd have ended up in the poor house. They helped him put food on our table."

Lew spoke up. "It's different in New York, Pop."

"Yes, New York is different," Esther broke in, picking off a hunk of a roll while looking in Toots' direction.

"Laboring with your hands is honest work," Marvin commented. "That's how I got started. It taught me a lot."

"Sure, now you own the business," Jacob said. "You're your own boss, nobody gives you orders."

"Pop, I've got different bosses. I answer to customers, creditors, and an employee committee. You always have someone giving you orders," Marvin replied mildly.

Esther ignored Marvin's observations, turning hawk-like back to the woman beside her brother. "Toots, we'd like to hear a little more about you. Tell us what you studied."

"Studied?" Toots repeated, pausing a beat. "Well, I always liked history in school, I was curious about where Mama and Papa came from, and why there are wars all the time. That was before the War had started, but everyone could see that Hitler was just biding his time. Mainly I stuck with practical courses like typing and stenography."

"History, interesting. What about in college, Toots?" Esther asked.

"I, uh, didn't get to college. My little sister came down with asthma and we needed money for her treatments, so I went to work. Then the war broke out and I landed a good job in Washington. As a secretary for the War Department," Toots said, glancing again at Lew.

"That was very patriotic of you," said Esther. "Unfortunate that it interrupted your studies, I suppose."

Lew put a hand on Toots' arm. "Toots is a real reader. She's probably read more history books than all of us put together. This girl could teach a college level history course better than some of my old professors," he said cheerfully, staring directly at his middle sister. Toots blushed.

"Well there's not much call for history professors in Point Pleasant, I'm afraid," Esther replied. "Most everybody seems focused on the future, and getting back to normal after the war."

Ann leaned forward. "I think it's just swell that you helped the war effort, Toots," she said earnestly. "Everybody sacrificed in some way. We had to deal with price controls in our business, that wasn't easy. But you — you did more than your part. Everyone, let's have a toast to welcome Toots!"

"A toast, good idea," said Lew, beckoning over a waiter who had been hovering near the door. "What will everyone have?"

The waiter circled the table, taking orders. When he reached Toots, she replied "Vodka and orange juice." The waiter looked quizzically at her, echoing what he'd heard "Awrange?"

Lew chuckled, saying to the waiter, "Orange juice with her vodka." "Ah," nodded the waiter, departing to fetch the drinks.

"Lew, you're going to be her translator around here," Esther commented.

Toots bit her lip. "I need to visit the powder room while he's getting our drinks." She stood up abruptly.

After Toots was safely out of the room, Lew turned to Esther. "You could be a little more welcoming," he said in a manner that mixed imploring with scolding.

"I'm doing plenty of welcoming. I'm talking to her more than anyone else."

"Talking or quizzing?"

"Someone needs to get the conversation going. You haven't told us much about her. How was I supposed to know that she'd never gone on to college?" Esther took up her fork and began picking at her salad.

"Oh ease up, Esther," Ann said, sounding irritated. "You always want to be the queen bee. You can't stand it now that a young and pretty girl is joining the hive."

Esther glared at her older sister. "I've been perfectly welcoming to the New Yorker, even if she does wear out-of-date styles. If Lew wants to marry someone half his age with a funny accent, that's his business."

"Hey, wait a minute," Lew wagged his finger at Esther. "She's not half my age, and I like the way she talks."

Toots appeared in the doorway then came to an abrupt halt, scanning faces. Smiles suddenly spread on six mouths, and Jacob spoke up. "Come back in, Toots. We are ready for that toast."

Shiva
Point Pleasant 1977

"Want to suck a duck? I made it the way you like it."

Toots stood squarely in the porch doorway, silhouetted against the bright overhead lights of the family room, bedecked in a floral print house-dress and hospital issue open-back slippers. A din of television sounds wafted out the door around her.

"Hi, Mom," Jake said cheerfully, a tinge of tightness infusing his voice as he gave her a quick kiss on the cheek.

"Sit. Eat," she commanded ."Where's the girl-friend?"

"Paige decided to stay with her aunt in Spring Lake," he answered, sliding into his place at the dinner table. He let out a long sigh while his mother loaded a plate with half a fowl and a huge mound of mashed potatoes.

"So, Jakele, was the putz at the *shiva*? That ghoul goes to every funeral. The *schnorrer* eats for free wherever there is grief. I hope you got the Estate work accomplished."

"Yes, Mom. Norm was there with the rest of them. It was a little awkward sneaking into a side room to get the signatures, but everyone agreed to paying for an accounting out of Estate funds. Now Norm has no more excuses," he said between mouthfuls.

"It's about damn time," she said. "Evelyn drove your father into his grave. Imagine, a niece suing her uncle for malfeasance that wasn't his fault! Though I can't blame her for demanding that after 25 years that schmuck Norman produce a full set of Estate financials. Just like in the store, the idiot shoves records into a shoe box and never gets around to keeping the books."

"Mom, you're a broken record. It didn't help having you rant on about Norman and the Estate to Paige last night," he said, licking his fingers.

"What, she's too delicate to learn the truth about your family?"

"You don't need to give my girlfriend chapter and verse about every relative you're feuding with the first time you meet her. And did you have to get into your grudge against Grandpop and call him the Old Bastard?"

"If she's going to hang around with you she might as well know who's who," she answered defiantly.

"I'm not sure she's going to be hanging around much longer," he said dejectedly.

"What's the matter, *bubbeleh*?"

He launched into recounting the day to his mother, beginning with giving Paige the full memory lane tour of his

hometown. They'd swung by the department store building, shuttered after decades as the domain of Itzkowitz
Department Store, the Store of Quality. They couldn't go
inside – it was on the market and the realtor wasn't around
to show it. But peering through the windows he'd narrated
a tour of the ancestral establishment: "That's the men's
store, where I sold bathing suits to the Bennies. There's the
women's department, we had cute high school girls working there part time. There's the scout department – I run
into people who hear my name and ask 'are you Itzkowitz
from the store? My parents took me there to get me my
scout uniforms!' And way back is the office where Norman
whacked my father with a phone book."

Then he'd taken her to what locals bragged was the
world's best donut shop. Enduring a long line snaking
down the block, he'd shown off by ordering without even
looking at the board. "Two bismarcks, an old fashioned no
sugar, two honey glazed, and an éclair, please." On their
drive she'd conceded that Hartman's were a cut above other donuts, way better than Dunkin'. They'd meandered
along the "scenic route", allowing him to show off more
iconic childhood sites. He'd pointed out the grand seaside
"cottages" of Bay Head and Mantoloking, that Barnegat
Bay was top of the world-famous Intercoastal Waterway
("you can go all the way to Key West and never be out in
the ocean!"), and where Aunt Ann and Uncle Marvin had
their furniture store.

He'd tried to prepare her before arriving at the shiva.
"OK, look, I know this will be a little weird," he'd said. "I'll
get pulled away to deal with the Estate stuff. Just get some
food, make small talk with anyone you meet, and I'll rescue you as soon as I can." She'd assured him that she was
a big girl who could take care of herself, as long as there'd
be good lox. They'd signed the guest book and navigat-

ed through the crowd to a dining room table stocked with the ubiquitous bagels and fish spreads, plates of rugelach and assorted other baked goods found at such gatherings. That's where he'd parked her before heading off on his mission to gather signatures.

Twenty minutes later, signatures in hand, he'd returned to the fish table but found no sign of Paige. Searching room to room, he finally spotted her sitting outside on the curb, head in hand. Ducking outside, he'd come up behind her and asked gently, "What's the matter?"

Ashen-faced, she'd looked up. "Get me out of here," she said in a flat, pleading voice. "Your family is fucked up."

"What happened?"

Out tumbled her account of what had transpired. She'd been carefully considering the options offered by a huge platter laden with assorted smoked fishes when she'd gradually become aware of a gravitational pull from across the other side of the dining room table. She'd looked up to see a woman peering at her intently. The apparition wore a dour countenance, a face that looked like it had long ago forgotten how to smile.

"I'm Minnie. You must be Jake's friend," the woman had said. Paige had replied that she'd come for the weekend and ended up at the shiva.

"Then things started to get weird," Jake said to his mother. "According to Paige, Minnie then blurts out 'Get out. Get out while you still can. This family's crazy!' Before Paige can react, the big woman continues, totally deadpan. 'You think I'm joking. They're crazy. Trust me, I know. Don't wait. I've told you, get out now.' Minnie then just turns away and glides into another room. At this point,

Paige said she's asking herself, was that real or am I becoming delusional?'"

"She got a real taste of the *meshuggenehs* in this family!" Toots interrupted.

"Mom, wait, it gets worse," he said, continuing the narrative. "Paige told me she'd stood there, heart beating wildly as if she'd just sprinted away from a dangerous animal chasing her. Then she'd sensed another presence looming, looked up, and discovered a tall, bald, bespectacled stranger staring down at her. She couldn't quite place who it was, until he opens his mouth and out tumbles 'You must be Jake's friend. You know Jake's taken a real interest in the family's genealogy, so he's probably told you about the trait for narrow feet. On both sides, the Itzkowitzes and the Moscowitzes. Not just Morton's toe, that's fairly common. Very narrow feet. His great-great-grandfather Israel was quite tall, maybe 6-7, almost a giant in those days in the Pale of Settlement, had to have special boots made for him in Kiev. My grandfather – you know, Jake is named for him – told me that he remembered his grandfather's special boots. Grandpop had narrow feet too, so the store's shoe department always stocked narrow sizes because he knew how hard it was to find a good shoe when your feet are narrow. That brought in loyal customers. My feet are double A, that's even narrower than we stock. I have to special order from Florsheim. Do you know Jake's width?'"

Toots guffawed. "Always with the feet."

"Luckily he paused to shmear a mound of cream cheese on an egg bagel," Jake continued. "All Paige can do is blurt out 'Very interesting about the feet! Nice to meet you, I think I have to get some air.' She'd had enough, and fled outside to where I found her."

"Nu, Jakele, what did you think was going to happen bringing her there?" Toots asked, cocking her head.

"You're right, Mom. I should have known that if Norman got hold of her, he'd bend her ear either about feet or inbreeding. I just never counted on Minnie descending upon her too. Unfortunately she got the full Itzkowitz treatment."

"Sorry, boychik," Toots said, serving him a big hunk of strudel slathered in icing. "Better she should get the whole story about your crazy family up front than be trapped like me before finding out. Trust your mother."

Reverberations
Point Pleasant 1944

"Mr. Itzkowitz, there's a man here to see you." Phoebe, the head salesgirl, was knocking on the door-frame of
his balcony hideaway office. The interruption irritated
him. He had been reviewing last month's accounts, trying
unsuccessfully to focus on the numbers. Shira could have
done this in her sleep, he said to himself absentmindedly,
then winced as wave of despondency passed through him.
The last few years he'd avoided dwelling on recollections
of his wife; that just dredged up confusion. It had been
very different early on, after the cancer had taken her. After the funeral he'd been wracked by a constantly revolving
wheel of unfamiliar emotions. Mostly he was overcome
with guilt, or what he thought was guilt. Why had he not
been kinder to her in her dying days? Why had he let his
anger dominate him, even after she fell ill? During the
week of sitting shiva the pain of losing her consumed him.
During the thirty days of shloshim that followed, observing the customs by neither shaving nor cutting his hair, the

rhythm of ritual helped distract. But during the next phase of mourning, when the bereaved mostly returns to normal life, painful thoughts would enter his head like thieves coming to steal his peace. His inability to soften and comfort his dying wife as he could see her wasting away haunted him for many dark weeks.

Little by little, applying the self-discipline that had benefited him so often during a lifetime in business, he'd learned how to banish the specters. He became adept at pushing troubling thoughts into a windowless room at the back of his mind. That worked well for several years. Yet here he was, conjuring Shira vividly, as if she were by his side poring over the columns of figures with him.

"What shall I tell him?" Phoebe repeated, perhaps for the third time. He dimly realized she was still awaiting his instructions.

"Who is he?"

"A Mr. Murray, from the OPA," Phoebe answered. "Will you see him or should I tell him to come back?"

The Office of Price Administration? Jacob tensed. They stick their nose into everyone's business. What could he want with me, he thought, feeling anxiety rising. I don't sell tires or gasoline or food, he reassured himself, that's mostly what they care about. "OK," he said finally, "send him back."

A minute later a tall, well-dressed man in a double breasted Victory suit appeared. Jacob immediately took in the quality of the cloth, which reflected a sheen signaling the requisite amount of rayon blended with sufficient wool. The wearer clearly enjoyed quality apparel on the more expensive side. The cut was impeccable, the pants leg tapering to a plain bottom cut the full nineteen-inch allowed diameter. This man's outfit is patriotic while still being fashionable, he noted with admiration. Having appraised the visitor's clothing, Jacob assessed the man's face. There's something familiar about him, he registered as he teased out the memory.

"Charlie?" he burst out, surprised and slightly disconcerted.

"Hello Jacob," the younger man replied. "It's been quite a while."

He sat dumbly, staring as if a ghost had appeared in his doorway. He recovered his wits, rounding his desk towards Charlie, who remained arms akimbo and smiling. Jacob's own arms began to rise almost instinctively in preparation for hugging his long absent relative. Then as if his body had been jolted by a current, his arms dropped, resolving into an awkward handshake pose. Charlie, unperturbed by the older man's nonplussed movements, took the outstretched hand firmly and pumped it twice. Up close, Jacob detected that Charlie's friendly smile was not entirely matched by the look in his cousin's eyes.

"Sit down, sit down," he said, gesturing to an armchair beside his desk. "You look, ah, very good."

"Well, you look pretty swell yourself, Jacob," Charlie replied. "Business been good for you?"

"You know, with the war on it's not the same," he answered cautiously. "But it's steady. People always need clothes."

"Oh they sure do, Jacob. Keeps me busy, too."

"The girl said a man was here from the OPA. Is that what you do these days?" he asked, struggling to make sense out of Charlie sitting across from him. "I haven't heard a word about you in years."

"I guess not. I've been away since about when the Oasis Hotel finally completed construction, back around '33 or so," Charlie answered blandly. "Say, Jacob, I was very sorry to hear about Shira. She was special to me. Papa was ill and couldn't travel for the shiva. I was up in New York then, and Papa didn't tell me until it was too late to get back."

Jacob absorbed this info as if he were reading a detective story. "New York?"

"I guess you really don't know what happened with me after."

"After?" he echoed.

"After the foreclosure," Charlie replied coolly.

He shifted in his seat. "Whenever I asked my wife, may her memory be a blessing, about you, she just told me you were tending to business. I thought she meant the tobacco store."

"She knew more than she was letting on," Charlie said. "I guess Shira had her reasons."

I used to think of him like a son, Jacob said to himself, dreading what Charlie had come to say. "My wife, she had her own mind."

"Then I guess she didn't tell you I wrote to her," Charlie said, crossing his arms. "After I figured it out."

"Wrote to her?" he was startled. Had Shira kept something else important from him?

"You know, that foreclosure almost wiped me out. For the longest while I believed it almost wiped you out, too.

After all, my investment amounted to tossing one lot into the pot. But you, as far as I knew, you paid top dollar for three other lots with your own money. I figured you had five times as much as me flushed down the toilet."

"We both lost a lot," he said softly.

"Ha. So I thought," Charlie continued, his mouth now more a smirk than a smile. "After the foreclosure I was crushed. Then I shook it off and said to myself, you took a gamble. Stop whining, get back to work and make some money."

"I taught you well," he interjected.

"Oh, you taught me a lot." Charlie was leaning forward, gesturing excitedly with his hands. "I learned to notice the little details. One thing nagging at me after the foreclosure was those two guys who showed up at the auction, the shorter one who looked like a bulldog, and the tall cadaverous one who said nothing. They looked out of place. What were they doing there? Lucky for me, I'd kept a copy of the auctioneer's roster from when people sign in."

He listened, feeling his jaw tightening.

"For a while I just licked my wounds and put my energy into running the smoke shop. Business was down but steady. Even in tough times people scrape up money for the little pleasures, like a smoke. Then the store next door went out of business. I snapped up his lease and expanded, made my operation more of a country store. I eked out a little more profit. Then I heard some odd news. Construction had started again on the Oasis Hotel. That got me curious," Charlie said, his eyes boring in on Jacob.

"What was curious? It was half built when they foreclosed. Somebody was likely to finish it eventually," he said, not looking away.

"That's true. But the bank bought the property at the auction, not some real estate developer. It seemed strange that the bank would get into the hotel business. Especially while everything was still going to hell. So I walked over to the land records, looked up the deed, and saw that the bank transferred the property to something called Oasis Hotel Corporation just six months after the foreclosure."

"So? No bank is in the development business," he broke in.

"Exactly, banks aren't real estate developers. So who was going forward with the hotel? Two things jumped out when I examined the documents," Charlie paused, letting his words hang in the air.

"The deed said the property sold for one dollar 'and other good and valuable consideration', whatever that meant. One dollar is a pretty sweet deal, even with land values in the crapper." Charlie held up his index finger on his right hand, and paused again. Jacob stayed mute.

"The other interesting detail was the Oasis address." He looked directly into Jacob's eyes. Jacob felt blood draining from his face.

"912 Barnegat Avenue. Sound familiar? You own that building, don't you Jacob?"

"What did you come here for?" He nearly shouted the question, slapping his palms on his desk.

Charlie leaned back, unperturbed by the outburst, seeming to be considering what to say next. The silence was more unnerving than the accusation he expected to hear.

"Let me tell you a story I heard at a family wedding a few years back. A Moscowitz cousin was marrying an

Itzkowitz cousin. That seems to happen often in this family. Very intertwined mishpocha. I think Shira was already quite ill, you weren't there." Charlie closed his eyes, as if inwardly projecting a picture of the event.

"Is this about Moishe's crazy wife Lottie and the store?" Jacob interrupted.

"Ah, right, Lew was at my table. He probably told you the whole saga. A very interesting illustration of the lengths a person will go to get revenge when they've been wronged, don't you think, Jacob?"

"Lottie was nuts. Pearl and Myron! They did nothing wrong to her. How could someone be so rotten?" he said, more to himself than to Charlie. Then, looking squarely at Charlie, he asked, "Why did you come here? Just to tell me that story?"

"Now you're curious." Charlie flashed a sardonic smile at Jacob. "Remember the clues I found out about the hotel construction? About Oasis Hotel Corporation? It didn't make sense at first. I saw the bank foreclose on us, I was there. Then, like I said, I eventually remembered those two odd fellows hanging around. I dug out a copy of the sign-in sheet from my files. Guess what? Their names were on the roster, listed as being with a company called Johannesburg Consolidated Investments at a Philadelphia address. Why were they there? It took me a while to puzzle out."

He sat motionless, thinking back to Shira's admonition, scolding him for swindling Charlie, her warning that someday the truth would get out. He'd reacted angrily at her accusing him of duplicity, nursing that anger even as she withered and died before his eyes. Now, seeing Charlie sitting in front of him, he viscerally understood that Shira had been right all along. He felt a lump of remorse in his throat, and an unfamiliar sensation in his eyes.

Charlie plowed ahead. "Those fellas weren't there to bid at the auction. They never uttered a word during the sale. It dawned on me that they were there watching what would happen to their investment. That only made sense if they were the real money behind you, your silent partners who'd put up the cash for the hotel venture. That meant your cash was safe in the bank, not tied up in the land."

"Charlie, you've got a wild imagination," he cut in. "So what if businessmen show up curious about an auction?"

"Oh, am I imagining things? Try this on. This is the big ticket item, the clincher that I finally worked out. You were double crossing them. You had them believing the fiction that the bank still held the loan, meanwhile you were getting rid of them without them knowing it. It all made sense if you had a side deal, where the bank was the public face of the foreclosure while behind the scenes you're really calling the shots."

"You've got no proof of anything," he burst out.

"No proof? Then explain how this brand new Oasis corporation buys the property for a buck just a few months later," Charlie said defiantly.

It took enormous self-control, but he sat mute.

"No? The answer is simple. You're Oasis Corporation. You must have gotten a good laugh out of it, duping your partner and ending up with the property for a song. And me? I was just a little fish caught in the net."

"I never wanted to hurt you," he said softly, almost in a whisper.

"You think I care? You hurt me badly just the same," Charlie's voice rose, his eyes flashing with anger. "It was one thing losing money, that I could handle. But you betraying me? I looked up to you, like my own father."

Jacob leaned forward, elbows on the desk, forehead slumped into his hands. "How can I make it up to you?" he croaked out the words, as if each syllable was barbed.

"You can't," Charlie snapped, coldly. "You know what you did to me? You wounded me, badly. After a while my pain turned to anger, and anger turned to a desire for vengeance."

He looked up at Charlie, a flicker of fear in his eyes.

"After losing the property, I figured I needed something more than my tobacco store to be successful. There was lots of talk after the market crashed about a need for accountants. I have a good head for numbers and started taking courses at night. I passed the CPA exam on my first try. That was before I'd figured out how you'd cheated me. Then I got a lucky break – one of my smoke customers had been hired to manage this new grocery store, Big Bear, opening up north in Hoboken. They were competing head to head with A&P and needed a financial guy badly. My customer got me in front of the owners, we hit it off, and they hired me."

He was listening intently.

"I started making good money. Pretty soon they moved me into a fancy office in Manhattan. The company kept growing, my salary got fatter, and eventually we sold stock to the public. My insider shares were worth a fortune. Finally I was way ahead of all my losses with the beach property."

"I'm glad to hear that," he blurted out, then realized Charlie was far from finished.

"Yeah, no thanks to you," Charlie almost sneered. "I figured out how you screwed me not long after the wedding I told you about. Hearing that story of revenge, that stuck with me. Lottie was crazy. But she was clever. I thought, if she can do it, so can I."

A look of glee crossed Charlie's face, as intense as if he were a kid tasting ice cream for the first time. A sharp feeling of dread, equal and opposite to Charlie's excitement, coursed through Jacob. "What are you saying?" he asked.

"You know the White Dunes Hotel that just opened down the street? Guess who's the major investor." Charlie was triumphant now, clearly enjoying this.

"You're going to ruin the Oasis? Like Lottie did to my sister?" he felt a surge of defiance mixed with fear.

Charlie chuckled. "I could if I wanted to, Jacob. Isn't it what you would do if you were me?"

"I told you, Charlie, I'm sorry you got caught up in the foreclosure," he said plaintively.

"You're only sorry now that I'm strong enough to ruin you! That's exactly what I planned, for years now. Thinking I wanted revenge drove me, pushed me to be more ambitious, work harder, climb the corporate ladder. But once I got to where I could do it -- can do it today with a phone call -- I realized something. Cheating people, hurting your own family, that's not strength. That's not what life's about, treating family like dirt. Not my life at least.

When I was young I wanted to be just like you, Jacob. To me you symbolized success. But I've grown up, Jacob. I've seen how people like you are willing to destroy even people close to them to make themselves feel like big men. And know what? I don't want to be anything like you anymore," Charlie said, demeanor transformed, tone almost prayerful.

He drew in a quick breath. Charlie's words cut at him almost as sharply as a knife. The young man who had idolized him had toppled him from the pedestal. He was deflated, at a loss for words.

"I don't forgive you," Charlie continued. "I won't forget. Who knows, I may even change my mind and exact my revenge someday. But right now, I look around, and there's a war on. Young men dying around the world. They're the strong ones, the big men, men willing to give their lives for the greater good. They're the ones I look up to."

"I'm sorry, Charlie," he said. "I should have listened to Shira."

"Yeah, you should have. A little late for apologies. I'll be watching you, Jacob. If nothing else, it's my job," Charlie said.

"Your job?" Jacob was reminded of what he'd meant to ask when Charlie first walked in. "I was wondering about that. What's with the OPA story?"

"Not a story, I'm the OPA regional director. One of those dollar-a-year-men. Big Bear loaned me out to the war effort. It's my way of doing something to fight the enemy. The OPA needed someone wise to all the retailers' schemes to get around the price controls. You're in my region. Better not let anyone buy too many rubber soled shoes or I'll be after you with a hefty fine."

"But why did you tell my shop girl your name is Mr. Murray?" he asked as if suddenly remembering an odd detail from a dream.

"The guys who started the grocery store were a couple of *goyim*. I wasn't sure what they'd think of a Moscowitz. So when I applied I used my middle name, signed the form Charles Murray. After a while, I figured it had worked, so why change it? A lot of guys in my generation have done the same thing. You do what you have to, to get ahead."

"I know, Charlie, I know."

Birthday Party
Point Pleasant 1952

"What kind of cake?" the boy demanded, following his mother into the kitchen like a puppy.

"It's a surprise, Adam. Stop asking questions!" Toots replied sternly, wrapping herself in a protective layer of a floral apron.

On the front porch, Jacob rocked, eavesdropping on the back and forth between grandson and daughter-in-law filtering through the screen door. The party is not until tomorrow, he mused, but the *kindele* is already excited. Not surprising, he thought, the boy's never had a real party before.

"Mom, will there be presents?" the five year old persisted.

"Presents? Adam, that's up to the guests. Isn't the party enough? Don't be greedy." She tousled his hair.

Toots was busying herself cooking dinner for the household, as always. Jacob actually liked her cooking, most of it at least, although he rarely offered a compliment higher than gesturing for seconds. He was happy to have her kitchen skills cooking for him these last seven years since Lew married her. Much better than the era when he and Lew had adopted the bachelors' routine of cooking for each other. After Shira's gravestone was unveiled and the ritual mourning period ceased, they'd resorted to hiring a series of housekeepers of varying quality. None in the parade of young women stayed more than six or eight months, as wartime jobs paid better, or fiancés returned from the service.

He'd been skeptical of Lew's choice of the much younger Toots for a bride. Yet Lew had seemed genuinely smitten with the girl, or at least with the idea of being married. So initially Jacob had bided his time, curious to see what she'd be like in person. First, however, he declared that he would pay for the wedding, even though tradition held that the bride's family footed the bill. It was no secret that her parents were short on money. Even before meeting Toots, Jacob had gleaned through a question here, a comment there, that her father was just a simple working man, the mother took in laundry, and they'd already married off two older daughters. Besides, he'd deliberated, I'll invite my business colleagues and the government guys and don't want her family crying poor. I had a lot less when we married off Ann and Esther and their weddings still were the talk of the community. Jacob Itzkowitz will show everyone how to throw a party!

After the honeymoon, he wrestled with adjusting to this strange woman sleeping in his house. Coming down in the morning to an ample breakfast she'd made for all of them was a *mechayeh*, that he had to admit. Her eggs were far superior to the ones he and Lew scrambled, and she brewed a decent cup of coffee. But unlike a housekeeper, Toots ate with them at the table, always trying to make small talk. "How is the toast and jam, Pop?" (She followed Lew's lead in what to call him, but it sounded strange in her Bronx accent). "Fine," he'd reply. "How's business been?" she'd ask. "Not so good. Ask your husband, he knows what I know," he'd reply, guarded about sharing business details with his young daughter-in-law. He still wondered if she'd married the much older Lew for his money. Was she hoping he, Jacob, would drop dead soon and leave the business to Lew?

As time wore on, he'd grown accustomed to her presence. Grudgingly he admitted, to himself at least, that Toots was smart and capable. She took better care of the household than had any of their housekeepers. She was no Shira, for whom a beautiful house was a labor of love, but she was no slouch either. Not that he ever told Toots he approved, but neither did he criticize her housekeeping. Yet over time, even as the novelty of having his daughter-in-law under the same roof wore off, her mere existence increasingly irritated him. He couldn't explain even to himself what rubbed him the wrong way, yet something did in a persistent low-level way, like a tiny pebble in his shoe. Maybe it was purely that Lew marrying had not been part of his plan, and disrupting plans was not something he tolerated well. Then, to top it all off, she started popping out babies.

Her fertility shouldn't have been surprising. After all, the girl was nearly twenty years younger than Lew. He could hear them going at it through the wall separating his bedroom from Lew's, an annoying sleep disruption he preferred not to dwell on. He nearly told Lew to move into the smaller bedroom at the other end of the house, but thought better of it. One morning at breakfast, however, in a particularly irritable mood, he found himself remarking that Lew should call an exterminator. To Lew's quizzical reaction he announced that there were squirrels loose in the attic who were disrupting his sleep, and then noticed the newlyweds exchange a look that seemed like smirks. Lew abruptly turned the breakfast table topic to business, commenting about the good news that the Office of Price Administration had finally lifted all price controls. After that, the racket from the next bedroom quieted down.

When Adam was born a year after the wedding, he savored the role of proud grandfather at the *bris*. He personally held the infant while the *mohel* performed the ancient ritual through which Jewish males are bound to their forefathers by the snipping of their foreskins. For that day at least, he reveled in knowing that the Itzkowitz lineage was extended even further. Throughout the ceremony he beamed at Adam, only the second male among his five grandchildren. With his own daughters well past childbearing years he felt temporarily grateful to Toots. Particularly since his older grandson Norman was turning out to be a bit peculiar.

He loved Norman, who'd practically grown up in the department store. When Norm was little, any day not in school was spent playing in the store. They'd walk side by side to Jacob's home for lunch. These were occasions to tell his grandson tidbits about life in the Pale, or the hardships and adventures of the Transvaal. Norm soaked up his stories, some more real than others. Jacob enjoyed having a captive audience, a doting grandchild hanging on his every word, and wove elaborate tales of daring escapes and unlikely encounters with celebrities. Then Norm grew up a bit, turning an age where he could be put to work in the store. To his chagrin, Jacob noticed that the young man quickly grew bored with the chores. Norman would show a burst of energy, offering up creative ideas about how to trim the display windows, inventing seasonal scenes to catch the eye of sidewalk shoppers. Yet the scenes were often unfinished, with the last mannequin left undressed, while Norm launched himself into the next briefly engrossing new project. Finally, out of embarrassment, one of the shop girls would badger Norm into clothing the naked dummy.

As Jacob rocked away on his porch cogitating over all this, his attention turned back to Adam's party. Write out the check, he reminded himself. He'd been a meager present-giver over the years. There was always something from the store for the other grandchildren when they were little. That is, on those rare occasions when he'd actually attended their birthday festivities. Growing up in Shavlan neither he nor Shira were given parties. At most the family might have a special meal, if times were good enough. But presents? Spending money on frivolous gifts was something entirely new to him, another omen of the prosperity of this country. By the time he'd caught on to the American fetish for making a big *tzimmes* over the anniversary of your child's birth, his offspring were fully grown.

His daughter-in-law seemed hell-bent on a lavish party for the boy. Toots made a big noise about being a "Depression baby", still upset that her family had to make due without birthday presents. He'd certainly felt the pinch of the Depression. Indeed, trouble with the bank had almost ruined him. Still, all in all he'd weathered that storm just fine. People still needed clothes, they couldn't mend everything. Enough of his tenants paid enough of their rent so that he lost only one property, not counting the beachfront ploy. Well, he thought, if she wants to make a ruckus for the little one, he could at least write out a $5 check for Adam.

Sunday, the day of the party, was overcast, although luckily the rain from overnight had blown out to sea. Toots had planned backyard festivities, but with the ground damp she shifted gears and instead adorned the double front parlor for the occasion. Nothing too fancy, just a spray of multi-colored balloons and bowls filled with jelly beans, plus a few dishes mounded with M&Ms topping the various side tables in the room. Coming down the front stairs Sunday morning for breakfast he spied the candies and smiled. He had developed a sweet tooth for the many new treats cropping up on grocery shelves after the war. At least I will have a good nosh during the party, he thought.

Promptly at two, guests began trooping in. First to arrive were Adam's playmates from down the street: Billy, who was Adam's age, and his younger sister Bernadette. The two were in tow behind their mother, Mrs. Dillon, whose lined face betrayed the strain of having a brood of seven under age twelve. The neighbor seemed quite ready to hand off two of her clan for a few hours, smiling at Toots as her children ran through the front door to Adam, who squealed with joy upon seeing them. Reaching into the pocket of her housecoat Mrs. Dillon removed a carefully wrapped box. "Here, Mrs. Itzkowitz, a little something for your boy," she said brightly as she handed Toots the present and departed.

The doorbell rang again. Toots opened the front door to reveal her sister-in-law Esther surrounded by her branch of the family.

"Esther, Bernie, come in, come in, so nice of you to come!" He heard Toots exclaim. "And Norman and Shirley, you're here too. Adam will be delighted."

"Hello, Toots," Esther said flatly as the Mettlers filed past their hostess. With Esther leading, the quartet made a beeline for Jacob. He'd positioned his high-backed easy chair at the far end of the room diagonally opposite the parlor entrance, providing a clear view of arrivals. He received his middle daughter and her family. One by one they bent wordlessly to give him a peck on the cheek.

"Sit, sit," he said. "I hope you've eaten, there's just candy and soda." Toots, hovering by the front door, glanced in his direction.

"We weren't expecting anything else," Esther replied, flopping onto the couch to his left. Bernie placed a wrapped package on a side table where presents were piling up, then wandered off, apparently heading for the bathroom. Norman and Shirley stood awkwardly, then drifted out of the parlor and up the front stairs, following the sounds of playing children.

Lew entered the room pushing a tea cart laden with soda bottles and glasses. "Esther," he said, nodding in greeting. "Lew," she responded blandly, remaining seated. Lew positioned his cart in the bay window to his father's right.

"Soda?" asked Lew, looking towards Esther. She nodded. "Seven-Up will do."

At the front door, Toots was greeting the McKendrys, who owned the house next door on the corner. Kate McKendry gave Toots a warm hug. "Is Adam all excited for the big party?" she asked effusively, as her husband Tom gave Toots a kiss on the cheek. Their teenage son, Eddie, shuffled in, emitting a barely audible "Hello, Mrs. Itzkowitz, thank you for inviting me." Tom, seeing Lew, strode across the room with his hand outstretched. "Lew, great to see ya," he said, pumping Lew's hand while clasping his shoulder with his old friend's free hand.

"Mr. Itzkowitz, you're looking well," said Tom.

"How else should I look?" he replied. Tom guffawed heartily. Jacob was fond of McKendry ever since the gentile courageously joined his band of Jews guarding the store during the Klan march. His fondness had its limits, though, as he found the man a little too rough around the edges. At least he wasn't drinking at this time of day, Jacob thought.

The younger children came running down the stairs, Adam leading the way as they all spilled into the living room. Norman and Shirley followed somewhat more decorously. The commotion caught Jacob's eye. Watching the procession, he noticed that when Shirley entered and caught sight of Eddie, she blushed and made straight for the boy. My granddaughter's flirting with the *sheygetz*, he thought with disdain. If that's what she does as a teenager, right under our noses, what will the girl do when she's out in the world on her own, he pondered.

"Everybody, take seats. It's time for presents!" Toots called out from next to the side table laden with presents. Adam scrambled over to sit on the floor next to her. Toots commenced handing the wrapped packages one by one to the boy, who eagerly shredded the festive paper to unlock each goody waiting inside. As Adam tore open a present, Toots called out what was inside, like a game show host to the audience.

"A watercolor set from cousin Shirley. Isn't that lovely!" Toots announced.

Adam pulled apart a smaller box, holding up the contents with a whoop of "wow."

"A baseball from the McKendry's. Lew, you're gonna have to learn to play catch," Toots rang out. "Maybe," replied Lew.

Picking up the next gift, Toots hesitated before handing it to Adam. She examined the outside, as if something odd had caught her attention. Jacob noticed her hesitancy, taking his own measure of the package. He could see it was scuffed or sullied in some way. Toots finished her brief inspection and passed the box along to the boy. "This is from Aunt Esther and Uncle Bernie," she announced.

Adam tore off the paper and opened a small hat box. "A Davy Crockett hat!" he yelled with obvious glee, holding it up for all to see.

Toots took the hat out of his hands. "It's damp," she said mostly to herself, sounding puzzled. Scrutinizing it closely, she burst out "What the hell is this? Some kind of animal tail? From a fox?" She scrunched her nose. "Ech. It's wet and smells!"

Toots cast an angry stare at Esther and Bernie, her mouth turned down in disgust. Her in-laws exchanged a glance, each looking with puzzlement at the other.

"What are you talking about? That's the hat that all the kids want these days. Just like the frontier heroes on TV wear. Norman tracked it down," said Esther.

Toots was shaking the hat. "Look at it. Did you find it lying in the gutter? It's just a damn animal tail sewn on to a cap to make it look new!"

"Mom, give me back the hat. I like it," Adam pleaded.

"Where did you buy this?" Toots demanded.

Esther looked at Norm. Norm shrugged. "What difference does that make?" she said.

"You couldn't afford the real thing?" Toots blazed at Esther.

"You're nuts. You're paranoid," Esther's voice was rising. Norm was edging towards the door.

"Enough!" Jacob yelled. "It's a party for the boy. Everyone stop the shouting. Toots, forget this foxtail nonsense, finish with the presents already."

Toots continued seething, but she took a deep breath, reached over to the gift table, and handed another present to Adam. Mother and son resumed their pattern with the final three packages. Toots duly noted a Hardy Boys book, a pair of striped pajamas, and finally the money gift from Grandpop. Each time Toots displayed another present, the tension in the room abated noticeably another notch. After the ritual opening of presents concluded, awkward chit chat ensued. Toots made a point of steering clear of Esther and Bernie, who made a point of hovering close to where Jacob sat. Toots finally exited, heading off to the kitchen to fetch the birthday cake. At her departure from the room, Esther and Bernie hastily said their goodbyes, called out "time to go" to Norman and Shirley, and trooped towards the front door. Norman followed dutifully, although Shirley remained rooted next to Eddie. "Shirley, now!" Esther called, and Shirley grudgingly fell in behind.

He sat stonily in his chair, fuming over what he'd witnessed.

The next morning Jacob was more taciturn than usual at breakfast, merely grunting as Lew read aloud items from the newspaper. Wiping crumbs from his mustache, he announced a need to visit the building inspector about one of his projects. As forays to Borough Hall were routine for him even at his age, the errand aroused no great curiosity in Lew or Toots. He set off dressed as usual, suit jacket buttoned up, silk neck tie knotted tightly against his collar, and hatless.

Walking down familiar streets, Jacob replayed the agitation brought on by the tumult of yesterday. He had long been vaguely troubled by a realization at the edge of awareness. His children would never carry on his legacy. Lew was a perfectly good manager, but he lacked the drive to expand his empire to its fullest. Esther and her husband possessed creativity, but they remained artists at heart. Real estate deals held no interest for them. Building up the Itzkowitz brand might offer an outlet for their passions, but he failed to see the ambition they would need to become the next Macy's. If anything, his daughter and son-in-law lately appeared tired and bored, more likely to pass their shares along to Norman and retire before too long than to do the smart thing and branch out across the state. His clever first born, Ann, chose the path of her hothead husband Marvin. The pair of them had the most sense as businesspeople, their furniture operation proved that, and for a while he'd considered anointing them as his successors. Marvin, however, was too much his own man to play by anyone else's rules. For Marvin and Ann, it was better to be captains in their own pond than to venture out into an ocean with him.

Yesterday's ruckus, however, had jolted him with a new realization. Toots and her fuss about a foxtail brought everything into focus. She was probably right, he thought. The tail did look like something retrieved from a ditch and sewn on to an old cap, a counterfeit of the ones in TV ads. That was beside the point. The intensity of her reaction was what shook him out of his lethargy. It was plain as the nose on his face that Toots would never get along with her in-laws, and vice versa. Maybe she was more than a little justified, he had to admit. Only Ann had welcomed the New Yorker, but they weren't close. He and Esther had both resented Toots showing up out of the blue with her hooks already deep into Lew. She was a little too rough around the edges, a little too loud, a little too pushy for his taste. He worried that when he was dead and buried, the girl would boss his Lew around even more, like Lottie dominated Moishe.

Then there were the grandchildren to take stock of. That Shirley is like a moth to a flame around the *goyishe* boys at this age, who knows who she'll end up with as a full grown woman. With a current of anger he thought, I didn't work like a dog so some gentile ends up with my money. Her brother Norman, certainly he's smart. I prayed he'd become more grounded as a man, but I don't see that happening yet. And Lew's boys, Adam and Dov? Who knows how they'll turn out, they're still little ones. His bride might even have more babies. The *ayniklach* shouldn't be in a hurry to get their hands on my money, he concluded with a sigh.

Jacob's reverie had carried him to his intended destination, a house converted to a law office nearby Borough Hall. He climbed the wide porch stairs, opened the ornate front door, and nodded to the assistant perched behind a sleek metal desk. "Tell Julius I'm here, Sally."

"He's expecting you, Mr. Itzkowitz."

A dapperly dressed man stepped into the foyer. "Jacob! Wonderful to see you. Come on back," said Julius Rosenblatt, now the preeminent attorney in northern Ocean County. "You're looking well. Still riding your bicycle?"

"Fine, fine. Not so much on the bicycle these days, Julius. Anyway, I want to get right to the point," he replied with impatience.

"OK, down to business. What's this about, Jacob?" Rosenblatt asked amiably.

"My will, Julius, my will. I've been thinking." He drummed the fingers of his right hand on the lawyer's desktop as he spoke.

Rosenblatt sat back in his leather swivel chair and arched an eyebrow. He'd been representing Jacob for nearly thirty years. "Go on."

"My kids, it's no good."

"No good?" Rosenblatt cocked his head.

"They're never going to build together. They're not like some families. I wasn't crazy enough to think they'd turn into Rothschilds, but maybe they could at least be like the Bergdorfs and the Goodmans? Or the Filenes up in Boston? But no, that's not them. I see it now."

"Uh huh. Jacob, what brought this on now?" The lawyer jotted a few notes on his yellow legal pad.

"It's a long story. A birthday party, the daughter-in-law, the whole thing."

"I'm not following Jacob. What party? What does this have to do with your will?"

"They don't need my money!" Jacob suddenly slapped the desk.

"You're cutting your children out of your will?" Rosenblatt leaned forward, peering.

"It's my money! They can make their own fortune."

"Jacob, yes, it's yours to do with as you please Still, there are certain norms, certain accepted principles.

Let's think this through." Rosenblatt leaned back, steepling his hands.

"I've thought enough. You're the lawyer, go figure it out. If I have to give my children something, make it as little as possible. They've all gotten plenty so far, they don't need any more from me."

"Alright, alright. Let me consider that. So then what? Where does it all go?"

"Ah, Julius, that's my problem. I've bought bonds for Israel, given some for the *shul*. The rest stays in the family. For the grandchildren I suppose."

"Good, good, Jacob. It would be a helluva mess if you gave it all to the cat and dog hospital."

"Why are you talking about animals?" He gave Rosenblatt a look as if he had suddenly started speaking Aramaic.

"Merely a figure of speech, Jacob," Rosenblatt murmured. "Anyway, good choice to keep the corpus in the family for the grandchildren."

"It's not like my grandchildren are any great shakes, Julius. I watched them closely at the party. I don't want my money pissed away. And I don't want it going to *goyim*."

Rosenblatt furrowed his brows. "What are you trying to say, Jacob? I know you well, but I'm not a mind reader."

"Tie it all up. Until the youngest is grown up," he declared, waving a hand as if swatting aside some invisible insect. "You know Lew married a young one, and she's already given him two little ones. Cute kids. The oldest one, Adam, he's a smart cookie. The younger one, Dov, is a little angel. But who knows how they'll turn out. So tie it all up until the littlest one is a man."

"Hmmm." Julius stroked his chin. "Your oldest grandchild, Evelyn is it? She's already an adult, married?"

"So?"

"So, if everything is tied up until the little one is grown, how old will Evelyn be? Don't you mean that each grandchild gets his share when he gets to a certain age?"

"No, Julius, you're not listening to me. I built everything myself. Well, with help from Shira, *zihronah livracha* if I'm honest," he said, staring absently out Rosenblatt's office window. "I don't want what I built split into little pieces. They'll all just have to wait until the time comes."

"Jacob," the lawyer protested, "you're making this very complicated."

"And they must remain Jewish!" he stood up as he said this.

"They are Jewish. You mean they can't convert?"

"Convert? Of course not!" He paced in front of the desk. "There's a tragedy in America, Julius, a *shonda*. Jews are assimilating. No one holds a gun to their heads, and still they go and marry *goyim*. Hitler couldn't wipe us out. Instead these modern kids go and do it for him."

"Please, Jacob, sit back down," Rosenblatt gestured to the empty chair. "Let's talk this through. I can't help you while you're wearing out my carpet."

"I saw it yesterday, right in front of my eyes. The *sheygetz* neighbor boy comes around and the next thing you know she's making goo goo eyes at him."

"Alright, Jacob. No need to explain, it's your money. Just let me think this through." Julius put his hands together as if praying, pressing index fingers to lips. The silence hung between them. "OK, I have some ideas. I'll write up a new will for you to review. Your Estate will be in a trust that will last until the youngest is, I don't know, maybe 21? 25?"

"Longer!"

"Longer? Thirty is as long as it should go," Rosenblatt replied.

"OK. And what about the *goyim*?"

"That's tricky, Jacob. The Supreme Court just struck down religious and race covenants. Everybody used to put them in deeds, and now you can't. I'm not sure if this would be viewed differently by a court."

"I don't care. Put something in my will to let them all know it's wrong. Jews should marry Jews."

"Alright, if you feel that strongly. Just remember, I cannot guarantee it will withstand challenge."

"Sure, sure, you've told me. I'll be lying in my grave by then." He gave a shrug. "Put it in anyway, they need to know it's a *shonda* to abandon the faith. You've got my wishes, write it up. I have to get back home before the nosy daughter-in-law starts asking questions."

"Jacob, I'll have this ready for your review in a week. Relax your mind."

The Negotiators
Point Pleasant 1982

The ornate oak table in the lawyer's conference room was littered with coffee cups and donut crumbs. Loose papers and yellow legal pads marked the territory of each of the six cousins, guarding their places during bathroom absences, walkouts in staged fits of anger, or just a stroll to get some air. Progress towards a deal had been made, then lost, with the tide turning on an insulting intonation or an ill-thought-out remark. Positions had been advanced, met by some with approval and by others with resistance. Trial balloons had been floated, only to be shot down by one or another relative, sometimes one's own sibling. In short, over the course of five hours on a Thursday in October, Jacob's grandchildren repeated the same dance steps they'd been gyrating to for years, as if some otherworldly choreographer had again taken possession of the troupe.

Jake surveyed the assemblage during a recess in the chatter. How'd I ever get stuck with this crew, he marveled ruefully to himself. At age twenty-five he was the youngest. Across from him sat his eldest cousin, Evelyn, a prim and proper lady turned family bomb-thrower when she filed her lawsuit five years earlier. A mask of makeup and well-placed nips and tucks gave Evelyn the appearance of a woman notably younger than her 60 years. She nevertheless inhabited the role of senior member of the cousins' club. Petite and well coiffed, Evelyn exuded an air of someone accustomed to a limousine now reduced by circumstances to riding a Greyhound bus surrounded by the masses.

Next to Evelyn was her younger sister, Janice, who clearly was unwell. He did not need a medical degree to diagnose that Janice was wasting away. Perhaps she's saving her energy, that's why she has been so silent today, he thought. Janice was one of his favorites among the extended family, in her day a warm and vivacious person who loved to laugh and play cards. Such evident joy for life was all the more remarkable given that Janice had suffered more tragedies than the rest of them combined, or so Jake had heard from his mother. A foolish first marriage ending in divorce within eighteen months. A much better second marriage was marked by the pall of multiple miscarriages before producing three healthy offspring. Then the terrible accident no one spoke of. The details of the tragedy which took one of her children were always vague to Jake. Surely it's accumulated grief eating away at her, he hypothesized. Anyway, he observed, her older sister was more than happy to talk for both of them.

To Jake's left, at the far end of the conference table, sat Norm. Ten minutes into their recess Norm was still struggling to compose himself. Jake found it hard not to feel sorry for Norm, despite the tumult for which he was responsible. Norm was the actual defendant in Evelyn's lawsuit by virtue of being executor of Grandpop Jacob's estate, and was the clear object of her venom. Evelyn could have named him in court papers as merely a functionary managing estate assets and records. Accomplishing her stated goal — of settling matters once and for all — required only an assertion that it was long past time for such a functionary to wind up the estate and distribute everything to the ultimate heirs. Yet Evelyn had gone out of her way to accuse Norman of all manner of malfeasance and breach of fiduciary duties in a twenty-page complaint employing dozens of multi-syllabic legal terms for lying schmuck. Jake had no doubt that Norm was sloppy in keeping estate records; he was notorious for that in his day job. Even so, he saw no reason for one cousin to slander another for blatant wrongdoing in a public pissing contest.

He detected in Evelyn's vitriol the hand of her husband, Herbert Schatz, a small town municipal court judge who carried himself as if he were the reincarnation of Justice Brandeis. Judge Schatz was famous for berating the average Joe charged with some unpaid minor debt, pontificating about the person's lax moral character. Herbert disdained Norm, so Jake assumed the good Judge had instigated his wife into the scorched earth approach. Norm, whom it would be generous to call high strung, predictably felt personally vilified by the claims of his elder cousin. During the necessary meetings throughout the course of the legal process Norm could barely sit in the same room with Evelyn. In these extended negotiating sessions his inner turmoil visibly manifested itself, his blood pressure rising, skin flushing until he appeared like a human thermometer on a brutal summer day. Recalling the bizarre scene years earlier when he'd witnessed an agitated Norm whacking his father over the head, Jake mischievously considered borrowing the lawyer's phone book in case Norm got out of hand. Thankfully, he noted, for the moment

Norm was keeping control, as his color had diminished more to soft pink than bright crimson.

Norm was flanked by his sister, Shirley. Shirley had all her brother's brilliance yet little of his ethereal resistance to the practical side of life. Slender and fit, she carried herself with a dancer's lightness. Good thing Shirley's sitting next to her brother, Jake mused; she exerts a leavening influence on him. All morning Shirley seemed to sense just when to reach over and gently touch Norm's arm. She was adroit at inserting a deflecting comment when the bickering started winding Norm up into a lather. Shirley played that smoothing role effectively with the other cousins as well, having somehow maintained good relations with each to varying degrees. This was to her advantage, as Shirley had perhaps the most to gain from a successful resolution among this group. Independent-minded, free of the prejudices of earlier generations, she'd broken one of the cardinal rules of their grandfather's will: Shirley had married out of the Hebrew faith. As revealed at the reading of Grandpop's will, in a codicil added near the end of his life, the patriarch disinherited any grandchild who dared stray from their religion. Shirley was not alone in being cut out – Jake's older brother Adam also had defied his Grandpop's controlling mandates. Adam, however, had become a wildly successful businessman. He lived all the way across the country, and showed little interest into whether or not he received a share of the estate. By contrast, Shirley remained enmeshed with the *mishpocha*. Both the emotional and monetary rewards of being reinstated as a full-fledged grandchild were especially meaningful to her. He was certain that Shirley was motivated to see a deal come together.

To Jake's right sat Dov, his middle brother. More precisely, Dov occupied a swath of the conference table. A large man, his gruff demeanor and often uncouth manner masked a wonderfully caring character. Dov was literally the guy who would give you the shirt off his back, or whatever you needed if he had it to give, if he deemed you a person truly in need. Through some odd intergenerational twist of fate, Dov was the closest in profession to their grandfather, a peddler of sorts. In Dov's case, fresh produce replaced dry goods, although the routine was remarkably similar. Like Jacob nearly a century earlier, Dov regularly set off for the big market at the beginning of the peddling week, then headed out to hawk his wares on the backroads of Jersey down unmarked lanes and into tiny villages. His odd assortment of customers were the ones feeling left behind by the economic forces, lives upended as their local shops were driven out of business by an invasion of corporate malls, characterless chain stores and fast food drive-thrus. Dov knew by name each customer's family and pets, their aches and pains, and felt their growing despair at transformations happening beyond their control. On long stretches alone in his modern horse and wagon, an Econoline van, Dov habitually tuned into the "hour of rage" talk show jockeys dominating AM radio. Their slant on politics matched his own well. Anyone Dov considered elitist – and a few were sitting around the table from him – evoked a level of disdain that often displaced his deeper empathetic side. Luckily for Jake, however, Dov's core sense of family solidarity overshadowed other considerations. Even if they differed bitterly politically, he could count on Dov's backing him up when the time came for voting on any final deal.

Jake was all too aware that his very existence added a major complication to the negotiations. As his mother had reminded him a thousand times while he was growing up, just by being born he'd thrown the validity of the estate into doubt. Old Grandpop Jacob had flaunted one last time his power over his family when dictating that nothing in his estate would pass to his heirs until the youngest grandchild turned thirty. Yet in doing so, Grandpop (or more accurately, his lawyer) embedded a potentially fatal flaw into the whole arrangement. Jake had learned well before starting law school that while a person may have vast control over disposition of his property after death, there are limits. Traditional Old English law turned a jaundiced eye on feudal entanglements across multiple generations. Americans might have thrown out the King of England through a revolution, but they clung to a lot of common law from the mother country, especially where property was concerned. One vestige was something called the Rule Against Perpetuities, a rule so convoluted that in some states it was not malpractice for a lawyer to get it wrong.

Grandpop's will stipulated that all his wealth would be locked away in his estate until the last of his grandchildren "to survive me" turned thirty. That wording may have tripped over the Rule -- which dictated that to be valid, an interest in property must "vest" within 21 years of the end of the lives of identified people who were around at the creation of the property interest. In the arcane world of property law, that meant spinning out hypothetical scenarios to test whether a property gift in a will would actually end up in the hands of an heir within 21 years of the death of all the other people named in that will. Because Jacob's will tied up the inheritance for thirty years, the highly technical prohibition on "perpetuities" now hung over the validity of the estate like a dead hand from an earlier era.

It was Jake's mother who'd unearthed this potential flaw in the estate arrangements. Toots began consulting lawyers shortly after Jake's birth to determine if her baby, born several years after Jacob's death, counted as a grandchild under the will. Frustrated by the first lawyer's "on the one hand, on the other" equivocation, Toots sought out several more legal opinions, yielding a collection of memos outlining varying degrees of optimism about the merits of a legal challenge. She had made no secret to Jake of her smoldering rage at her father-in-law, "the Old Bastard", insisting to her teenage son that he must pore over everything in her extensive files and carry on her fight for vindication. Consequently, he'd been virtually the only first year law student who had not only heard of the opaque Rule Against Perpetuities, but actually knew how it worked. Nevertheless, on most days even he got bollixed up trying to explain the Rule. Now, having prepared for the negotiation by consulting the state's foremost expert on the topic, the Dickensian octogenarian Judge Goodhart, Jake felt confident that he'd come armed to the familial knife fight with the legal equivalent of a bazooka. If he challenged the validity of the will, he could very likely get it thrown out altogether.

Not that getting the will thrown out would be easy, or even accomplish what any of them wanted. The real beauty of having this card to play was the threat to embroil the entire group in years' more litigation. As the youngest cousin, he could wait the longest. Legal expenses would drain the coffers further, but now that he was a lawyer, he could do much of his advocacy himself. He anticipated still more leverage as the country was evidently slipping into a recession of uncertain duration. The grandchildren were meeting this time because their broker had finally produced a solid offer from a credible buyer to acquire the crown jewel of Grandpop's remaining properties, the stretch of beachfront that included the Oasis Hotel Jacob had built decades earlier. The substantial cash offer might well evaporate if they did not accept it in the next day or two. If that happened, as the economy worsened there might not be another buyer for a while, certainly not one at anywhere near the price that was on the table. Jake smiled to himself as he wondered what might be going through minds of the rest of the *mishpocha.*

"How's everybody doing?" called out the jovial attorney, old Mr. Malloy, as he shuffled into the conference room. Resembling a bulky Atticus Finch in his cream-colored three-piece suit, but too rumpled to fit the part, counselor Malloy had represented the executors of the estate since Evelyn had filed papers. To date he was the only one in the room actually getting any money out of the process, so he had reason to be jovial. He smiled cheerfully at the exhausted negotiators, as if expecting a coherent answer. Seeing only glum faces, Malloy plunged ahead with his nugget of news. "They've upped their offer!"

Six heads snapped round towards the grinning attorney, like a pack of prairie dogs startled by a predator.

"Increased by five percent and shortened their financing contingency by fifteen days. Clearly they want the property. In exchange they insist on an answer by close of business tomorrow. They say this is their last and best offer," Malloy reported. "Have you all made any progress?"

Six bodies shifted in their seats. Dov blurted out, staring at Evelyn "We'd be done if she would get off her high horse! And that schmuck at the end of the table isn't helping matters either."

Evelyn, eyes on Malloy, spoke in her most polished nasal tone. "As the one here who knew Grandpop the longest, I adhere to the principle that we must respect his last wishes. It is only right to hold fast to the terms he set down. I'm disappointed some won't give their grandfather the respect he's due just because it is to their personal advantage."

Shirley, perhaps noticing Norm's leg now jiggling under the table at the frequency of a hummingbird's wings, spoke up. "We all respect Grandpop, he was a wonderful man. Of course we all owe him a great deal," she said calmly. "But there are also principles of fairness and justice involved here. We shouldn't perpetuate religious discrimination that violates public policy. I am sure that if Grandpop had better legal counsel, he would have understood the implications of certain clauses in his will. As a man who stood for justice, Grandpop would agree if he were here today."

Janice looked down at the table and mumbled, as much to herself as to anyone, "Can we just be done with all this?"

Jake sat back assessing the room. We're going around in the same circles, he said to himself. Evelyn seems strangely ready to hang tough. Has her legal genius husband convinced her that I won't challenge the will, he wondered? Or maybe they're even more cynical, assuming that I will bring a lawsuit to throw out Grandpop's will, but counting on her sister dying before that verdict comes in? It would be just like Schatz to play those odds if it would put a lot more money in their pockets.

He recalled Goodhart explaining what would happen if the will were overturned. If the will is voided, all of Jacob's estate would get split equally among his three children. If any child of Jacob's is dead, that child's share passes down one generation to his or her children who are then alive. Evelyn would calculate that her branch of Grandpop's descendants would inherit a one-third share through her deceased mother Ann. Splitting that with her sister would only leave Evelyn (and the good Judge) one-sixth of the estate. But if Janice were gone by the time a court got around to voiding Grandpop's will, Evelyn would inherit the full one-third herself. One-third is certainly much better than being one of seven grandchildren with a share, Jake mused. No wonder Evelyn is playing hardball, resisting the deal on the table to cut in all seven cousins no matter what Jacob's will says. For the hundredth time he played out various scenarios in his mind, each time circling back to one persistent conclusion: Evelyn is cold enough to play that hand and count on outlasting her poor sister. Especially with haughty Herbert egging her on. Well, he concluded with a deep inhale, if it's come to this, then it's time for me to play my ace in the hole.

"Evelyn, I just remembered," he said pleasantly. "My mother found an old photo she wants me to pass along to you. It's out in the car. Come get it with me. Maybe folks can use a bathroom break while we step out."

Evelyn turned quizzically toward him, wearing an expression as if he'd spoken in a foreign language she only half understood. "A picture? Now?"

"Actually a couple of photos," he replied. "You know Mom, always finding something for someone."

"Well, alright, I guess stretching my legs is a good idea." Palms on the oak surface she propelled herself to her feet, taking time to arrange her designer outfit to its intended elegant lines.

As they cleared the rear door of the lawyer's office into a parking area, Evelyn squinted in the sunlight. "How is your mother? Still suffering with the asthma?"

He clenched his jaw and thought, as if you actually care. "Fine. Mom gets by. With the store closed down she has more time for herself."

He opened the rear door of his Chevette and reached in for a briefcase, as Evelyn stood by expectantly.

"They're not exactly photos, Evelyn," he said, unzipping the case. "Photocopies. We found a copy of the letter."

"The letter? What letter?" Evelyn replied calmly but with a hint of wariness.

"The letter you thought no one else knows about."

"You're talking in riddles, Jake.I don't like being misled. You said you had photos from your mother. This is quite rude." She turned as if to go back into the building.

"You're going to want to stay and discuss this here, not in front of everyone," he said.

Evelyn slowed her walk, as if debating whether to turn or not.

"Or maybe you want me to bring in copies of Grandma's letter to your mother? I'm sure the cousins would love to read it."

Evelyn wheeled around. "How dare you!!" She was seething. "You have no right to go rummaging around in my mother's life."

"Seems that Grandma liked to keep copies of correspondence. She was pretty meticulous about it. Maybe a habit from keeping records and acting as Grandpop's private secretary for so many years? Except this letter just happened to be in a box in the attic. It had gotten buried under some piles of store records. I only found it while tidying things up after Pop died."

Evelyn was rooted where she stood, breathing shallowly and rapidly. He'd never seen her lose composure, let alone edging towards panic. His arrow had hit its mark, Evelyn looked almost like a wounded animal. He pressed on. Picking a sheet of paper out of a manila folder and scanning down the page, he started reading aloud.

" *'My dear daughter....you are special to me blah blah blah... now that the cancer is eating away at me and I do not have long to live, I need to tell you something etc. etc. But I cannot bring myself to talk about this out loud or face you, so if you are reading this you will have found it in the box of jewelry I left specially for you.'* You recognize which letter we are talking about now, cousin?" He paused, glancing to catch Evelyn's expression.

"Here's the good part: '*...the truth however is that your actual father is a boy I knew many many years ago, back in the village. As far as Papa knows, you are his special firstborn. He knows nothing of the boy. There was no reason to tell him. Blah blah ....But I could not leave this earth without letting you know the truth.'*" He dropped his hand to his side, and looked up. He could see Evelyn's eyes glistening.

"You little bastard," she spat out. "That's none of your business. Why the hell are you bringing that up now?"

"Oh, I'm afraid it is my business."

"My mother has nothing to do with this. She's gone, just like your father and Aunt Esther. Leave them in peace."

"Sorry, cousin," he pointed at the letter, "your mother has everything to do with this. I didn't realize it at first. Then I looked closely at Grandpop's will. His lawyer maybe made one big error, but he was very precise with terminology. The will specifies clearly in several clauses that everything passes to 'the children of my issue.' Most lay people would not think twice about that wording. A lawyer, however, would recognize that 'issue' are not the same as 'children'. I'm betting that after your mother died, you found the original of the same letter. You don't seem very surprised by the shocking revelation I just read to you."

Evelyn's face betrayed a peculiar mix of contempt and fear. "You brat. You've always thought you were clever. Now you're just flailing around with nonsensical theories."

"Am I? Let's see how this theory strikes you. You find this letter among your mother's things. You're shaken by the truth. You share it with Herbert. Your smart lawyer husband realizes you have a big inheritance problem. If Ann is not Jacob's biological child, she is not his 'issue'. If she is not his issue, you are not his heir. You get nothing." Jake crossed his arms. He noticed Evelyn swallow.

"Good so far? Herbert, being an aggressive kind of guy, figures that the best defense is a good offense. If you are the one suing, nobody will be looking at whether you deserve to inherit or checking into family history. So you go on the attack, file a lawsuit demanding a full accounting and distribution of the assets, and here we are. Of course no one ever would have imagined Grandma sleeping with anyone but Grandpop, that's too weird. If Grandma wasn't a meticulous record keeper that angle would certainly never have crossed my mind. But you must have figured, why take any chances?"

"You little snot-nosed shit," she seethed. "Herbert always said you were too full of yourself."

"Oh yeah, Herbert, who thinks he's some towering legal mind. Remember when you invited me over for dinner when I was in college? Herbert asked me about law school, insisting on knowing my LSAT scores. He badgered me into telling him, and the first thing he said is not, 'Good for you' but 'You're going to take them over, aren't you?' I just sat there looking at his smirk, him thinking he's an admissions expert. Well, I got into the top law schools in the country, thank you very much. But Herbert's the brilliant one I suppose."

He noticed his heart beating faster and heard his voice rising. Get a grip, he told himself. You're not here to pay back old slights. Or maybe I am, it occurred to him. He turned his attention back to his cousin, who was clearly boiling over with her own surge of resentments and old scores to settle. They locked eyes.

"Well hooray for you, Jake. You got into good law schools. So what. Grandpop never knew you existed! You don't deserve a share of anything. He left it to his real grandchildren, the ones he knew. Grandpop loved my mother the most, his eldest, his little girl. No letter from a demented dying woman is going to change anything."

"No? I think the law would beg to differ." He noticed Evelyn had started rubbing her hands obsessively.

"Maybe you should have done a little more research before trying this little power play." Evelyn spoke as if reciting lines from a script. "A child whom the parent treats as their natural child has the same rights as a biological child. That's the doctrine of presumed parenthood."

"Oh, so Herbert hit the law books on this, eh?" he chuckled.

"Go ahead and waste your time. You won't cut me and my sister out of Grandpop's will."

"Sorry to disabuse you of the notion that Herbert knows what he's talking about. I know he likes throwing around impressive-sounding legal words. Like when he accused Adam of "barratry and champerty" just for writing a letter trying to settle all this. I admit, we had to look up those fancy legal terms," he said. "But Herbert's mistaken again. Presumed parenthood is just that, presumed. Here I'm holding in my hand clear evidence rebutting the presumption, to use the technical term."

"Like I said, it won't work."

Jake smiled and held up the letter. "*Nu*, what's it going to be? Do we go back and tell the group you'll agree to the offer for the property and settle? With all cousins cut in equally, seven ways? Or do I hand out copies of Grandma's letter? I've prepared a little dissertation on inheritance law, which I would be delighted to share with the cousins."

Epilogue
Princeton 2013

"Mom. Mom, wake up! Aaron's here." Sherry's piercing voice startled Evelyn out of her doze. She felt someone gently stroking her shoulders.

"Aaron?" she mumbled, eyes fluttering open. "Aaron's here?"

"Yes, Mama. The cab from the Dinky just dropped him off. Wake up!"

Evelyn shifted around in the floral bergere chair, her legs stretched out on the matching ottoman. Wriggling, she methodically hoisted herself into a sitting position. "Is my hair in place, Sherry?" Evelyn inquired, patting her close cropped curls.

"Your hair's fine, Mom. You always look put together!" her daughter answered reassuringly.

The whoosh of the front door bursting open was quickly followed by a bellow. "Mom, Sherry, I'm here. Where are you?"

"Back in the sun room, doofus," Sherry called out playfully to her younger brother. " Where else this time of the afternoon?"

"Don't start with me, Snotty!" Aaron replied light-heartedly, wrapping his sister in a bear hug. "And you, beautiful lady! How's my favorite nonagenarian?" A portly man in khakis, Aaron knelt beside Evelyn, who had stiffened her back to pull herself up to her full sitting height. He planted a kiss on his mother's rouged cheek, holding her shoulders in a light embrace.

"Sherry didn't tell me you were coming!" Evelyn said, looking up at her daughter with pursed lips. "Sherry, close the window, the damn cicada brood is buzzing so loudly I can't hear myself think."

To Aaron, Evelyn flashed a broad smile. "Stand up. Let me look at you!"

"It's the same me, Mom."

"You look more and more like your father every time I see you. Very distinguished," Evelyn opined, her eyes slightly glistening.

"Aw, Mom, thanks. We all miss Dad. Hey look, Mom, I'm really sorry I missed the birthday bash. We're working on this huge bankruptcy case and I had to stay and supervise the associates. Maybe you heard about it? The City of Detroit, can you believe it!"

"Your mother's not senile yet! I still read the Journal every day, just the way I did with your father at breakfast.

No wonder Detroit is bankrupt, those people can't manage their own city…"

"It's more complicated than that, Mom," Aaron cut her off. "Anyway, it's the biggest case in the office right now."

"Mr. Big Shot lawyer, too busy to even come to his mother's ninetieth birthday party," Sherry tried to sound good natured but struck more of a mocking note.

"Quiet, Sherry, your brother's a senior partner in one of New York's most prestigious law firms, doing important work. Herbert would be so proud."

"Mom, it's OK, Sherry's right. I should have been at the party, I just couldn't get away. But I brought you something special!" Aaron grabbed one of a pair of brocaded faux Louis XIV chairs standing against the wall, pushing it close to Evelyn. Dropping his bulk into the seat, Aaron reached into his maroon leather briefcase and extracted a sheaf of papers.

"You brought me legal documents?" Evelyn said perplexedly, putting on the half-glasses hanging around her neck.

"Not documents Mom, history. Family history! I've been doing our family tree." Aaron waved fifteen pages of names listed in outline form. "It took me nearly a year, Mom, but I think I've finally gotten all the relatives into one big tree! Happy Birthday, Mom!"

Evelyn blinked. Her thoughts skittered back to the birthday party her daughter had thrown for her yesterday. She'd forced herself to hide her disappointment after Aaron had sent last minute regrets. The confusing mix of joy and deep sadness she had felt during the party returned, as she recalled the faces of the twenty or so well wishers who had gathered. Her three grandchildren had come, as well as her niece and nephew, surviving children of her long-dead sister Janice. Also her few friends from the synagogue who were still alive, and a couple of *alter kockers* she could not place. How the hell did I ever get to be ninety, she had wondered, hurt that her favorite child was absent. Now Aaron had surprised her by making the journey down from Manhattan, and for a present he'd compiled a list of dead relatives. "That's so thoughtful, Aaron. Thank you."

Aaron grinned. "It was fascinating, Mom. Remember last year I arranged for us all to use this Ancestry thing to figure out our DNA history, where we come from?"

"Sure, I remember. You made me spit into tube, it was disgusting," Evelyn said, scrunching up her lips.

"Yeah, but the results were fascinating! Sure, we're all mostly European Jewish, but there was five percent Spanish/Iberian in your results," Aaron replied, animatedly.

"I have no idea what that was about," Evelyn said briskly. "You know everyone came from the old country, what used to be Russia. Now it's Lithuania."

"Right, Mom. But maybe way back someone was kicked out of Spain, with the Inquisition? Jews wander all over, you know. Anyway, turns out there's lots more to Ancestry than just finding out where your ancestors came from."

Evelyn merely smiled without affect, waiting for her son to share a discovery that apparently excited him. She sensed the slightest quickening of her pulse.

"You can do a whole tree on Ancestry, and it has all these tools for doing research. Here's the best part! When other people take DNA tests, they match them with you.

I won't go into all the technical details, but Ancestry can tell you if somebody you've never heard of is a relative."

"How accurate is that?" Sherry, who'd been sitting quietly to one side, was now leaning forward with interest.

"Oh, it's getting more and more accurate. If you share above a certain amount of DNA, you're definitely related."

"How interesting," said Evelyn, straining to sound blase. Has Aaron turned up a match for my mother's father? The thought induced a chill up her spine.

"You OK Mom?" Sherry asked. "You're looking pale."

"It's nothing, dear. Just a little hungry. It's getting late, shouldn't we have some lunch?"

"Hold on, Mom, I'm getting to the good part," Aaron plowed ahead. "You remember how as a teenager I got really into family history? It started when we went to one of those weird *mishpicnic* things that the cousins organized every decade or so."

"Those gatherings were tedious," Evelyn said, stretching as if to yawn. "It was nice to see some cousins who lived far away from time to time. But Norman always jabbered on and on about some story he'd heard from Grandpop Jacob. Probably made up half of it."

"Sure Mom, I know what you mean. The thing is, as a kid I thought those tales were really fascinating. I had Norm give me a copy of this tree he'd created, about eight pages on old mimeographed paper showing how everyone was related. The names were fascinating to me, especially the ones with little annotations, like that great great-great-great-grandfather Israel de Greiser was nearly seven feet tall. Who knows what's really true, but back then I thought that was cool."

"You were always getting excited about some new hobby, and then a minute later jumping to the next one," Evelyn said, patting Aaron's hand.

"That's me, Mom. Well, it used to be. Anyway, after we got the Ancestry results, I remembered that mimeographed tree was in a drawer. So I dug it out. It got me started on our tree, then I tracked down more relatives from the databases. Norm had all of great-Grandpa Jacob's siblings listed. But since he'd done the tree nearly fifty years ago, before DNA matching, there were a lot of gaps. He had hardly any info about relatives in later generations."

"He kept everything in his head, the same way he kept the Estate's books," Evelyn said scornfully. "He probably had the details. Knowing him, he just never got around to writing it down."

"Well, Mom, it doesn't matter. You see, Ancestry does all the work for you," Aaron said excitedly.

Sherry cut in, "How so?"

"This is the great part! I finally checked the DNA section, where Ancestry shows you DNA matches. And guess what? Two people popped up named Itzkowitz, showing them as second or maybe third cousins!"

"What's special about that?" Evelyn asked warily.

"Well, in DNA terms, it means a highly accurate match. It has to be, to be that close. Because they're named Itzkowitz, I figured they're probably descended from one of Jacob's brothers. It wouldn't just be coincidence they have the same last name."

"There are a lot of Itzkowitzes in the world, not just my grandfather's family," Evelyn offered, puzzled at the idea of new relatives on Jacob's side.

"True. But remember, these people have matching DNA. They're *mishpocha*! Anyway, Ancestry reveals details about your matches, like their age. If the matches are really old, say from Grandma Ann's generation, they'd likely be Ann's cousins. We don't have her DNA, but we do have your DNA in the system Mom. So I checked the results against your DNA, and the matches are even closer to you than to me. One of them is your actual second cousin, Mom!"

Evelyn knitted her brows. What's he telling me, she wondered. This doesn't make sense. He doesn't know that my mother's real father was some *yeshiva bucher*. "Tell me this again, Aaron. I must be a little tired. How is this person related?"

"Let's take it step by step. Your grandfather was Jacob. Jacob passed his DNA down to Grandma Ann, and then from Grandma Ann that DNA passed down to you. Jacob also shared DNA with his brothers. A DNA match named Itzkowitz must be from Jacob's side of the family. Turns out the guy I found is the grandson of Jacob's youngest brother Avram." Aaron paused.

"Avram? Wasn't he the brother who died mysteriously?" Evelyn asked.

"Sort of, Mom. Avram died young, an accident in South Africa. Norm's tree didn't have any info about Avram's family, so originally I just assumed Avram must have died before getting married and that was the end of his line. But I was wrong! Avram did marry. He had a son named Beryl who was born a few months after Avram died. Poor fella grew up without a dad, I don't think the mother remarried. Beryl Itzkowitz got married later in life and had two sons. His youngest son is the DNA match on Ancestry, a guy named Abe Itzkowitz. So even though Abe is about my age, he's actually your second cousin. Does that make sense, Mom?"

"Your telling me you found a man and we have some of the same DNA?" Evelyn said quietly, starting to feel lightheaded.

"You got it Mom. Isn't that amazing? I bet you had no idea this branch of the family existed."

"And you're sure this Abe, this stranger, he's actually the grandson of Grandpop Jacob's brother? Maybe he's adopted? Could it be a mistake?"

"It's not a mistake, Mom. I found the birth certificate for Abe, and also for Beryl. Ancestry is terrific, you can find all these documents on line!" Aaron grinned from ear to ear at his mother.

Evelyn said nothing, just stared at her son. Grandpop's brother had a son. That son had a son. He and I have the same DNA. The same DNA? My mother had Grandpop's DNA? Evelyn noticed that Aaron's face was getting blurry. And that noise she was hearing, was it cicadas? It sounded like a buzzing inside the house. The noise was getting louder and louder. She felt empty all of a sudden. I'll just close my eyes a rest a second, Evelyn said to herself. As her lids closed, she could hear a terrified voice not quite drowned out by the buzzing. "Mom? Mom??"

"That little bastard, he fooled me," she murmured. "If it's the last thing I do, I'll get even."

Glossary

The definitions in this glossary reflect the author's understanding of the meaning of each term as it was used in the The Foxtail Legacy. As with all colloquial terms, different speakers might offer differing interpretations.

Alter kockers — old farts.

Ayniklach — grandchildren.

Babas — babies.

Baruch hashem — blessed be the Holy One.

Bashert — fated; destined to occur.

Bedeken — a Jewish wedding ritual, when the groom places a veil over the bride's face.

Bimah — the place in a synagogue where the Torah reading occurs, generally a raised platform.

Boerverneukers — a derisive term castigating persons who cheat or swindle the Boer.

Bris — the Jewish circumcision ritual.

Bubbeh — grandmother.

Bubbeleh — a term of endearment, usually for a child, akin to "sweetie".

Bubbemeises — akin to "old wives' tales", implying self-deception.

Chevre Kadisha — the traditional Jewish burial society.

Chuppah — the canopy under which a Jewish wedding is conducted.

Chutzpah — brashness, gall, audacity.

Der kinderlach — the little children.

Dybbuk — a mythological evil spirit; a lost wandering soul.

Farshtunken — lousy, no good.

Feter — uncle.

Gey gezunt — go in good health, with a hint of "good riddance".

Goniff — thief; swindler. While the formal plural of go-niff is *gonuvim*, the more colloquial version is *goniffs*.

Goyim — non-Jews, in particular Christians.

Goyishe — distinctively non-Jewish in character.

Gut in Himmel — an exclamation of distress, literally "G-d in heaven".

Ha shem — literally "the name", used to avoid taking the

name of G-d in vain.

Hondling — haggling, bargaining, dickering.

Kaffir — a derisive racist Afrikaans term for a Black African.

Ketubah — the Jewish wedding contract.

Kindele — an endearing term for a child.

Kippah — ritual Jewish head covering; yarmulke.

Kittel — a white, plain burial shroud.

Kvell — swell with pride.

Landsmanshaft — a mutual aid society, generally limited to persons from the same hometown or region.

Landsmen — persons from the same hometown or region; fellow countrymen.

Lignerisher shvester — lying sister.

Macher — big shot.

Mamaloshen — the mother tongue, generally applied to Yiddish.

Mamme — mother.

Mamzer — bastard; scoundrel.

Mechayeh — a special pleasure; a real joy.

Mensch — a good person; someone with integrity.

Meshugenneh — crazy; mixed up.

Mevrou — a respectful term of address to a woman.

Mishpicnic — a family reunion, the contraction of "mispocha" and "picnic".

Mishpocha — an extended family network.

Mitzvah — a good deed.

Mohel — the person who performs the ritual circumcision at a bris.

Muzhik — a peasant, usually applied to a Russian.

Naches — great pride; satisfaction.

Nu — an inflected term implying a questioning "so what".

Olev ha'sholom — a term of remembrance of a deceased loved on, meaning "peace be unto" the person.

Ponds — Afrikaans for "pounds" in currency.

Shadchante — a female matchmaker.

Schlemiel — a klutzy or awkward person, with an element of unluckiness.

Schlepper — implying a simpleton, but can mean someone who hauls around heavy objects.

Schlub — a stupid, boorish person.

Schnorrer — someone who mooches off others.

Shacharit — the morning prayer service.

Shehecheyanu — a prayer of thanksgiving, generally marking reaching a milestone or new accomplishment.

Shema — the prayer that reflects the central Jewish creed.

Shicker — a drunkard.

Shidduch — an arranged marriage.

Shiksas — non-Jewish females, generally applied to

Christian women.

Shiva — the mourning ritual of receiving people offering condolences at the home of someone who has lost a love one.

Shloshim — the thirty days after the burial of a loved one during which religious Jews refrain from many activities of life.

Shomer — the person who guards or watches over a dead body, as part of the rituals of preparing the corpse for burial.

Shonda — something that is a disgrace or a scandal.

Shtetl — a small town or village, commonly referring to towns and villages inhabited by Jews in Eastern Europe.

Shtick drek — piece of shit.

Shul — synagogue.

Simcha — a joyful occasion.

Smouses — a derogatory Afrikaans term for a Jewish peddler.

Taharah — the process of preparing a dead body for burial, involving the ritual purification cleaning of the corpse.

Tante - aunt.

Tekiah gedolah — the longest, final blast of a shofar, ending a portion of a religious service.

Tzedakah — charity and good works.

Tzimmes — a traditional Eastern European Jewish stew typically made from root vegetables and prunes; also used to connote a big fuss over something.

Tzuris — trouble or distress.

Uitlanders — a foreigner or outlander.

Yahrzeit — the anniversary of a person's death, and the memorialized recognition of the anniversary.

Yeshiva bucher — a dedicated student of Torah and Talmud, generally studying in a Jewish academy called a yeshiva.

Zihronah livracha — may her memory be a blessing.

Acknowledgements

This novel didn't write itself, and my portion of the work was only a part of the finished product. I would never have completed the manuscript without the gentle steady guidance of my writing coach Jill Riddell, the excellent thoughtful developmental editing of Raghav Rao, and the beautiful formatting of Sophie Lucido Johnson, all of the Office of Modern Composition. Their support through every step of the process kept me going even when I could not see the finish line.

No one had more roles along the way or played a bigger part in transforming me from a guy musing about writing a novel to an author sitting down and putting words on the page than my wife, Joan Ruttenberg. She listened (countless times) to all the yarns over the years, encouraged me to undertake the project, brainstormed critical plot points, journeyed with me to scope out sites, gave feedback on early drafts, and copyedited the entire manuscript. Every page has benefited from her excellent input.

I cannot thank enough the friends and family who read drafts and gave me invaluable feedback. Hillary Weisman, Dan Janis, Ed McKenzie, Phil Abromowitz, Rich Ruttenberg, and Madeleine Abromowitz all willingly devoted their precious time to a work in progress, providing insights and reactions that greatly aided me along the way. And to my departed Cousin Nate goes gratitude for passing along much family lore and the gift of a grounding in the *mishpocha's* genealogy.

About the Author

David Abromowitz is an advocate, policy shaper, believer in opportunity youth, affordable housing attorney and writer. A frequent author of op-eds and policy papers during his career as an attorney at Goulston & Storrs, as the Chief Public Policy Officer of YouthBuild USA and as a Senior Fellow at the Center for America Progress, David's writings have appeared in the Boston Globe, Los Angeles Times, Baltimore Sun, USA Today, Huffington Post and many other publications. An active civic leader, David serves on the Board of the Jewish Community Relations Council of Greater Boston, B'nai B'rith Housing New England, and the Princeton Class of 1978 Foundation, and he previously served on the boards of The Equity Trust, YouthBuild USA, and the New Economy Coalition, among others. A graduate of Princeton University and Harvard Law School, his contributions have been recognized by numerous awards, including the Affordable Housing Vision Award of the National Housing & Rehabilitation Association, the Distinguished Achievement Award of B'Nai B'rith Housing New England, and the Lifetime Achiever award of the National Law Journal.

David is a proud New Jersey native now living in the Boston area; *The Foxtail Legacy* is his first novel.

Made in the USA
Middletown, DE
02 May 2023

29901468R00227